A Disreputable Scandal

Nick Meyer

For Jake, Dia + Leila
with lots of love
Dad, Nick, Opa.

Dedication

To the memory of E. G. E. Meyer.

Acknowledgments

Many thanks to Joyce and the gang, to Dia for the cover design and to Tim for all his tech support.

Chapter One

Esther Hart's Diary

Tuesday 2nd January 1940

Douglas gave me a leather bound diary for Christmas which has a lockable clasp on it. Said he bought it when we were in Florence two years ago and was waiting for the right time to give it to me. I wonder why now is the right time. Perhaps because he knew I was so upset at the children not being allowed home for Christmas. They could have come; after all thousands that were evacuated last September have made their way home to London, but Douglas was adamant and said that they are far better off with his sister. He can be thoughtlessly unkind sometimes. But then I saw that there were thirty thousand people killed in an earthquake in Turkey and that does rather put one's own worries into perspective. Still I do worry about the children being cold and it is far colder in Rutland than it is here. Last night it was so bitter that part of the Thames was completely frozen over.

I think Douglas has given me this diary now because he wants me to be able to share my private thoughts with it, rather than bothering him with them. Also he has been very secretive lately and simply won't tell me what's going on. I know there are things happening that he can't talk about at home, or anywhere else for that matter, but he seems so weighed down. Then I think of all those women whose men have been called up in the last couple of days and really think I should count myself lucky because Douglas will at least come home each night. The Government is advising everybody to take cod liver oil capsules. Better get some in before they are rationed as well.

Saturday 6th January

Very strange evening last night. Douglas came home terribly late with two of his colleagues, Mr Jeffries and Mr Mason. Mr Mason had a bottle of whisky and he said they were celebrating. Douglas seemed rather discomfited. We sat in the drawing room as the only one that is being heated and the easiest to black out. I had some sewing to do. Apparently they were drinking to Mr Hore-Belisha's resignation as Minister of War. They drank quite a bit and Mr Mason said he should have been sacked before the war ever started, and if it wasn't for him we might never have gone to war at all but that being a Jew he wanted us to go and protect the German and Austrian Jews at the expense of our boys, because he wouldn't be risking his own life. I don't know if that can be quite true. Mr Jeffries was of the opinion that it was the army generals who had him sacked because he was far too generous to the soldiers and they didn't like his idea about building pill- boxes all along the Belgian and French borders. He thought they were right to resist him because it was the generals who were the trained soldiers. Douglas kept looking at me nervously and said something in a voice I couldn't hear and Mr Jeffries laughed and said they would stop talking shop now and invited me over to share the whisky. It was horrible and tasted like petrol. Apparently he had a phone call from a friend in the Home Office who said they were looking for JP's to attend tribunals for refugees from Germany and Austria to see whether they should be interned as enemy aliens or can be left free. I was quite surprised when Douglas said he was sure I'd be glad to help. It's true, I would.

Monday 8th January

Rationing starts in earnest today and there were long queues outside the butcher's. Walking out in the morning it all seems so unreal. The sky full of barrage balloons and the cold make it feel as if we are in a giant refrigerator. It is quite beautiful and surreal. Looking out of the window last night in the dark I saw a yellow light bobbing along. I couldn't make out what it could be for ages and then gradually it dawned on me that it was a dog wearing a bicycle reflector on its collar. The woman in front of me in the butcher said Herr Hitler doesn't need to attack – there are so many accidents in London because of the blackout that we'll quite defeat ourselves.

I've just had a phone call from Sir Ralph Spiers asking if I can be available for a tribunal on Thursday. He'll meet me before the first hearing at eleven o'clock to explain the process, but as this will be my first one I'll only be expected to listen and if I want to ask any questions I can write them down and pass them to him and he'll read them out. I forgot to ask him what I should wear. It's in the school, which, apparently, is terribly cold.

Thursday 11th January

Arrived at the school and was shown into the hall by the caretaker. On my way passed the three internees sitting on a bench in the corridor. Sir Ralph said this should all be quite straightforward. He didn't think that any of them were active Nazis, and in his view anyway, Communists are a much bigger danger and a lot more cunning. As well as Sir Ralph there was the lady acting as secretary, another man, Dr Rogers who is also a JP, and me on the committee. We sat in the hall behind a table with a one bar electric fire. We, in practice, Sir Ralph, had to decide whether the internees should fall into category A, meaning that they are a danger to national security and would therefore be sent straight to an internment camp, a B, in which case they would be free but wouldn't be allowed to travel more than five miles from their place of residence, would have to report to the police every week and would have any cameras or radios confiscated; or C, in which case they would be as free as anyone else.

The first person Franz Niedermayer, I guess was about forty-ish, an Austrian. It seemed to me that part of the problem was that he was also terribly nervous. He shook throughout and the thin jacket and shirt he wore would hardly keep out the cold. As far as we could ascertain he is from Graz and had escaped into Czechoslovakia when the Germans entered Austria. He has a wife (not Jewish) in Czechoslovakia who had to remain behind because their daughter was too ill to travel and he obviously desperately wanted to get them all to England. He said with such a desperation, "Please, you can help," but of course it was pointed out to him that the committee's remit was to ascertain whether or not he personally posed a danger to our national security. He stared at us for some time, either in disbelief or incomprehension and then said, "I am no Nazi, I am socialist." Sir Ralph gave me a knowing look and asked him if he had a job. Apparently the Austrian Centre is providing him with help with his English lessons and he is training to be a welder. I wanted to know whether he had any contact with his family and passed a note to Sir Ralph who glanced at it and then said, "Well Herr Niedermayer, I'm putting you down for a category B. You will report to Paddington police each week and they will also search your premises to ensure you have no proscribed possessions. If you do, you will be given a receipt for such items as are confiscated and they will be returned to you when your status changes or when the war ends. Is that clear? If and when you secure employment and can present evidence from your employer as to the legitimacy of your contract, then we will consider re-categorizing you as a 'C'".

The man had been straining to understand, and looked at each of us with an expression of complete bewilderment on his face. Sir Ralph put out his hand and the secretary tore of the top copy of the form and handed it to him. He leaned across the table, "Take this to your police station tomorrow. And you may find this useful too." He handed him a leaflet. "Dismissed."

Herr Niedermayer looked at the leaflet and then back at us. Sir Ralph turned to the secretary, "Show the man out," he said and hen turned to me. "I understand your concern for the chap's family, my dear, but we can't allow ourselves to become sentimental over these things. I know it's hard to remember sometimes, but there is a war on. I gave him this pamphlet that I give to all those who come before me." He handed me a leaflet, *'Helpful Information and Guidance for Every Refugee.'* I glanced at it. It was produced by a Jewish organisation and exhorted Germans not to speak German in public or to be seen reading German language papers, not to criticize government regulations or the way things are done in England. *"Englishmen attach very great importance to modesty, understatement in speech, and quietness of dress and manner. They value good manners far more than the evidence of wealth."*

"It always helps when they can understand us a little better," said Sir Ralph.

The next refugee was a student who had been studying at the University. Her English was excellent and she brought with her testimonials from her professor and her landlady. She was given a 'C'.

Finally a well-dressed man of about sixty and wearing a monocle came in. He seemed very sure of himself and smiled at me in a way that I found quite uncomfortable. "I don't understand why you haven't appeared before earlier tribunals," said Sir Ralph, "You seem to have slipped through the net, rather, Mr Reinhardt. He explained that he had recently moved from Harrogate to London and his post hadn't been forwarded. He had been in the country for over forty years and while he had never bothered about becoming a naturalised Briton, his mother had been very keen for their sons to be English, and he had recently heard that in fact his eldest son had wanted to join the RAF. He was working as a self-employed expert on racing car fuel. His wife was English, but they had separated a number of years before. Sir Ralph asked a number of questions about racing cars that I didn't think were strictly necessary, but he explained to me that he needed to convince himself of the man's bona fides.

Walking home afterwards I couldn't stop thinking about poor Herr Niedermayer and his wife and child. I must find out more about what the Council of Austrians does.

Visited Douglas's father on the way home. Suggested he should move in with us, at least until the weather gets warmer, but the old man is as stubborn as his son. Seems ridiculous to me that he is freezing in that flat when we could halve the fuel costs, but he was adamant and to be honest I don't want him with us. He gets so bad tempered.

Wednesday 15th January

Listened to Mr Chamberlain making a speech that was supposed to boost everyone's morale but it seemed to have the opposite effect because there were an awful lot of complaints about the trains all running late owing to the blackouts and the bad weather. If anything it's getting even colder. Said to Douglas that I thought we should insist that his father move in with us- I'm sure he's not eating properly and one does have to be quite enterprising in the kitchen with the rationing which, I am sure he isn't. I didn't like to press the point, but Douglas was not really in the mood to talk about it- just said I should talk it over with Charles and when I said I had and he wanted to stay in his own flat, Douglas simply said, "Well then, I don't see that there's a problem."

He worked all Saturday so I went for a walk along the Embankment. The days drag for everybody. We've now been at war for four months and it feels as though we've all been holding our breath all that time and only now are gradually beginning to feel that we can relax. It still seems surprising to see so many men in uniform. There were girls with their sweethearts all along the river and some of those boys looked as if they should still have been at school.

Douglas came home and said the Belgians had refused permission to the British and French armies to enter their country, but along with Holland was mobilizing its own. The war is coming closer. For some reason this seemed to make Douglas more angry than usual, but it seems to me completely understandable. It was only just over twenty years ago that their country was devastated by the German, French and British armies. Why would they ever allow such a thing to happen again if it can be avoided? I didn't disagree with Douglas, there's no point. Careless talk causes rows. And probably wars as well.

Saturday 20th January

Woke up to find Douglas gone to work by seven and he hadn't left a note. At least I assume he's gone to work. Had supper at the Vaizey's last night. A taxi journey to South Kensington that would have taken fifteen minutes before the war started now takes the best part of an hour. The taxi driver said he'd had a couple of 'gents' earlier that evening, one of them a doctor. They'd been talking about the blackout and the doctor said that so far three soldiers had been killed in action and four thousand people died in accidents during blackouts. The taxi driver said the government doesn't tell you things like that. In his opinion it isn't a war between us and Germany, it's a class war. I looked at Douglas to see how he reacted to that but he wasn't listening. The driver said there was probably at that very moment a taxi driver in Berlin who was driving a couple round in the dark so that he could support his wife and family and whose own father had also been killed at the Somme. He couldn't see why they would want to kill each other.

6

The other 'gent' said it was essential for people to remember there was a war on and that was the real importance of the blackout. And this had so incensed the taxi driver that he'd stopped in the middle of Westminster Bridge and lowered his window, hoping the gentleman would get his point. The searchlights reflecting off the barrage balloons cast a silver light that twinkled all along the Thames, like stars laid into the frozen river, he said. And if the Germans come with their flying boats, it couldn't be any clearer where to land than London airport runway on a sunny day. When he dropped us off he apologised for having gone on. But he didn't go on as long as Henry Vaizey. The meal was a bore, except for the syllabub which was delicious.

Chapter Two

Reinhardt woke up slowly and found himself focusing on a strange ceiling. He dimly recalled that this must be New Year's Day and that there had been a woman. The room smelt of paraffin and eau de cologne. He turned his head and a sharp pain shot up his neck, but he'd seen enough to know that there was no woman there now. He was relieved. It would give him time to remember what had happened. He looked back at the ceiling. The weight of the blankets and eiderdown pressing on his chest was making him nauseous. He pushed up the blankets to let in some air and peered down under the covers. As far as he could see he was completely naked. He rubbed his feet together; no, he was wearing his socks. He sighed. It hadn't been satisfactory, he remembered. She had said it really didn't matter, it was such a long time since she'd even had a cuddle. She had insisted on getting undressed in the dark but had had to get him to undo her zip, which he had done with difficulty.

"Must cut down on the booze," he said aloud, "Die in bed at ninety-four, shot by a jealous husband? Not unless you stop drinking so much. And it's important for a man to have an ambition."

He pushed the covers aside and gingerly put his feet on the floor. The room swam a little to his right. He stood to turn on the light, but to his surprise found that it was already on. He squinted at the twenty watt bulb hanging from the centre of the ceiling and then at the window. The curtains were drawn open, but the window panes were painted black. He suddenly felt claustrophobic and went to find the lavatory. The hall was equally gloomy but there was light coming from the farthest room. He was almost completely sure there was no one else in the flat, but he covered himself with his hands just in case, and shuffled forward. It was the kitchen and it was empty. On the table there was a note. He picked it up to read it, but even with one hand slapped over one eye and holding the note at arm's length, he couldn't make out what it said.

When he'd wanted to get undressed in a hurry he'd got into the habit of putting his monocle in the breast pocket of his suit jacket. Now he hurried back to the bedroom praying that the previous night he'd remembered to do the same. His jacket was hanging neatly over the back of the chair and he breathed a sigh of relief when he felt for his monocle. He put it on and scrutinised the letter by the light of his lighter.

Dear Links, the writing was in a large copper plate,

I promised to visit my daughter in Wandsworth this morning. Make yourself at home. Tea's in the caddy by the kettle. Sorry, no milk. Hope to see you again. Mary.

PS leave your number if you feel like it.

PPS If you leave before I get back, don't worry, I've got the key so you can drop the latch.

He found his watch in his trouser pocket. It was gone twelve. He dressed quickly and wondered about leaving her a note. Then he recalled that he couldn't leave her his number. It was all coming back to him. There'd been a party in 'The Feathers'. She'd come with a friend and he'd been watching them at their corner table. Then at midnight everyone had sung 'Auld Lang Syne' and he'd managed to hold hands with both of them as the tables were cleared and a circle formed. Actually, it was Mary's friend that he'd taken a shine to and he offered to buy them both a drink. But her friend said she had to go and he noticed her give Mary a wink. So he and Mary had found a table in the corner and she said she had a daughter and a son who was in the territorials and training somewhere and how her flat now seemed so empty, at which point he said he was afraid he'd missed his last tube to Cockfosters and really wasn't sure what he should do and she said, after a pause, that she had a spare room, which is what he's hoped she'd say. They had a few more drinks. She accepted his offer of a cigarette, though she said she didn't really smoke and they had a few more drinks and then went back to her flat, where he produced his whisky flask, which, it had turned out, had been a very bad idea indeed. She had told him about how hard it was, suddenly finding herself living alone, especially the long winter evenings, and he sympathised. He was good at sympathy. She had asked him how he got the name 'Links' and he had explained his golfing pals had given it to him because it was his favourite kind of golf course, where he always seemed to play especially well. And this wasn't exactly true either. He had never played golf, though he would like to have done and was sure that he would have been good at it, but, of course, it was far too late to start now. His English nanny had tried to get him to use his right hand to write with when he was little, and she'd say, "Nicht links, Ernst, " and he would stick out his bottom lip stubbornly and say, "Doch, links. Links ist gut." And 'Links' had stuck.

He stuffed her note in his pocket, turned off the paraffin heater and let himself out of the flat.

Outside the cold seared his nostrils. He breathed deeply and set off down the empty street, wondering what to do about breakfast, or by now it was lunch time. He'd have to go home to Mecklenburg Square for a wash and brush up and then perhaps treat himself to a snack at the Savoy, or possibly the Ritz.

There was a freezing fog that quickly penetrated the bones and numbed his ears and fingers.

He took the bus to Gray's Inn Road. It had started to snow in great flurries so that when he got off at his stop there was already another covering on the pavement. He was just wondering whether to try and warm himself with a cup of tea in Lyons when he heard a voice calling him from the entrance to 'The King's Head'.

"Links, my dear chap, you look frozen. Let me buy you a snifter. Happy New Year and all that."

Monty Jennings, pint in hand and a large cigar between his lips was grinning at him from beneath a cloth cap.

Reinhardt went over to him.

"Hello, Monty, good to see you. Happy New year old man," They shook hands.

"You're absolutely blue, dear chap. What's it to be?" He ushered Reinhardt into the saloon bar.

"Actually, I had a skinful last night."

"Exactly. Hair of the dog and all that, that's just what you need. Lily, a whisky chaser for me and a large brandy for my friend. He needs defrosting." He slid his heavy frame onto a bar stool. Lily turned to the optics and poured their drinks before returning to drying up the beer glasses from the previous night. Monty raised his glass, "Bottoms up and down the hatch."

"So," he said, "What've you been up to? Thought we'd see you here last night. Some of the chaps thought you might have been called up."

Reinhardt looked at Monty's reflection in the mirror behind the bar to see whether he was joking and downed his brandy.

"Too old, I'm afraid, by about thirty years."

"No, I didn't mean that, I meant, with you being a Kraut and all that…"

Lily, who was wiping a wisp of hair away from over her eyes with her sleeve, glanced up. "You German, then?"

"Lily's been telling me she's from Sutton," said Monty, as if by way of explanation for her question.

"Sudbury," said Lily. "But are you? German I mean. You don't look like one."

"Oh?" Reinhardt smiled, "What does one look like?"

"Oh, I dunno. Sort of big and blonde, and I don't mean to be rude or anything, but younger than what you do."

"Ah," said Reinhardt, "You're talking about Bavarians. They live in the south of Germany. They're all big and blonde. You'd have a great time there, Lily. They wear leather shorts with braces called lederhosen under their uniforms and drink five pints of beer for breakfast. A beautiful blonde waitress like you can earn a thousand pounds a year just working the early morning shift."

Lily looked doubtful. "Yeah, but you're not blonde, you're more ginger like."

"And that's because I'm from Silesia, in the east."

"Who," said Monty, are womanising…."

"Sensitive souls who just want a quiet life and peace," interrupted Reinhardt. "And then there's Herr Hitler, who is neither blonde nor red-headed, as you will have noticed, Lily."

"So where's he from, then?"

"Hitler? He's from Austria, where everyone has flat hair and a little moustache. Even the women. They're all born like that."

Lily started to rub vigorously at a glass. At last she said, "I can't tell if you're taking the mickey or not."

"Tell you what," said Reinhardt, "Here's half a crown. Get Mr Jennings another pint of stout in and another whisky chaser, get me a large brandy and yourself whatever your tipple is, keep the change, and then I'll tell you the truth." He slid a coin across the counter.

They watched, smiling as Lily poured the drinks and pocketed the change.

She set out the glasses in front of them and looked at Reinhardt expectantly.

"The truth is, Lily, you're an absolute sweetheart," laughed Reinhardt, and took his brandy to a table by the window. Monty followed him as Lily protested loudly, "You bastards."

"But seriously, Links, I've been meaning to ask you. You're in the petroleum business. I mean this rationing is killing me. And at two bob a gallon I can't hope to survive. Can't you help a pal?"

Reinhardt didn't really see Jennings as a pal and had been vaguely wondering what all this bonhomie was about. He shook his head. "Not that kind of petrol," he said. "We were developing stuff for racing cars. Stick that in your old Austin 7 and it would blow your roof off."

"Oh," said Monty, and he downed the whisky, "I didn't know that." He took a long draught of his beer." When he looked up again his voice was slurred.

"So we're just supposed to sit around and wait for the bombs to start falling."

Reinhardt shook his head. "You know Monty, it's a funny thing but until this so called war, what do they call it? The bore war started, I felt like an Englishman. I mean I've been here for over forty years, for Christ's sake. But since September the third I've felt like a German. Look, as long as Chamberlain's in power there isn't going to be any fighting, not in this country, anyway. Hitler wants lands in the east, you know, Poland and Danzig and Czechoslovakia. Since Britain declared war what has happened? Sweet FA. Hitler wants England to have the empire and he wants Europe. Chamberlain's happy about that. With the majority he's got in Parliament, who's going to shift him? And if he does go, the Tory grandees will make sure we get another gutless wonder who won't fight. The only danger to this country is if we get some gung-ho Charlie like Churchill. Relax, old man, it's not going to happen." He leant forward and whispered conspiratorially, "Anyway, I have it on the best authority that Hitler is a great admirer of this country."

"How do you know that?" demanded Monty.

"Good God, Monty, the man reads 'The Tatler'," and he roared with laughter."It's true, Binky Burns' wife works for the magazine and Hitler has it sent over every month."Monty looked at him slyly over the rim of his glass before slowly putting it down. "They interned all the Germans during the last war," he said .

Reinhardt waved the remark away dismissively, "They won't do it again, they realised their mistake. For one thing, just think how many Jewish refugees from Austria and Germany have come over her in the last seven or so years before the war even started. I mean, where would they put them all? For another, Chamberlain is terrified of antagonising Hitler. If they interned the Germans, what do you think Hitler would do to all the Brits stuck in Germany? What was the government's response when the Nazis invaded Poland? They leafleted the German population saying they couldn't win the war. And the pilot who got back to base two hours earlier than expected, and was asked if he had dropped the leaflets in bundles, and he admitted he had, was told, "Good heavens, man, you could have killed someone." He downed the dregs of his brandy and stood up, "But if I am interned, I'll send you a postcard from the Isle of Man. Thanks for the drink."

The pavements were slushy with dirty snow. He looked down in disgust at the dark, wet stains that were forming on his tan brogues and he cursed. He didn't like the idea of going back to an empty house that would be cold and where it would take an hour for the boiler to heat up sufficiently to heat the water. He prayed that he wouldn't get back to find burst pipes.

It was a fine Georgian terraced house that he had a twenty year lease on, though he had taken no part in choosing it, or any of the furnishings for that matter. He'd signed the contract without even having seen it and all the furnishings which were very much to his wife's taste, were both expensive and, in his view, tacky, with all the chintz and brocade and the heavy floral curtains. Still, the friends he bought back to the house would enthuse wildly over his wonderful taste- the female ones would, anyway. They knew that he was divorced (or thought they knew. Reinhardt was unclear about his marital status, even in his own mind) and that his ex-wife was living in Yorkshire. It was true that she had taken the two boys back to Richmond to be near her parents, having failed to secure an allowance from Reinhardt. At that point, he had moved in. He had long ago decided that, having been sent to England himself at the age of fifteen, and therefore missing out on a relationship with his father, who he remembered as a distant figure with a shotgun and a beard, he wasn't very good at paternity, and that the upbringing of her sons was much better left to their mother. He hadn't seen them for eight years. He'd provided the money, which she had spent. She had provided the love and support and affection, which had all gone on the boys, so he didn't really see reason to blame himself; he simply found it elsewhere.

Still, he reflected as he wandered round the cold and empty house, it had been nice to come back to a warm fire and a good meal prepared by the cook and hear the boys playing in the nursery or being shooed up the stairs to bed by their nanny. The house was now more of a mausoleum than a home. Maybe he should employ a full-time housekeeper.

The following week, along with the pile of leaflets exhorting him to keep his chin up, not to listen to idle gossip, to listen to government announcements and to take no notice of propaganda coming out of Berlin (though everyone knew that was the only way of really finding out what was going on in the war) he opened an official letter summoning him to a tribunal for aliens. If he did not attend he would be arrested. The tribunal was scheduled for the eleventh at eleven in the morning.

Reinhardt took the letter and slumped down on the sofa. He had tried to erase the memory of the last time from his mind, but now it came flooding back. There had been no tribunal. He had been taken to Olympia along with thousands of other Germans. His abiding memory was of standing in a queue for the latrines while a guard said to each prisoner in turn, "pisserashit?" Depending on the response he got he jabbed with a tobacco stained finger towards one of two lines. The ignominy had almost been too much- he was not sure that he could cope with such treatment any more without losing his temper. It was then that he promised himself that he would become more English than the English.

"Pull yourself together, old man," he said aloud, "Things have changed." But for the next couple of nights he awoke with nightmares of having to sleep in horse boxes at Newbury, of being so cold that he didn't know what to do with himself.

On the morning of the eleventh he got up early and wondered what to wear. He'd had the brainwave of taking his umbrella, although the sky was cloudless. But he reasoned that Chamberlain's umbrella had become the symbol of appeasement and of the peace loving Englishman. He would wear his double-breasted dark suit and his best overcoat that normally he reserved for the theatre. And if they let him go free he would go to the Ritz to celebrate.

He took a taxi to the school in Bayswater.

He had never been in a state school before. It had obviously been closed for some time. A notice directed him to the hall, and apart from a guard standing at the gates, the place appeared deserted. The guard asked, "Can I help you, sir"

Reinhardt said he'd been asked to attend a tribunal.

"Are you Dr Rogers? Here to interview the Jerries."

"No," said Reinhardt, "I am a Jerry. Here to be interviewed."

The guard covered his confusion by searching inside his pocket and pulling out a crumpled piece of paper. "I'm sorry, sir, I thought you were one of us. So are you Mr Reinhardt?" He pronounced it 'Reenhardit'.

Reinhardt said he thought he recognised the name, and that that probably was him, yes.

The guard drew himself up to his full height, but even with his tin hat on was a good six inches shorter than Reinhardt. "I shouldn't take that attitude with you in there if I were you. Go through the double doors, at the end of the corridor you'll see my colleague. You can wait there to be called.

Reinhardt thanked him. The corridor smelled strongly of fresh paint and varnish. Wet footprints had had left grey stains down the centre. At the far end another man was huddled on a bench. A guard stood looking out of the window at the empty playground. He turned and nodded towards the bench.

Reinhardt studied the man next to him who was completely frozen, his arms wrapped round his chest and trembling.

"What's your name?" asked Reinhardt.

"Niedermayer." He thought long and hard about what came next. He nodded at each word he spoke, as if ticking it off. "I not speak English, but I learn, ja?"

Reinhardt frowned, "Aber, warum sind Sie nicht mit einem Freund gekommen?"

"Oy," protested the guard, "No German. You've got to speak English. I've got to be able to understand what you're saying."

Reinhardt stood up and smiled at him, "The thing is, major," he paused, just long enough for the compliment to register, "We've had a letter saying we can bring a friend or someone to vouch for us. I can show you if you like. This man speaks no English so I was simply asking him why he hadn't brought anyone with him."

"All right, but I'll know if you're not telling me his answer straight."

Reinhardt repeated his question. Niedermayer said that someone from the Austrian Centre had agreed to meet him there this morning at ten o'clock but he hadn't shown up. Someone said he'd got flu, so Niedermayer had had to come alone.

Reinhardt dutifully translated, and then asked Niedermayer if he wanted him to translate for him in the tribunal. The guard shrugged, "You can ask if you like, but you'll be wasting your breath. They're very good at making theirselves understood, like."

Niedermayer was making placatory gestures, "Nein, danke," he said to Reinhardt, and "Thank you, thank you," to the guard.

The doors to the hall opened and a young girl brushed past them. Reinhardt watched her go, her bare ankles pink above her heavy shoes.

"Student at the University," said the guard. "Lovely girl, perfect English. She'll be all right."

A severe looking woman with her grey hair plaited on her head put her face round the door and barked, "Mr Niedermayer" and marched back, leaving the door swinging behind her. Niedermayer stood and gave a little nod to Reinhardt and then followed her.

"Think I'll pop outside for a smoke," said Reinhardt, "Care to join me?"

"Well, why not, you're the last and he'll be in there for ages."

They stood under the covered entrance to the school and watched the snow land in heavy flakes across the playground. Reinhardt offered his cigarettes, "How many people on the committee? Any idea?"

The guard took a cigarette, "Senior Service. Very nice. Well, there's the secretary, Miss Bobbitt, a right old biddy, but of course she's got no power. Then there's the chairman, Sir Ralph Spiers, who's done a lot of these. He's some bigwig in the local Tory party, and Dr Rogers who never says much. And there's a new lady," he consulted the paper in his pocket, "Mrs Hart, haven't seen her before, so it's her first time, first time I've seen her, anyhow."

Reinhardt felt he'd got a slightly better idea of what he'd be facing.

They stubbed out their cigarettes and went back inside to find Niedermayer standing in the corridor consulting a piece of paper. The doors swung open behind him and Miss Bobbitt announced imperiously, "Mr Reinhardt."

Reinhardt leapt forward, and as she stood with the door open, looking at him with some surprise, he smiled, held the door and said, "Thank you so much."

She led the way across the large and dimly lit hall and took her place at the small table. The three members of the committee sat behind what Reinhardt assumed must be the headmaster's table. A single chair had been placed an intimidatingly long way from the committee and completely outside the range of the single bar electric fire that glowed more with hope than conviction, Reinhardt thought.

Sir Ralph Spiers was busily organising his papers, Dr Rogers was holding his glasses up to the light and was trying to clean them by rubbing them vigorously with his handkerchief. Only Mrs Hart paid him any attention as he walked in.

"Sit down," said Sir Ralph, without looking up. Reinhardt laid his umbrella across his lap, sat down and smiled. She was, he thought, just the kind of woman he should have married. She was elegantly, though not ostentatiously dressed, and that combination of modesty and attractiveness that he always found irresistible. He glanced at her hands which had been resting on the table and noticed her wedding ring before she slipped them out of sight onto her lap. He wondered about her husband- probably some pompous businessman who was big in bakelite or something and who had lost interest in her years ago. What was she? Forty-ish? A ten year old son who has been sent away to school. Empty nest syndrome, so she's got to find something to do with her time and for the war effort. Obviously well-educated or she wouldn't be here. I bet she's ripe for an affair.

He caught her eye and smiled and she looked away hurriedly and then at Sir Ralph who coughed, put down his papers and looked up at Reinhardt.

"Can't quite understand why we haven't seen you before, Mr Reinhardt, did you not receive a summons?"

Reinhardt, in all honesty, wasn't sure. He had gone through a period last autumn when he had avoided opening his post on the basis that it was either news he didn't want to read, or demands for money that he didn't want to pay.

"I've been away in Harrogate quite a bit. On business," he said.

"Oh, so you work, what line of business are you in?"

"My partner and I have developed a high performance petroleum for use in racing cars, actually. Of course, with the start of the war and Brooklands closing as a result, there's no immediate demand…"

"Are there no other uses for this fuel, I mean, couldn't it be adapted for military uses, for example?"

Reinhardt smiled, impressed by the question. He'd noticed little pockets of paranoia in the press, and the idea of a German using British money and labour to make fuel for planes that would one day bomb Britain would make a great story in the Sunday Sillies. "My partner, Charles Knowles is the scientific brains. I find the capital and do the marketing, but he has developed it with the needs of high performance cars in mind. It is added to the fuel, and of course the fuel in military vehicles is quite different."

Sir Ralph nodded, "I see. And who uses your fuels. Anyone we may of heard of?"

"You may have heard of Delage, and Bugatti, for example. And the ERA Voiturette won the Swiss Grand Prix in'36 with it."

"Really, " Sir Ralph was impressed, "Good to hear of a British success. And did you race yourself?"

"Only in a very small way, one or two races, oh a number of years ago, but I do find speed very seductive." He glanced at Esther Hart, but she was busily watching the chairman who said, "I do agree. Well, I don't think we need to detain you any longer. I'm awarding you a 'C' which means you are at liberty to travel as you wish, and good luck with your business."

Reinhardt thanked him and left, feeling relieved. Outside the school he hailed a taxi. "The Savoy," he said.

Chapter Three

Lotte Staengl sat with a copy of 'Der Zeitspiegel' open on the table in front of her. She turned the pages absent-mindedly, hardly taking in what she was reading and kept glancing up at the open door of the reading room. The old man beside her had given up trying to engage her in conversation and had returned to his book with a sigh. Eventually she became aware of his presence.

"I'm sorry, Herr Jütte, "she said, "I'm a bit preoccupied, what were you saying?"

Before he could reply, Franz Niedermayer walked through the door. Lotte jumped up to greet him.

"Franz, I am so sorry. There was a mix up. Otto Bauer told me he was coming to the tribunal with you but by the time I heard he'd got flu, it was too late. Was everything all right?"

Niedermayer sat down at the table beside her and shrugged his shoulders, "I didn't really understand- they spoke so quickly. But they gave me this paper."

He passed her the chit he'd been given.

She glanced at it. "It's a 'B'. Did you show them your visa?"

"They didn't ask for it, I don't think."

By now the other men in the room had put down their books and newspapers and were listening to the conversation.

"A 'B's' all right, said Herr Jütte, "I'm a 'B'. So they took my radio and my map of the underground, so I got another map and when I want to hear the news I just go round to Bauer's flat. His radio's a lot better than mine was. He's a 'C' so he can have as many radios as he wants. And I go to Paddington police station every week on Fridays. You can come with me if you want. I'll be glad of the company. At least we're not going to be locked up. Locked up is not good. I'm speaking as one who was in Dachau, you know."

"But I should have been there with him," said Lotte, "It's crazy. Did you tell them you left Austria because you were a union official?"

Niedermayer shook his head, "I didn't know how to say that. I said I was a socialist."

A voice from the corner interrupted, "You shouldn't have said that, that's why you got your 'B'. Some of these Englishmen are more worried about Stalin than they are about Hitler. They think if you say you're a socialist that means you're a communist. It's true."

Niedermayer looked at his watch. "Don't worry, Lotte, it's not your fault. Look, I'm on duty at one so I'm going to get some lunch. Come and eat with me."

The living room of 126 Westbourne Terrace had been knocked through to next door and been converted into a Viennese style restaurant. Herr Jütte shuffled after them. Standing in the queue he tapped Niedermayer on the shoulder and pointed to a mural that had just been completed, showing a scene from the Prater. He shook his head. "You know," he said in a whisper, "I was there when the Germans came and I saw what they were like." He looked up into Niedermayer's face. "They made an old man strip to his underclothes and crawl on the ground and then they told him to bark like a dog. And when his wife tried to stop them they put a ladder up against a tree and made her climb up it and sit on a branch and make noises like a bird. All those young soldiers with their uniforms and their rifles thought it was a great joke. We were so embarrassed for them we couldn't look and we were too ashamed and too frightened to protest. It's better to die than suffer such humiliation."

Niedermayer had heard the story before, and about the treatment of prisoners in Dachau. And each time he heard it he felt his throat tighten and wondered about Ilse and his daughter in Prague. He, too, had felt ashamed at leaving them, but his wife had pleaded with him to leave because he was in danger, not they.

He had learnt that he had to keep busy, and in the Austrian Centre that was not difficult. His friend, Willi Stölz was serving and greeted him in English,

"Good afternoon, sir. Today we have wiener schnitzels à l'anglais. They are not too bad. And they are not too good. Man can eat them. This is good English, no?"

"One can eat them," corrected Lotte.

"Ach, so, my teacher." He reverted to German, " Franz, you're relieving me in

21

twenty minutes, so you'd better eat quickly. I don't want to be late for my class."

They found an empty table. Herr Jütte had seen a couple of old friends eating at another table and had gone to join them. Before starting his food, Niedermayer asked, "Is there any news?"

Lotte shook her head, "I've spoken to the people at the Czech Trust Fund and to the Thomas Mann Society. I'm sorry."

They completed their meals in silence. Finally he said, "You will let me know."

"Of course,"

"Even if the news is bad."

"Yes. I'll see you tonight."

He took his plate to the kitchen and went to the counter to take over from Willi.

"Do you want to come up to 'Das Laterndl' tonight? asked Willi.

"But we've got our English lesson with Lotte."

Willi clicked his tongue, "Damn, I forgot. She won't mind if we miss one."

"No, it's not fair. Anyway, I need all the help I can get. You go if you want to, anyway, it'll be on other nights."

"OK, they're showing 'The Beacon.' It's supposed to be really good."

He took his coat from the back of the door and put it on, and said in stilted English, "Bloody English weather, I'm coming."

Willi and Niedermayer were sharing a room in a guest house behind Paddington Station with Johannes Roth, a Bavarian musician who had left Munich after Kristallnacht. Their room consisted of a bunk bed, a single steel framed bed, a small table with a wooden chair and a chest of drawers with one leg missing. A window so covered with soot and grime from the trains that they felt no need to black it out overlooked the roof of the station. Three similar rooms, also on the fourth floor, were occupied by other refugees from Germany and Austria . The twelve men shared a lavatory, but to wash they had to go down to the third floor where a notice on the back of the door said that baths could only be taken once a week and that the management reserved the right to confiscate any towels or washing materials left in the bathroom. On the back of each bedroom door a notice reminded guests that it was forbidden to hang pictures on the walls. In consequence, Niedermayer, Willi and Johannes had small framed photographs of their wives and children on the table, each one facing its owner's bed.

When Willi got back at just before six, he found Niedermayer studying his 'Guide for refugees' that he had been given earlier, a dictionary open at his side.

"What does 'attach importance' mean?" asked Niedermayer

Willi shook the snow from his greatcoat. "Show me."

He took the slip of paper. "Attach- festmachen, I think. But how can you attach a thing to something that's not a thing. I've no idea. Ask Lotte."

Niedermayer sighed, "I'll never understand this language. Sometimes I think I should have taken my chances and stayed in Prague. At least I could understand what they were doing to us."

Willi sat on the bed beside him. He was scornful. "Did you know what they were doing to people like us in Dachau and Buchenwald? Have you heard what Johannes says about Kristallnacht? Have you even been listening?"

"Of course I have, but I feel so guilty."

"About Ilse?" Willi's tone had softened. Niedermayer leant forward and put his head in his hands. "Yes, and about you."

"About me? Why me?"

"Your English is better than mine- read what it says." Niedermayer passed him the judgement again"

Willi scanned it and his eye lit upon the word radio. "But you don't have a radio."

"No, but you do."

"Ach, that's nothing. If they take my radio because you're sharing a room with me, well, so what. Still it's six o'clock. Let's use it while we've still got it."

He reached under his bed and plugged it in. Big Ben was striking and the BBC accent intoned, "This is the six o'clock news for today, Thursday, 18th January. In a review of territorial troops, the King and Queen…."

23

"Not that," said Willi. He knelt down and turned the tuning dial. The radio whistled and crackled until he found the station he was looking for. The familiar nasal tones of William Joyce announced, "This is Jairmany calling, Jairmany calling. You millions all over Britain who wish to know the truth about this war, also know that you can only find out what is happening by tuning into Berlin. Your government is deceiving you. The BBC has been taken over by the Ministry of Misinformation. They dare not tell you the truth. And the truth is that when spring comes, when Germany's troops have returned from subduing the East, it will be your turn. Do not let your little tin pot prime minister deceive you. This is a war you cannot win. We have supporters at the highest level in your government who will welcome the Führer when he leads his victorious army through the streets of London. Why only today our secret troops successfully destroyed a munitions factory in Essex. Has your government told you that? We know who our supporters are. People of Britain, join us, cast down the pathetic government that is betraying you. Let us together create a new and better world. This is Germany calling."

Willi switched off the radio. "Come on," he said. "I'm starving. Let's get something to eat before class."

Chapter Four

The snow was swirling in the darkness. Müller hurried across the compound. The beams of light criss-crossing from the guards' watch- towers and illuminating the snowflakes reminded him of something. He stopped at the door of hut seventeen, his hand on the door handle. What was it? And suddenly he remembered. As a small boy he'd been given a torch by his father for Christmas and a snow scene of Neuschwanstein that when you shook it, the snow floated around the castle that was on a tiny mountain. In his room that night he had shone his torch on it. You could change the colours on the torch to blue or green or red, and he had spent ages deciding which one he liked the best. He had loved the fact that it had been so silent, the snow shining blue as it drifted down. Now the wind was howling in the barbed wire and beyond the barbed wire, the sea. Sometimes the search- lights would, just for a second, light up the horses' tails. He wouldn't have liked to have been out on it on a night like this.

He pushed at the door and the force of the wind forced it out of his hand and it slammed open against the wall.

In the tiny hut six of his crew mates were huddled around a radio. They looked up in surprise, and his cabin mate, Busch, who was sitting a little way away from the others snapped at him, "For fuck's sake, Müller, can't you look what you're doing?"

Two of the other men turned on Busch, "Shsh."

Captain Burfeind sat with his ear pressed to the radio, the others watching him intently. After a few moments he switched it off and said, "Not much. A munitions plant blew up somewhere in Essex. Five dead."

Busch smiled, "And that means we did it. We've blown up one of their armament factories. It won't be long now."

Captain Burfeind looked at Busch thoughtfully. "Here," he said, "Let me show you something. He stood up from the bed on which he had been sitting and pulled it away from the wall. He prised the skirting board away and from behind it pulled out a map that he opened on the floor. Glancing up, he said, "Müller, keep an eye."

Müller went to the window and peered out.

"Now," said Captain Burfeind, "This is the English Channel, here is northern France, and here southern England." He placed a forefinger on the map. "We are here, in Seaton, on the coast. Now, it's just off the map, but as I remember, Essex is here, on the east coast, just north of Kent." He looked up, "What does this tell us?"

Busch said excitedly, "That we landed troops, by boat or plane, and blew up the factory."

Captain Burfeind looked at him and shook his head. "It's possible, but unlikely. You've seen what the weather's been like for the last month- how could they have got across? No, in my opinion it was an accident. But suppose it wasn't, or more importantly, the British government thinks it wasn't. They would conclude that the coastal areas are unsafe- in fact, they may have decided that already. In that case, they will be taking steps to move us inland and to the north. In which case, Seaman Busch, your escape plan is a waste of time."

Busch reddened and said, "How did you know?" Then he looked accusingly at Müller who was staring fixedly out of the window."

"It's my duty to know," said Captain Burfeind, "In Dachau, so I've been told, for every prisoner who tried to escape, the SS shot ten more. Why do you think the British are any different?" He folded up the map, replaced it behind the skirting and stood up. "I don't think I need to say any more. "

The seven men wrapped themselves up and stepped out into what was now a blizzard. Though they'd swept the path only a couple of hours earlier, the drifting snow had already covered it.

"Mind the pool," said Captain Burfeind over his shoulder, "We don't want to have to pull anyone out," and then, under his breath, "except Busch."

The dining room held three hundred people, and still had the décor it had had when it was a Warner's holiday camp before it was requisitioned at the outbreak of war. A life size painted clown, the paint peeling off it's nose had had written under it 'Ein Englischer Soldat.' The brown panelled walls had become browner with cigarette smoke, but at least the heat from the ovens meant that the place was warm.

The room was only a quarter full which added to the moribund air of the place. The one person who seemed to be happy was Hans, who had been the ship's cook when their ship, the SS Woermann had been scuttled off the coast of Angola. Since then he had been preparing meals for the German sailors who tried to avoid eating at the same time as the Jews and anti-fascists and who had taken the chalets as far away from the Germans as they could.

Busch ate in silence, still smarting from the reprimand he had received, and as soon as he had finished his meal rushed out of the room, barging his way between the two guards who were standing in the doorway. "I hope we are moved," he muttered to himself as he tramped through the snow, "Why should we have to share the place with Jews and communists. They make me sick. And Burfeind isn't a Nazi, he's a coward and a disgrace to Germany." He was still smouldering and shivering in his bed when Müller returned an hour later.

Busch sat up, shouting, "You betrayed me, you bastard. Why did you have to tell him?"

Müller was unmoved. "Because he's right. Suppose you had managed to get out. You don't speak English. You didn't even know where we were before you saw that map. At best you would have been recaptured and brought back and put in solitary- at worst you would have got yourself, and ten of us shot. Your duty is to do as you're told."

Busch wasn't listening, "My duty," he yelled, "As a Nazi, is to fight for the Führer. How can I do that, trapped in this place with that scum?"

"Otto, let me tell you something. There's another camp, not ten kilometres from here. The Captain was offered a place there- it's called Paignton, or something like that. For twenty Deutschmarks a day he could have had his own room, received letters, have proper food three times a day, got the news in a place that is warm and comfortable. He could even have received guests. He saw it as his duty to turn it down so that he could be with his men. So don't talk to me about duty, just do yours."

Busch was silent while he thought this over, and then said, "How do you know this?"

"One of the guards told me. He was working there before he got transferred here. And he told me that the only people in there are Germans. So if the Captain is here it's because of us. Don't you forget it." And he turned out the light.

By morning, when the internees lined up for the roll call, a crisp frost lay on the ground. The men's breath made little clouds as they stamped their feet in an effort to get warm. On the far side of the compound, Busch could hear the hated Jewish names being called and the answering grunts. One of them, a young man of about his age had jeered at him the previous day as he was clearing snow. It was all he could do to stop himself from going over and smashing him with his shovel. As the guard called out the names of the Germans, they either answered, "Hier," or "Ja," until Busch's name was called, and he replied, as he did every day, morning and evening, "Heil Hitler," and clicked his heels together and gave the Nazi salute. Busch could never understand why the roll call always took so long- didn't they know that the Germans had been forbidden to try and escape by their own commander? At first he had started to make the Nazi salute to infuriate the guards; the fact that to begin with they had just looked at him quizzically and after a few days simply ignored it, enraged him.

After the roll call Captain Burfeind took the place of the guard and said that as it was so cold he would be having a shortened service that morning, "Let us pray." He opened his prayer book and started to read, but after only a few sentences, Busch could hear loud jeers coming from the his right, where the Jewish internees were billeted. He glanced over- there were three of them, including the lad who had been mocking him only the day before when he had been clearing snow. And the shouting and hoots of derision grew louder when Burfeind announced the hymn they were to sing. Everybody except Busch seemed to be ignoring them as they sang with enthusiasm, the pent up emotions of frustration and boredom of the last week releasing into the frosty air. Busch didn't sing. After the service, the Germans trooped off to the dining room for breakfast, but Busch hung back, wishing he had taken his revenge the day before. The three boys had moved closer and Busch waited. When one of them shouted, "That's right, crawl way you filthy

Nazi schmuck," he ran at them. The boy he had wanted to hit fled, but his friend slipped as he turned, held up his hand to protect himself and fell heavily on his arm. He gave a cry of pain but before he could get up, Busch stamped on his wrist. He was about to throw himself on his opponent when he was caught from behind.

"Idiot!" shouted Müller, who had him by the neck. The scream had brought a dozen Jewish internees running and behind him, Busch could hear shouts in German, of "Get back, get back!" He struggled to free himself, but a panting guard with a rifle pointing at his chest was yelling at him in English. Another was telling the Jews to get back to their part of the camp while a third was kneeling down and staring at the boy's wrist. Busch felt a surge of satisfaction at seeing it was broken as it hung limply and at a strange angle from his arm.

Major Stimpson was sitting behind his desk, smoking his pipe and frowning. "Bloody Admiralty, what the hell do they expect me to do about it?" he said aloud. Ten minutes before, his secretary had come in with a telegram.

"Bad news, I'm afraid, sir." He read it and sighed.

'Seventeen German seamen taken from US ship. Stop. Arriving 1700 hrs. Stop. Please accommodate."

He looked up, "Do you have a cat, Miss Higgins?"

"No, sir, why do you ask?"

"We do, you see, a large ginger tom that I have just renamed 'Winston.' It never answers to its name anyway, so what we call him doesn't matter a fig to him. But he brings rats into the house which he then releases. It's as if he's bringing us a present and wants us to praise him and say how clever he is. It's just like that with the Admiralty. They keep sending me these German seamen as if I should be grateful, but quite frankly, I've no idea what to do with them. And what on earth were they thinking of, boarding an American ship? I thought they wanted America to be on our side. Still, at least that's not our problem."

Miss Higgins smiled. She liked her boss, but she wasn't sure he was cut out for this job at all. "Will there be anything else, sir?"

"Yes, can you get me a coffee, and not in one of those ridiculous little holiday camp cups. You know, in a proper tin mug. And I think this is a four sugar job."

When the coffee arrived he slid open a desk drawer and took out a bottle of whisky and poured the remainder of the bottle into his mug. "Where the hell am I to put them?" he said aloud.

He was still pondering the problem twenty minutes later when there was a loud knock on the door, and before he could say, "Come in," Corporal Hutchinson burst in. He saluted, "Begging your pardon, sir, it's happened again." The corporal was panting and red faced from running.

"What has?"

"It's that man again, sir?" said Hutchinson, staring at the wall behind the major, and then, as if suddenly realising what he'd said, he took a deep gulp of air and stood frozen.

"I see," Major Stimpson sat back in his chair and put his fingertips together, enjoying the corporal's discomfort. "I take it we're not talking about Hitler here, corporal. It's not that he's been captured and is being sent to us as a POW."

Hutchinson glanced at the major to see if he was joking and then returned his gaze to the wall. "Yes, sir, I mean no, sir, we're not talking about Hitler. It's Busch, sir."

"Oh, well I suppose that 's a relief. What has Busch done?"

"Broken a man's wrist sir, one of the Jewish prisoners."

The major sighed, "And how did this happen?"

"There was a fracas, sir The Jewish lads were taunting the Germans during their service. Busch chased one who fell and he might have broken his wrist then, but Busch stamped on it, sir."

"And where is Busch now?"

"Outside, sir. Ross and White are guarding him. Shall I send him in?"

"No, corporal, you will not. Put him in 73. Tell Ross and White to stand guard, they can each do hourly shifts. Ask Miss Higgins to come in and then get Mr Biedermann and Captain Burfeind to report to me at ten o'clock. Then I want you to write me a full report and let me have it this afternoon. Is that clear? Or are we referring to Captain Burfeind as 'Colonel Chinstrap' now?"

Hutchinson grinned. "We could do, sir."

"And make sure ITMA gets his tea to take in with him. I don't want him dying of hypothermia."

Hutchinson grinned again, saluted and left. A minute later Miss Higgins entered. Ah, Sophie Tuckshop, thought the major unkindly, glancing at her ample figure,

"Miss Higgins, I need you to phone Dr Dobel and ask him to come and see me as soon as he can make it, and tell him to bring his bag."

Dr Dobel had been working as a GP in Seaton for the last seven years. He was the Stimpson's doctor and had been at the house every day for a week when the Stimpson's eldest child, Freddie, had suspected meningitis. They lived next door to each other and as a result the two families had become close. The doctor had asked the major to come and support him at his tribunal just after the outbreak of war. And frankly, the major had far more confidence in Dobel's skills than he did in those of Dr Elton, the official doctor to the camp. He had tried to assuage Elton's resentment by pointing out that Dobel, being German, could communicate with the internees, and this surely, was helpful. Dr Elton hadn't agreed and still referred to him as 'Jerry Dobel.'

The guards at the gate were familiar with Dr Dobel's Morris Minor. Most of them had had to push it at some stage. Being very short-sighted he drove slowly and erratically, his nose pressed to the windscreen. The camp was at the end of a long road and when they saw them coming the guards swung open the gates as he careered through. He went straight to the major's office.

"Thanks for coming so quickly, Walter," the major said, standing up and shaking his hand, "I've got a problem and need you to interpret for me. Have a seat."

"I was told to bring my bag."

The major grimaced, "Elton's dealing with it, but I may need a second opinion. There was a fight this morning, and a lad's wrist got broken. Busch was responsible."

Dobel frowned, "The young seaman I saw a few weeks back? He's been in trouble before hasn't he?"

The major nodded, "Yes, a couple of times, but this is the most serious."

"What are you going to do with him?"

The major looked embarrassed. "Put him in the cooler for a couple of days-same as before."

Dobel was aghast, "It won't be the cooler, it'll be the freezer. Philip, you can't do that, you'll be killing him. It would be murder. I can't condone that."

The major shrugged, "I'm not asking you to condone it and, frankly, I wish I hadn't told you. It's not why I asked to see you."

Dobel leaned forward in his chair and stared across the table. "Last night it was minus seven degrees. I had two deaths from hypothermia and seven patients with severe pneumonia. Come to think of it, you probably know one of the women who died, Miss Chadwick, lived with her sister in our street. She was found on the beach this morning. What you're doing is not punishing this boy, but condemning him to death."

The major shook his head, "We'll get some heating put in there. Look, Walter, I've got seventeen more seamen coming in at five, and nowhere to put them. If even five of them are Nazis there's going to be more trouble than we can deal with. As it is they go around giving that ridiculous bloody salute every time they see each other and the other night apparently kept the camp up half the night singing that stupid song, what's it called?"

"The Horst Wessel song."

"Yeah, whoever he is, or was. No, I need you to translate for me. I'm having Burfeind and Biedermann in here at ten," he glanced at his watch, "And I'm going to read them the riot act. They're the elected leaders, they've got to control their own groups. But I need you to make sure they understand."

"OK," Dobel agreed," But before they come in, will you make sure that Busch at least gets hot drinks every hour and that he gets a chance to exercise every two hours. At least do that. I don't want to be the doctor who has to sign his death certificate."

The major nodded reluctantly, feeling suddenly tired. "I'll tell the guards responsible."

There was a knock on the door and Miss Higgins announced that Captain Burfeind and Mr Biedermann had arrived. Biedermann was tall and thin, deep furrows in his sallow complexion and with a thick white beard. He was at least nine inches taller than Captain Burfeind whose presence the major always found reassuring. His men clearly respected him, all, it seemed except for Busch.

"Gentlemen," said the major, "I've asked Dr Dobel to be present in order to translate and so that we all understand each other." He paused and waited for Dobel to repeat what he had said in German. He went on, "I have asked you to come and see me as the leaders of your respective groups. One of your tasks is to maintain discipline. That is your job, not mine. This incident this morning was not the first but it was the most serious. The hostility between your men has reached dangerous proportions and I am concerned that the next time someone may be seriously injured, if not worse. Do I make myself clear?"

Neither Biedermann nor Burfeind could bring himself to look at the other.

Eventually Biedermann said," The Jews should not be in the same camp as the Nazis. We came to this country to escape from them, and they put us in a concentration camp with people who were wanting to kill us back home. I don't understand."

The major shook his head, "That isn't the issue here. I can only do as I am ordered. I want to run a peaceful camp and it's not up to me who is interned, Herr Biedermann. But I must insist that you take the appropriate action against those men who were involved in the incident this morning."

Biedermann snorted, "What action should I take against a man who is lying in the medical hut with a smashed wrist? You treat the Nazis much better than you do the refugees, that is a fact."

The major stood up, "I've made my point, and I expect to see an improvement. You may go."

When they had left, he turned to Dobel. "The trouble is, Biedermann is right. The Swiss camp inspectors assure us that the names of the Nazi internees are not passed on to the Germans, but we have our doubts. If the Germans thought we were not treating their people properly, they'd take it out on the British people they're holding. I know the refugees have a tougher time of it, but the authorities won't hear of it. There's nothing I can do."

Dobel nodded and then said, "Look, if there's nothing else, I must be going. I've still go my rounds to do." He left the major still trying to figure out where to put the new arrivals.

Busch was taken back to his hut to collect his blanket and wash bag and was then led along to perimeter fence to hut 73. It stood beyond the line of occupied huts and before the war had been used as a store when the place had been a holiday camp. Now it held a single bed, a pile of deck chairs and a three broken desks. Busch was familiar with it. He wrapped the blanket around his great coat and lay on the bed, waiting for the cold to numb his senses. Above him a cracked window pane let in the light. He felt angry with Müller and was much better off here than sharing a room with that little shit. He closed his eyes. The worst thing was the boredom, the second worst was to be able to hear the sea and not be on it. It was where he felt free; he couldn't show it, but being a member of a crew made him feel for the first time in his life that he belonged. Even when he had joined the Hitler Youth he had felt like an outsider, just as he had felt like an outsider in his own family as the second of three sons. Drifting off to sleep he was often woken again by a memory. He had come home from school and gone into the kitchen. There was nobody there. He could hear somebody moving about in the living room. He went into the kitchen where a fresh loaf of Graubrot was lying on the sideboard. He broke a piece off and as he did so, he heard the swish of a belt as it caught him across the wrist. The buckle had torn his skin. With the shock and the pain, he put his wrist to his mouth and tasted blood on his tongue as he spun round. His father was staring down at him. He was still angry and ashamed at what he had felt at that moment. He had wanted his father to hold him and love him, because, he realised, that's what he felt for his father- love and gratitude. Yet he despised those feelings in himself, they were weak and effeminate. His father had turned without saying a word and walked out of the room, and the boy had run up to his room, thrown himself on his bed and cried, burying his head in his pillow so that he couldn't be heard. When, an hour later, his mother had come up to find out what was wrong, he had refused to answer. It took his father's voice, barking his name from the bottom of the stairs to bring him down. The incident was never mentioned, and he had never told anyone about it.

That was three years before the Führer came to power to rescue Germany from the Jews who had made her weak. He had seen troops of soldiers in their smart uniforms marching through Bremerhaven, but he hadn't wanted to join them. He wanted to serve the Führer in his own way, so at the age of seventeen he had joined the merchant navy. He had it in his mind that he would become a submariner and this ambition was reinforced when, last October, they had got the news that the Royal Oak had been sunk at Scapa Flow. Busch would have given everything to have been in that U boat with its captain Günther Prien as it manoeuvred its way through Ross Sound. He had memorised every word of that news broadcast, how the attack was completely unexpected, how the first torpedo had failed to do any real damage and how Prien had spent twenty minutes reloading three more torpedoes, each one of which had been on target, and how they had escaped without anyone realising that he had even been there.

Busch turned over onto his side. A few moments later he didn't hear the door quietly open and see the mug of hot tea placed on the floor.

Chapter Five

It was well after midnight when Franco Baldini came off duty. He couldn't see a thing and stood on the pavement blinking his eyes to get accustomed to the darkness. A bus rumbled out of the gloom and he took his normal seat, slipping in behind the driver. The conductor greeted him but he only nodded distractedly and stared out in to the blackness. Usually this was his best time of day, when he could get a few minutes to himself, a bit of peace and quiet. He imagined it like a journey across a suspension bridge that was swaying gently in the breeze and that was suspended between two towers full of light and frenetic activity. But tonight it felt as if one end of the bridge was going to shear away from its moorings and he was going to be plunged into an abyss. How could she do this to him? He ran the scene back over his mind. It was just as awful this time as it had been the first.

He had just come off his tea break at the Savoy and was entering the restaurant when he saw his daughter, Francesca walk through the doors on the arm of a tall and fair man. Before she had a chance to see him he had ducked behind a pillar and beckoned to Federico. "See that couple who have just come in, over by the window. Do me a favour and go and serve them," and Federico had obligingly gone off, only to return two minutes later saying that the young lady knew he was on duty and had specifically asked for him. So he had pulled down his waiter's uniform, checked his moustache and run his hand through his hair, and smiling awkwardly walked over to their table.

"What are you doing here?" he asked his daughter in Italian, but she had ignored the question and said, in English, "Papa, this is Eric."

Eric had stood up and offered his hand, which Franco had taken briefly, looking round nervously to check that he hadn't been seen.

"Papa," went on Francesca, smiling, "Eric has something to ask you."

Franco looked from his daughter to Eric, "Yes?" and then he felt that spasm of fear up his spine that had hardly left him all afternoon and evening. He could still feel it.

"What, now?" he asked, dry mouthed.

Eric had smiled nervously, cleared his throat and said, "Mr Baldini, I should like your permission to ask for your daughter's hand in marriage."

Franco had stared hopelessly at him and then at his daughter. Finally the only thing he could think of saying was, "What would you like to drink?"

Sensing that a celebration was probably premature, Eric ordered an Earl Grey tea. Francesca ordered the same and Franco went off to the kitchen, thinking,

"Earl Grey, the girl had never even heard of Earl Grey before he mentioned it."

Federico was collecting a pot of coffee, and Franco stopped him. "You've got to help me, that's my daughter and she wants to marry that Englishman."

"Ay ay ay," said Federico, "And how is Giovanna taking it?" and he took up his tray and left. Having ordered the tea, Franco put both hands against the wall and dropping his head between his shoulders, took several deep breaths. "If I say 'no' she'll make my life a complete misery. If I say 'yes' her mother will kill me." Federico reappeared, "Perhaps he'll join the army and not come back," he said cheerfully. Franco nodded, "Grazie." But he had had an idea. It might be clutching at straws but it was all he had.

He returned to the table with the tea to find the couple gazing into each other's eyes in a manner that he found quite repellent. Laying the tray down he asked, "Are you planning to join the war effort?"

"Papa, Eric is a lecturer in English Literature. That's how we met. First he made me fall in love with Chaucer and then I fell in love with him," and she squeezed Eric's hand across the table.

"As a matter of fact, sir," said Eric, "I applied to join the RAF but I was turned down as I have rather poor sight, but I am an ARP, when I'm not teaching."

"I see," said Franco. He was aware he had spent too much time at this table and decided it was time to clutch at his last straw. Addressing Francesca in Italian he fell back on the strategy he had been using ever since his daughter was old enough to speak. "And what does your mother say?"

She moved her hand from Eric's to his, "Papa," she smiled, "It will be so much better coming from you." She stood up and Franco watched as she was helped on with her coat, leaving the tea untouched. Eric fumbled in his pocket and placed a two shilling piece on the table while Franco said, "I'll have to discuss it with Francesca's mother, you know, before I can give you…" But Francesca was already leading Eric out of the door. He knew that his daughter had done what she had come to do.

Letting himself in through the front door he stopped and gave a little groan. Weddings are expensive and she would expect the best. He had £171 saved, but that money was so that Giovanna's sister and her husband could be brought over and to set them up in their own flat just around the corner that Giovanna had found for them. He climbed the stairs and opened the front door. The place was dark and quiet. He had hoped somehow that he would come back to find that Giovanna had already discovered their daughter's intentions and that there would be screams and yells and throwing things. The silence was worse. Outside their bedroom door his pyjamas were neatly folded on the floor where Giovanna always left them when he was on the late shift, so that he could undress in the bathroom and get into bed without waking her. Mechanically he washed his face and cleaned his teeth and then, opening and closing the bedroom door as quietly as he could, he slipped into bed beside his wife. "That you, Franco?" she asked sleepily.

"Who else would it be?" The joke had been repeated thousands of times. It was a way of saying "Good night."

Lying in the warm bed he felt as if he were lying next to a time bomb. One word from him and it would go off, sending him running for shelter. But if he didn't tell her tonight she would only accuse him of keeping secrets from her, one of the many things she couldn't abide above all others. He had an image of standing before a firing squad and being told that he had to give the order to fire. He simply couldn't do it.

The next morning Franco woke up with a headache and alone. Giovanna usually left him to have a lie in when he had been working the late shift, and he had hardly slept. He could hear his wife moving about in the kitchen and scolding Francesca who was also, apparently still in bed. He pulled the covers up over his head. A few minutes later she was standing over him, "Franco, here's your coffee. Are you ill?" she asked. He poked his nose over the blanket. In her black pinafore and with her curlers in she looked as forbidding as she did when he had imagined having to tell her that her daughter was wanting to get married to an Englishman who probably wasn't even a Catholic. He sat up and took the coffee. "And there's a letter from the Fascio that arrived yesterday that you'll have to deal with, it's probably about that land that you want to buy."

"About time too," said Franco, "I'll go and see Eugenio about it this morning." He didn't actually need to discuss it with Eugenio at all, but he did want his brother's advice on how to deal with his problem. Once dressed he went into the kitchen where Francesca had her head in a book and Giovanna was berating her, saying she needed the pasta made and that there was all the washing to be done and that she needed to get ready for mass. Francesca looked up and smiled at her father, raising her eyebrows as if asking a question. Franco shook his head, frowning.

"We've got to go in an hour," said Giovanna, wiping the flour off her hands on to her pinny and then taking it off. "Francesca, light the oven and finish off this pasta and when you've done that go and get dressed. I want everything ready when I come back- Julia's setting my hair for me. Franco, go and shave and get clean. You can't have a bath, there's no water." And she went out.

"Why haven't you told her?" Francesca was whispering as if her mother were in the next room. Franco was also whispering, "I have to choose the right time. I'm not sure this is a good idea at all, I mean how long have you known him?"

"Just over a year, why?"

Franco scratched his head, "Well, it's a shock, you know. You've never mentioned him and then suddenly you want to get married. We, I mean, your mother had other plans for you." The moment he said it he regretted it. His daughter stopped whispering, "It's my life and I'll marry who I want. In eight months I'll be twenty- one and you won't be able to stop me. Don't you want me to be happy?"

Franco sat next to her and took her hands in his. At all costs he must stop her from crying; he could never cope with his daughter crying.

"Of course, more than anything else," he said consolingly, "It's just that you're so young."

"I'm the same age as Mama when she married you and you were younger than Eric when you got married and you're happy. Aren't you?"

The question was unanswerable. Franco had never thought that being happy had very much to do with anything. Sometimes he was happy and sometimes he wasn't. He had never given it much thought. Right now he knew he wasn't.

But money was a constant worry and that made him unhappy.

"The thing is," he said, dreading where this bit of the conversation might go, "Weddings are so expensive."

Francesca smiled, "Oh Papa, I love you. You don't have to worry about that. I'll be happy to get married in a register office and Eric says he would too. We don't want a big Italian wedding. He'll even pay for the licence. You wouldn't have to pay for anything."

She'd thought it all through. Franco shook his head despairingly, "You mother would never stand for that, and, to be honest, I wouldn't be happy about it either." Another appalling thought came to him, "Francesca you're not...." He couldn't bring himself to say the word.

She looked at him, clearly shocked and hurt, her eyes filling with tears, and then she pushed herself away from the table and stood up, "You don't understand at all, do you?" she stamped off to her bedroom and slammed the door.

Franco stared blankly at the picture of the Blessed Virgin calendar hanging on the wall by the sideboard. There was no point in going after her. He must speak to Eugenio. Wearily he got up and put on his coat. He tiptoed to his daughter's bedroom door. He couldn't hear a sound. Then he went to find his brother. He crossed the landing that separated their two flats and opened the door without knocking. Julia was brushing out Giovanna's hair at the kitchen table. Franco ignored them both and spoke to Eugenio who was reading a newspaper.

"Eugenio, venga," he said, "I need to talk to you." Without moving her head, Giovanna protested, "You'll have to do that this afternoon, there's plenty of time later. Go and get ready for mass. We've got to leave in forty minutes."

"Five minutes," said Franco, "We'll only be five minutes." Eugenio looked bewildered, "What's this about?"

Franco frowned and nodded towards the door, "Venga," he mouthed. The two men went down the stairs with Giovanna calling, "Mind you are, and has Francesca finished that pasta yet?"

Outside on the pavement, Franco breathed a sigh of relief and started walking down the Gray's Inn Road."

"What's up? Where are we going?"

"It's Francesca," burst out Franco, "She wants to get married to an English boy who isn't a Catholic even and she wants me to tell Giovanna and she says she'll soon be twenty-one and they'll get married in a register office and she doesn't need my permission and how am I going to tell her mother? I don't even know where to start." He stopped and stared at his brother, "What am I going to do? You've got to help me."

They were standing outside a newsagent. "I need cigarettes and a paper," said Eugenio, and he went into the shop. Franco fidgeted on the pavement until his brother reappeared waving the headlines at him, "What's Mussolini up to now? The man's mad, he's talking about joining the war. Well, Ceni is and he wouldn't have said it if Mussolini hadn't told him to."

"Eugenio I really need your help," Franco said, taking the paper from his brother and putting it under his arm. "What am I going to do?"

"Well, suppose I tell Julia that Francesca wants to marry this English boy. She's bound to tell Giovanna and that let's you off the hook. Giovanna will forbid it and you can side with her. Problem over."

Franco thought this over and then shook his head. "That won't do. It'll take Giovanna two minutes to work out that I told you and that you told Julia and then she'll be furious that I didn't tell her first."

"So," said Eugenio, taking his paper back and opening the door, "Tell her yourself, like Francesca wants you to, or else," he turned halfway up the stairs and looked down at his brother, "Tell Francesca that if she's old enough to get married, she's old enough to tell her mother herself. Or I'll tell her, I'm not frightened of my own sister-in-law. Do you want me to do it?"

Franco stopped short of the landing, thinking, but Eugenio simply nodded. "I'll do it," and before Franco could stop him he had gone into his flat. Franco stood frozen to the spot as he heard Eugenio say, "Hey, Giovanna, congratulations, it's great news about Francesca." There was a silence that seemed to Franco to stretch into next week, and then a scream and Giovanna shot across the landing so fast, half her hair still in curlers, that she didn't notice her husband standing on the stairs. The door to their flat slammed shut and he heard his wife shouting and then his daughter shouting back. He knew that the right thing to do would be to go home and he fumbled for his key but thought that he must have left it in his work trousers. The yelling grew louder and more persistent. Franco reasoned that even if he knocked on the door he probably wouldn't be heard, and that anyway, it was better to let the storm run its course without his interference. He turned to take shelter in his brother's flat but before he had a chance to knock on the door he heard Julia's voice rising to a crescendo, "Es stupido, Eugenio!" and a flood of invective following that made him retreat as fast as he could down the stairs.

On the pavement he wondered where to go for a second, and then headed off down the Gray's Inn Road for the Fascio Club. He needed a glass of wine, if not something stronger.

By the time he reached the club he was frozen and realised that not only did he not have his coat, but he also had no money with him. The place was deserted, since everybody would be getting ready for mass. Only his old friend Paulo was there. He looked up and held out the morning's paper, showing Franco the headlines he had already seen.

"Have you seen this, Franco?" He did a double take. "Whatever's the matter, you look as if you've had the whole of the German army after you."

Franco slumped down beside him, "It's worse than that, Paulo, much worse."

Chapter Six

"Happy New Year, Mr Hickey," said the vicar, stamping his boots on the door mat to get rid of the snow. He looked round the shop, at the half empty shelves and pulled out his ration book.

"If it is, it's likely to be the last," replied the shop keeper, wiping the counter with a grubby cloth, "Reckon by this time next year we'll all be singing 'Deutschland Uber Alles' at gun point on the village green."

The vicar laughed, "Oh, come now, you surely don't think it'll ever come to that."

Mr Hickey wiped his hands on his brown apron and looked at the older man.

"I wouldn't say it if I didn't. And if you don't believe me perhaps you'll believe Mr Harold Nicolson." He reached across the counter and took a book off the top of a pile. "I bought forty of these for a pound," he said, "It's my way of doing my bit for the war effort, trying to make people see sense."

He passed it to the vicar. "Here, take it. Look on it as a late Christmas present, and when you've read it, pass it on and then tell me I'm wrong. It's all in there."

The vicar examined the cover 'Why Britain is at War' a Penguin Special. Anxious to change the subject, he said, "Jolly good, these Penguins, aren't they, getting people to read. Have you read many of them, Mr Hickey?"

"Just that one, and I've read it four times. And every time I read it, it makes more sense." Making a convert of the vicar would give him no end of satisfaction. "He says Hitler is just like that murderer, George Smith, you remember? who married three women and killed each of them in the bath on their honeymoon and he was only caught because one of the girl's uncles read a newspaper report and saw that his niece had died in exactly the same way as the two earlier girls. And Hitler's just the same, Czechoslovakia, Poland and Austria, always the same tactics. It's all in the book."

"Oh," said the vicar, not sure that he had quite followed the logic of the argument, "Well thank you, I'll read it with ple…well, with interest, anyway."

Do you have any eggs?"

He was aware that Mr Hickey was examining him with an expression that he didn't find altogether comfortable.

"Only powdered."

"Oh. Ah. Well, my wife didn't say anything about....but she did give me a list." He fumbled in his pockets and at length sighed and said, "Oh dear, I must have mislaid it somewhere. Not to worry, I'll just take two stamps, please. How is Mrs Hickey?"

"Her nerves are still playing her up," said Mr Hickey in the tone of someone who has heard quite enough about nerves and has no intention of discussing them further.

The vicar left the shop clutching the book and stepped out into the snow. Since the war started he had discovered a great solace in poetry and he found himself reciting under his breath, to the rhythm of his footsteps crunching along

"He went like one that hath been stunned

Te dumty dum forlorn

A sadder and a wiser man

Te dumty dumty morn."

Saturday night in the Queen's head was always busy, especially the public bar. Across the green from the village shop, the pub was standing room only. Maurice Hickey must have told at least ten people that the seat next to him was taken and he had almost finished his beer. He had drunk the first half pint quickly- he was nervous, but he was reluctant to finish his glass and go back to the bar because he would lose his seat, so he stared into the bottom of the glass, trying to think of the right form of words to say to her if, that is, she turned up. But then, suddenly, there she was, standing over him and smiling.

"Hello, Maurice, why such a long face?" She was ruddy cheeked and wiping a dewdrop from her nose with a sleeve. He thought she had never looked so beautiful.

"Here, he said, I've been keeping this seat for you. What d'you want to drink? The usual?"

He pushed his way to the bar and rehearsed his lines for the hundredth time as he waited to be served, glancing over at her every couple of seconds. He frowned when he saw that she was already chatting to Mavis Roberts- tonight he really needed her to himself. Taking her half of sweet cider and his pint back to the table he stood embarrassed and angry as the two women apparently carried on their conversation oblivious to his presence. Eventually Rose said, "I think Maurice wants a word in private, Mavis. Will you excuse us" and she giggled. Mavis gave her a knowing smile and winked at Maurice, which made him blush. He waited for her to turn away to talk to her friends before sitting down. He looked across the table at her as she drank. Then putting down her glass she said, "Well you do, don't you? What is it?"

The embarrassment he had felt a moment before had turned into a burning sensation in his face. "It can wait," he muttered.

"Oh, OK then." She stood up and took off her coat and looked round the bar and then back at him. "It's bloody freezing out there and my chilblains are killing me."

He nodded and looked down at the table.

"Oh come on Maurice, if you're not going to talk to me I'll go and talk to my friends. It's Saturday night for God's sake."

He leaned across the table and took hold of her hand. "Rose, I think we should get married."

She frowned and squeezed his hand, and after a pause said, "Why?"

"Why?" he exploded. That wasn't the answer he'd been expecting, and he went on in a fierce whisper, "Why? We love each other, don't we?"

She shook her head. "I didn't mean that, I meant, we're not ready that's all. Of course I love you, silly."

"Well," he said despondently, "I'm ready. That means you're not, I suppose."

"Look, Maurice, we haven't got any money. We haven't got anywhere to live. We'll just have to wait."

He looked at her over rim of his glass and finished his pint. "Right, well I've been thinking about that. Your Dad's got those three empty cottages at Frogmore End and last week I earned four pounds fifteen. I gave my Mum two quid for food and stuff and I won't have to give her anything if we're living in one of your Dad's cottages. If your Dad charges us rent, say thirty bob a week, we'll be better off and you're working as well, so we can manage. You think it over while I get them in."

Without waiting for her to answer he took the two empty glasses to the bar.

If she says no that means she doesn't love me at all and I'll bloody well go and join the bloody army and see how she likes that, he thought angrily.

"Well?" he said, standing over her as he put the drinks down, "And what do you say now?"

"Listen," she took his hand as he sat down," I'm not saying no for ever. In the first place, the ministry has what d'you call it, requisitioned those cottages for a load of land girls. They're coming to work on the farm just as soon as the weather clears, so we can't have them. So we still haven't got anywhere to live. And I'm not living in your Dad's shop, that's for certain. And suppose you get called up. I want a husband who's there with me."

"Well, I'm not going to get called up, am I," he said bitterly.

"You might, you don't know. It's not like you're in agriculture. If you were, they couldn't call you up, but you're not."

"Yeah, well, if you really loved me you'd have asked your Dad to give me a job, but anyway, I wouldn't have taken it if he had." He was furious at her reasonableness.

"Anyway, they won't have to call me up because I'm going to volunteer. What do you say to that?"

Rose removed her hand from his, leant back and shrugged. "If that's what you want," she said. "Look, I'm bored with this. Your Dad has been on at you to join up for months and you've had bloody great rows with him about it and your Mum says it'll be the death of her if you do. As far as I see it, it's your decision. So don't try and make out that I'm forcing you to do it because I'm not. Think about what you're going to do and let me know- if you want to."

She stood up and put on her coat. "And another thing, my Dad can't just give out jobs, he's not made of money. I'll walk home by myself."

She shoved her way through the crowd. A group at the bar were beginning to give a drunken rendition of 'Smoke gets in your Eyes'. It made Maurice feel even more sorry for himself. After the first couple of verses he staggered over to the bar and began to join in

'Now laughing friends deride

Tears I cannot hide

So I smile and say

When a lovely flame dies

Smoke gets in your eyes'

Maurice was roaring the words when the barman called 'Time, gentlemen please'. He'd had another two pints and a brandy bought for him by Jim Evans who helped him on with his coat. "The thing of it is," he said, fumbling with the door handle, "She's a cold woman, Jimmy."

"Mind the step," said Jim, but it was too late. He fell into a snowdrift, his head spinning suddenly as the cold air hit him. He lay on his back hiccupping, "As cold as..as Eskimo Nell." He started to shout again,

"When a man grows old and his balls grow cold

And the tip of his knob grows blue..."

A light appeared above his head and a voice said, "Keep it down, lads, I'll lose my licence. Go home."

Jim tried to haul him too his feet but Maurice was too heavy and his friend slipped and fell down on top of him. Maurice went on singing,

"And it's bent in the middle like a one string fiddle

he can tell you a tale or two."

"She doesn't love me, Jim. I'm going to join the army and then I'm going to get killed and I'll die a virgin." Jim hauled himself to his feet and, with difficulty, managed to get Maurice to stand up. He staggered towards the road and then said, "I feel sick." Jim put his arm round Maurice's waist and, with Maurice's arm hanging over his shoulder started to bundle him across the green towards the shop. They were both breathing heavily when Maurice stopped and said, "Have you ever done it, Jim?"

"Done what?"

"You know, been with a woman."

Jim pulled him forward, "I'm not going into it. Come on, you'll die of cold at this rate."

Maurice shook his head, "I don't care, I want to die. Just leave me here."

Jim dragged him on and led him round to the back of the shop where Maurice fell over the wheelbarrow and banged his head on the wall beside the kitchen door. He knocked on the door until the light went on and his mother opened it.

"I'm afraid Maurice is a bit worse for wear," said Jim, "I've brought him home.

Mrs Hickey, in dressing gown and nightcap nodded curtly. "The door was open, Maurice, there's no need for all that racket, waking the whole village. What have you done to your head?"

Jim left and Mrs Hickey led her son to the kitchen table and pushed him down onto a chair. "Have you been in a fight? Sit there, don't you move and wait till I've found the iodine and a bandage." While she searched the cupboards for the iodine Maurice swayed gently; the light hurt his eyes and his head was throbbing.

"Yeah, I've been in a fight, but she started it."

He flinched as she dabbed the iodine on his forehead. "Rose hit you? Sit still."

"With a crowbar, Ma. She said she didn't care if I went away and never came back and just because I…." His voice trailed off. She wrapped the bandage around his head, "Just because you what?"

"I asked her to marry me, if you must know."

He glanced up. His mother's eyes were welling with tears and then he heard his father's voice. "What in God's name is going on here?"

"Maurice claims that Rose hit him over the head with a crowbar," said Mrs Hickey, "I don't believe a word of it, now sit still, I don't want to stick this safety pin in your head, so just you go back to bed, Stan. We'll talk about it in the morning."

Mr Hickey didn't move. Maurice said, "No, some idiot left the wheelbarrow on the path and I fell over it. Mr Hickey snorted, "The only idiot around here is you, son. You left it there when you used it to get the logs in last night, if you remember. You're always doing it and I've warned you it would cause an accident and now it has. So what's this nonsense about Rose? If you've finished with him, Mother, you go on up to bed. I'll help him up."

His wife gave her son a last look and wiped her eyes and went out. He waited for her to be out of earshot before whispering to Maurice, "I'll not have your mother upset, Maurice. You know what her nerves are like. Why did you say Rose hit you?"

Maurice could feel the tears well up again. He sniffed, "Dad, I've decided to join up, that's all."

"Well," Mr Hickey couldn't conceal his look of pleasure, "Well, your mother's right. We'll discuss it in the morning."

But in the morning Maurice wasn't in a state to discuss anything. The needle sharp pain in the back of his head was balanced by the throbbing ache in his forehead. Feeling that he was going to be sick, he rushed across the landing to the bathroom. His father's voice was coming up from the kitchen- he was shouting, nothing new in that, and though he desperately needed some aspirin, Maurice couldn't face going into the kitchen and facing his father's anger. He assumed that as usual they were arguing about him, his mother in that quiet, almost apologetic way she had; his father with that hectoring, bullying tone of moral outrage that he used. Maurice opened the door to the shop and took a packet of aspirin from the shelf, opened it and stuffed four of them into his mouth. They tasted disgusting and made him gag. He'd have to get some water but on his way back to the stairs he found his mother standing in the hallway.

"Maurice, dear, are you all right?"

"Of course he's all right, mother, just a bit of a hangover, eh son? Come in the kitchen and your mother'll make you a cup of tea and you tell me what you got up to last night." He followed them into the kitchen and sat down.

He watched his mother fill the kettle and light the gas ring. "Leave the boy be," she said quietly, "He's upset about Rose."

"Well he's better off without her if you want my opinion."

Maurice closed his eyes. He was used to his parents talking over his head as if he wasn't there. "And what's more," said his wife, "You shouldn't have spoken like that to the vicar."

"What are you talking about woman? I didn't talk like anything to the vicar. I just gave him a book."

Mrs Hickey turned round and glared at him, "Well he didn't come into the shop for a book, did he. He came in for a dozen eggs and you said we hadn't got any, and they were right there on the counter where anybody could see them and he did too, I shouldn't wonder. I was so embarrassed when Mrs Earnshaw came in. She said he'd left the shopping list at home and that the only thing you offered him was powdered eggs. Powdered eggs indeed. We've got two dozen chickens out in the back Stanley Hickey, and well you know it. We've got eggs enough for anyone that wants them.

"Eggs are rationed," said Mr Hickey weakly, "and I'm not selling my eggs to them as won't support the war effort. In fact they don't deserve to be served at all in my opinion."

"Well, if we had to rely on your opinion we'd all starve because we'd never have any customers. Eggs are not rationed and you're not God, even if you think you are." She took of her pinafore and straightened her hair. "Now I'm going to church and to apologise to the vicar." She took her coat from the back of the door and put on her hat.

"Before you go, you ought to know that Maurice is going to join the army, aren't you son."

Mrs Hickey paused at the door, "You're only saying that to spite me," and she looked at Maurice, "You wouldn't do that to me, would you Maurice? With Don at sea, and if anything happened to either of you..." She shook her head, "I couldn't bear it." Maurice saw her wiping her eyes as she passed the kitchen window.

Chapter Seven

Esther Hart's Diary

Saturday 20th January 1940

Had letters from Lydia and Gordon this morning. I think the children are all right but I can't understand why Ada felt the need to correct Gordon's spelling. Having one's children's letters censored by one's sister-in-law is somehow rather galling, even if Gordon should be able to spell 'presents' correctly by the age of twelve. Finished his balaclava and Lydia's scarf and sent them off. The thermometer read −10, so it must be even colder in Rutland. As Douglas was working again I went round to Charles's and cooked him lunch and then went on to Fortnum's. Bumped into Jenny Brownlow and had tea with her. She said I must be delighted by Douglas's promotion to the Home Office. I didn't like to point out that I knew nothing about it, so I just said I was. Told her about being on the panel for interviewing aliens and about poor Mr Niedermayer. She said if I was interested The Austrian Centre is putting on performances of 'The Good Soldier Schweik' at the Hampstead Concert Studio, just round from where they live. Said she'd get tickets and ring me.

Awful news at six. An explosion at the Royal Gunpowder factory at Waltham Cross and the police suspect German and Austrian refugees. Mr Churchill gave a broadcast to what he called 'the neutral countries', but everyone must know he means Belgium and the Netherlands, saying they were like a crocodile's victims, each one hoping to be eaten last. I know Douglas can't stand the man, but I think he is much more impressive than Mr Chamberlain.

Must stop as I can hear Douglas coming in.

Sunday 21st January

Douglas not working for the first time in what seems like weeks. He went out and bought the Sunday papers while I cooked breakfast and then we went for a stroll in St James's Park. Didn't bring up his promotion- he will when he wants to, but did suggest he might visit his father since he hasn't seen him since New Year. That's where he is now.

Banner headline in 'The Sunday Express'- 'Those Influential Friends of Dangerous Aliens' and then the article went on to say that officials were 'gravely concerned' that foolish British people were vouching for refugees that they didn't know and who might well be German spies, and that the best thing would be to intern all refugees who, were not absolutely genuine. Then it talked about a highly placed Jew who was interned as the police knew him to be a spy, although his friends claimed that he was anti-Nazi. Apparently some official told the paper that lots of refugees had relations in Germany and though they were not paid spies, they did pass information to Germany through neutral channels in order to protect their friends and relatives from the Gestapo. It must be true that most of the refugees do have relations in Germany and Austria but I find it hard to believe they are not on our side.

Jenny phoned. She's got tickets for the theatre on Wednesday and invited me for a meal after.

Tuesday 23rd January

Douglas now does not have one shirt that doesn't have a frayed collar. Asked him if he shouldn't buy some new ones and he said he didn't have time to go shopping. Was on the point of saying it was important to be as presentable as possible in a new job, but bit my tongue just in time. Offered to go and buy some for him but he just said he'd heard that the German government had forbidden Jews to buy shoes or shoe leather. It's unimaginable.

On the lunchtime news the Metropolitan Commissioner of Police said that there was absolutely no evidence that any refugee aliens were suspected of sabotage or espionage. I suppose the government is anxious not to create anti-refugee feeling, though to be honest, I've never heard anyone feel anything but sympathy for those poor people. It does seem that there is a campaign against them by those papers that were all for appeasement before the war started. Perhaps now they'll show a bit more sympathy and understanding.

Thursday 25th January

I don't know where to begin with this, because last night's play was so extraordinary it makes me cry to just think about it. After the darkness of the blackout the tiny theatre was so brightly lit that it hurt one's eyes, and it was absolutely packed out. Stupidly I hadn't thought the whole thing would be in German and mine is so rusty that I would never have been able to follow it if they hadn't kindly thought to provide us with a synopsis of each act. Actually, it was really a series of sketches dealing with a solder (Schweik) who is keen to join up with the Austro-Hungarian army during the last war. He has got terrible rheumatism so he gets his charlady to take him to the recruitment centre in a wheel chair where he is arrested and imprisoned as a malingerer. It was done as a sort of anti-war farce that made the whole audience howl with laughter, but I couldn't work out whether he was an imbecile or was really clever and undermining the authority of the army. Then there was a scene when I thought I recognised Herr Niedermayer. I had to check my programme notes and it was. But he was completely confident, unrecognisable as the frozen, dejected man who presented himself at the tribunal only days ago. His voice was strong and he was so convincing in the part of a cook in the army who had been the editor of an occult magazine before the war, and who was now trying to avoid active service by writing long letters home to his wife in which he described in detail all the meals he was planning to cook for the senior officers. And I kept imagining him now, sitting in a grubby little bedsit somewhere, in real life, writing real letters to his real wife. So while the audience was laughing at his performance I was also laughing, but crying as well, because it was so heart-breaking. Then, in the final scene, Schweik was arrested by his own troops because he was wearing Russian uniform. I don't think the irony of that was lost on anyone. There was complete silence at the end, then someone started to clap and then we all got to our feet and gave a standing ovation that went on and on. The cast seemed both pleased and embarrassed by such applause. I pointed out to Jenny that the man standing at the end of the line was the one I'd seen at the tribunal and she said we could go back stage because she is a patroness of the theatre. She introduced me to Eleanor Rathbone who must be nearly seventy by now but who is as sharp as mustard and said if I was interested, the refugee organisations need all the help they can get. I said I was on the alien tribunals and she was awfully huffy about that and said she'd never met a single tribunal chairman who had the foggiest idea what he was about.

The cast were still all in their make up. I spotted Herr Niedermayer and with some trepidation went over to see him- I wasn't sure how pleased he would be to see me. I don't think he recognised me at first, but when he did he called a young woman over. For a ridiculous moment I thought she might be his wife, but it turns out that she is called Lotte and works for the Austrian Centre. I said I just wanted to say how marvellous and moving the performance was. I don't think she liked me very much- she was quite offhand, but anyway, translated what I said for him, and he seemed very pleased and through Lotte again, invited us to visit the Austrian Centre. So it's arranged. We're going to see it next Tuesday.

Douglas was in bed when I got home. Told him about it and about meeting Eleanor Rathbone. "Bloody woman," he said, "We used to duck behind pillars at the Foreign Office whenever we saw her coming." His first admission that he doesn't work there any more. Didn't tell him that in my excitement I'd left the shirts I'd bought him at the theatre.

Friday 26th January

Looked out this morning and couldn't see more than a few feet for the blizzard blowing from the east. It's gone on all day and then at I heard a crash and the sound of breaking glass from the back of the house. The snow on the silver birch had become so heavy that it broke off a large branch that smashed into the green house. I braved the storm to go to a matinee showing of "Brother Rat" at the Gaumont with Emily which had Ronald Reagan and Jane Wyman in it. It was all very loud and after last night seemed a bit silly. At the end of the performance someone, presumably the cinema manager, announced that the film had been especially chosen to celebrate the marriage today of the two stars who met on the set when they were making the film.

They've reduced the speed limit from thirty to twenty miles an hour in the hope of preventing all the accidents that keep happening. Still, since I was nearly run over by a car on my way home that was sliding down the road at about ten miles an hour, it's somewhat academic. Keep hearing reports that we are going to be attacked at any minute and Mr Chamberlain has promised the Belgians every support if they are attacked. I wonder what the Belgians think of that, since we declared war on Germany when it attacked Poland and we haven't lifted a finger to defend them. Presumably the Belgians don't think very much of it because their response to Mr Churchill's plea to join the allies has been point blank refusal.

Saturday 27th January

Received letters from Lydia and Gordon this morning. Lydia's picture showed her wearing her new scarf, Gordon's him in his balaclava with only his mouth showing. I think it is his way of saying it's too big. Half the page was empty with his signature at the bottom, so on a hunch I held it over a candle flame.

In invisible ink he'd written 'Auntie Adas blamonj is diskustin and all lumpy.'

A bit like Ada, then. Wonder where she got the lemon from. Wonder if I dare reply to him with invisible ink.

Listened to Mr Churchill's broadcast from Manchester. He said he couldn't understand why we haven't been bombed yet and talked about 'each to his station'. It's difficult because one has the impression that he is only in the Cabinet under sufferance, but he seemed to say it with some relish, as though he can't wait for the action to start properly. But we've had two days of continuous blizzards. I daresay the Russians and Finns can fight in these conditions because they're used to it. Douglas back from the office early saying he was feeling unwell. Think he may have bronchitis and I'm sure the number of cigarettes he smokes can't be good for his chest. Gave him some Vick to rub on. There was a time when he'd have let me do it for him. There was a time when I'd have offered.

Sunday 28th January

Douglas had a temperature of 103 so at two in the morning took myself off into the spare room and then couldn't sleep for the cold. He's a bit better this morning and asked me to go out and get the papers. Big headline in 'The Sunday Pictorial'- 'Arms Expert Loves A German.' It seems a German refugee girl has fallen in love with an Englishman who has some top job in an armaments factory. They want to get married, but she says she knows it might be difficult and that they could just be friends. The paper says that the romance might be genuine, but it might not and that it's not worth the risk. The British public, it says, is alarmed at the seventy thousand potential enemies at large and that this kid glove handling of enemy aliens had to stop. There was great wave of uneasiness sweeping across the country and that we couldn't take any risks just for the sake of being polite. Best to intern them all.

Asked Douglas what he thought. He said Sir Philip Game, the Metropolitan Commissioner had said he wasn't worried, but he's heard through the grape vine that M!5 was concerned about spies because with that number of refugees it would be surprising if there weren't quite a few.

Told him he couldn't go to work if he was still bad in the morning. He said he'd got no choice, as if we're going to lose this war because a bald man in his forties in a bowler hat has got a cold.

Monday 29th January

I'm a bad wife. Listening to Douglas sneezing and snuffling his way through Sunday and refusing to eat any supper because he felt too ill, I was quite relieved when he took himself off to work because I couldn't stand another day like yesterday. Still, if he has to play the martyr, I do wish he'd do it without the sound effects.

Apparently the weather forecast has been censored so as not to give information that the country has been at a standstill for the last month to the Germans. Now the ban on the broadcast of the weather has been lifted, it's been revealed that this is the coldest winter since 1894. It was −13 in Buxton last night.

I'm sure that's not very far from Rutland. Better knit the children some warmer socks.

Heard on the news that the Polish government in exile claim that the Nazis have murdered eighteen thousand prominent Poles since the country was occupied.

Tuesday 30th January

Got to the Lyons tea rooms early to meet Jenny and read the paper till she arrived. When I pointed out the lifting of the censorship on broadcasting the weather forecast, she laughed. But I thought there was a serious point. If there are Germans sending information to the German government as some of the papers are saying, what's the point of banning the weather forecast because the Germans will find out anyway. She thought that was vastly amusing and said she had an American journalist friend. When the RAF dropped leaflets all over Germany at the beginning of the war, he phoned the Foreign Office to ask what the leaflets said, and was told that the information was strictly confidential. He asked why and they replied that they didn't want such information being put into enemy hands. He pointed out that the leaflets were being dropped on the enemy, so that couldn't be true. They answered that they agreed, something wasn't quite right, but still insisted they couldn't tell him.

At the Austrian Centre we were met by Herr Niedermayer and Lotte. She was very distant again, until she asked me why Hans should have got a 'B' at the tribunal. I said it really hadn't been my decision, I had only been an observer and that I was partly here out of concern for him, his wife and his daughter. At that she became a bit warmer. She said she's written to the Czech Embassy who were trying to trace his wife and that Eleanor Rathbone had also contacted them but there was no news. So many Austrians had come over after the invasion of their country that they were overwhelmed by the amount of work. She herself was German, from Munich and had come to England as a student to study English. Her father had written to her in '37 telling her to stay in England if she could. So she's got a job as a German teacher and then, through a boyfriend, started to work for the Austrian Centre. It had started with £15 in the house that was due to be demolished, but a group of volunteers had renovated it and it was given to them by the Paddington Council. They were both obviously very proud of what had been achieved as they led us from the reading room that contained, as far as I could see all the English papers and a German one which was a digest of the English press. There was a library of thousands of English and German books and a restaurant.

Lotte said they serve up to 13000 meals a month. The food is Viennese and they have over two thousand paying members. There are also classes in English language, literature, shorthand and very popular lectures in German on a whole range of subjects. I asked if the German refugee community has anything similar and she said they had, but on a much smaller scale. Most of the Austrians had fled after the Anschluss in '38, whereas the Germans had come over a six year period. The tribunals caused a problem especially for the 'B's'. There doesn't seem to be any consistency among the tribunal chairmen. She knew of one man who had been a member of the Austrian Parliament and who is now living in Barnes. He was given a 'B' and so was prevented from coming to the Centre any more as it is more than five miles away. He was having English lessons at the Centre and looking after the library but had to give it up. She hadn't seen him for weeks.

They showed us a room where men were learning to repair their clothes and shoes. When we left I said I'd like to help in any way I could. I'd love Douglas to visit and see what's going on there, but I don't suppose he'll have the time.

Wednesday 31st January

Government's starting a huge campaign to use 120 million tons of household waste, especially scrap iron, waste paper and steel. Started sorting the rubbish. Douglas still not good but refuses to stay at home and get better.

Chapter Eight

Niedermayer was euphoric when he arrived at the Centre to meet Herr Jütte. He had understood the English lady when she had said that she would do everything she could to help. He hadn't grasped a lot of what she had said to Lotte the previous day but he was sure she meant what she said and she had a kind face and she had liked the play.

Before leaving his digs he had checked that he had got his visa and his college enrolment form. And the previous night he had written a long letter to his wife and hoped that the next time he saw the English lady he would be able to give it to her and she would somehow be able to get it to Prague. He and Herr Jütte had walked to the police station last week. It had been hard for the old man and Niedermayer wondered whether they shouldn't take the bus today. Herr Jütte's feet were bad. They met in the reading room.

"We must walk," said Herr Jütte, "I'm fine, never better," when Niedermayer suggested they took the bus. He pulled himself up with difficulty, leaning on his stick. "Now," he said, putting on his cap, "If you'll let me take your arm I'll manage."

It hadn't snowed for a couple of days but the slush lay thick on the pavement. The old man shuffled along, wheezing. He seemed less well than he had a week ago as they walked slowly along Westbourne terrace and turned into Bishop's Bridge Road. "Are you sure you wouldn't like to take the bus?" Niedermayer repeated, but Herr Jütte dismissed the question with a wave of his stick. "It's important to exercise at my age," he said, "I'll be sixty eight next birthday. When I was a young man I was a great walker. Weekends we used to go to the Tyrol. That's where I went to University, you know. Innsbruck. That's where I met my Magda. You know," he squeezed Niedermayer's arm, "Slow down a bit, She, she wouldn't go out at all towards the end." He was struggling for breath. They went on a few more steps before he stopped again. "Forty two years we were married. She died on our wedding anniversary. I thought I couldn't live without her, but I think she's better off dead. She couldn't have coped with this."

They were passing over the railway line and he waved towards the station. A chill wind was blowing along the track. "I had to leave her to go to work. It was only down the stairs. I had a little bookshop in Neubadgasse. On the twentieth March a young man came in the shop. I'll never forget it. I thought he was a student or something. Asked if I'd got any books by Heine, you know? So I showed him the poetry section and he took the book and tore it up. Just like that. Then he spat on it and dropped it on the floor and stamped on it. Then, without a word he went to the door and called in three soldiers in uniform and they ransacked the place." He was wheezing heavily. "Asthma" he said. "I can't think of it without getting breathless. I'll be all right in a minute." Niedermayer watched in concern, "Shall we find somewhere to sit down?"

Herr Jütte ignored him. "I thought I must see this man who is responsible for so much suffering so I went to the Heldenplatz and there were people waving flags and flowers. Were you there? Did you see him?"

"No, I was in Graz, are you sure you don't need to sit down?"

"I went home and told Magda I'd seen him. She was in bed by then. She never got up again. I tried to get her up and come with me to vote. I'm glad she didn't. I'd have been too ashamed. Did you vote? Of course you did," he said, answering his own question. "I was determined to vote against the Anschluss. After what I'd seen I didn't want anything to do with my country being part of Germany. It wasn't Schuschnigg's fault. He was a good man. A bit right wing for my tastes but he did what he could. Hitler tricked him you know. He was at the same University as me at Innsbruck. But I think I told you that already. Of course, he was a lot younger than me, but I did see him once. Not in Innsbruck. No, in Dachau. Must keep walking."

They were passing the Grand Union Canal. They stopped and looked over the bridge. In the oily waters, small lumps of ice were drifting. He sighed, "We had our honeymoon at a place called Rorschach on the banks of the Bodensee. It was in May I remember and one night we took out a rowing boat. Magda had never been on a lake before and I didn't tell her but I had never rowed before either and she had a parasol and a beautiful cream dress on. She was very nervous but she couldn't help laughing when I pulled too hard on the oars and fell over backwards in the bottom of the boat and then she panicked when the boat rocked, but it was all right and I remember the full moon and the lapping of the water and her laughter when we got back to shore." He nudged Niedermayer, "Our little Heinrich was conceived there. But he died when he was five. TB. And we didn't have any more children after that though we tried. It's very sad, but now I think it's probably for the best. What kind of world is this to bring children into? Not far now."

They stood waiting to cross the road. A bus sent up a grey slush that sprayed Niedermayer's trousers. They passed a group of refugees who were standing talking outside the police station and joined the queue inside. Niedermayer examined the posters stuck on the wall. "Careless talk costs lives.", "Look Out in the Blackout." "Coughs and Sneezes Spread Diseases." He read them slowly, pleased at how much he understood.

When Herr Jütte was called over by the desk sergeant, Niedermayer stepped forward with him.

"Just be patient, sir, I'll call you in a minute," the policeman held up his hand.

He waited and watched as Herr Jütte put his papers on the desk. The policeman scrutinised them and then handed them back. "Next" he called.

Niedermayer stepped forward and handed over his papers.

"Is this your first registration visit here?"

"I'm sorry?"

The policeman repeated the question more loudly, "Have you been here before?"

"Yes, I come last week."

The policeman looked at him suspiciously and then at the tribunal certificate. "Obviously an oversight," he muttered. Then he reached under the counter and stamped the visa 'Not to take employment paid or unpaid.'

"Employment?" asked Niedermayer.

"Work," said the policeman, "A job. You must not work, not even if you are not being paid."

"But I must work," protested Niedermayer. "My wife and my daughter are in Czechoslovakia. I must work to buy them a ticket to come here to England."

"Sorry, cock, not my problem," said the policeman. "Next."

Niedermayer took the papers and put them in his pocket. Herr Jütte was sitting on the floor examining the sole of his shoe that he had taken off. There was a large hole in the centre and the sock was soaking. That settled it for Niedermayer, "We're getting the bus back," he said. Herr Jütte shook his head, "I haven't got any money with me." He put his shoe back on and hauled himself up, "I'll be fine. We'll walk."

But Niedermayer insisted, "I've got enough for the bus for both of us. Come on."

"I'll pay you back. You know old Oskar Wiemann? He used to be a cobbler in Krems, you know. I'd mend it myself but I can't see as well as I used to. He'll do it for me if I ask him."

Standing by the bus stop he looked up at Niedermayer, "You've been very quiet. Is anything wrong?"

Niedermayer said, "I don't understand. The man at the tribunal said if I get a job they'll change me from a 'B' to a 'C'. Now they've stamped my visa and it says because I'm a 'B' I'm not allowed to work. I just don't understand. I'm training to be a welder, but even if I pass the course I still won't be able to work. And I'll never be able to get the money to bring my family over. There must be some mistake."

The bus arrived. Herr Jütte needed help from the conductress to pull himself up and slumped down on a seat, "Tell you what," he said after a long pause, "I've got a visa to go to America. You can have it if you like. It's no good to me any more. What would an old man like me do in America. I can't speak the language and I'm much too old to learn. But you're young, how old are you?"

"Forty two," replied Niedermayer.

"Exactly. You've helped me and 'eine Hand wäscht die andere. Hilfst du mir, so helf ich dir.'"

Niedermayer smiled. A penny bus ride seemed an awfully cheap price to pay for a visa to America. He smiled at the old man as the bus crawled through the slush along Westway. He and the conductress helped Herr Jütte down and they shuffled slowly along Westbourne Terrace.

"It's very kind of you but I can't accept. For one thing your visa is not transferable and for another, I must find my wife and daughter. How can I ever find them if I'm in America? When they arrive in England they'll be looking for me."

"Ach, the British authorities are hopelessly confused. You just change your name to Jütte till you get to America. Anybody with any sense is going to America. I know at least ten people who have gone. The Germans are going to win this war. Within a year they'll be here, you mark my words. That man, what's his name, Moseley, he'll be Prime Minister. Think about it. Even the Royal Family is German. And when they have come they'll set up camps for the likes of you and me in places like Dachau and Sachsenhausen. It's terrible I know, but we have to face the facts."

Niedermayer looked at him. He thinks he's really ill, he thought. He thinks he's going to die. The euphoria that he had started the day with had completely gone and left him with a cold and empty feeling, but he couldn't possibly go to America as long as there was a glimmer of hope of getting his wife and daughter back.

Chapter Nine

"Are you sure you want to do that?" asked Captain Burfeind, looking across the table. Busch stroked the stubble on his chin and glanced up. "I've got a plan- you don't know what I'm going to do next."

"Richtig, but I know what you have to do now," and the captain moved his knight to the centre of the board, "Check."

Busch frowned. He lifted his hand to move his king out of danger and stopped. "If I move my king you'll take my queen, but I have to move my king to get out of check. But I think I can still win." He moved his king back a square. "You're still in check there from my bishop."

Busch examined the board. "There's only one place where I can go." He moved his king back another square. Burfeind brought his queen up next to Busch's king, "Checkmate." He smiled. "The thing you have to remember is that though you need a plan of what you are going to do, it is about taking into account what your opponent is likely to do. You have to balance defence and attack. I understand you. You just want to attack, that's your nature. But in that case, you leave yourself defenceless. Another game?"

They replaced the pieces. Busch had watched Müller laboriously carve a chess set out of pieces of broken deck chair. He had coloured the black pieces with boot polish and made the squares from an old table that he had inlaid with cut up cigarette packets and gold foil. "Teach me to play," Busch had said when the whole thing was completed, but Müller had shaken his head, "I don't know how to." Two months' work had led to his exchanging the set with a guard for an old pair of pyjama bottoms and a packet of cigarettes. Busch had collected up the off cuts and used them as a base into which he stuck cardboard chessmen and then he had gone off to find someone who could teach him the game. It had kept him busy for a day.

Captain Burfeind had taught him the rudiments. He saw it as a way of trying to keep him away from the young Nazis who had arrived at the camp four days earlier. There had been an immediate problem. The seventeen seamen who had been allocated three huts between them had refused to acknowledge Captain Burfeind as the group leader. They insisted that Rudolf Wirth, a civilian who had been travelling to North Africa as a government ambassador when their ship was taken, should be the elected representative of the German prisoners of war. A delegation of five of them had stormed into his hut at six in the morning, given the Hitler salute and insisted that he write out a letter of resignation which they would deliver to Major Stimpson. They also said that the voting system had previously been unfair since non- Nazis should not be entitled to vote.

Burfeind had asked them to leave while he got dressed and said he would go with them to see Major Stimpson when he came on duty. They answered that they were not leaving without his written resignation, at which point Burfeind had said, "Very well, " and turned over and closed his eyes. The seamen withdrew into a corner, undecided what to do and they were still arguing among themselves in whispers when reveille was called. Finally one of them left and went to find Wirth. He told them to attend the morning parade- he would see Stimpson himself later.

Dr Dobel arrived at the camp early. He had wanted to see Busch after his release from hut 73. The sailor had said nothing while Dobel listened to his chest, and examined his hands, ears and feet for signs of frost-bite. Having satisfied himself that, under the conditions, Busch had suffered no lasting ill effects, the doctor went to Major Stimpson's office. They were talking when Miss Higgins knocked on his door and announced that Wirth wished to see the major as a matter of urgency. "Stay, if you have the time, Walter. I need you to translate."

Rudolf Wirth was in his early forties, tall and slenderly built with black combed back hair that was receding at the sides. "I am representative of men of the Third Reich," he said in a thick accent. "I want with you alone to speak." He glared suspiciously at Dobel.

Stimpson picked up his pen and began to write. There was a long silence before he eventually put it down and looked up coldly, "In the first place, Captain Burfeind is your representative in the camp and so any representation is to be made through him and in the second place, this is Dr Dobel who is German and while I am willing on this occasion to hear you out, I suggest strongly that we communicate through him, for the sake of clarity, you understand." He said the words as quickly as he could and then waited. There was another long pause before Wirth said, "I do not understand. Speak more slow. Please."

Stimpson glanced towards Dobel who gave a barely perceptible nod. Stimpson said slowly, "The internees have, after a lengthy election process, deemed Captain Burfeind their most appropriate elected representative and therefore any representation to the camp authorities are to be made through him and in the second place Dr Dobel, as a linguist of note should, I suggest, be accepted by us both as the most able to facilitate our mutual understanding. Is that clear?"

From the expression on Wirth's face it certainly was not clear. Dobel stood up and spoke to the ambassador in German. Wirth, clearly unhappy, replied, also in German that he wished to state that Burfeind could not possibly represent the majority as he was not a Nazi, and that under the terms of the Geneva Convention of 1929 prisoners of war were entitled to the same living conditions as the host nation's army, that the conditions in the camp were not fit for purpose and different religious and ethnic groups were entitled, where possible, to be kept in different camps. Finally, that internees should be kept well away from the area where fighting might take place.

Dobel translated. When he had finished, Wirth said, "I therefore demand an election in order that prisoners of war can elect a representative who will ensure that the British government abides by the agreement it made when it signed up to the Geneva Convention, which would mean a new election." Dobel translated.

"I am quite satisfied as to the legitimacy of the last one," said Stimpson, "Make your requests through Captain Burfeind." Wirth listened to Dobel and then, giving a thin smile, clicked his heels and left.

"Well, I'm quite surprised he took that as well as he did, " said Stimpson. Dobel looked sheepish, "You know, Philip, some things can get lost in translation."

"What do you mean?"

"Well, for a number of reasons another election would be a good idea. Wirth is going to be a very disruptive influence in the camp. You either have to get him on your side, which is going to be difficult, or you have to..what is your English expression?..clip his wings. Do you trust me?"

"I trusted you with my son's life. So…."

"Excellent. Then I suggest you have the hustings at, say, two o'clock, followed immediately by the vote and the count, as usual, at five, in your office. And tell Wirth that I've had to go but explain slowly in words of one syllable that under the Geneva Convention, all internees are entitled to be represented. I'll have a word with Miss Higgins about getting the voting slips ready."

Three hundred and seventeen men crowded into the refectory that afternoon. Within minutes the air was thick with cigarette smoke mixed with the smell of cabbage soup and unwashed bodies. The English guards were muttering that getting all the men together was craziness, that the situation could easily get out of hand. Major Stimpson was now also sure this was a bad idea. Wirth had agreed that all the what he called 'Aryans' should have a vote and had spent the rest of the morning preparing for the election with a dozen of his supporters. Captain Burfeind needed persuading to even stand again but eventually shrugged. "I will lose."

Now he was standing on a table in front of the hatch, holding up his hands for quiet. He was not a natural speaker. What he said was short and difficult to hear among the heckling from the Nazis. He stepped down and was replaced by Wirth who leapt on the table to loud cheers from the front and a sullen silence from the back. He started quietly, almost whispering, stopping occasionally for dramatic effect. Dobel suddenly appeared next to the major. "He's good," he whispered, "Same tactics as Hitler- start slowly and thoughtfully. He's talking about the injustice of sharing a camp with the Jews. How hypocritical the British are interning them having taken them in as refugees and now treating them like scum. At least the Germans made no bones about not wanting them. "

Wirth raised his voice and started pummelling his fist into his hand. "Now he's talking about the Treaty of Versailles and what an insult it was." Wirth began to shout. The Nazis who had surrounded the table on which he was standing were looking menacingly at the back of the room. "Jews again," said Dobel.

Wirth finished by brushing the hair from his forehead and shouting, "Sieg Heil!" and those around him took up the shout, stamping their feet and banging on the tables, while those at the back of the room looked around nervously. Some began to chant reluctantly, others shook their heads and cowered as the Nazis pushed their way among them. Wirth held his hands up to quieten them.

"He said it's time for the vote," said Dobel. The Nazis were pushing men into lines and the ballot box was placed on the table. Four of them distributed the ballot papers while several more stood around the table. The first man in the queue was given a pencil. He looked at the men who were watching him, made his cross and went to put the ballot paper in the box. The paper was snatched out of his hand scrutinised and then placed in the cardboard box.

"No, I really must protest, the ballot must be secret," said Stimpson. Livid, he pushed his way over to the corner of the room where Wirth was being congratulated by his supporters. "This is an absolute outrage," he shouted. Wirth stood up looking surprised. Stimpson looked around for Dobel, "Translate," he spat, "The ballot must be secret." Dobel translated.

"My dear major, I was present at the referendum in Ostmark, what used to be known as Austria. The procedure being followed here is just the same. No German is ashamed to show who he has voted for. We are all Germans here. The Austrians voted for a Greater Germany because that is what they want. Not all of course, but 99.7 per cent voted freely to join again with the Fatherland. This is how it is done in Germany and we are all Germans."

It took almost two hours until the last man had voted and left the hall.

There was a sudden crash and a cry from the kitchen. The seven men ran in to find Hans, the cook, rolling on the floor in agony and clutching his chest. Broken shards of glass lay around him. Dobel grabbed a broom and thrust it into Wirth's hand. "Sweep up the glass before anyone cuts themselves and you," he pointed to Wirth's aide, "Help me get on him on his back and hold this spoon between his teeth. He mustn't bite his tongue. I'll get my bag." He ran back into the refectory and a couple of minutes later came back with his stethoscope on and listened to Hans's chest. "We need to get him to the Infirmary. " Hans was heavy and it took five of them to carry him.

As they got him into the refectory Dobel said, "Major, be so good as to bring the ballot box." Hans was still moaning as they laid him on a bed and Dobel closed the curtains. "Here, take this," he said, handing Hans a bottle. "I'll be back in a short while."

He glanced at his watch. "I think I'll stay for the count, it's nearly five. "

Major Stimpson asked a guard to go and find Captain Burfeind and to report to his office. He arrived shaking his head as the ballot box was opened on the major's desk.

"A representative from each candidate will make the count, witnessed by those present," announced the major portentously, "Mr Wirth's votes on the right and Captain Burfeind's on the left."

The two men each took out a handful of voting slips while Wirth looked on and smiled, his arms folded across his chest. Captain Burfeind examined a map on the wall. The expression on Wirth's face changed from one of self-satisfaction to one of incredulity and then of horror. By the time the first hundred voted were counted, he had gained precisely two. He had not added any by the time the second hundred was counted and when the final vote was declared, of the 317 votes cast, Wirth had three. He stormed out of the room closely followed by his aide.

"Pity," said Dobel, "I was hoping to point out to him that he did even better than those who voted against the Austrian's unification with Germany."

"Would you mind telling me how that happened?" said Stimpson, "Or is it best that I don't know."

"Miss Higgins was kind enough to lend me the ballot box this morning and one of the voting slips. I had them roneoed at the stationers in town and my wife and children spent a happy morning voting for Captain Burfeind. Unfortunately I had a number patients to see, so I didn't have time to cast more than three votes for Herr Wirth."

He opened his large doctor's bag and pulled out a paper bag and emptied it on the table. "These are the votes cast by the men under coercion. I fastened it under the opening of the ballot box and removed it when I went back to the refectory to fetch my things from the refectory, and these," he pointed to the voting slips that had been counted, "Are the votes freely cast by my wife and children that I put in the bottom of the ballot box."

"This is highly irregular," said Stimpson, smiling.

"Miss Higgins told me how many men were entitled to vote and Hans didn't know why he had to feign a heart attack but agreed to do it in exchange for a bottle of schnapps. I needed to create a diversion in order to retrieve the men's votes." He sat down. "I've never mentioned this before, but my father was also a doctor, in Koblenz. One day he received an anonymous letter that said that if he didn't stop treating Jews, he would have to face the consequences. Of course he ignored it. Coming home one evening he was so severely beaten up by a group of Nazis that he died of his injuries. The authorities did nothing. That's why I came to England. I couldn't think of bringing up a family in Germany. You've no idea how much satisfaction this has given me. Like my father, I took the Hippocratic oath, but as far as I'm aware, that doesn't extend to elections."

He stood up to go. "If it's at all possible, I would get Wirth transferred to another camp. If he stays here he will cause trouble."

Major Stimpson spent the following morning on the telephone. At lunch time he sent for Wirth who listened sullenly. "Herr Wirth, the authorities have heard your complaint. In order to comply with the Geneva Convention of 1929, you will be sent to another camp."

"I have the right to know where."

"That is also true. You are to be sent to Swanwick Camp, in Derbyshire. A guard will escort you."

That had been two days previously. Now Busch was scrutinising Captain Burfeind across the table as he tried to rub the shoe polish off his fingers.

He had no idea how his captain had won the election so convincingly but he was beginning to understand how he could beat him at chess.

Chapter Ten

Franco felt he had no good reason to celebrate his forty fifth birthday.

Between long periods of tearful silence, Giovanna would suddenly erupt and berate him just as he was dropping off to sleep and harangue him for not having told her of Francesca's intentions, and then ask him questions to which he could not possibly know the answers, and then, when he said he didn't know whether Eric's parents were Catholic or not, she would accuse him of keeping the truth from her. For four days after her argument with their daughter, she refused to speak to Francesca at all.

Meanwhile, for the first time ever, the Baldinis had seen nothing of Eugenio and Julia who were also at loggerheads over what Julia saw as Eugenio's stupid interference into the Baldini's family life. As a result Eugenio had taken to going to the restaurant early each morning and dropping off at the Fascio club, where interest in the war had been superseded by the drama of what was happening at the Baldini's.

Everything changed when Giovanna went to buy some vegetables at the market and she bumped into Paula Montale, a woman she couldn't bear at the best of times.

"Mi dispiace, Signora Baldini," Paula said, "It must be terrible for you, quite terrible, but I can only pray it's not true."

"What's not true?"

"Allora, it's what Attilio tells me is being said at the Club," said Paula, "That your Francesca has run away from home and is living in sin with a Scottish soldier in Bermondsey and she's expecting his baby and that Franco is keeping them until the baby's born."

Giovanna had not dignified this remark with a reply, but scuttled off home and sat at the kitchen table in her coat and waited for Franco to get home from work. I should have hit the malicious old crone with my shopping bag, she thought, and the more offended she felt at this gross slur on the honour of her family, the less angry she felt with Franco and Francesca.

Francesca was the first to arrive. The experience of the last few days had taught her that it was wiser to be around her mother only when her father was there, so she was on the point of slipping into her bedroom when her mother stopped her.

"Francesca, we need to talk. Come and sit down."

Francesca sat down reluctantly.

"Tomorrow's your father's birthday and we mustn't spoil it for him. Go and tell Julia that they're invited for his birthday supper and then go down to the pawn shop and redeem grandfather's watch. I'm giving it to him because he has always liked it. The money's in my purse. I won't have my family insulted and talked about behind my back. And…" she found the words hard to say, "That young man you've been seeing, invite him too." Francesca left, too surprised at her mother's change of mood to ask what had caused it, while Giovanna started to prepare the evening meal, thinking that the next time she saw Signora Montale she would give her a piece of her mind. "No, no, she would say, "I have no time for people who spread wicked gossip. Francesca is living at home with us, Franco would never agree to such a thing and I'll thank you to mind your own business. And if Francesca has a fiancé who is English he is an honourable young man who is quite independent who we all like very much. In fact, he has been round for supper. You just tell your Attilio that."

By the time that Franco got home she had laid the table and cooked a large meal for the first time since she had heard the news.

"I'll just say this," she said, "You're my husband and I won't have anybody say bad things about you- that's my job and nobody else's." And then she filled him with trepidation again by saying, "And tomorrow you will get a special surprise, and Francesca, you are not to give it away."

Franco was indeed surprised the following night when he got back from work. The kitchen table was laid with the best lace tablecloth. Eugenio had brought four bottles of Frascati from the restaurant and was wearing his best suit. He put a carefully wrapped parcel at the head of the table next to a smaller one from Giovanna.

"Go on on, open it," he said.

"No, we must wait for Francesca," said Giovanna, she'll be here in a minute.

There was an embarrassed silence. Giovanna beamed at Franco and then at Eugenio and Julia, "We're all family. We shouldn't fall out. It's Franco's birthday, so let's have no more unpleasantness, va bene?"

Eugenio opened his mouth to reply but after a stern glance from Julia thought better of it.

The door opened and Francesca came in. She had been to the hairdresser and had had a perm. She was wearing lipstick and was smiling broadly. "Everyone, this is Eric." Franco and Julia glanced nervously at Giovanna who nodded and smiled. "Benvenuti," she said. Eric smiled back,"Thank you, I mean 'Grazie'" and then to Franco, "Er.. Buon Natale, sir."

"Hey, so you speak Italian," smiled Eugenio, shaking Eric's hand vigorously.

"Eric's learning, I'm teaching him, Uncle Eugenio," said Francesca, "He's a very quick learner, but can we all please speak English tonight. We've only just started his lessons."

Giovanna sat down. "Franco, open your presents," she said in Italian, "And Eugenio, please open the wine."

"I have something for you, Papa," said Francesca in English, "and so does Eric, don't you Eric."

Eric took a cigar out of his breast pocket and placed it with the other presents.

"Molto gentile," said Giovanna, "But he'll have to smoke it outside. The smoke is very bad for my asthma."

"I thought he could smoke it at the club," said Francesca.

" He won't have time to go to the club any more, there's too much to do in the house. I don't want him going to the club any more." Giovanna stood up and went to the oven. "Open your presents and then I can serve the lasagne. And I've made a tofu. It's your favourite, isn't it Franco."

Franco tore the paper off the present from Eugenio and Julia. It was a small water colour of the square in Bologna.

"I commissioned it especially from Pietro Draghi and then I framed it myself. I thought it would remind you of home," said Eugenio proudly.

"Thank you, it's lovely."

"Please, Papa, speak English."

Giovanna put down the lasagne dish. "Francesca, it's your father's birthday. He can speak in whatever language he pleases. Besides, if Eric is learning Italian, it will be good for him to hear it spoken. If you are worried that he can't understand, then translate for him by all means, but I'm not speaking English. It's not fair to expect it."

Eric looked quizzically at Francesca, who whispered, "Mama's English isn't very good. She's embarrassed to speak it in front of you."

Giovanna frowned at her daughter, "Francesca, it's rude to whisper. If you've got something to say, say it so we can all hear, per favore. Now, Franco, open your last present before this meal gets cold."

Franco obediently opened his present from Giovanna and held up the watch with a beam of delight.

"Go on, put it on, I want to see how it looks on you. It's got a new strap."

Franco strapped it on to his left wrist and held it up.

"It's very big," said Eugenio.

"It's very valuable," said Giovanna defensively. "It was presented to my grandfather in 1918. He told me that they invented wrist watches in the first world war so that soldiers could have both hands free. They were called trench watches in those days and that is one of the first. Are you pleased with it, Franco? You can say if you're not."

"It's very nice," said Franco, "and I will wear it on special occasions. It's too good for every day."

"Yes, but you'll have to wind it every day, otherwise it'll stop and it must be kept going. It suits you."

Giovanna served the food while Eugenio poured the wine. "So, Eric," he asked in English, "How's the war going? What's going to happen do you think? Are you going to join up?"

Eric looked to Francesca for help and then said, "Well, I think we've got a much stronger navy than Germany and to attack us and France they'd have to break through the Maginot line and to be honest I can't see that happening. They say that France has got the biggest army in Europe. I don't really understand why the Belgians wouldn't let us help them. I don't think the Germans would dare to fight on two fronts."

He looked nervously round the table, "But of course, I'm no expert...."

He became aware of Giovanna studying him closely. She suddenly put down her knife and fork and rushed from the room. Franco made as if to follow her, but Julia beckoned to him to stay where he was and she got up from the table and went after her. There was a long silence. Eric wore an agonised expression. "I'm sorry," he said, "Did I say something I shouldn't? I mean, if I offended...I really didn't mean to. Perhaps I should go?"

"No, no, it has nothing to do with you," said Francesca, putting her hand on his. The sound of sobbing was coming from the bedroom and Julia's urgent whispers could be heard before the bedroom door was slammed.

Eugenio stood up, "A toast," he said, "To my brother and to an end to all this madness. I don't mean...you know what I mean. Anyway, happy birthday, Franco." He sat down again.

Franco smiled thinly. "Thank you." There was another lengthy silence.

"Eric, you must have had some interesting experiences. Francesca tells us you're an air raid warden."

"Yes," said Francesca, "Tell them that story you told me, you know about your friend."

"Well, I don't really know if it's true or not, but my friend said he knocked on a woman's door during a blackout and when she answered he said, "Madam, there's a chink in your upstairs window." She looked at him and said, "Oh no, sir, that's not a chink, that's a Japanese gentleman."

He looked round. Francesca gave a forced laugh; Franco smiled benignly. Eugenio looked confused. "Yes, and what happened then?"

"Oh, Uncle Eugenio, don't you understand?"

"No," said Eugenio, "Is that it?"

"You explain, Eric," Francesca said.

Eric was covered in confusion. He stared at the protuberance on Franco's wrist, "My goodness is that the time. I'm sorry, but I really have to be going, I'm on duty at nine. Signor Baldini, please give my apologies to your wife." He leapt up and grabbed his coat and rushed out of the door, closely followed by Francesca who was calling after him.

Eugenio shrugged and took a large gulp of his wine.

"Did you understand that, Franco?"

Franco shook his head forlornly, "I don't understand anything anymore. I don't understand my wife. I don't understand my daughter and I didn't understand that boy's story. And I don't understand why everyone has disappeared."

He poured them both another glass. "I don't understand why there's a war or why we can't get the food we used to have when the people who come into the hotel can eat exactly as they've always eaten."

"Because they're rich," replied Eugenio, "Don't complain, they keep you in a job. I can't get half the stuff I used to get for my restaurant. I don't understand Julia either. She's been in a foul mood with me for the last week."

The door opened and Francesca came in. She had obviously been crying. Franco put a protective arm around her.

"Why did Mama have to behave like that. When she told me to invite Eric, I thought everything would be all right, but then she had to go and spoil it all. If she didn't want him to come, why did she tell me to bring him? He'll never be able to come again."

Franco shrugged, "Maybe she thought she would be able to cope and then, when it came own to it, she found that she couldn't. It's a lot to ask, you know. And I'm sure she will get used to the idea. Just give her time."

"Time to do what?" asked a voice from the door of the bedroom. "I hate it when people talk about me behind my back." Giovanna sat down at her place at the table and pushed her cold plate of food away. "Time to do what?" she repeated. Franco said, "I was only saying…"

"I know what you were saying. You were saying that I'll get used to the idea of

Francesca marrying that boy. You want to know why I told Francesca to invite him? I'll tell you. Because they're saying at your club that she has got herself pregnant and that they're living in sin somewhere and that you're supporting them. That's what they're saying and that's why I don't want you going there any more, Franco, not while this family is a laughing stock."

"I've never heard any of that," interrupted Eugenio, "And I've been at the club a lot lately."

"Shut up, Eugenio," said Julia.

Eugenio looked hurt. "Why 'shut up'? What have I said now? I'd have noticed if there were stories like that going around."

Julia looked at him contemptuously, "You wouldn't notice if I was pregnant."

"I would," he protested.

"Well, said his wife, "You haven't."

"I haven't what?" said Eugenio, looking bemused, but before she could reply, Giovanna had leant across the table, knocking over her wine glass as she did so, and was clutching her sister-in-law to her bosom.

"I'm expecting a baby, you big oaf," said Julia in a muffled voice.

"I don't understand, the doctor said we couldn't…"

"Well, we can. Francesca, get some salt to put on this wine before it stains."

"Not too much, it's rationed," warned Giovanna, "Oh, I'm so happy, this is such wonderful news. Franco, more wine for everybody. How long, Julia?"

"Four months. I didn't say anything before because, you know, I'm quite old to be having the first one, and I couldn't believe Eugenio didn't notice how sick I was every morning."

"I thought it was something you ate," said Eugenio. "I can't believe it, I'm going to be a father. If it's a boy we'll call him Silvio."

"We certainly will not," said Julia shortly.

"No, all right." He took his wife's hand and kissed it, "We'll discuss it, and then when we've finished discussing it, you'll decide, as always." He winked at Francesca who looked embarrassed.

The wine had stained the salt red. Giovanna clicked her tongue, "We'll need some more salt, I'm afraid this tablecloth is ruined. Pour some more wine, Franco, let's celebrate."

Chapter Eleven

Maurice was in a dilemma. The truth was that he had received his call up papers back in September. He had thought about ignoring them, hoping that in all the confusion he would be overlooked. He had spent sleepless nights agonising about what to do, until it occurred to him that unless he presented himself at the recruitment office, they would send a couple of people round to find out why he hadn't responded and then his father would accuse him of being a coward and his mother would cry. He wasn't a coward and he couldn't bear the thought of being accused of being one. His brother Don had joined the navy in '37 and their mother had been distraught. The last thing Don had said to Maurice before he left was, "You're what holds them together now, Mo, you've got to be there for them."

The more he watched and listened to his parents, the more he thought it was true. They only ever seemed to argue, and what they mostly argued about was him. So he had taken the van one day and presented himself at the recruitment office and explained that he was exempt from call up because he was an agricultural worker. "I'm working on the harvest," he'd said.

"If you're exempt I need a letter from you're employer," the sergeant had said.

"Well, it's temporary work, I haven't got a contract or anything like that."

The sergeant looked at him suspiciously," So what do you do when you're not harvesting?"

"I'm self-employed. I can write you a letter."

The other man shook his head. "I need a letter saying you are permanently employed on the land. And I need it by the end of next week. You got that?"

"Yeah."

"That's 'yes sir.' I think we'll be seeing you in uniform soon."

On the way home Maurice wondered if he could get Rose's Dad to write him a letter, but he didn't think he would be able to bring himself to ask. That was back in September. Now, four months later, and a week after his relationship with Rose was apparently over, he hung around the shop doing odd jobs- cutting up wood, checking stock, sweeping the snow off the paths and making deliveries. His mother kept giving him sidelong glances and shaking her head and making as if wanting to say something and then thinking better of it.

On Friday morning he put together Cassie Bawden's delivery and carried it to her cottage on the outskirts of the village. It was a tiny timber framed house with a corrugated iron roof and a picket fence. He knocked on the door. A reedy voice called out, "Who is it?"

"It's Maurice, Mrs Bawden, I've brought your weekly delivery."

She opened the door and pulled aside a heavy brown blanket that hung down behind the door. "I have to keep this drawn to keep out the draught," she said, "I just can't get warm. Look." She held up her hands. Her fingers, bent by rheumatism were blue under her fingerless green mittens. I daren't go out to get some wood in for fear of falling. Did you bring me some kindling? I can't light the fire without kindling." She pulled her coat tightly round her. "I've taken to sleeping in this as well. I swear to God, Maurice, this cold is going to be the death of me. Just put the box down on the kitchen table and I'll make you a nice cup of tea. Did you bring tea?"

Maurice put down the box. "I'll get you some wood in and light the fire for you if you want. The tea's here." He stopped in the tiny sitting room. "It's awfully dark in here Cassie."

"I like to keep the curtains drawn to keep out the cold and then yesterday the light bulb blew. I can't change it, Maurice. I can't stand on a chair at my age. What would happen if I fell? I don't see anybody from one week to the next. If I fell I'd just lie there till I died of the cold."

"If you've got a spare I'll change it for you."

"Oh, you really are a love," she said and hobbled off to the kitchen and came back, dragging a kitchen chair behind her. She took a torch out of her coat pocket and shone it on the ceiling. "Can you see what you're doing?"

The forty watt bulb cast dark shadows across the dark furniture. "There," she said, "That's more homely. Now, if you'll get the logs in, I'll lay the fire and put the kettle on. They're round the back, by the privy."

Having lit the fire Maurice was studying a sepia photograph of a young man in uniform when Cassie brought in the tea. "That's my Harold," she said. "He was wounded at Ypres. He died in that chair behind you. That was always his chair but you can sit in it if you like." She passed Maurice his tea. They sat on either side of the fireplace and drank in silence until she said, "What's troubling you, Maurice?"

"Me? No nothing, really."

She lay down her cup and looked up at the photograph. "I had him for six months when he came back. He could never make the stairs. It was his lungs. The gas, you know. But there was never a cross word between us, except once. Once I said, "I wish you'd never gone to that war," and he shouted at me, well shout's too strong because he could never talk above a whisper, but I could see how cross he was because he went red and gasped the words. I'll never forget. He said "If I hadn't've gone I wouldn't have been a man. I couldn't have lived with myself. I'd rather die like this, knowing I did the right thing than stayed and have the guilt kill me."

Maurice looked at the picture and then at Cassie. "Yeah, but what about you? D'you think he did the right thing?"

"I didn't used to but I do know, because as it was, we could share the suffering. But you can never share guilt, can you."

Maurice thought about this, and then said, "My problem's just the opposite. I'd feel guilty if I go." Cassie waited for him to go on. "Dad wants me to go and I think it would kill Mum if I did. I don't think they'd cope without me."

"Is that your job?"

Maurice looked confused. "What do you mean?"

"I'm asking if it's your job to keep them together."

Maurice hesitated. "Well if you put it like that…" He stared down at the flames dancing in the grate. A log sizzled its sap and spat a spark out onto the carpet. Cassie stuck out a foot and trod on it. "What does Rose say?"

Maurice watched as she dragged her foot back across the ash stain.

"I …we're not together any more." He wondered what he was doing, sitting in this gloomy room with an old woman that he had always thought was a witch when he was small. Now he felt like telling her everything that had been keeping him awake and miserable for the last week, if not months. He was so far into his own thoughts that he hardly heard Cassie's question. It was its directness that shocked him.

"Why not?"

"Why not? She said we weren't ready."

Cassie went on relentlessly. He thought he detected the glimmer of a smile. "Not ready for what?"

He blurted it out. "I asked her to marry me and she said we weren't ready. Look, thanks for the tea, I've got to be going." He didn't move.

Cassie hauled herself to her feet and leaned over to take his cup from him. "I'll get us both some more." While she was out of the room Maurice stared into the fire and then looked around him. He felt strangely relieved, as if something inside him was being lifted. She came back with the tea and settled back into her chair.

"She's a sensible girl that Rose," she said and lifted her cup to her lips, "But she turned you down, did she? Did she say why?"

"She said she wanted me to be there and not away in the army, that was one reason. She said she wouldn't live in the shop with me. I mean, I thought we could have one of her Dad's cottages but she said that some land girls are having them. She said her Dad couldn't get me out of being called up by giving me a job."

Cassie contemplated her cup and then said, "You know, Maurice, it sounds as if you are minding everybody's business except your own."

"No I'm not, I don't know what you mean."

He glared at her. Her sunken cheeks and eyes, gleaming in the firelight brought back his childhood memories of her as a witch, but she had a kindly smile. "Is your parents marriage really your business? Surely it's theirs and if it's not, then there's no hope for them no matter what you do. But you say you don't want to go on living there anyway, because you want one of Rose's father's cottages. What kind of message do you think that gives Rose? You want to be around, but you don't want to, you want her because you think her father might give you a job. Have you asked him? I bet you haven't. So Rose probably thinks that you want to get married so you can move out. No sensible girl would get married on those terms."

"Oh," said Maurice, "I hadn't thought of it like that. What do you think I should do?"

Cassie put her head back and laughed. For the first time he noticed that she had two teeth missing. "That's your business, not mine. The question is, what are you going to do?"

Maurice sighed. "I don't know. If I really thought I could do any good, I suppose I would join up. If …." He hesitated.

"Yes? If we go to war, that's what you were thinking, isn't it?"

Maurice nodded.

Cassie nodded towards the radio standing in the corner. "That's just about the only human voice I hear from one day to the next, and there's never much news. But it's more important for what isn't said, than for what is. We declared war on Germany because Hitler invaded Poland. How crazy is that? Gesture politics. But Hitler wasn't gesturing when he invaded Austria and Czechoslovakia. He knows how confused our politicians are and the ones in France are even worse. Oh, he'll attack us all right. I don't know when, but he will. He knows our army is weak and that, if anything the Air Force is worse. I remember Baldwin saying, "The bombers will always get through." He was right. The people will show the politicians that we have to fight. If they don't, we'll lose the war."

"You sound like my Dad," said Maurice.

"Well to be honest with you, I've never thought your father was the sharpest knife in the drawer. He's always been too angry and that's because he was too young to fight in the last war. If he's pushing you to go, it's for his own reasons. That's no good. If you go, you have to do it because you think it's the right thing to do."

She looked at him searchingly. "And if you go, you have to know that you might be killed."

Maurice nodded, "I know, I do know that."

Cassie bent down and put another log on the fire. "There's nothing glorious about war, Maurice. It's a disgusting, evil business."

"I thought you were trying to persuade me to go just now. Now you're saying I shouldn't."

Cassie shook her head. "I'm not trying to persuade you of anything. I'm saying whatever you decide to do or not do, do it for your own reasons and not because your father wants you to or because you want to get back at Rose, falling gallantly in battle and imagining her going round in widow's weeds for the rest of her life."

"I've never thought that," protested Maurice.

Cassie laughed. "Of course you have, you're a boy."

"I'm nineteen. I'm a man," he said angrily.

Cassie laughed again. "It's the same thing. All men are boys at heart. That's what's so lovely about them. Unfortunately it's also why there will always be wars. I've got some sympathy with Mr Chamberlain because he is really trying to be rational and to behave in a civilised manner. It's just that he can't understand that he's dealing with a juvenile delinquent who has turned millions of Germans into delinquents as well. Still, I've kept you long enough. Come and see me again if you've a mind to."

Maurice trudged back up the road feeling somehow both bruised and relieved.

It occurred to him that perhaps his Dad was right with all his gloom mongering. Until now he has always thought that the world would always go on like this, with the buzzards hunting over Johnson's Spinney, with his parents arguing, with people in the pub complaining about everything that it was possible for them to complain about and then some. He would change and grow older but he somehow always imagined that the life of the village would go on for ever, just as it had always been.

He went into the shop. His father was cutting up some cheese for Jim Baker. Maurice looked at the pile of books on the counter. He counted them. There were nineteen. He took one off the pile.

"Oy, what are you doing with that?" demanded Mr Hickey, "and where the hell have you been for the last hour? There's a whole pile of deliveries to do."

"Well, they'll just have to wait, I'm going to read this first." He went off to his room.

"If my boy spoke to me like that I'd give him what for," said Mr Baker.

Mr Hickey chose to ignore the remark, but silently added a penny to the cost of the cheese.

Chapter Twelve

Reinhardt was furious with himself. He slumped down into the seat in the railway carriage and stared out of the window. "How can I have been so stupid?" he said aloud. An elderly woman sitting opposite him looked up.

"I beg your pardon?"

"Sorry," said Reinhardt, "I was thinking out loud."

Two days before he had received a letter saying that his business partner, Charles Knowles, had been killed in a car crash. The funeral was to be today.

That had been a shock though not altogether unexpected- Charles always drove recklessly and tore round the Hertfordshire lanes as if he were still competing at Brooklands. The stupid thing was that Reinhardt owed him nearly a thousand pounds. He told him that it was only temporary- he had over two thousand in his German bank, which had been true enough. Except that Reinhardt had made a point of not opening any letters from Germany or looking at anything that might be a bill. Letters from Germany had been either from his father, until his death in 1917, which stated that he would be stopping Reinhardt's allowance, or from his mother, imploring him to come home and help manage the estate, or, most recently, from his younger sister. He had stopped opening them along with any official letters from Berlin. He had run up a few debts when he had last been there and suspected that these were being called in, and stuffed the lot into the bureau in the dining room.

But the news of Charles's death had galvanised him into action. He needed the address of the bank in Berlin because he was going to need that money. Ignoring the hand written envelopes (he was astonished at how many there were) he eventually found four from the bank. The first two showed how his investments had appreciated. The returns still seemed to be reasonable, though not as spectacular as he hoped, presumably, he assumed, because of the lower inflation in Germany. The third one made him swear and sit down. It was dated the 5th September 1939 and stated that as he was living in England his investments could not be withdrawn until the war was over.

The train hissed and pulled slowly out of Kings Cross. Reinhardt lit a cigarette and tried to read the book he had bought at the station. It was the new Agatha Christie, 'Ten Little Niggers.' The girls in the office had been following it avidly when it was serialised in 'The Daily Express' the previous year. He had listened, amused, at their conjectures as to who the murderer might be, and then at their astonishment that it wasn't William Henry Blore because he had been found with his skull crushed by a clock. But he couldn't concentrate, he just prayed that Charles's son, Anthony wouldn't be at the funeral because he would be sure to ask him about the money.

The train pulled into Hatfield and he glanced at his watch. He was going to be late; he'd have to go straight to the church and depending whether Anthony was there or not, he would either make his excuses and leave, or go back to the house.

The countryside was covered in snow. He could never understand why anyone would want to live in the country, it was so quiet and boring. He'd spent the first fifteen years of his life cooped up on an estate in Silesia. He joked that he'd been interned twice, once four for years during the Great War, and once for fifteen years in his father's house. The fifteen years was infinitely the worst.

At Hitchin he got off the train and took a taxi. Although it was only three miles to the village, the driver drove painfully slowly, so that by the time Reinhardt slipped into the back row of the tiny church they were already over half way through the service. He searched for faces that he knew. Maureen, Charles's widow was sitting in the front pew, and Laura, their daughter, had her arm around her mother. There were two other women that he didn't recognise beside them. No sign of Anthony, he thought, and breathed a sigh of relief. The coffin bearers, hands folded in front of them and looking appropriately mournful carried the coffin out of the church, their soles clicking on the stone floor as they moved past him. Maureen, beneath her black veil was sobbing and holding a handkerchief to her face.

When Reinhardt joined the mourners at the Knowles' house he looked around and realised that he hardly knew anybody. He'd been to their home a few times, especially when they were planning the business. "Maureen's the homemaker,"

Charles used to say, "She's the one with the passion for antiques." It was furnished to be entirely consistent with the Georgian architecture of the house. In the drawing room, with its classical décor, there were highly polished oak coffee tables and deep- buttoned chairs. The guests stood holding their wine glasses uncomfortably, clearly unsure what to say beyond what a marvellous chap Charles had been and what a terrible loss and how they really didn't know how Maureen was going to cope, and how sorry they felt for the children. Reinhardt wandered across the hall into the dining room. A large man in a double breasted suit was mopping his brow as he held court in the far corner, gesticulating with his wine glass as he addressed the room. "Hitler's right in this regard," he was saying, "It all comes down to race. It makes no sense for us to go to war with Germany because we are of the same racial stock as the Germans. We are all Aryans. This is why we've always been at loggerheads with France, whereas there is a biological link with the Germans that is more important than culture. Hitler knows that and that's why he'll do anything to avoid war with us. I wouldn't say it too loud, but our downfall is that we live in a democracy. We're far too soft, letting all these Jews into the country. They're just as much a burden on the state as the physically handicapped and the mental defectives. Huxley said it years ago, they weaken the race from within. The politicians know that and they'd love to have a programme of euthanasia and sterilization like they've got in Germany, but they know the public wouldn't stand for it- too damned squeamish." He paused and refilled his glass.

"Oh, for God's sake." muttered a woman standing next to Reinhardt and she turned and shook her head. Reinhardt looked down at her, "I beg your pardon?"

"Oh, he's such a pompous ass when he's been drinking."

"I don't know who he is," said Reinhardt.

"You don't know Sir Ralph Coates?" She gave an ironic smile, "I thought everyone knew him. And you are?"

"Links Reinhardt."

"Ah," she said, "The disreputable Mr Reinhardt. I've heard all about you."

Reinhardt studied her. She was, he guessed, in her mid-forties, attractive in a vulnerable sort of way, though her expression suggested an aloofness that he found appealing.

"I don't know who I'm defending myself to," he said

"Elizabeth Coates," she smiled.

"Ah, so you are…"

She nodded, "His wife, for better or worse." She looked at her empty glass and glanced up at Reinhardt.

"Let me get you another," he said taking it from her.

She shrugged, "If you can't beat them join them, I suppose," and followed him into the kitchen. "So how do you know Maureen?" asked Reinhardt.

"We've known each other for years, in fact we were at school together. I was a bridesmaid at her wedding and she's always been an enormous support." She glanced back into the dining room. Sir Ralph had moved on to the talks that were apparently going on behind closed doors to secure a peace settlement.

She looked up at Reinhardt raised her eyebrows and smiled, as if to say, "My God, I've needed it." "But then, I've been a support to her as well. Charles wasn't easy either. She blames herself for his death, though as far as I can see he brought it entirely upon himself."

Reinhardt filled her glass and passed it to her, "What happened?"

"Well, as I understand it, he went out for a spin. Maureen said they'd had a row and he took the sports car. He'd been doing something to increase its acceleration, or something, and though it wasn't snowing it was very icy. Barbara asked him not to go and apparently he got cross. Anyway, the upshot was that he skidded on a bend and hit a tree on the Whitwell Road. Was killed outright. Neck broken."

She moved closer and looked round, "I say, do you have a cigarette?"

Reinhardt offered her a Senior Service. She put it to her lips and then withdrew it, leaving a smudge of red lipstick on the tip. "Perhaps we shouldn't smoke in the kitchen, we'll go out onto the veranda. I'll get my coat." They squeezed their way through the throng of guests in the drawing room and into the hall. Charles's study was full of photos of racing cars and models. At the far end the French windows led on to a veranda that overlooked the length of the garden. Reinhardt opened the doors and was struck by the chill air. Elizabeth didn't seem to notice it. She touched Reinhardt's hand lightly as he lit her cigarette, inhaled deeply and looked turned to look at the snow.

"Maureen said that yesterday morning the deer came right up to the house. Usually they're far too timid, but I suppose it's the cold makes them desperate. They can't get down through the snow to get enough food."

She drew on her cigarette again and then said, "No, things were very difficult. Maureen discovered that someone had been going through her things. She thought it was the charlady, and told Charles, and he said, as coolly as you like that it was him. When she asked him why, he said he was trying to find out who she was having the affair with. I mean, it's perfectly ridiculous, you simply couldn't meet anyone more uxorious than Maureen. But it made her suspicious, though she's never say anything to him, of course. But she did tell me that she was pretty sure that Charles had another woman. She had no idea who it was and I don't think was very interested in finding out. If it were me I'd be itching to know."

Reinhardt smiled, "You mean, if Sir Ralph…?"

Elizabeth laughed, "Well yes, I'd be frightfully curious. I think it would have to be an enormous blonde German hausfrau with her in a plait on top of her head who mothers him all day and tells him how wonderfully intelligent he is and makes him cakes and cocoa at bed time." She suddenly looked serious, "I'm cold, can we go in?"

Reinhardt felt there was something unutterably bleak about the dead man's study, or maybe it was simply his own aversion to the idea of death. He stared at a photograph of Charles sitting in an ERA, smiling triumphantly, his face black with dust except where his goggles had been so he looked like a photograph of a panda in negative. Elizabeth stood beside Reinhardt.

"Is that the car he died in?" she asked.

"No, no, I don't think there's a picture of it here."

"I've never really understood what your company does," she said.

"We developed high performance fuel for racing cars, but since the war started and the race tracks all closed, there's been no demand and so we're in something of a financial pickle, frankly. And with Charles dying, well, there are going to be difficult decisions to be made."

"Well, can't you adapt it for other things, like, you know, things to help the war effort?"

Reinhardt thought back to the same question that had come up at his tribunal. "I don't think someone with a name like Reinhardt should be seen developing fuel for tanks and planes, do you? I think it would look a bit suspicious."

"No, I wasn't thinking of that, I was thinking more of tractors and combine harvesters. That kind of thing."

"Well, I think the research costs would be very high but it's a possibility I suppose."

At that moment Sir Ralph Coates could be heard calling his wife's name. "Oh, there you are, " he said, "We should be going." He looked at Reinhardt suspiciously. Elizabeth went over to her husband and slipped her arm through his. "Darling, I want you to meet Mr Reinhardt, you know, Charles's partner. Mr Reinhardt has been telling me that he's developing a type of fuel for farm equipment that will be far more economical than what's currently being used. They just need a bit of investment to research the necessary changes. Isn't that interesting?"

"Yes," said Sir Ralph, "But we really must be going. Perhaps we could talk about it on a more appropriate occasion. Um, do you have a card, or something?"

Reinhardt took a card from his wallet and handed it to Sir Ralph. Elizabeth took it and slipped it into her handbag. "Well, it's been very nice meeting you, we'll be in touch," she said, and led her husband to the front door.

Reinhardt watched them go and wondered at the boredom of some wives and the ease of their duplicity. It was a quality he had cultivated, and to see it passed off with such nonchalance made him smile with admiration.

Maureen was not only incapable of that kind of dishonesty, she would not have believed it possible in anyone else either. He also admired those qualities of honesty and directness, and found them attractive, but only, he suspected, because it made such women unobtainable.

"Thank you for coming, Links," she said, "It means a lot. Charles always regarded you more as a friend than as a business partner. Do stay in touch."

He kissed her lightly on the cheek, "Of course I will. How are the children?"

She sighed, "You know, Anthony's in Canada, training with the RAF, so it was impossible for him to get here. The weather's held up his return twice now, but he's due leave. I know he'd like to see you too."

Reinhardt nodded; that's what he was afraid of. "There'll be plenty of time for that. Tell him not to worry- I'll be in touch."

All in all, thought Reinhardt, as he settled back in the railway carriage, that was a pretty good day. He took his book out of his pocket and tried to read, but found himself wondering whether it really were possible to adapt their performance fuels for farm machinery. The idea was absurd, though, of course if someone was putting up the money for research he was sure that a plausible case could be made. He would enjoy explaining to Elizabeth what might be done to make it possible.

Chapter Thirteen

Esther Hart's Diary

Sunday 4th February 1940

Douglas has gone to take his father out for lunch and has finally seen the sense of trying to get him to move in with us, at least temporarily. I don't suppose the old man will allow himself to be persuaded- he likes what he calls his independence far too much, but it's obvious from just looking at him that he's not eating properly- how could he be? Rationing makes it almost impossible to create a halfway decent meal even for those of us who have been cooking for years. Sometimes I do wonder if it's all necessary. We get bits of information about the Soviet war with Finland, about terrible things happening in Germany and Poland but nothing tangible about why we have to put up with so much hardship. It's like a very distant thunderstorm that we're constantly warned is coming our way but of which there has been no sign. I was beginning to wonder if the government was crying wolf, but then I read in the paper that a German plane has been shot down somewhere over England. Perhaps that was the first drop of the storm to come. Who knows? Anyway, I thought I was beginning to win the argument about bringing the children back home, but Douglas pointed out in what I felt was a rather nasty triumphalist way, that this plane meant that an attack was imminent and so it was out of the question to bring the children to London. Sometimes I think he just doesn't want them around.

Tuesday 6th February

Oh God, the whole world is going mad! Russia has bombed Helsinki, so our government along with France has promised help to the Finns and I suppose that means that we are now at war with Russia as well. So we've offered help to the Poles and to the Belgians and now to Finland. It's all empty words and all it does is to antagonise the enemies of the countries that we've offered to support. Now they've launched a big campaign with posters saying 'Careless Talk costs Lives' It shows two old gentlemen in a railway carriage, one saying to the other, "But of course you mustn't say I told you." And above them, in the luggage rack, what looks like the legs of a Tommy sticking out, and on the other side, a huge fat German general, who, if he were really up there, would break the rack and collapse on top of the two old men.

Men and women seem to feel so very differently about the war. The government tries to chivvy us along, like a rather grumpy nanny and we (women I mean, because God only knows what's going on in men's heads any more) react like sulky children. We're not grown up enough to be told what's really going on, so we have these puerile posters thrust in our faces.

Had a phone call from Rosie Aldred, who said she wanted to come up to London to visit her brother and would I be free for lunch next Monday. Said she was quite worried about it, and when I asked why, her answer surprised me, though having thought about it since it makes perfect sense. She said she has a friend who came up from Salisbury for two days and who was horrified by the changes to London. For one thing the blackout is so much stricter here than in the west country, and she felt there was a really threatening atmosphere, especially after being followed by a couple of very dubious looking fellows along Blackfriars Road. Apparently, though I didn't know this, the blackout has led to an enormous increase in crime. The government is hardly likely to publish the fact, but thinking about it, I have heard more women, especially, say they've felt threatened, and of course both Linda and Deirdre Stokes have had their handbags snatched. She also said that London just looks so seedy, with sandbags everywhere and a general air of the whole city being run down. I don't know one female friend who isn't heartily sick of the war and who isn't utterly got down by it all.

I felt too apathetic to get up and make Douglas's breakfast this morning, so I stayed bed and said I had one of my heads. Don't know if he believed me or not, but I watched him get dressed, straightening his tie in the mirror with his 'Well, I'm off to bash the Bosch expression' and then he said he'd bring me a cup of tea. Told him not to bother- we are out of milk. He took out of his breast pocket some extra food coupons and lay them on the eiderdown with a look of triumph before touching his nose and going out. I don't know where he got them from but I remembered the lecture I got from him the other day when he was leading off about these criminals who are thriving on the black market. Spivs he called them.

Thursday 8th February

I hate to admit it even to myself, and I certainly wouldn't to Douglas, but I think he's right about the children being better off out of London. Four people were injured when the IRA let off a bomb at Euston. I heard about it from a woman in the grocers who was telling her friend. She thought that the explosion was caused by German spies who were masquerading as refugees. They sometimes still publish that sort of rubbish in the rags. I felt like saying to her, "If the Germans are so clever, don't you think they'd have their spies know how to speak English, and be able to infiltrate the government, rather than dress them up as refugees when all they would be able to report on to Hitler is our miserable weather?" Presumably the bomb the IRA let off was to protest against the execution of Barnes and Richards who were hanged in Birmingham gaol yesterday for the Coventry bombings last year. That seems to be what it's about, "You hang two of our men who are guilty of murder, and we'll let off a bomb aimed to kill whoever gets in the way. That'll teach you."

If they ever find my diary I expect I'll be tried for treason and probably found guilty. Anyway, the Irish are now up in arms and hate Chamberlain; obviously he's treated with disdain by Hitler and most of Europe, and he's not too popular here either, except in the right wing press and presumably his cabinet, so you do have to wonder why he wants to be Prime Minister any more. Douglas doesn't seem to think too much of him, but then Douglas wasn't too keen on Halifax when he was at the Foreign Office. He seems to support Chamberlain if only to keep Churchill out, but I don't really know what he thinks, just that from odd snippets I've picked up from him when he's been talking to colleagues.

Perhaps I should be like Lysistrata and persuade all my friends to withdraw conjugal rights from their husbands (and in the case of Alice, from her lovers) until they stop organising the war. I wonder what would happen if I asked them.

Alice would refuse and probably say it was her duty to increase her contribution to the war effort. Jenny would say it would make a welcome change from having to have migraines. I think if I told Douglas, he'd just shrug his shoulders and say, "As you like," which would be absolutely mortifying. Not that I want him, but it would be nice to be wanted occasionally. Enough of this, I'll go and have a nice hot bath in two inches of water.

Monday 12th February

Realise I was feeling excessively gloomy last week because I was going down with a fever. Spent three days in bed reading Isherwood's 'Goodbye to Berlin' that the children gave me for my birthday last year. It brought back memories of when we went there in '34, the year after Hitler came to power. People we met were so welcoming, something I'd completely forgotten with all the propaganda there's been since the war began. Perhaps to go to war with people you have to demonise them, to make them far less than human, so killing them is not only all right, it is a duty. That's what the Nazis have done to the Jews after all, persuading the German people that Jews are sly, cunning and plotting the downfall of the State, as if they are genetically evil. The government and some of the papers try to persuade us that the same is true of Germans, that somehow they've become monsters to a man (and woman) who want to destroy us. How did an entire population change so much between that described in 'Goodbye to Berlin' and now?

They haven't of course, but in accepting this caricature of Germans as evil and sinister, we lose part of our humanity. Douglas accuses me of naivete and always has, but in my view, far better that than the cruel cynicism that seems to permeate the wireless and papers.

They've started paper rationing today. Supplies have been cut by 40%. Glad I've got my diary.

Friday 16th February

Went out today for the first time in over a week and felt much better for it, though it was very foggy and chilly. Still, it feels as though spring is in the air, and

I always look forward to that. Met Jenny for lunch in Oxford Street. Asked me if I'd had a reply to my letter for Herr Niedermayer. I haven't and feel I should go and see him again. I'll go next week.

She also showed me a magazine called US that she's subscribed to and asked me if I wanted to get it as well. She receives it because she keeps a journal that she sends regularly to the Mass Observation Unit. They collate the views of the members of the public who write to them- there are thousands apparently, so it acts as a barometer for public opinion. Not surprisingly it reflects the fact that far more women are disillusioned by the war than men and that "practically nothing has been done to deal with female situations and their neurosis." Must be edited by a man then.

Didn't tell her that I'm keeping a journal as well - I prefer to keep my neurosis to myself.

Jenny said she surrendered her membership of the Communist Party yesterday. I didn't even know she'd been a member, but she said that she'd been really disillusioned by the Nazi/Soviet pact last August, but she persuaded herself that it was only about non-aggression and economic aid. Now they've agreed to trade arms it's the last straw. She says she was very naïve and the whole affair has caused a huge rumpus in the British Communist Party. And now the government has called for volunteers to go and fight in Finland against the Russians. It seems that all those people who visited Russia and came back saying that the Soviets had created a truly socialist society where everyone was equal were having the wool pulled over their eyes.

I followed a woman back to the tube. She was wearing an incredibly threadbare fur coat and a fox fur stole. I caught a glimpse of her face as she turned to look in a shop window. She had lashings of scarlet lipstick on and masses of eyeliner. The thing that really struck me, though, was her legs. From a distance I took her to be about twenty five. When I saw her face she was obviously over forty. What I initially took for silk stockings was a black mascara line drawn down each calf over her bare legs and down to her high heels. When she reached the top of the steps going down to the tube a soldier stepped forward and said something to her. He was perhaps in his late thirties and had a beer paunch. She smiled at him, slipped her arm through his and they made their way down the stairs. For some reason the scene made me feel inconsolably sad. Then I noticed a young couple watching them, leaning over the railings. He was an ARP, very tall and good- looking. She was dark and very beautiful and was watching the first couple in wide-eyed amazement. Then the ARP said something that made the girl laugh and she buried her head in his chest. He kissed her on the top of the head, put his arm round her and they wandered off towards Marble Arch, still laughing.

I can't work out what it was about the made up woman that made me feel so sad. Perhaps I unconsciously admired her defiance in the face of so much abject dreariness. I feel so plain and dowdy and can hardly bring myself to make an effort with my appearance any more, so maybe also she just made me recognise how unwanted I am. I haven't even heard from the children for over a fortnight. But she was grotesque. I don't know if she was a prostitute – I assume so, though I might be doing her an injustice. Certainly her soldier seemed delighted to see her, and he was pretty unprepossessing as well. And she must have been aware of the pretty young girl's look of complete amazement- I should imagine that she attracts that reaction all the time, and just doesn't care. Maybe I should try it – put lashings of make up on tonight for when Douglas gets home, stick down his spam and mash in front of him and say, "Well, Douglas, you work for The Home Office. What are your plans for dealing with the situations of females and their neurosis?" And then show him my calves where I've put on my 'silk stockings'.

Just put on the news. The government has announced that all merchant ships will be fitted with guns. I expect they thought the Germans would reply by saying that in that case they had better stop attacking merchant ships. If so they were disappointed. The German government has just announced that in future all British merchant ships would be regarded as enemy combatants. I wonder how the mothers of British merchant seamen are feeling after hearing that.

Chapter Fourteen

Every afternoon at three o'clock, Captain Burfeind and Otto Busch sat down to play chess. Busch was right- he had worked out how to beat his captain, though it took longer than he had anticipated. But he had won their last four games. This wasn't altogether surprising, since, as the Germans' representative in the camp, Burfeind was constantly having to sort out disputes, have meetings with Major Stimpson and listen to complaints about the running of the camp from the internees.

Busch had no responsibilities. He locked himself away in his cabin as soon as breakfast was over and played matches against himself. He recorded each move in a note book.

"The thing is, Captain," he said at the end of their last game, "Chess is war on a board. That's checkmate. You were right when you told me that I had to learn to defend, but you also have to see the enemies' weakest point and then strike like lightning when he's least expecting it. If you don't mind me saying so, you are so busy building up your defences and always in the centre that you don't think about attacks coming from the flanks. And you castle too late. "

Captain Burfeind smiled and shrugged his shoulders, It's a game, it's just a game."

Busch leaned forward and shook his head, "That's why you lose. It's not a game, it's war. I bet the great masters want to destroy their opponents psychologically, that's how they become great."

Burfeind sat back and looked at him quizzically, "Is that what you want to do to me?"

"I want to become a great chess master. If you think it's just a game I'll always win, there's no pleasure in that. Don't you think Günther Prien felt the greatest pleasure when he sank the Ark Royal at Scapa Flow? That's war. That's the ultimate. I wish I'd served under him."

Burfeind stood up. "Well, if there's no point in our playing any longer, I'll have to find you a worthier opponent." He left Busch re-arranging the pieces and taking out his note-book.

Over the following week they scarcely saw one another. The tacit understanding that their games were over came as something of a relief to the Captain. There was something in Busch's intensity that Burfeind found disconcerting and over the following days he wondered if he had made a mistake. Busch stopped joining in with any of the camp activities. He had been an enthusiastic member of the football team, but dropped out complaining of an ankle injury. He stopped attending the lectures that were held in the dining room after supper on most evenings. He remained in his cabin. Even Müller found him withdrawn and sullen and mentioned the fact to Burfeind. " I shouldn't have stopped playing chess with him," said Burfeind, "I'll have another go."

At three that afternoon he knocked on the door of Busch's cabin door and went in. Busch was crouched over the board, making notes. He didn't look up.

"Come on, let's play." There was no response. Busch moved a knight and made a note. Burfeind watched him for a few minutes and then said, "I've been thinking. There's a weakness in your theory. I know how to exploit it."

Busch paused and then put the pieces on the board for the start of a game. Then he turned the board around so that Burfeind was playing the white pieces. In the half- light of the cabin, and crouched over the board, he reminded Burfeind of a cat waiting to spring. Burfeind moved his queen's pawn two spaces. Busch moved a rook's pawn one space and then took one of his bishop's and placed it on the side of the board.

"What are you doing?" asked the captain.

Without lifting his face from the board, Busch grunted, "Go on, your move."

"Arrogant little bastard," said Burfeind under his breath. He wished he'd never taught him the game. He played slowly, remembering what Busch had said about protecting the flanks, but Busch didn't seem to give a thought to his own moves, lifting and putting down each piece almost carelessly, and then making a careful note in his book. Eventually Burfeind saw an opening- Busch had left his queen unprotected and Burfeind took it triumphantly with his bishop. He glanced up. Busch immediately moved his knight- "Checkmate," he said in a dull voice and sighed. Burfeind stared at the board and shook his head. "I really thought I had you, but you're too good for me. I shouldn't have taken your queen."

Busch looked up for the first time, "If you hadn't I would have beaten you in four more moves." The certainty with which he said this took Burfeind aback.

"Look, I'll show you." Busch replaced the pieces as they had been. "if you had done that," he moved the pieces rapidly, "I would have done this, on the other hand your best move would have been to do this and to leave your bishop in place, but I would have countered that by doing this..." he moved the pieces too fast for Burfeind to follow, "You think, what? Two, maybe three moves ahead? You think the queen is like the general in the army. If you capture the general you win the war. There's only one piece that's important. That's the king. The king is the Führer. In chess you can sacrifice everything for the king so that he can win. It's the same in life. Sacrifice everything for the Führer so that he will triumph. We're just pawns, captain." Burfeind was disturbed by the flat, matter-of-fact tone and the deadness in the young man's eyes. He got up and went to the door. Glancing back, he started to say, "You should,"... but noticing that Busch had gone back to his chess board, simply finished the sentence under his breath, "get out more."

The last of the snow had gone some days before, leaving mud-caked pathways to the huts and the dining room. There was still a thin layer of ice on the swimming pool. He had suggested to Major Stimpson that it should be emptied several times, and the major had agreed but, he noted bitterly, nothing had happened. It wouldn't take much for someone to fall into it, and they would quickly die of hypothermia unless immediately pulled out. Major Stimpson had agreed that it was dangerous, but nothing had happened to empty it. Now he was late for their weekly meeting.

When he arrived at the office, Dr Dobel was there, discussing the agreement to trade war materials between the Soviet Union and Germany.

"I don't know what to make of it at all," Major Stimpson was saying, "I thought Germany was supposed to be a bulwark against the Communists, and then they start signing treaties together. I don't get it."

"Dictators collaborate- they're as bad as each other," replied Dobel, "The

Soviets want Finland and Hitler is happy for that to happen because it gives him access to the North Sea in a way that he didn't have before. They're carving up Poland between them."

When Burfeind entered the room, Dobel greeted him in German. "How are you? How are the men?"

Burfeind sat down, "Mostly all right. The boredom gets everybody down. We've had a few incidents but not anything to really worry about, but I am concerned about one or two. The tedium is making some very depressed."

Dobel translated and then asked, "What form is the depression taking?"

"Well, take young Busch, for example. You might remember you examined him after he was put in isolation last month. I taught him to play chess to try and channel his energies. It seems I did rather too good a job, because he's stopped joining in with any of the other activities. He spends all day in his cabin working out moves. He's got some idea that chess is really war and he wants to be a grand master. I played against him this afternoon. He gave me a bishop's start and still beat me easily."

Dobel translated, and Stimpson said, "I seem to remember that one of the Jewish internees is something of a whiz at chess. Never learned to play myself, wouldn't have the patience for it. What the devil's the chappy's name?"

He lifted the phone, "Miss Higgins, one of the Jews is a crack chess player, could you check out who it is, please, and bring in three coffees."

Dobel frowned, "If you're thinking what I think you're thinking, Major, I think it would be a very bad idea indeed."

The major looked surprised, "Really? Why so?"

"Well, the flu epidemic amongst the Jews separated the two groups more effectively than you've been able to achieve and to that extent has been a blessing. To deliberately arrange a match between a professed Nazi and a Jew is asking for trouble, in my opinion."

"Which I respect, I really do," said the major rapidly, "And you may be right. But don't they have correspondence matches, where players write to each other. I just thought if we could find a common interest, it might be a way of reducing the animosity between the two groups. It's just a thought."

Dobel translated for Burfeind, who shook his head. "Nein," he said emphatically.

Miss Higgins came in with the coffee and put the tray on the table. "The chess player is Aaron Rosenbaum, Bavarian champion from Munich from '28 to '31. She took a file from under her arm and passed it to Major Stimpson. "Yes, that's the chap." He examined the photograph that was clipped to the file. An unsmiling face stared myopically at the camera. He had a small beard and thick pebble glasses. "Looks a bit of a boffin. Wonder why he got a 'A'." He flicked through the file. "Oh, research physicist- shame we can't use brains like this instead of locking them up." He sighed. "Well, this doesn't get us any further in deciding what to do about your man, Captain."

Dobel translated and then said, "There's a second hand bookshop in town. I noticed it had got some old chess magazines when I was in there the other day. I could probably pick up a dozen or so for tuppence."

"It's kind of you, but they'd be no good to Busch, he doesn't speak any English and refuses to learn."

"Well, I don't think that matters. The problems are quite self- explanatory because they're set out graphically. And if he wants to understand more fully, then perhaps he'll be motivated to learn a bit of English. But the main reason is that I think it's very important psychologically for him to be given something, and something that he wants- it would make him feel valued and I suspect part of his depression is caused by feelings of uselessness. I'll see what I can do."

After Dr Dobel and Captain Burfeind had left, Major Stimpson lit his pipe and went back to the problem that had been worrying him for the past few days. He knew that he was due a visit from the Swiss Camp Inspectors. They always took an interest in the physical and emotional well being of the men, even going so far as to attending the lectures that were put on and examining with more zeal than the major thought strictly necessary, the sanitary arrangements.

On the last visit, the chief inspector, an unsmiling and immaculately dressed man had said in his emotionless voice, "The men cannot receive letters from their loved ones. This is well understood and the reasons for it known. However, this lack of communication has adverse effects on the mental health of POW's and internees, and therefore it is incumbent upon the camp authorities to make provision of diverting activities. This is not something that can be solely left to the men."

Major Stimpson had vaguely wondered what the Chief Inspector knew about having 'loved ones', and he was stung by the criticism. He'd known for weeks that he'd have to come up with some kind of activity that would be seen to involve the men. Then it came to him. He was the camp commander, after all, not Dobel or Burfeind.

He picked up the phone, "Miss Higgins, can you find the carpenter and ask him to come to my office immediately."

Chapter Fifteen

It had been a difficult couple of weeks for Francesca and Eric. He had been on duty a lot, and since after what she regarded as her father's disastrous birthday party, Francesca was sure that Eric had been avoiding her. So she wrote to him, saying that they had always known that it would be difficult for her family to accept him, that she loved him and wanted to marry him, but that if it was too difficult for him she would rather that he let her know than say nothing. She signed it and then added a PS. "Please Eric, tell me that I can still hope."

Every morning for a week she waited for the post with a mixture of anticipation and despair, and when there was no letter from Eric, she spent the rest of the day in despair. Then on the tenth day after the party, after a tearful conversation with Julia who counselled her that all men are insensitive cowards, that she would never hear from him, and that it was best to forget him, to which Francesca had replied that in that case she would die a spinster, the letter arrived. It was brief. It read simply, "Please meet me next Tuesday at the café in King's Cross Station at noon. We need to talk. Eric."

For a day she kept the letter to herself, read it twenty times and finally decided that Julia was obviously wrong, at least about her Eric, and went off to show it to her.

Julia's morning sickness had got worse, and in the last few days had been accompanied by splitting headaches. Also she had begun to find Eugenio's sudden attentions rather trying.

"Do you know," she complained to Giovanna, " last night when I was putting the pasta on the stove, he wouldn't even let me lift the saucepan. I preferred it when he ignored me."

Giovanna was crocheting a jacket for the new baby, and simply nodded. "I know," she said, "But it'll wear off."

"Why are you so sure it'll be a boy?" asked Julia, looking at the blue skein of wool. "It might be a girl."

Giovanna looked up and smiled, "By the shape of you," she said, "I can always tell."

Julia looked down at her stomach, "But it doesn't even show yet, does it?"

Giovanna smiled knowingly, "You'll see," she said, "I'm always right."

Back in her own flat, Julia was wondering with some trepidation how much interest her sister-in-law would take in the baby when it was born, and was saying a prayer to God, that if it wasn't too late, could he please give her a girl, when Francesca rushed in.

"See, Julia," she said, "It's all all right. Eric's written to me. He does love me, I knew it would be all right. I'm so happy. Do you want to see the letter?"

Julia read it and looked at Francesca.

"Well?"

"Hmmm," said Julia.

"Hmmm? What do you mean 'hmmm'. You said he wouldn't write and he has, so you were wrong. He wants to see me and talk. He's not a coward. He's not like other men."

Julia put her hand on Francesca's. "Why do you think he wants to meet you at King's Cross?"

"Why? Well it's quite close to where we both live, that's why."

"Is that where you usually meet him?"

Francesca shook her head, "No."

Julia leaned forward and took Francesca's hands in hers, "Listen, bambina, I just don't want you to get hurt, that's all."

Francesca looked puzzled and withdrew her hands, "Why should I? It's going to be all right, I just know it is."

"Good," said Julia, "Well that's fine then, after all you know him better than me. I only met him the once."

But Francesca sensed that Julia wanted to say something and was holding back. "Why did you ask whether we usually meet at that café?"

Julia sighed, "Francesca, it's the end of the line, isn't it. He might be meeting you there to say good-bye and because he's getting on a train. He might have been called up and be going away."

"Oh," said Francesca, looking crest-fallen, "I hadn't thought of that."

When Franco arrived home from work an hour later, he found his daughter sitting at the dining table, a book open in front of her, and sobbing. He put a consoling arm around her and looked round for Giovanna, "Where's your mother?"

Francesca wiped her eyes on her sleeve, sniffed, and said, "I don't know, shopping I expect." Then she started crying again.

"Whatever's the matter?" asked Franco. He always hated having to try and deal with Francesca's crying and it seemed terribly unfair that his wife should be out just when he needed her most.

Francesca took out Eric's letter from the back of the book, which is where she kept it, and handed it to her father. "Read that and tell me what it means to you," she said and began sobbing again.

He was going to protest that he didn't really like to read other people's letters, but it was so brief and to the point that he struggled to see what the problem was. "Well, it just means that Eric wants to see you next Tuesday. What else can it mean?"

"Julia says he wants to meet at the station to say good-bye because he's going away."

"Does she?" said Franco, "But Eric doesn't say that. He seems a very decent man, I think he would have said in his letter if he was going away. "

This made Francesca brighten. "Do you?" but a second later she darkened again. "But I told him when I wrote to him that I love him. And he doesn't say he loves me. He doesn't even finish the letter, "With love, Eric." Julia says he would have said it if he did."

Franco sat down next to his daughter and wiped a tear stained wisp of hair away from her eyes. "You know, when Eugenio was courting Julia he would write her poems and sing to her and bring her flowers and she loved all that stuff. And your mother used to say to me, "Why can't you be more romantic like your brother?" And she was right, I'm no good at it, so I'd say, "Which would you rather have, a man who can unblock your sink, or one who can sing you 'Nessun Dorma' when you're knee deep in water?"

Francesca laughed, "I expect she said she wanted both, a man to sing Nessun Dorma while he was unblocking the sink."

Franco smiled and stroked her cheek, "Si, é vero. We both know your mother. But then sometimes I think I should have been born an Englishman, or maybe it's just that I've lived here so long, but, well, I love your mother, but I don't have to tell her every five minutes like Eugenio tells Julia. It sometimes seems to me that they spend the other four minutes fighting. So Eric's an Englishman. Englishmen don't do all that stuff like Italian men. Anyway," he added knowingly, "He couldn't be sure who was going to open his letter."

"So you think he does still love me?"

Franco smiled, "I'm your father, so I'm biased, but how could he not?"

Francesca kissed her father on the cheek. "Thank you Papa, you've made me feel so much better. But Eric is very romantic. You know he's translating this old poem by Chaucer into modern English, and when he gets to a beautiful passage he gives it to me. It's the story of Troilus and Criseyde. Do you know it?"

"No," said Franco, "I'd never heard of Chaucer until you mentioned him to me."

"Well, it's about the Trojan War, you know, Helen and all that. Well Criseyde's father is called Calchas. He's a Trojan and because he can see into the future, he knows the Greeks are going to win, so he goes over to their side and leaves Criseyde in the city. And one day she's in the temple and then Troilus comes in with all his soldiers. They're all very macho and they walk up and down looking at the girls and then Troilus catches sight of Criseyde and immediately falls in love, but he's too embarrassed to say anything, because he didn't believe in love before he saw her and he's afraid that his men will laugh at him. It's such a beautiful passage when he sees her- do you want me to read it to you?"

"No, no," said Franco hurriedly, "Just tell me what happens."

"Va bene. Troilus persuades Criseyde's uncle Pandarus to arrange a meeting in secret, but Criseyde is very shy and she resists for a long time, but then finally she gives in, and they meet, and Criseyde falls in love with him and they become lovers." She stopped, "What's the matter?"

Franco frowned, "Francesca, you won't do anything silly, will you."

She blushed, "Papa, it's a poem. And anyway, I... do you want to know what happens?"

"Si, go on."

"Then the Greeks and Trojans exchange prisoners, and Calchas persuades the Greeks to send Antenor back in exchange for Criseyde. Of course she doesn't want to go, but she promises Troilus that she'll come back to him within ten days. Troilus gives her a brooch just before she leaves. But once she is back with her father she realises she can't go back and she is wooed by Diomedes. In the end she begins to forget about Troilus. In a battle, Troilus finds the brooch he gave her on Diomedes' armour. He kills lots of Greeks in his fury, but before he can kill Diomedes, he is killed by Achilles."

The door flew open and Giovanna and Eugenio came in.

"Just put them down on the table, Eugenio, that's very kind."

Eugenio set the bags down. "What are you two up to?" he demanded.

"Francesca's just been telling me the story of Troilus and Criseyde," said Franco, "Her young man is translating it into English."

"Then his Italian must have improved a lot," said Eugenio, "It's very hard, even for an Italian. I know. We had to read it at school."

Francesca took her book, stood up and showed him the spine. "Look, Uncle Eugenio, it's by Geoffrey Chaucer. An old English poet. How can you have read it at school?"

Eugenio shrugged, "Then your Geoffrey Chaucer must have stolen it from our Boccaccio. It's in his stories, what's it called, 'Il Filostrato.' It's all about how fickle women are. And that Criseyde, she was one of the worst."

Tears welled up in Francesca's eyes. "No, she wasn't like that. She had no choice, you don't understand."

She stared at Eugenio defiantly. He sat down and laughed. "What are you saying? That I don't understand women? Just show me a man that does."

Francesca turned on her heel and ran from the room, closely followed by her mother, who hadn't yet had time to take off her coat. She stopped at the door of Francesca's bedroom, "Thank you for carrying my shopping, Eugenio…but honestly." And then she closed the door.

"What can you do?" said Eugenio, shaking his head. "I help your wife carry her bags and that's the thanks I get. Julia's just the same. She won't let me lift a finger to help and when I do, she bites my head off. Have you seen the paper today?"

"The thing is…" said Franco, but Eugenio had pulled the paper out of his pocket and was flattening it on the table, "Look here. Mussolini's got a billion- a billion, do you see that? A billion lire to build up the defences along the Austrian and German borders. And only six million along the French border. You see what this means, don't you. It means he doesn't trust Hitler any more. It means there'll be no war. He finally understands that the Italian people don't want to get involved in this stupid war. Isn't that good news?"

Franco looked doubtful. "So why did he attack Albania then?"

Eugenio snorted in derision, "That was nothing. What did Ciano say? Albania was as good as ours anyway. "Like raping your own wife," that's what he said. Anyhow, what good's taking Albania anyway? What use is Albania to anybody?"

Franco didn't feel inclined to argue. He wanted his brother to go so that he could see how his daughter was, so he stood up and said, "Look, we both hate Mussolini and who knows what he's going to do. In my opinion he's just biding his time to see who comes out on top. If the Germans do, he'll side with them, whether the Italians like it or not. All we can do is wait and see."

"Va bene," said Eugenio, "but you'll see, I'm right."

When they heard the door close, Francesca and Giovanna emerged from Francesca's bedroom. "Sometimes that brother of yours…" started Giovanna, and she shook her head vigorously.

Franco held up his hands in a gesture of surrender, "I know, I know."

"Well, speak to him about it, will you," she said, and disappeared into their bedroom.

Four days later Francesca left the flat at ten thirty. There was a thick fog that made her eyes and nose smart. She had lived the previous few days in a state of elation, interspersed with periods of gloom. Her mother had taken advantage of the elation by getting her to clean the oven and re-arrange the kitchen shelves. She hadn't asked Francesca the reason for this roller coaster of emotion, and hadn't thought to ask Franco, assuming he wouldn't know anyway, but she kept giving Francesca sidelong glances that hadn't gone unnoticed, but which were unacknowledged. The trouble was that in those moments when she was most sure that everything would be all right between her and Eric, the memory of Julia's voice kept interrupting, "Well, it's the end of the line, isn't it."

She had hardly slept the night before, took over an hour to get dressed and put on her make up, and decided to walk the nearly two miles to the station. By the time she reached the junction of Clerkenwell Road and Farringdon Road her feet were painful and she chose to catch a bus, though this meant she would arrive far too early.

Once in the station she hurried to find a ladies' lavatory. "That'll be a penny, dear," said the elderly attendant, "are you all right?" Francesca scrabbled around in her handbag and gave the woman the coin, and then rushed to a mirror. Her worst fears were exceeded. "Oh, God, I look like a panda," she said aloud. The woman who was washing her hands at the next basin turned to her.

"Let me see, ducks. Oh, you've smeared all your mascara. Let me see if I've got a hankie, I'm sure I've got one somewhere." The two women searched their respective handbags to no avail, until the woman eventually produced one from her sleeve. "Here we are, though I'm afraid I have used it."

Francesca thanked her but decided to decline the offer. She dabbed some water on her finger, but only succeeded in smearing it further.

"No," said the woman, watching her attentively, "I'm afraid you've made it worse. Try Boots, they might have some."

Francesca rushed out and was rushing past the café when she stopped. Through the open door she saw Eric. For a second she hardly recognised him. He was wearing spectacles with small tortoiseshell frames. She had never seen him in spectacles before. And he was holding up a paper to his face and peering at it. She went in and sat down opposite him. He was so engrossed in what he was reading, that he didn't look up until she said, "Hello, Eric, you're here very early."

He took off the glasses hurriedly, "Francesca," he said, "I'm so pleased to see you. I was so worried you wouldn't come. What have you done to your eyes?"

"Oh, that," she said, rubbing one eye vigorously with the ball of her hand, "Why did you think I wouldn't come?"

"Well, I made such an ass of myself at your father's party. I thought you might not be able to forgive me. I say, I don't think you should rub your eye like that, it's making it worse. You look like a panda. Would you like a cup of tea?"

"No thank you. But you took such a long time to write. I thought you didn't want to see me anymore because my family was so…so...well. I didn't know you wore glasses."

Eric looked at his glasses and put them away in their case. "And it took you such a long time to write. It was ten days before I heard from you."

"No, well I wrote that night as soon as I went on duty. But then I didn't know whether to post it and so I carried it about in my pocket because I didn't like what I'd written. And then I tried again and I still didn't like it so I gave up trying to, you know, and in the end I thought I'd just have to see you and keep the letter as simple as possible. Sorry."

She studied his face. "Put your glasses on again, I want to see you in them."

Reluctantly he took them out of the case and put them on.

"Now we both look like pandas," she said, and leaned across the table and kissed him.

"I've got something for you," he said, and passed her the sheet of paper he's been reading when she had arrived. "It's the part when Troilus and Criseyde spend the night together for the first time."

She took it and read it quickly. "It's lovely. Do you still want to marry me?"

Eric sighed deeply, "More than anything. Can we go and buy you a ring to prove it?"

She leaned forward and held his arm, "But Eric, you do know that I won't sleep with you before we're married, don't you?"

He nodded his head several times, "Oh absolutely, yes of course." And then he laughed.

"Why are you laughing?"

"Well, even if I wanted to, I mean if we wanted to, which we don't, what I mean to say is, we might want to, but we wouldn't even if we could, which we can't. I mean there are always people around in both our houses and there's nowhere else, so we can't anyway. If you see what I mean."

"Eugenio says there's all sorts of hotels round his restaurant in Soho that let out rooms by the hour," said Francesca, "But I wouldn't want us to be like that, would you?"

"Oh, I couldn't agree more." Eric nodded several times.

"Oh," said Francesca, "Shall we go then."

They took the tube to Oxford Circus. At the top of the steps a heavily made up woman in a threadbare fur coat and a fox fur stole was walking towards them and smiling at someone. Francesca gaped. "Don't laugh," said Eric, "That might be you in forty years' time.

Francesca giggled and buried her head in his chest.

Chapter Sixteen

Maurice spent two days lying on his bed reading 'Why Britain is at War.' He read slowly- some of it he didn't understand and skipped whole passages, but those that he did grasp seemed so important that after thirty pages he felt compelled to go and find a dictionary and a red pen and start again.

There were two books in the house, a Bible, that his mother took to church every Sunday, and an old dictionary with the spine missing.

"Where have you been hiding?" asked his mother, "The orders are piling up, Maurice, and what are you looking for?"

"This is really important, Mum, I need the dictionary," he said, leaning over the back of the sofa and scrabbling amongst the magazines and catalogues.

"You don't need the dictionary now, you've got work to do," she said emphatically.

Maurice retrieved the dictionary from underneath a seed catalogue. "I need to know what 'galvanic' means."

"What?" her voice rose in a shrill yelp. "You're not reading a book, are you? Nobody reads in the daytime. If you want to read a book you can do it in the evening. I never heard such a thing."

Her raised voice brought Mr Hickey in from the shop. "What the hell's going on in here?" he roared, "It sounds like bedlam. And there's customers in the shop. What do you want people to think?"

"Maurice is reading a book," said Mrs Hickey, as if no other explanation were necessary.

Mr Hickey looked at his Maurice patronisingly, "Are you son? What are you reading, then?"

"That book you're selling in the shop. I want to know why we're at war. I think it's really important."

"You see? But I told him…."

Mr Hickey cut his wife off, "Are you then?" He nodded, "That's all right, Mother. Leave the boy be. He's right, it is important. You come and serve the

114

customers and I'll see to the deliveries."

Mrs Hickey shook her head in annoyance and clicked her tongue, but followed her husband into the shop. Maurice felt a pang of guilt and then ran upstairs to his room.

He lay on the bed and pondered. He didn't know where Poland was, or Czechoslovakia either for that matter. He wished he'd got a map so that he could see where all these places were. He'd only been to London once in his life, and that was to his uncle's funeral in Finchley. He hadn't thought much of the place to be honest. On September 3rd, when they'd all crowded around the radio in the lounge to hear Chamberlain announce that Britain was at war with Germany, that posh voice might have been coming from another planet, as far as he was concerned. It was only the fact that his father had gone white and given a grim nod of satisfaction and his mother had burst into tears, that it had seemed important to him at all.

He picked up the dictionary and went through the alphabet until he came to the letter 'g'. 'Galvanic'- it seemed to be something to do with electric shocks. He read the sentence again

"Although galvanic, he (Hitler) is brittle." He sighed. Maybe the next chapter would be easier. But he couldn't even understand the title of the next one. The word 'Mein' wasn't in the dictionary. Then he looked up 'Kampf.' No luck with that either. Why couldn't the man write in plain English?

Discarding the dictionary he decided to try and read each sentence as a whole. His Dad said he'd read the book four times. If his Dad could understand it he was damned sure that he could, and there was no way he was going to ask him to explain it. But it was hard work. Still, if he was going to decide to join the army and get killed, he felt he owed it to himself to understand what he was going to die for and in any case, he felt it was important to explain to his mother why he had to go and fight. And if he wasn't convinced then he's stay at home or be sent to prison as a conchie. He wondered whether Rose would visit him in prison if he did. Not that he cared, one way or the other.

He read on slowly. Some sentences were just too hard, and then suddenly one would leap out at him, and that encouraged him to go on.

"Why, therefore are we now at war? The answer to that question can be given in two words: "Adolf Hitler."

That was easy. The next bit wasn't, but then Maurice worked out that 'Mein Kampf' was the title of Hitler's autobiography. And in it he said that

"Man is a fighting animal and the nation is therefore a fighting unit...."

Then there was something about how pacifists and Jews are weak and sinful.

"Only brute force can ensure the survival of the race....The race must fight; a race that rests must rust and perish. The German race, had it been united in time, would now be master of the world today. Is it too late for Germany to realise that mystic function?"

Was it true that man is a fighting animal? He'd only ever fought somebody once and that was when Jimmy Jones had said he was going to ask Rose to go to the village dance with him. Maurice had punched him on the chin, and he simply couldn't believe how painful it had been. He'd stared at his hand in astonishment as Jimmy lay on the ground looking dazed. It had frightened them both. Later Jimmy said he'd only been joking and Maurice said he couldn't understand it-he'd seen the cowboys on the flicks punch each other for ages and not even flinch. Jimmy had said that perhaps cowboys were different. Now Maurice was wondering if Germans were different. After all, in the book he says that the English hate war and the people are peace loving. But if the Germans wanted to fight, then it was up to people like him to make sure that they didn't win the war. But what could he do? He was a good shot. He went pigeon shooting with Rose's Dad and he was handy with a 12 bore and a 410. But shooting another human being was different, he wasn't sure he could do that, not when another soldier was looking at you. He supposed he might be able to do it if it meant the difference between living and dying, but did he really want to put himself in that place at all?

The reading and thinking about it hurt his brain and he dozed off and dreamt that a pigeon was sitting on a fence. But it had a human face and was looking at him scornfully and was mocking him in another language. He looked along the sights of his gun. The bird didn't move, as though daring him to shoot. His arm was trembling. The bird seemed to laugh and that infuriated him. He raised the gun to his shoulder, and without thinking, aimed and fired. The sound of the shot shocked him awake.

He rubbed his eyes and looked around him, and then ran down the stairs into the kitchen where his mother was preparing the evening meal.

"Mum, I know you're not going to like this, but I've decided and I'm not going to change my mind. I've got to join up"

Without waiting for her reply he went out of the door and walked up to Cassie Bawden's house.

"She'll understand," he said aloud.

Chapter Seventeen

"Suppose we meet in the tea room at the National Gallery," she said, "There's a concert at five, and I thought we could go to it if you're free and then catch a bite to eat, say at the Ritz?"

"That's an excellent idea," said Reinhardt, "I'll look forward to it." He paused, wondering how he was going to get the money to pay for a concert and a meal at the Ritz. He was terribly stretched just at the moment and owed money in a few places, but he'd have to get it somehow. He'd had a cheque bounce at the Ritz just before Christmas so he'd have to pay cash. How much would he need? Twenty-five quid ought to cover it, but where would he get that kind of money?

"Hello? Are you still there?" Her voice was impatient.

"Yes, I was just wondering whether we shouldn't go somewhere a little quieter."

"No, I've been promising myself the Ritz since this damn war started. Good then, see you at four."

He hadn't really believed she would get in touch with him. He pictured her leaning on the arm of her husband in the doorway of Charles's study, and smiling coquettishly while Sir Ralph stared at him like a blinking idiot. Reinhardt smiled at the memory. Oh, well, Carpe Diem, he thought, I'll just have to see if I can bluster my bank manager.

He wasn't sure what he should wear to an early evening concert. Before his second wife left him they used to enjoy going to the opera, he in his evening suit and she in her best gown and the diamond brooch that he'd bought her for their final wedding anniversary before she'd finally had enough of what she called his "endless philandering." She'd taken it off and thrown it at him.

Halfway through dressing he suddenly remembered he'd locked it away in his desk. It was still there. He slipped it into his suit pocket, put his bowler on and hurried to the pawn shop.

The old man behind the counter examined it with his eye glass. "Fifteen," he said, "It's a nice piece, but I'm getting more jewellery than I can handle."

"Make it twenty and it's a deal," said Reinhardt.

The old man went to his till and took out three five pound notes, placed them on the counter and, licking his thumb, counted them out in front of Reinhardt.

"Take it or leave it," he said.

Reinhardt reluctantly put the money in his wallet and waited as the receipt was laboriously written out.

"Miserable old bugger," he said to himself as he left the shop, the bell clanging behind him.

He took the tube to Trafalgar Square. He hadn't been to The National Gallery since the boys were small. Now, walking along the long corridors, the place seemed unutterably bleak, the cream walls bereft of pictures and sheets hanging from the ceilings. He followed the signs to the café which was already half full. Sitting alone by the far wall, Elizabeth Coates was waving to him. He sat down opposite her. She laughed. "I'm afraid we may both be fearfully over-dressed," she said, "I mean, just look." It was true. There were a number of Tommies in uniform, other people who, he suspected, were far more interested in the sandwiches and tea that were being served at the counter, than they were in the music, women with shopping bags, and elderly men who, it seemed, had simply come in to shelter from the cold.

He looked back at her. She was wearing a red beret and matching lipstick, an expensive black coat and red dress. She took a cigarette from her handbag and lit it nervously.

"I say," she said, still not looking at him, "I hope you don't think I'm in the habit of doing this sort of thing." He raised an eyebrow. "You know, phoning up strange men that I hardly know and asking them out. The thing is I've read about these concerts and always thought I'd love to go to one. Do you like music? I thought of you because it's all your fellow countrymen, you know, Bach and Beethoven and Schubert. For some reason I assumed you would."

"And do I take it your husband doesn't like music?" Reinhardt asked innocently.

She stubbed out her cigarette in a saucer and laughed scornfully. "Ralph? Good

God, no. The only things he's interested in are his horses, whisky and his BPP cronies."

Reinhardt hadn't heard of the BPP.

"You know, the British People's Party. Still trying to coddle up to Hitler. Back to the land and all that tosh. He's gone to some conference, that's how I could get away." She glanced up at him and took another cigarette. "I told him I was going to visit my sister in Richmond. Do you think that's very wicked?"

"Very," smiled Reinhardt, "And are you?"

She leaned back in her chair and for the first time looked at him carefully, and then exhaled the smoke. "That depends," she said, "Perhaps." She stared at him for a few seconds and then pulled her chair closer. "The thing is, well, I'm sure you've read the papers, and I bet they don't tell the half of it. The things that are happening in Germany are just too dreadful. And the more Ralph says the papers are exaggerating about the way they're treating the Jews, the more I think we're not told the half of it. You're German, you must know."

Reinhardt shook his head, "I haven't been back since the boys were tiny, well before Hitler. It's true that I have a sister in Berlin, but I'm afraid she regards me as being far too, what was the word you used? Disreputable?"

Elizabeth blushed. "Did I? How very impolite of me. You know, I was always brought up to mind my P's and Q's and my mother drummed into me that when I grew up I would marry a wealthy man and have children and a nice house and my role would be to be a good and obedient wife. I've got a nice house, a wealthy husband who ignores me, and no children. I'm forty- four years old. To be brutally honest, I can't see that being good and obedient has got me very far, so when I saw this concert was on, it really made me think. I mean, only a year ago, I wouldn't even have dreamt about it. But the way I see it now is that in a year we could all be dead. Do you worry about that?"

"So," said Reinhardt, ignoring the question, "Your philosophy now is 'Carpe Diem?'"

"Precisely."

"Mine too," said Reinhardt, "Do you think we should go and get the tickets?"

Elizabeth squeezed past an old man who was wiping the crumbs from his beard. She grimaced. "Not exactly how I imagined how it would be," she said.

She took Reinhardt's arm as they stepped outside There was already a long queue forming, and a cold drizzle was drifting from a grey sky. "Oh, God, poor London," she said, "When I used to come up before all this started it was so bright and lively, you could feel the excitement in the air everywhere and now look at it." They stood on the steps surveying Trafalgar Square while Reinhardt put up his umbrella. "I think it's like some great animal that's lost the will to live. All those horrible sandbags everywhere and the rubbish. It's quite pitiable. Don't you think so?"

They joined the end of the queue which was shuffling forward slowly. Reinhardt paid and took a programme. The place was packed. The piano was on a platform with the audience sitting round, and lit by two enormous lights suspended above the piano. They found seats near the stage. Elizabeth studied the programme. "Is Myra Hess Jewish?" she asked.

"I've no idea," said Reinhardt. The man sitting in front of them turned round and said gruffly, "Part Jewish. Is that significant?"

"No, not at all," said Elizabeth apologetically, "I just wondered, that's all."

"Well," said the man, who had a strong German accent, "Mahler and Mendelssohn were both Jews and banned by that barbarian. He would have said more but the audience was beginning to applaud the pianist as she strode to the piano.

Elizabeth whispered in Reinhardt's ear, "She's jolly imposing, isn't she."

Reinhardt smiled and nodded, less at the remark than at her warm breath on his cheek. As she played she seemed to be glancing at music that wasn't there, but the violence of the 'Appassionata' and the way she seemed to register no emotion apart from the occasional raising of an eyebrow or slight sway added to the impact it had. Reinhardt glanced at Elizabeth who was sitting stock still and tears flowing down her cheeks. At the end of the movement the audience burst into applause, much to the disgust of the man sitting in front of them. "Ridiculous," he announced, "Wait till the end of the piece, damn it."

Elizabeth was shaking her head as she searched in her handbag for a handkerchief. She looked up at Reinhardt, "Oh, God that was awful, don't you think that was awful?"

"Awful? I don't think..." but the next movement was starting, and she squeezed his hand and held it.

They stayed in their seats during the interval. "I didn't mean awful as in terrible. I meant awful as in, you know..awe-ful. How else could you describe it? It's terrible, as if he's fighting against his fate, or his deafness, or, I don't know, death I suppose. And then in the slow movement it's like an undertaker's steps and it transforms itself into something so beautiful." She paused as if remembering, "And then the rage, as if the music wants to end, to die, and it goes on and on, like a person drowning, and those terrible cries for help." She looked up at him helplessly, "Does that make any sense, or am I just being silly?"

"No, no, it makes perfect sense," Reinhardt lied.

"And don't you think she's wonderful, I mean, what an amazing woman. What do you think?"

Reinhardt pictured Myra Hess at the piano, a large figure in a rather shapeless black dress with chiffon sleeves, her severe parting and her bun.

"Well, she's not really my type, to be honest," he grinned, "But I agree, she's an extraordinary woman."

"Look," said Elizabeth, "Would you mind terribly if we went. I know, it's only the interval, but I don't think I could listen to any more. Is that terribly selfish of me?"

"I'm at you command," said Reinhardt, "Where would you like to go?"

"Just walk, if it's not raining.

Outside it was dark, the sky overhead lit up by the search lights reflecting off the barrage balloons that rose above St James's Park. Elizabeth put her arm through Reinhardt's and they walked in silence, following the white line along the kerb.

"I was talking about me in there I realise," she said, "I think what affected me so much was the way she was so composed but at the same time producing all that emotion- that rage and despair and terrible sadness from her fingertips. I feel all those things, except I've got no way of expressing them. Sometimes I think I'll go mad. And I've got no skills." They walked on in silence until she suddenly stopped and said, "Do you know, last September, the billeting officer came round with a couple of little girls from Isleworth. They were sisters, about six and eight. It was late and these poor children were dead on their feet and hadn't eaten since breakfast. And the woman said she couldn't place them because it's only a small village and she just had these two to find a home for. Doris and Elsie, that was their names. And without thinking I said of course we'd have them. I cooked them omelettes and they were wolfing them down when Ralph came home. He hit the roof when I told him. He didn't even let them finish their meal. He dragged them to the car and took them off to the Pritchard's. He's the local gamekeeper. She cleans for us.

While he was gone I thought, He's right. We've got six bedrooms, only two of which are used. The Pritchard's have got three bedrooms, two children of their own, two evacuees and now these two, and still Doris and Elsie are better off with them than they would've been with us. He just could not have begun to tolerate them. Their lives would have been a misery, as well as mine."

She sighed, and looked up at Reinhardt. He put his arm round her and kissed her lightly on the forehead.

"What a shit that man is," she said, and started walking again. In the darkness of Green Park, a dozen or so men were grappling with an anti-aircraft gun. Others were rolling out barbed wire. "Mind yourself, lady, keep to the path."

"Why are you doing that?" asked Elizabeth, "Isn't it dangerous?"

The ARP came over and laughed. "I hope so. The AA guns are just for show, we've got no ammo. So if the Germans do come we're just going to have to trip them up with this barbed wire, see?"

Reinhardt laughed, "And then beat them to death with your helmets, I suppose."

The ARP nodded. "We would have to leave that to our colleagues over there. There's only three helmets between the eight of us. But my mate Bill pissed in one, or at least he said he did, so as he's the only one who'll wear it now, there are only two that are strictly operational. Operational is defined by ARP's as completely useless but is capable of being passed around."

"Thank you so much," said Elizabeth, "Most enlightening."

The Ritz was almost deserted. When Raffaeli saw them come in, he hurried over to get their coats. "Hello, Mr Reinhardt, how are you. We haven't seen you for a while. I was afraid- you know, we hear things."

"No Raffaeli, I'm fine, thanks for asking. I don't think the government is going to be much concerned about a man who has lived forty years in this country, do you. But aren't you worried about Mussolini? He's making quite aggressive noises."

Raffaeli shrugged, "Mussolini? He knows. Italians are not fighting people. Italians don't like war. They like good food and wine. Let me fetch the menus."

He disappeared and met Matteo carrying a bottle of champagne and two glasses on a tray. "Hey, Matteo, Mr Reinhardt's here. He's got another woman with him? He's not good-looking. He's old. How does he do it?"

"Easy," said Matteo, "He's German. So he's mysterious, a bit dangerous maybe. Women love that."

"Oh, so we should hope Mussolini joins the war, then we'll be mysterious and a bit dangerous and have his luck with women. Va bene."

Elizabeth was looking intently at Reinhardt. "You know, before we eat, I really ought to make a phone call."

"To your sister in Richmond?"

"Yes," she said.

"The phone is through the lobby, do you need change?"

She frowned, "Am I doing the right thing?" She laughed, "Why am I asking you?" Then she straightened a crease in the table cloth. "Would you mind, I mean, would you like me to stay with you tonight?"

Reinhardt nodded, "What a silly question."

Chapter Eighteen

The last of the customers had left the Austrian Centre and the café staff were clearing the tables and washing up. Niedermayer had been on his feet all day; they had been unusually busy. It was his day off on the following day. He would have to go and report to the police station at Paddington. Lotte had offered to come with him to ask why he couldn't get a job, there was clearly a mistake. The chairman of the tribunal had said that if he found work, he could have his category changed from a 'B' to a 'C'. As it was, the policeman last week had said that he couldn't do any work, whether paid or voluntary. He was wiping down the last of the tables when the thought suddenly occurred to him. He called over to Lotte who was sitting at a table correcting exercises from her last lesson, "Lotte, if I'm not allowed to do any kind of work, I shouldn't be working here, should I?"

She looked up. "I wouldn't worry about that," she said, "How are they going to know?"

He went and sat next to her, "But what would happen to me if they found out?"

"Franz, the whole of the Centre was done with volunteers, and with money from the Council. If it wasn't for people like us, the place wouldn't exist. Don't worry, but don't tell the police when you go to the station either. They're not going to close us down. Anyway, there are too many important people on the Board, Members of Parliament and people like that who wouldn't let the police touch us. It'll be fine. This isn't Austria."

Willi Stölz came from the kitchen and joined them. "Es tut mir leid," he said, "Am I interrupting something?"

"Yes," sighed Lotte, "Me, I'm trying to correct your work." She passed him the exercise book. "It's not too bad, but you can't say "I am the Willi" in English. It doesn't sound right, you have to say, "I am Willi, or my name is Willi."

"Ach so," smiled Willi, "But I can say, "I have a willy, nicht wahr?"

Lotte gave him a withering look, "If you must."

"Very good," Willi went on in English, "This is a new word I learn, no, I am learning today."

"Have learnt," corrected Lotte. "Look, I'm tired, and I want to go home. Franz, do you want me to come with you tomorrow?"

Niedermayer thought about it. He hated to make himself conspicuous. On the other hand there was no point in him going on with his welding course if he was not going to be able to get a job at the end of it.

"Yes, thank you," he said finally, "But it takes a long time because I go with Herr Jütte and he is very slow and won't take the bus. Have you seen him today?"

Lotte shook her head. "He's always here, but I don't remember seeing him yesterday either. Have you seen him Willi?"

Willi said, "The last time I saw him was two days ago. We should find out where he lives."

The names of all the members were held in a filing cabinet in the reading room. Niedermayer went and looked it up. "36 Craven Road. We should go round there and see that he's all right."

"Do you need me to come?" asked Lotte, and then answered her own question. "If he's ill and we have to call a doctor or an ambulance I'll have to do it. Come on, let's go."

It was a cold, foggy night. They couldn't walk fast because of the blackout. The streets were deserted except for a couple of drunks who were tottering along the pavement, pointing down at the white line along the kerb as they held each other up.

They peered at the numbers on the doors until the came to a row of shops. "It's here," called Willi, "It's a shop. His place must be above it." He banged on the shuttered window and tried the door. "It's locked, we can't get in." He stepped back onto the road and looked up. "He must be up there, but how do we get in?"

They walked to the end of the row and then back again.

"Here," said Lotte, "there's a gate." She lifted the latch and they fumbled their way along a narrow alley, feeling their way against the high wall. At the end of the alley they turned the corner that led to the backs of the shops. Empty cardboard boxes had been thrown out that they stumbled over. They stopped when Willi said, "This must be the one. It's the fourth one along. This is thirty-six." He lit a match in order to see the handle. That door, too was locked, so he gave the door a shove and it sprang open with a clatter.

"Shsh, for God's sake, Willi, you could have knocked first," protested Lotte.

"It was only secured with a little hook," said Willi. He lit another match. A narrow hallway led to the front of the shop. The whole place stank of damp. Willi led them along the hall. They found a flight of stairs. Willi was about to start up when Lotte put her hand on his arm. "There might be other people up there," she whispered, "Hadn't we better call first. They might be armed."

Willi clicked his tongue. "Nobody would choose to live in a place like this unless they had to," he said.

Reluctantly they followed him up. At the top there was an open space with a table and a single gas ring, to their right, a closed door. Willi pushed it open.

"Herr Jütte," he whispered, "Are you there?"

A groan came from the far corner of the room. Willi felt for the light. A dull glow lit the room from the ceiling. The old man was lying in bed, his hands in fingerless gloves lay on the threadbare brown blanket. He was wearing his overcoat. He was breathing with difficulty, a hollow rasping sound coming from his throat.

Lotte sat on the edge of the bed and took his hand. "You're frozen," she said, "I must get a doctor. What's the emergency number for doctors?" Nobody knew. "Then I'll have to go and find out. While I'm gone, Willi, put on some hot water to boil."

The old man looked up at Niedermayer and shook his head. "Sit down," he whispered, "I don't want a doctor." His chest heaved as he spoke and he gasped before saying, "I'm glad you came. I want you to have something."

Niedermayer was alarmed at the whiteness of the old man's face and the deep shadows in his sunken cheeks. He felt the same resignation, the same sense of total helplessness that he's felt when he's said good-bye to his wife and daughter in Prague almost exactly two years earlier. " Please don't say anything," he'd said to her as he'd left. They'd looked at each other in mute desolation before he turned and left.

"Don't try to talk," he said to Herr Jütte. Willi's going to make you something hot to drink and then you'll feel better. Lotte's gone to find a doctor."

The old man shook his head. "I'm glad you came," he repeated. He tried to struggle up onto his elbows but fell back into the bed. The effort caused him to start panting. He stared at the ceiling and Niedermayer could feel the old man's hand groping across the blanket, searching for his own.

"No doctor," he said, and then, after a pause, "A priest, perhaps."

Niedermayer squeezed his hand. "Don't talk." He wondered what was keeping Willi. Herr Jütte took a deep breath, "Listen, you must do this for me." For the first time he addressed Niedermayer in the familiar 'Du'. You must do this. Promise."

His voice was getting weaker. "By the chair, there's my suitcase. Bring it here." He let go of Niedermayer's hand. Niedermayer leant over and pulled over the suitcase that appeared so light as to be empty.

"Open it. In the top there's a flap. You'll find an envelope. I want you to have it... .no. You must use it. Look at it. Promise me you'll use it."

Niedermayer opened the envelope. It was a visa for America.

Through half closed lids Herr Jütte was scrutinising him. "You will, won't you. Tell me you will."

Niedermayer didn't know what to say. He knew he couldn't go without his wife and daughter. But he also knew he couldn't deny the old man, but it felt so wrong to lie to him. He took his hand again. Herr Jütte seemed to be smiling.

"Es muss sein!" he whispered.

Niedermayer felt himself shiver and looked up. Willi was standing above him, looking over his shoulder. He lay the cup of steaming water on the floor and felt the pulse on the old man's neck.

"He's dead," he said. Niedermayer stared at his hand, still clasping the old man's. He withdrew it carefully. He stood up and turned to Willi and put his arms around him. Then he burst into tears. The two men held each other,

Willi, staring down at Herr Jütte, until he finally drew away whispered, "I didn't know you were so close," he said, "I'm sorry."

Niedermayer shook his head. "We weren't, it's not that. It's, I don't know, it's… everything, I suppose."

Willi said, "I don't know what we should do now. We can't just leave him here, we must tell someone, but I don't know who."

Niedermayer nodded. "And we can't go until Lotte gets back." Ten minutes later they heard her running up the stairs, "I can't find a doctor, there's no one about," she said, bursting into the room. She stopped when she saw the expression on the two men's faces."

"Oh, God, poor Herr Jütte." She walked over to the bed and looked down at him. "Oh, you poor man." She closed his eyes, and then, after a last glance, covered his face with the blanket.

"We can't do anything tonight," she said, "I'll get someone to inform the authorities tomorrow."

They went back to the Austrian Centre, nobody speaking on the way back. "Look," said Lotte as they reached the door, "I don't know about you, but I don't feel like going home tonight, so if either of you want to stay here…I mean, there's nowhere to sleep, but I don't think I'll sleep tonight anyway.

Niedermayer and Willi agreed. It was getting on for three o'clock.

They went into the reading room and slumped down. The chair that Herr Jütte always sat in was left empty.

Chapter Nineteen

Esther Hart's Diary

Saturday 17th February 1940

The government has announced that it wants to evacuate 400,000 children to rural areas. Where on earth will they find to put them all? Can't write any more now. Douglas has just rung to say he's bringing a couple of colleagues home for supper and told me to make sure that I put out 'a good spread.' I don't think he realises that I'll have to spend ages queuing and how rationing makes a decent meal so difficult, especially for four. We'll just have to go without next week.

Sunday 18th February

Managed to get a couple of rabbits for the meal last night and a fish starter. Douglas's old colleagues from the Foreign Office, Mr Sands and Mr Atkins came for supper and they were all in high spirits when they arrived. The brought a bottle of Cointreau and a bottle of sherry, and had been to the pub to celebrate the release of the English prisoners from the Altmark. Nearly three hundred sailors were captured in the South Atlantic before Christmas during the battle of the River Plate. The Altmark was the Graf Spee's supply ship and our sailors were taken prisoner before the Graf Spee was sunk. The Altmark was trying to get back to Germany and was stopped in Norwegian waters. It seems that it was examined by Norwegian inspectors who failed to find the men since they were being kept in the hold. A British destroyer, the Cossack, tried to force the Altmark out of Norwegian waters, but it was being accompanied by two Norwegian torpedo boats. In the end, the Altmark tried to ram the Cossack, but ran aground. A boarding party of British sailors leapt across and there was a fight with guns and cutlasses. Four German soldiers were killed and the 299 English sailors were rescued. Apparently a couple of English officers dived into the sea to rescue a German, but he was already dead. Mr Churchill had ordered that the Norwegians shouldn't be attacked, but it's a major diplomatic incident because if the Altmark had really been an unarmed merchant ship as it claimed, and was not holding any prisoners, we would have been violating Norway's neutrality. As it was, the Germans violated it first. Mr Sands said Mr Churchill had insisted on the boarding and was cock a hoop at the whole expedition and was sending out press releases left right and centre and what a great day this was for the Navy. He wants to have some sort of national celebration. But in Mr Sands' view, the whole thing had been terribly risky, because it could mean the Norwegians would side with Germany and this would be a disaster since the Germans get their iron ore from Sweden and have to transport it through Norwegian waters. Much better that we should keep quiet about the whole incident.

Mr Atkins laughed and said, "It's not in Winston's nature to keep quiet about anything." Anyway, he thought it was good for morale. I'd made a rhubarb crumble that Mr Atkins said he couldn't eat as he is allergic to rhubarb. "Projectile vomiting" he explained. Douglas gave me a dirty look as if it were my fault. Anyway, it made me decide to dispense with the idea of dandelion coffee and so I used up what remained of the stale coffee we had left from before Christmas.

While I washed up the men got into quite a heated argument. Mr Sands said the whole affair should have been hushed up because it would make Hitler worry that as we had not respected the Norwegians' neutrality and were making much of having rescued our sailors, Hitler would move on Norway to protect his sea routes. Mr Atkins said the people preferred Churchill to anyone else, especially Chamberlain. It would of course be a disaster if Churchill had power over anything but the Navy, and he wasn't sure that even that was a good idea. After all, last time he'd been First Lord of the Admiralty he'd made such a mess of the Dardanelles Campaign that he'd had to resign. At least then he could go off and fight, but he was much too old now. As usual, Chamberlain had got it right. Give Churchill a job where he could make the maximum amount of noise while leaving him with the minimum amount of power. Douglas and Mr Sands were of the view that there was a growing disquiet among young Tory MP's about Mr Chamberlain's leadership and that they were coalescing around Mr Churchill who wanted to be much more active in pursuing the war. "They may well be right," said Mr Atkins, which infuriated Douglas and Mr Sands. But he refused to get embroiled in an argument and, I suspect, in order to escape, came into the kitchen and offered to dry up. "Between you and me," he said, "I think the young Turks will force Chamberlain out before the year's out. If they do, and I'd be prepared to put money on it, I think the King will want Halifax to take up the reins. They're great chums, you know, but I'm not sure he'd want the job. Anyway, I don't think he'd have a taste for the, what shall we say, seamier side of politics. Far too morally upright. Neville's got Joseph Ball working for him. He's a one man dirty tricks department all by himself. He did his damnedest to get Winston de-selected from his constituency, you know. He loathes the anti-appeasers, and Jews. He did for Hore-Belisha, because he was a Jew. Had Neville kick him out of the Cabinet. I'm not saying that was a bad thing, necessarily, but he's not a man it pays to be on the wrong side of. But you must know all this from Douglas, he works quite closely with him."

I muttered something about Douglas not bringing his work home, and Mr Atkins suddenly back-tracked and started talking about his wife. "Daphne's one of those women who would have been handing out white feathers during the last war, but then women can't know what war is like. I was at Ypres. I'd do anything to stop us getting into another situation where we're sending our young men off to get slaughtered. But I'm beginning to come round to her way of thinking. It is different this time. Hitler's not to be trusted, he's proved that again and again. But over 50,000 of our boys killed at Ypres alone. I still have nightmares about it. You can't get away from the fact that anyone who went through that would do anything to avoid it happening again."

Went to bed and left the men to it.

Monday 19th February

Before Douglas went off to work, I asked him about what Mr Atkins had said to me on Saturday night- whether it was true that there was a move among some of the young Tories to get rid of Mr Chamberlain. Douglas was in an unusually good mood, and laughed and said that Atkins was a fine civil servant but would have made a lousy diplomat as he could never keep his mouth shut. So I asked him if it was true that he worked with Sir Joseph Ball and what he did. He said Sir Joseph Ball was a confidant of the Prime Minister's and went on fishing trips with him, and that for the last twenty or so years had been involved in 'things that it is better not to know about.' As he was leaving he said, "Certainly there are MP's who would like to see Chamberlain go. Ball knows who they are and what they're plotting. He's got their phones tapped, including Churchill's I shouldn't wonder. He hates the Jews, he hates Churchill and the Americans. He's a deep dyed pacifist, like most of us are. We can't always approve of his means, but his ends are sound. And you are never to breathe a word of this to anyone."

Tuesday 20th February

Went to the Austrian Centre, feeling somewhat guilty that I hadn't visited earlier. Lotte said that an old man had died and that they were all quite upset. Herr Niedermayer had been with him when he passed away and had taken it very badly. She asked if I'd had any news about his wife, and I had to admit I hadn't. The funeral's on Friday. She asked me if I would go. That way I could also speak to Herr Niedermayer.

Friday 23rd February

The funeral of Herr Jütte took place in 'Our Lady of Sorrows' in Paddington. There were no other English people there as far as I could make out. There were very few mourners at all, in fact. Herr Jütte was a widower; his wife had died in Vienna some time ago. It was a bleak and cold day and the church was icy cold. Went back to the centre for coffee afterwards, and didn't really get the chance to talk to Herr Niedermayer who looked exhausted and terribly gaunt.

In the afternoon caught the tube into town. There had been a huge explosion in a dress shop in Oxford Street yesterday. Met a lady who said lots of people had been injured. At first people had thought it was a German bomb and that the war had come to London, but it seems it was another IRA attack. At the Guildhall there was a victory parade celebrating the sinking of the Graf Spee in the Battle of the

River Plate. There were hundreds of people waving flags and cheering, and Mr Churchill was to give a speech and hand out medals to the sailors who had shown exceptional bravery. Saw one sailor surrounded by shop girls who were getting his autograph. They were laughing and flirting with him, and needless to say he was thoroughly enjoying their attention. Going from the funeral to the parade seemed to encompass the extremes that characterise our lives at the moment- an awful sadness on the one hand and jubilation on the other, and death at the centre of it all.

It's been such a long time since I've heard from the children. Thought I'd go and see them but learned that because of coal shortages there has been a drastic reduction in train services.

Sunday 25th February

Obviously the Germans aren't short of coal because they've just signed an agreement with the Italians to increase the latter's coal supply. The clocks went forward at 2am, so an hour less in bed. Everybody now thinks the war will come to us in the spring. The only thing that has stopped it so far has been the appalling weather.

Douglas somehow managed to find a copy of The New York Times. Researchers have discovered that the human eye can identify two million different shades of colour.

Tuesday 27th February

On the news this evening Mr Churchill said that half the German U-boats have now been destroyed. Douglas said that may be true, but for every one we destroy, they build two more.

Spring is finally here. The daffodils are out and several trees are just coming into leaf in the back garden, but I fear that the poor old silver birch that had a branch brought down by the snow may have given up the ghost. There was a strange bird, black and white with a red tail climbing up it this morning. It flew off when it saw me coming, but later it returned and was drumming where the branch had broken. It must have been a woodpecker. So already the insects had got into the wound and now are food for the birds.

Reports are coming out of Poland that don't bear thinking about. I wonder if they have a centre in London like the Austrians.

Chapter Twenty

It was Franco's day off. He would have liked nothing better than to have gone to the Italian Club and spent the morning talking to his friends and reading the papers, but Giovanna was adamant that she didn't want him going to what she called 'that hotbed of gossip and tittle tattle.'

"Take me out," she said when she had finished her coffee. "Eugenio's always taking Julia out and you never take me anywhere. It's all right for you, you go out to work and see other people all the time. I never see anyone except Francesca, when she's at home, and that isn't often since she met that Englishman. And Julia, of course, and she's in a dreadful mood most of the time. Come on, let's go out for the day."

Franco knew better than to argue with his wife and simply said, "It's very cold out, are you sure? And where do you want to go?"

Putting her hair up, she shrugged, "It doesn't matter where. I've been cooped up so long I just need to get out. Here, put your coat and hat on. We'll get the bus into the city."

The bus trundled down Goswell Road towards the Barbican. Franco thought that there was an unusual number of people out on the streets, and all going in the same direction. A couple of women sat down behind them. One of them was saying, "Poor Bert, he's so proud, but he just couldn't have come. It's gone right to his chest, you know. Even he could see it would have been the death of him. Do you know, when Stan went up to say good-bye to him this morning, there was tears in both their eyes. Mine too, I don't mind admitting. Bert said, "Son, I'm proud of you." He's never said anything like that before. Honestly, you'd think Stan was going away for another six months the way they carried on. But he did look smart. Got up at five this morning. Spit and polished his shoes till they was like a mirror."

The other woman made appreciative noises and asked, "D'you think we'll get to see him then?"

"I should ruddy well hope so. Said he'd be near the back on the second row in.

I ain't come all this way for nothing. But do you know what he said to me? He said Ma, I don't want you going all soppy and making a fool of me in front of me mates. As if I would, but as a mother you can't help being proud."

"Course you can't, "said the other woman.

From the way she was sitting rigidly upright, Franco knew that Giovanna was trying to understand what was going on behind her. He was about to explain, when the second woman said, "And do you think we'll see Mr Churchill? I've always wanted to see him. My Brian says he should be Prime Minister. He says in a war you need a soldier to lead the country. He said Mr Churchill was proved right when he said the Munich thingy brought shame on a proud country. Bert's given me his camera so I can take some pictures. Says it's dead easy, but I'm terrified. I've never taken a picture in me life. I told him, I can't work that, and what if I break it? He said he'll risk it. Do you know how to use it, here, I'll show you."

"Don't give it to me," said the other woman, "I'm useless."

There was a pause, and then the first one tapped Franco on the shoulder. "Excuse me, love," she said, "Are you going to the parade?"

Franco glanced at Giovanna who shrugged, "If you want to," she said."

"Yes," said Franco.

"Well, the thing is me son is marching. He was on the Exeter, and his Dad wants me to take a picture. Would you be so kind? I've got no idea how to use the darn thing."

Franco took the Brownie Box camera and looked at it. He had taken several photographs for people who had come to the restaurant and wanted pictures for their birthday celebrations or parties. "Thanks awfully," said the woman, We should be getting off here."

The bus had stopped at the end of Gresham Street. Crowds of people were hurrying along the road towards King Street. The woman who had given Franco the camera turned to Giovanna. "Have you got a flag, love? I've got a spare in me bag, here. It's a great day, the proudest since the war began. We've got to get a good place. My Stan says the place to be is on the corner. That way we'll see them coming up the road and they'll walk right past us and if we're lucky we'll see Mr

Churchill. They say he's going to greet them on the steps. And my Bert said to Stan to make sure he gets a menu and see if he can't get it signed by Mr Churchill, but I don't suppose he'll be able."

The crowd was jostling for position, standing on tiptoe and everyone craning their necks to look down King Street. They could hear a roar in the distance and the strains of a brass band gradually getting louder. The ripple of waving flags moved towards them as the crowd began to crane forward to look down the street and cheer.

"You get in front, you're quite short," said the lady who'd given Franco the camera, "I'll point him out as soon as I see him."

The crowd was pressing forward as Franco tried to steady the camera against his chest. He was finding it difficult. Giovanna was clinging on to his arm and he was being pushed in the back. The band came into sight, rows of smartly dressed sailors behind it, each man trying to hide his smile as they marched towards the Guildhall. The men from the Ajax came first, followed by those from the Exeter. As the last column approached, the woman shouted in Franco's ear, "He's there. Look, the second one in, next to the tall fellow with the blonde hair."

Franco clicked the shutter but at the same moment received a push in the back. He wound on the film hurriedly and tried again.

"Did you get him? Did you get a good picture?"

Franco turned and gave her the camera back. "I think so, I hope so." He shrugged. "I did my best."

She put the camera in her bag, and glanced at the receding columns.

"I'm so proud of him, but he said it didn't mean nothing really cos his best friend was killed in that battle. Tommy Jones, his name was. They was at school together. Joined up on the same day. But Tommy was killed on the Exeter. He was only nineteen. Training to be a master baker. Stan said he was on the turret when it was hit. He never stood a chance. Lots of them were killed. All of them buried at sea. Stan said during the service all he could think about was that it could have been him. The ship was so badly damaged that it had to go down to the Falklands for repairs before they could bring it home. I pray he won't have to go back to sea again, but he says he wants to on account of his mates. They say the captain of the Graf Spee committed suicide after he'd scuttled it. It was the dishonour of it. Have you got any boys?"

He could feel Giovanna squeeze his arm.

"No," said Franco.

"Some might say that's for the best," said the woman, "You coming up to see if we can get a sight of Mr Churchill? If you can get a picture of him and you tell me your address, I could send you one."

Giovanna squeezed his arm more tightly. "No, that's kind of you but we must be going," he said.

"OK," said the woman brightly, "Thanks again anyway," and she and her friend joined the crowd that was pushing up behind the parade.

Franco and Giovanna started to walk towards London Bridge. She was clutching him tightly and they had to shuffle as people jostled around them. He could feel her tension, and every now and again she brushed her face against his shoulder as he tried to steer them a path through the crowd.

When they reached London Bridge, he stopped and looked down at her. She was crying.

"Cesare?" he asked.

She nodded and wiped the tears from her cheeks with her sleeve. Then she said angrily, "She shouldn't have said that. How can it be better to have a son that's died?"

Franco put a protective arm around his wife. "She wasn't to know, I don't suppose she meant anything by it."

"But it still hurt, Franco. You're much too quick to think the best of people. You don't go asking strangers questions like that. And he'd have been nineteen next birthday, just like the boy who died on that ship."

"Maybe that's what she meant," said Franco. "Think how we'd have felt, how we'd be worrying all the time if our boy was in the Navy and at war."

But Giovanna wasn't to be placated. "Cesare was Italian. What business have any of us with this war. It's nothing to do with us. No, no, he'd have married a nice Italian girl and stayed out of all this. "

Franco had never been able to console his wife over the death of their son. He'd been only three when he died of tuberculosis, but it was as if she contained an unfathomable well of grief which hadn't diminished with time. They rarely spoke of it. Giovanna had spoken almost no English when Cesare was taken ill. Franco had had to translate what the doctors were saying, and Giovanna somehow managed to make him feel guilty that Cesare was so ill and there was so little that could be done for him. She was almost totally dependant on him in any dealings with the outside world, and Franco often felt she more than compensated in their home life.

She looked down at her hand. She was still holding the Union Jack that the woman had given her. She looked round, and seeing no one was watching, dropped it in the gutter.

"Let's go and have some lunch," said Franco.

Giovanna shook her head. "I'm not in the mood any more. I want to go home."

"You really wanted to go out for the day…"

"No," she said, "Take me home."

Chapter Twenty One

Maurice was cold. He leaned back in the railway carriage and stared out of the window. Leaving home hadn't been as difficult as he thought it would be. His mother had been resigned to his going and fussed about his taking enough warm clothes and busied herself making sandwiches for the journey, while his father kept stepping back and looking at him and smiling approvingly. His mother packed his case and little had been said in the hours before his father drove him to the station. She'd stood on the door of the shop and waved until they were out of sight.

"Make sure you write and tell her how you're getting on," was all his father had said, "She'll worry no end if she doesn't here from you."

Maurice had felt suffocated and now his overwhelming feeling was, apart from the cold of the third class carriage, one of relief. It was an adventure.

At Trent two boys of about his own age entered his carriage. They nodded and the taller one asked, "You going to Leeds?"

"Yes," said Maurice, "You?"

"We've been conscripted. You been conscripted as well?"

Maurice said he had.

"My name's Joe. Joe Harper, and this is Ray Evans." They shook hands and Maurice introduced himself.

"So, where do you think they'll send us?" asked Joe. My Dad says France. After all, the B.E.F. is there already. He was in France. Says the food's really good there, and the wine and the women. You speak any French?"

"Not a word," said Maurice. "But my Dad says we'll be kept here to fight if there's an invasion. He says there's bound to be one in the summer. Or even the spring. He thinks we'll be sent to protect the ports. Dover, or somewhere like that."

"I don't know what to think," said Joe. "Here, have a sandwich."

When the train reached Chesterfield they had eaten all their food and the carriage was thick with cigarette smoke.

By the time they reached Leeds they were stiff with cold and hungry. The Gibraltar Barracks were half an hour's walk.

"Blimey," said Joe, "Looks more like a prison." The turreted building had its portcullis raised. Uniformed officers were standing outside in small groups and smoking. They approached a soldier and asked where they were to report.

"Conscripts?" he asked, looking at them disdainfully. "Through the large door and the office is on the left."

Maurice was feeling relieved that he wasn't alone. The place did feel like a prison to him, but the sergeant who took their details seemed to be friendly enough, though his parting words filled Maurice with panic. "Right," he said, "Medical, uniform, a meal and then we'll be shipping you out. Medical first, you'll find the doctor at the end of the corridor on your right."

"Looks like my old man was right," whispered Joe , as they went to find the doctor, "I didn't think we'd be sent straight off without any training."

The doctor listened to Maurice's chest and examined his teeth. He made notes on a clipboard and then said finally, "You'll do. Out of the door, turn left, across the yard. Go and get fitted up for your uniform."

The three of them joined other recruits in a queue. Each man was handed a uniform and told to go and try them on. Maurice's was obviously made for somebody a lot taller and thinner than he was. The sleeves came down over his hands, but when he suggested he needed he needed a slightly smaller size he was told that he was in the army and not at a bleeding fashion parade.

They joined the queue in the mess hall which Maurice thought was the biggest room he had ever seen. Stew was being served from enormous tureens, and they joined a group of other recruits who looked equally daunted by the place.

"Could be our last meal in England," whispered Joe, "Tonight we'll be eating frogs' legs and snails washed down with a bit of the old vino. Better see if we can get some more fags before we get there. My dad says French fags taste like burning socks."

A sergeant major told them to fall in outside in the yard where three army trucks were waiting. He looked at them and shook his head.

"Well," he shouted, "Looking at you it is difficult to believe that you are men. But miracles do happen. We'll make soldiers of you. Right, fourteen to a vehicle."

Maurice was waiting to climb in the back and was standing next to the cab.

He swallowed and looked up at the driver.

"How long does it take to get to France?" he asked.

The driver scratched his head. "To France? Let's see. Seven hours by road, say three by boat. Ten hours about."

"So we'll get there in the middle of the night, will we?"

"You think we're going to France?" He winked at the Sergeant major over Maurice's shoulder. "No, son, we're going somewhere much more dangerous than that."

Maurice felt his mouth go dry. "What, Germany?"

The driver shook his head. "No, son. Leicester. Now get in before the sarge puts you on jankers."

It was getting dark as the convoy left Leeds. The trucks travelled in convoy through the city before speeding up as they reached open countryside. The men were subdued and talked listlessly for the first few miles but gradually, with the rocking of the truck and the difficulty of making themselves heard above the noise of the engine, fell into a kind of torpor. The smell of diesel and the constant shaking was beginning to make Maurice feel sick. He put his head out through the canvas flap and sucked in the air.

"Don't do that mate, " said his neighbour, "It's freezing enough already."

Maurice closed the flap and leaned back and closed his eyes. He knew there was no way he could have avoided this, but it wasn't at all what he had expected. He'd thought that they would have been given guns by now, and been for shooting practice on a range, have been shown how to camouflage yourself and done at least one assault course. Instead of that there was being driven from one part of the country to another; after all, why couldn't he have had his medical and got his uniform in Leicester in the first place?

He opened his eyes and looked around. He'd expected to be feeling exhausted but happy, full of having made new friends at the end of his first day in the army, bonded by singing songs as they went to their barracks. Instead he was feeling sick and alone and miserably cold.

Chapter Twenty Two

Reinhardt thought it was the perfect arrangement. Elizabeth got away at least once a week and brought fresh meat, either pork or beef, that he could never have bought, but that she got from her husband's farm. And she seemed to enjoy cooking and rearranging the furniture so that the place felt much more comfortable and not, as she said 'a bachelor pad plonked in the ruins of an old marital home.' When they went shopping, she bought a nightdress and dressing gown that she hung on the back of the bathroom door and which stayed there when she was back in Hertfordshire. Reinhardt smiled when he saw it for the first time. He wasn't sure whether it was a claim she was making on him and the house, or whether it was to warn off other potential women visitors, that the place was already taken. Reinhardt liked that, whichever way it was. He liked feeling spoken for, for the first time in his life. He liked the way Elizabeth tried to alter his behaviour, and while saying that he was too old to change, he listened to her and carefully considered what she said. For his birthday she bought him a book.

"We'll go out and have a really good meal and then perhaps go to the pictures," he'd said, but she had shaken her head. "No, we'll stay in. I've brought two steaks and a bottle of the best wine I could find in the cellar. Then we'll have a fire and make it lovely and snug during the blackout. And you can read to me."

So while she knitted in front of the coal fire he had lit, he read to her from the book she'd given him- Robert Graves' 'Collected Poems.'

"I've marked my favourites- read those first," she'd said.

Reinhardt smiled to himself as he read the last verse

'His wiles were witty and his fame far known,

Every king's daughter sought him for her own,

Yet he was nothing to be won or lost.

All lands to him were Ithaca: love-tossed

He loathed the fraud, yet would not bed alone.'

Elizabeth lay down her knitting and took a sip of her wine. "I think all lands to you are Ithaca," she said, "and I love that line about his wife and his whore being the same. Read that bit to me again." He read

"To the much tossed Ulysses, never done
With woman whether gowned as wife or whore
Penelope and Circe seemed as one:
She like a whore made his lewd fancies run,
And wifely she a hero to him bore."

"You don't like sleeping alone, do you?" she said, looking at him directly.

"I've had to get used to it," said Reinhardt defensively, "but then I'm sixty-one today, and I suppose it's the nature of things that I mind less than I did. But it's true, I used to hate it."

"Mm," said Elizabeth, "We'll take that as a 'no'."

Reinhardt laughed and moved to open a second bottle. "And if you open that you may as well sleep alone, because you'll be too drunk to do anything else."

Somewhat to his own surprise, Reinhardt put away the corkscrew.

"I won't be able to get away for another fortnight," said Elizabeth, "so let's make the most of this evening."

So Reinhardt was surprised to find her standing on his doorstep two days later. She was very agitated, looking in both directions up and down the road. She gave him a peremptory peck on the cheek as he opened the door.

"I didn't dare phone," she said, "I didn't know what to do." Reinhardt went to take her coat, but she shivered and slumped down on the sofa. "No, I'm freezing," she said, "Have you got any whisky left? God, I need a drink."

Reinhardt poured two whiskies and sat down next to her. "Whatever's happened?" he asked.

She seemed not to hear him, but sat shivering and distracted.

"Elizabeth," he repeated, "What's wrong? He's found out about us?"

She looked at him, shook her head, and then said, "Coates has been arrested." She always referred to her husband, rather disparagingly, as 'Coates' in protest at the way all of their acquaintances deferentially called him 'Sir Ralph'.

Reinhardt was confused. "Start at the beginning," he said," and drink your whisky."

She downed the glass. "Two detectives came to the house this morning. They were very polite and said they wanted to ask him some questions. They asked me about his contacts and whether I'd been on any trips with him lately. Of course I said I hadn't, because I haven't. Whenever he's been away I've always come to see you. But it's true that that's only been possible because he's been away such a lot. Anyway, when he's come back he's always seemed very, how shall I put it, smug, I suppose. He said the other day that that if it wasn't for his contacts Hitler would have invaded by now, and that they deal directly with Goering who has assured them that Germany has no quarrel with us and that there is no question of Germany attacking us unless we attack them first. God, he kicked up such a stink when he realised that they'd come to take him away. Said he'd got friends who would get them sacked on the spot. And the language he used was simply frightful; they almost had to wrestle him into the car. He shouted at me to phone his solicitor, but they said that on this occasion that would be no help since he was being arrested under Section 18B. Do you know what that is?"

Reinhardt shook his head. "Go on."

"No, so I didn't, I was going to phone you, but then I thought, supposing they've tapped our phone."

"Then they'd know about us already, wouldn't they?" said Reinhardt. "I know it was over a month ago, but they didn't seem at all suspicious about me at my tribunal. They certainly wouldn't have given me a 'C' if they were."

"I've been racking my brains to remember what we've said to each other on the phone. I can't think of anything, though just the fact that we've arranged to meet so many times is pretty incriminating."

"Elizabeth," Reinhardt smiled at her affectionately, "What we're doing may be immoral, at least I suppose some people might think so, but it's certainly not illegal."

She shook her head. "That's not it. Suppose they somehow think that you're involved in whatever he's up to. I'd feel so guilty."

He put his arm round her. "I wouldn't worry about that. He's probably forgotten all about me by now. He'll certainly have forgotten my name."

He drew her closer to himself, but she pulled away, frowning.

"No, that's just it. I've been nagging him to invest in your project for weeks."

"And what does he say?"

"He always says he's got more important things to worry about, or he's fobbed me off with some excuse. But he certainly knows who you are."

"Well," said Reinhardt, taking their glasses and refilling them, "if they've been tapping your phone they'll know I've never spoken to your husband, and if I ever had, I'd have told him….," he held out her glass to her and smiled down at her, "what an ass he is for not keeping an eye on you."

She looked up at him. "Links, you're not taking me seriously. I'm frightened."

"I can see that, " he said, sitting down beside her and taking her hand, "but I'm not sure exactly why. That if they know we're having an affair that they might tell your husband?"

She shook her head. "No. I told him years ago that I wanted a divorce and he laughed and said, 'My dear girl. You can't have one so let's just stop this silliness'. He didn't even want to know why. No, I'm frightened for us, that they might think that I'm tied up in whatever he's doing and that you are too."

"All right." Reinhardt was confused. "So what exactly do you think he has been doing?"

Elizabeth reached down into her bag and took out a magazine. "Have you ever seen this?"

"'Truth'?" No, I've never heard of it."

"He told me it's in all the officers' clubs and is even supported by Chamberlain. I'm not even sure it isn't edited by an MP. Anyway, it's one thing to be against the war- probably most people are. It's quite another to be collaborating with the Germans and the sentiments in this are so anti-semitic that they could have been written by a Nazi. Look at this." She flipped through the magazine and pointed out the page to Reinhardt. He read aloud,

"Land of dope and Jewry

Land that once was free

All the Jew boys praise thee

Whilst they plunder thee.

Poorer still and poorer

Grow thy true born sons

Faster still and faster

They're sent to feed the guns."

Reinhardt grimaced. "Well, it's not Robert Graves, is it? I mean, it's nasty, but I'd have thought it was harmless."

Elizabeth stared at him. "You still don't understand, do you? You were interned in the last war. You know what it's like. These people want Hitler to invade. They want him to run the country. You must know what they've been doing to people in Austria and Poland."

"Well," said Reinhardt, "as I understand it, Hitler has no interest in invading England. He wants what he calls 'Lebensraum' in the east. He's happy as long as Britain and the Empire stays out of it."

Elizabeth shook her head. "God, Links, you're so naïve. How can we keep our Empire when U-boats are sinking our ships in the Atlantic? Do you want Britain to become like Germany?"

The question stung him. He suddenly had an image of the last time he had visited his sister in Berlin in 1923. A little girl, perhaps three years old was lying at the feet of a prostitute. The woman was oblivious to everything, her eyes rolling as she held out her hand for money to by cocaine. There were 3.8 billion marks to the dollar that day.

"No, of course not, but it can't happen. Times have changed. We were interned regardless of who we were, and it's true, it was hard. But things are so much more liberal this time. What's his name at the Home Office- Anderson, he might be a dry old stick but his heart's in the right place. I'm sorry to say this, but if there are a few right wing fanatics who want to see the country run by Hitler, then they're deluding themselves if they think it's going to happen and they deserve to be locked up. But I don't think they'll hold your husband over night even. They're just giving him a warning shot across the bows."

"Well, in that case, I must go," said Elizabeth, glancing at her watch, "If I leave now I'll just manage to get the 4.05. I must be there when he gets back, how ever could I explain not being?"

Reinhardt felt that the bubble that they had inhabited in their relationship up until that moment had suddenly burst. "When will I see you again?" he said forlornly.

She picked up her bag and opened the door. "I don't know. If they've frightened him enough to give up this nonsense, he won't be going away. I'm sorry, I've got to dash. I'll phone you." She stopped and stared at him. "No, I won't, oh, look, I'll be in touch somehow."

Reinhardt watched her run across the street and turn the corner towards Kings Cross. Feeling suddenly cold, he closed the door and wrapped his arms around his chest. Then he slumped down where moments before, Elizabeth had been sitting, and put his head in his hands.

Chapter Twenty Three

He awoke with a start and listened. In the distance a train was shunting quietly into a siding. Usually he found the familiar clicking of the tracks and the gentle sound of the steam being released, like a giant's sigh, somehow reassuring, but now he had a premonition of dread. Perhaps it was a dream, though he couldn't remember it. Maybe he was woken by an unfamiliar sound outside the room and his body had alerted him to danger. He strained his ears, but apart from the train there was only Willi's soft snoring and Johannes's snuffling and the odd words that he seemed to mutter all night in his sleep.

He turned towards the wall and suddenly realised how it hurt to move. Every joint in his body ached. And he was trembling. He had thought that his depression of the last few days was a reaction to Herr Jütte's death, and to the fact that he still hadn't any news of his wife. Now he knew that he had also been sickening for this. He was cold. He didn't like to get up and get Willi's coat to put on his bed for fear of waking them.

For the next few hours he drifted in and out of consciousness. He was asleep when he felt Willi shake him and say, "Franz, wake up, it's time to go to work. Are you ill? Oh, God, you are ill. "

Willi looked down at him and shook his head, "You've got a temperature. You need a doctor."

"I can't afford a doctor," Niedermayer protested, "I'll be all right. I'll get up in a few minutes."

"Don't be ridiculous," Willi appealed to Roth for support, "Johannes, tell him. He needs a doctor. The centre will pay. I've got some aspirin somewhere, but I'm going to find a doctor." He was hurriedly putting on his clothes.

Roth yawned and got up. "You won't have to pay. There are at least four doctors at the centre. Schepke was really helpful when I cut my hand and it got infected. He's around most days. Look, it's almost healed."

He held up his palm for Niedermayer to look at.

"My eyes hurt too," and Niedermayer turned to face the wall with a groan.

151

Willi came crashing up the stairs and through the door. He told Niedermayer to sit up and drink the water that he was holding out to him along with a couple of aspirin. "Take these and let me turn your pillow over, it's all cold and wet. Are you cold?"

Niedermayer nodded. "Frozen." He lay back heavily and shivered.

Willi pulled the blanket from his own bed and covered Niedermayer. "You've got three blankets and your overcoat on you now, so I'm going to find a doctor and I'll be back as soon as I can. I would have been a lovely nurse, but on second thoughts, looking at you, I'm glad I'm not one."

Niedermayer smiled thinly, "Thanks," he said.

He drifted in and out of sleep and was suddenly aware that there were a lot of people in the room. Some were whispering in German, but one was speaking loudly in English. It was a woman's voice, and though he couldn't understand everything she was saying, he knew she was angry. When he opened his eyes, Lotte was leaning over him and looking at him with a concerned expression.

"Franz, how are you feeling? I'm sorry to disturb you like this, but she insisted on coming and she's got some news for you. And Dr Schepke's here. Willi's really worried about you."

"What news?" said Niedermayer.

"You know Mrs Rathbone," Lotte went on, "She came to the play. She's got a letter for you, it came through the Swiss delegation, I think. " She turned to the elderly woman who was examining the wall around the window at the end of Niedermayer's bed. She turned to Lotte, "It's a disgrace, she said, "Look here, mildew on the walls, a gale coming through the crack between the window frame and the plaster, running water here, look, and that's been going on for some time. I'm making a note of this," she scrabbled round in her bag while she talked, " and it's impossible for anybody to stay healthy in a place like this. I shall have very strong words with the landlord, but first of all I shall be asking questions in the House this very afternoon, if they'll let me, which I very much doubt. But I will not be made to keep quiet on this." She was writing hurriedly as she went on, "It's a scandal the way we're treating the refugees. We had to fight to get a pittance from the government to support them. That's the Tories all over, no understanding at all, and what's worse, no desire to understand. They're all the same, except Winston, of course. You know where you are with Winston. Of course he's a reactionary old beggar, hates to have women in the House, I mean, good Lord, he's still living with the Boers" (she pronounced it 'boors')," but at least he knows what the Nazis are up to and wants to fight for what he believes in, but Chamberlain, hah! He's got all the fight of a wet dishcloth. The man's more slippery than an eel." She put away her pencil and notebook and snapped her handbag shut, and then looked up. "Sorry, where were we?" she asked.

Lotte said, "This is Franz Niedermayer. You've got a letter for him."

"I have, that's right, it came through the Czech refugee council." She opened her handbag again and sat down on Niedermayer's bed. She passed him a large brown envelope. He squinted at the official looking writing on the cover.

"I can't see without my glasses," he said, looking up at Lotte, "I can't see at all very well at the moment."

"Do you want me to open it?" she asked and he nodded. Inside the envelope was a smaller white one. She opened that too and looked expectantly at Niedermayer who nodded. She read,

"My dear Franz, I don't know if you will get this, but if you do, you must know that we are safe. Clara was very ill for a while after you went and kept on asking for news of you. We stayed in Prague, but I was told just before Christmas that you were being looked for by the police. A friend said his sister lived in Switzerland, and he knew someone who could get us some papers to go and stay with her. Her name is Anna Raub. So now we are in Geneva and we are desperate to come to England and are trying to find a way. I pray you are well and that you will receive this and be able to write to us at this address. I have found some part-time work as a secretary and Clara is going to school and is enjoying it, though it is hard work for her as it is French speaking. We are both trying to learn English so that when we are all together again we can enjoy our new lives in England.

We both hug and kiss you, Ilse."

Lotte folded the letter and put it in the envelope. She looked at Niedermayer who was lying with his eyes closed, but she could see by the way his chest was heaving that he was desperately trying to hide the fact that he was crying.

"Is everything all right?" asked Mrs Rathbone, "I gather it's from his wife, but is it good news?"

"It's very good news," said Lotte, "And I know he is very grateful to you, but I think we should go and let the doctor examine him now." She put the letter on the bedside table, but Niedermayer immediately took it and held it to his chest. Then he sat up with a struggle and took the old woman's hand and kissed it. Mrs Rathbone blushed. "Yes, well now look," she flustered, " I mean, if you want to write back to her I dare say we can send it through the same channels." She stood up and looked at her watch, "Good Lord, is that the time? I'm meeting that odious little prig Hart in twenty minutes. I sometimes think the civil servants are worse than the politicians," and she strode out.

The doctor, who had been waiting patiently by the door, pulled a chair over to the side of the bed. "Well," he said, "I think the best thing I can prescribe for you is a pen and paper, and maybe a small drop of brandy. And once you've made use of them, we'll see how you are. It may be that you've just received better medication than any doctor could ever offer. I'll come back tomorrow an see how you're getting on," and carefully replacing the chair, he went out.

"I'll bring you some paper," said Willi.

"Now?"

Willi frowned, "I've got my course to go to and I really don't want to miss...OK," he said, "Now."

Chapter Twenty Four

Busch stooped at the door of the dining room and looked in. They'd moved the table he always sat at for his meals, the one nearest the door. He frowned. They'd done it deliberately to annoy him, and they'd succeeded. It was his table. They'd no right. There were few enough things that he could rely on, and where he'd sat for his meals was one of them. There was a small crowd of men standing inside the door all looking at something, but without entering, Busch couldn't see what it was. Reluctantly he pushed the door open and went in. His table had been moved to support a huge chess board which was leaning against the wall. Each square of the board had a small shelf so that the flat pieces could stand up. Someone had made the first move of a game, moving the white queen's pawn two spaces. The whole board was about four feet square. Busch lifted it carefully off the table and leaned it against the wall. Then he took the table and returned it to its rightful place before going to the hatch to get his morning coffee and bread.

Sitting in his usual place he looked thoughtfully at the board. Then he noticed a typewritten notice on the wall next to where the chess board had been. It was in English. He didn't understand it, and he certainly wasn't going to ask, though it clearly referred to the chess. Feigning nonchalance, he looked around, and caught Captain Burfeind's eye. He was trying to suppress a smile.

"If you don't make a move, somebody else will," said the Captain, leaning across the table. You've read the rules?"

Busch shrugged.

"White and black, each makes two moves a day."

"Is that what it says?" Busch could have kicked himself for having appeared so interested.

"If you'd started to come to the English classes you'd know," the Captain said, "and he's a good teacher. Sent here from Oxford University. He speaks the language like an Englishman."

Busch looked at the board again. "Is he the one who set this up, then? Is this his idea?"

Captain Burfeind shook his head, "I don't know who set it up."

"Well you must know who is playing white," said Busch.

"I don't, I've no idea. But if you're not going to do it, I'm going to play black." With that he got up and went over to the board, and having moved the king's bishop's pawn two spaces, he went out.

Busch waited until he was out of sight and then replaced the pawn and moved the queen's pawn two spaces, and then followed his captain out into the cold.

When he returned at lunch time, the board had been put back on to the table and pushed over to the wall. Somebody had made white's second move, and it was a strange one. The king's rook's pawn moved forward one space. He was torn. Nobody who could play properly would make such a negative move, not unless it was some kind of trick. He reminded himself to look it up in the magazines he'd been given. But he decided to leave the table where it was, and having got his lunch, he went over and joined Müller and some of the other crew members who were discussing the chances of their being moved to another camp in the spring.

"They'll have to move us," Müller was saying. "The British have already got an army in Northern France. They can't allow us to take the Belgian ports so they're going to have to protect their interests there. That means we'll have to take Belgium and the Netherlands. Then the French and English will try to defend them which means that we'll move against France and we'll win easily. The English and the French have never got on. Once we take the French ports we'll be just across the Channel. The English would be crazy to leave us here. My bet is that they'll move us in the next few weeks. And they're still interning people. Look at that lad that's just arrived."

He nodded in the direction of a young boy who looked no more than seventeen who was in earnest conversation with Captain Burfeind on the next table.

Busch clicked his tongue in annoyance, "The weather's improving. Our army and air force will be across here before they have time to move us. It's only a matter of days now, I'm sure of it." His crew mates looked at him disdainfully. "Wishful thinking," said Müller dismissively, "You don't know what you're talking about." He turned back to his colleagues.Felling angry and resentful,

Busch scraped his chair back and went and sat down next to his captain. "Busch," said Burfeind, "let me introduce you. Alexander Weiss. Our new English teacher." Busch nodded stiffly. Weiss smiled warmly and held out his hand, which Busch took reluctantly. "Weiss was just telling me how he comes to be here, and he's got some interesting news about what's going on."

Busch judged him to be about the same age as himself, maybe twenty-two or three. He was tall and wore an expensive English overcoat and Busch was suspicious of his easy manner. He also thought he detected a slight Bavarian accent. "You know, when the English declared war, all Germans had to attend a tribunal. I had my professor from the University attend with me so I wasn't really worried, most of my friends were interviewed and not seen as a threat, so I assumed it would be the same for me. That was back at the beginning of September. Also I was living with an English family just outside Oxford and they were what the English would call 'pillars of the community'. Anyway, the chairman of the tribunal asked me what I was studying and I said I was doing research on the influence of the thought of Karl Marx on the English working classes in the nineteenth century. He asked me if that meant I was a socialist, and I said no, I'm a historian. Then he asked me what I thought of Hitler, and I gave a non-committal kind of answer. I couldn't believe it when he gave me a 'B', which meant that I wasn't allowed to go more than five miles out of Oxford, or own a camera. Apparently he thought that if I didn't give my complete support to Hitler, it meant I was a socialist. I thought that if I said I supported him completely, he'd think I was a Nazi and intern me for that. Anyway, I owned a camera which I gave to Kate, who is the daughter of the people I was staying with. When her brother joined up there was a parade of troops through the city. She wasn't well, so she asked me if I would go and take a picture for her. I was standing in the crowd, and bumped into the secretary of the tribunal I'd been at and she remembered me. We had quite a chat, she was very charming. I took some pictures and next morning at six, there was a knock on the door and I was arrested for violating the conditions of my 'B'. I was taken to the prison. Poor Kate. She felt terribly guilty. The worst thing was that there was an article in the local paper with the headline, "Nazi free to 'shoot' our troops. So when I appeared before the judge, he told me that I was to be interned 'for my own safety'. So that's how I got to be here. Still, they let me bring my books and papers, and he's probably right. I don't know what's going to happen now. There was some talk of deporting me back home but," he shrugged," who knows. Anyway, it shows how nervous they are. And it's impossible to know what's really going on in the war because the BBC is being run by the Ministry of Information, but I know they are appealing for volunteers to go and help the Finns fight the Soviets. But they can't arrest everyone- there are thousands of refugees and students like me. Wherever can they put them? And now, apparently, they're wanting to move all aliens away from the coast in case of the invasion when it comes. The whole thing is a mess."

"Where are you from?" asked Captain Burfeind.

"Augsburg," replied Weiss." The irony is that I got a letter from my father just before the war started telling me to stay in England. Now I've got no choice." Busch frowned. "Why did he say that?"

Weiss smiled. "I've no idea. Perhaps he thought that if I returned home Himmler would have me arrested as an English collaborator." Busch was about to reply angrily, but Burfeind interrupted, "But you know a lot of English people. What do they think about the war?"

"Difficult to say. Most people I talked to were more worried about food rationing and the terrible winter. Blackouts and having to carry their gas masks everywhere gets everybody down. They've lost faith in Chamberlain, that's for sure, and while the people who were all for Munich suddenly went very quiet when war was declared, I'd say the overwhelming feeling is one of futility. It's hard to explain, as if no one is in control and events are taking over, but then nobody really knows what those events are. Like I say, there's no real information, and nobody believes the propaganda. Most English people tune in to William Joyce, who the papers call 'Lord Haw Haw' for the only news they believe."

Busch laughed disdainfully. "Well, at least they get the truth from somewhere. At least our government doesn't have to hide behind lies and propaganda." Weiss was about to reply but thought better of it, instead he raised an eyebrow quizzically and gave a slight smile. "Anyway, I thought for tonight's lesson we could do something about the English class system. What do you think?"

Captain Burfeind agreed. "Anything that helps us to understand the country better is helpful he said.

"And will you come to the lesson tonight?" Weiss asked Busch.

"I don't think so, Herr Busch is rather too busy working out how to win this chess match," said Captain Burfeind, "He doesn't really have time for anything else."

Busch rose to the taunt. And he had also been thinking over what he had heard Müller say earlier. Perhaps they were all going to be moved, at least those men who were seen as helping in any invasion when it came. And Captain Burfeind had been right when he had said it was useless trying to escape from the camp because he didn't know where they were and nor could he speak the language. But if they were going to do be moved it would either be by train or by truck, and then maybe his chance would come. If he could just get enough English to understand a few words and to read some signs, perhaps he could slip away and find his way back home. But he would have to be a lot cleverer than he was last time.

"Yes, I'll come," he said. "Do you play chess?"

"Me? A little, and not well, I'm afraid, "But I'll give you a game if you like."

"No, it's not that," Busch hesitated, "I've got some chess magazines but they're in English. Can you help me understand them?"

"I'll do my best, why don't I come to your hut and I'll have a look at them for you."

Over the next few days the game progressed. The moves that white was making were being made by someone who went into eat in the shift before his. Busch had no idea whether he was playing against one man, or a whole committee, and he resisted fiercely any advice about his best move from the men who were in the dining room at the same time as him. On a couple of occasions he got into fierce arguments with men who made a move without his agreement. He was following the game with the board in his hut, trying out alternatives and making notes on his strategy.

On the last day of February Major Stimpson received a telegram and gave a whoop of joy. His constant pleading with the War Office had at last paid off. The following morning at roll call he announced that the following internees were to collect their kit from their huts and to report to the dining room for further instructions. Included in the group of forty seven men was the entire crew under Captain Burfeind's command, as well as twenty-three others. "Told you," said Müller to Busch as they packed, "We're going to be moved." Busch said nothing. He was pleased, but he was also on the point of winning the game, and right at the last minute it was being snatched away from him. He stormed into the dining room and glared at the chess board. Weiss was studying it, smiling to himself. "It's white to move?" he said.

"Yes, and there's nothing he can do. I've got check mate in four no matter what he does and by tomorrow night, I'd have won. I could smash the whole thing," said Busch. "Look, I'll show you. He's got to defend his queen and by blocking my bishop with this pawn which is protected and that lets my rook in. Then he does this" he moved a knight, "and then I've got a pin that is fatal. If he was honourable he would have surrendered last night. There's nothing he can do."

"I see," said Weiss, "but what if... ?" he moved the bishop's pawn.

"What does that do?" Busch said scornfully.

"Well, just stand back for a minute and put yourself in white's place. There's nothing to lose. It seems that sometimes the most innocuous looking moves are the most lethal, just because they look harmless."

Busch suddenly saw. It was as if a beautifully intricate bridge he had created had suddenly had its keystone removed. There was no way of stopping it. The foundations had been removed so clinically that it was almost as if his plan was destroying itself. "That's brilliant," he said, in horrified admiration. "But who is it?"

"I'll tell you on the way," said Weiss.

Chapter Twenty Five

Esther Hart's Diary

Friday 1st March 1940

There was a letter from Ada this morning that was addressed to Douglas. I was afraid it was some terrible news about the children, so, feeling somewhat guilty, I steamed it open. She complained that she couldn't keep the children on the allowance he was paying her and could he send her at least ten shillings a week more since she was going to have to buy Gordon a new pair of shoes. Then there was a tirade about their terrible table manners and how Lydia was always crying and how Gordon had become very insolent and said "You're not my Mother" when she told him to take his elbows off the table. I don't know what she expects Douglas to do. He hasn't written to the children once since Christmas. Feeling very low.

On the one o'clock news there was an appeal from the government for women to wear light coloured clothes so that the dyes could be used for uniforms. We've been invited out for a meal tomorrow night with Douglas's new boss, Herbert Radcliffe. I expect it would be seen as unpatriotic not to wear white. I'd better watch my table manners as well.

Sunday 3rd March

The usual talk about the war over supper. Sweden and Norway have refused our government and the French the right to cross their territory which means we can't go to the aid of Finland who are at war with Russia. But the men agreed that the real problem is that we can't now establish a base at Narvik, the purpose of which was not to help the Finns at all, but to stop the Germans transporting iron ore from Sweden, which they need to manufacture their weapons. At first I thought Barbara Radcliffe was a complete flippertygibbet, but I grew to like her as the evening wore on. She put her hand on her husband's once the coffee was served, and said "Darling, this is frightfully interesting I'm sure, so why don't you take Mr Hart into the drawing room with your cigars so that Esther and I can get to know each other better." I don't think Douglas has ever given me the melting look he gave her. She was completely different once the men had left the room and full of surprises. She said her husband was full of admiration for Douglas's work and that she had persuaded him to invite us for dinner. He particularly admired the way Douglas had managed a meeting with all the Chief Constables! I must have looked astonished because she laughed and asked how long we have been married. When I said fourteen years she said that probably explains why I don't get told things. They've only been married eight months. His first wife died five years ago of cancer. He is twelve years older than Barbara. I don't really understand why she married him because she is very beautiful and reminds me of someone, though I can't think who. She asked me about the children, and I found myself close to tears talking about them. I even admitted I'd opened Ada's letter and how much I hate her. Barbara said she would have done exactly the same thing in my place, and that made me feel better. Said she was going to see 'Algiers' at the Odeon on Wednesday, and did I want to come. When she said it was starring Hedy Lamarr, I suddenly realised who it was that she reminded me of. I think it's the way she holds her cigarette and rests her head on her hand when she's listening. Anyway, we're going to meet for lunch and go to the matinee performance.

Tuesday 5th March

Prepared the evening meal last night and blacked out the flat. When Douglas wasn't home by eight, I began to get worried and the supper was quite ruined. At ten I phoned the police- there have been so many accidents because of the black out that I was sure that he must have been run over and badly injured, or something worse. The police were very sympathetic but said that they hadn't heard anything and gave me the numbers of all the local hospitals. He still wasn't home by midnight and the hospitals saying they had no one of his name I started to suspect that he must be with another woman. I went to bed with my book, but couldn't concentrate and eventually fell asleep. He came in at twenty- five to two. I said we needed to talk and he said very aggressively 'Not now,' and turned over and went to sleep. He left early this morning. I didn't know what to do with myself and then the phone rang. It was Barbara Radcliffe. She was laughing and said didn't I think it was the funniest thing I'd ever heard. When I said, rather crossly, I'm afraid, that I didn't know what she was talking about, she said that Douglas and her husband had had a meeting at five o'clock with some chap from M15 at Wormwood Scrubs, which is where M15 is based. After the meeting Douglas was finishing off his notes, the chap left and inadvertently closed the door behind him, so they were locked in. It wasn't until the night duty guard came on that they could make themselves heard. Douglas had been terribly embarrassed because he had had to use the chamber pot that had been left in the corner. I was so relieved, but can't understand why Douglas should be having meetings with M15 when he works for the Home Office.

Wednesday 6th March

Asked Douglas if he has replied to his sister yet, hoping he would tell me what was in her letter. Said he hadn't had time.

Thursday 7th March

Lunch with Barbara. We talked so much that we nearly missed the film. She studied German at Newnham College and was travelling in Bavaria in '37.

She was in a church in Munich when the Papal Bull criticising the Nazi regime was read out, and she said she'll never forget the anguish on people's faces as they listened. She was staying with a Catholic family. After mass they'd invited a friend to come over for lunch. She wanted to understand why people had reacted as they did, but when she asked, the Mother gave her such a look of terror that she said nothing. After the guest had gone, they explained that the friend was in the army. If he knew how they'd felt about it he would undoubtedly have reported them and they would have been arrested. The Gestapo confiscated all copies of the Bull from the churches and closed down all the presses that had printed it. Hundreds of priests were arrested, allegedly for 'corrupting the youth'.

There was an enormous queue for the film, and since it was a matinee performance I was surprised at how many men were there- soldiers, mostly, and a lot of older men as well. Barbara giggled and whispered that they were probably hoping to see a repeat of 'Ecstasy'. When I looked nonplussed she said that in her first film Hedy Lamarr had appeared naked. There was also a love scene, which was rumoured in Germany not to be simulated, though she said it was. At the critical moment the producer had stuck a pin in her bottom. I enjoyed the film which also starred Charles Boyer. Went for tea afterwards. Barbara said Hedy Lamarr was something of a role model for her- they had both married much older men- perhaps it was something to do with the fact that for both of them, no man could be as important to them as their fathers. Told her about being on the tribunal and it suddenly occurred to me as odd that I'd only been asked the once. She said that there were lots of ways that women could help with the war effort and then, after a pause, said that Herbert had told her that Douglas had come to him and asked whether he didn't think that my attending further tribunals wouldn't be 'a conflict of interest', since he was now working at the Home Office. Mr Radcliffe had said he didn't really think so, but Douglas must have stopped my being asked again. I don't understand why he couldn't have told me that himself. It's both hurtful and annoying and I'm quite jealous of the fact that the Radcliffes share everything, Suppose that's what my diary's for.

Saturday 9th March

The 'Queen Elizabeth' has arrived safely at New York after crossing the Atlantic at high speed to avoid U-boats that are patrolling the seas to try and cut off supplies to and from Britain. It must have been an horrific journey. The government is terrified of the Finns making peace with Russia since that would deprive us from having an excuse for establishing a base at Narvik. We've offered troops and materials to the Finnish government. Douglas brought a lot of work home and scarcely spoke a word last night. Awful atmosphere. Feel I must pluck up the courage to say something.

Monday 11th March

All meat has been rationed. Long queues at the butcher's and still bitterly cold. Got 6 ozs of meat and the butcher helpfully asked all his customers if they wanted some whale meat that's been imported from South Africa. Big discussion in the shop about what to do with it. I didn't see anyone take up his offer, though if things become desperate, who knows? Wrote to the children as Douglas still hasn't replied to Ada and sent them a book each. Sent Lydia the copy of 'The Babes in the Wood' that I had as a child. Don't know if she'll get the joke.

Wednesday 13th March

The Finns have surrendered to Russia. That war cost nearly 100,000 lives and now hundreds of thousands of Finns are leaving the territories that have been claimed by the Russians. It's news like that that make me feel ashamed of being sorry for myself.

Went to the Austrian Centre to see if I could do anything to help. Herr Niedermayer has been ill but has received a letter from his wife, and so is now feeling elated. He spoke to me in English without an interpreter and says he has written back and is praying that somehow his wife and daughter will be able to come to England soon. They are staying in Switzerland where at least he knows they are safe. I was feeling very buoyed up by the news. I told Douglas, thinking that the Home Office must have had something to do with it, but all he said was that it wasn't a good idea for me to get too attached to 'these people.' I was fuming, but bit my tongue and phoned Barbara for a chat when he'd gone to work.

Sunday 17th March

The Germans launched a bombing raid on Scapa Flow yesterday, and a civilian was killed. I suppose this is just the beginning, because there are bound to be reprisals and more civilian deaths. Haunted all morning by what Stanley Baldwin said years ago, "The bombers will always get through."

Chapter Twenty Six

Saturday 2nd March 1940

Dear Mum and Dad

You can write to me at this address because this is where our new billet is. I'm OK and I've got some new friends, especially Joe Harper who is a good mate. Most of the time we have to do drill. Yesterday we had to march up and down between the goal posts for hours but mostly we have to do route marches all over the place. The worst is when we have to do route marches wearing our gas masks, like on Thursday. We had to take off our gas masks when we were coming out of the Gas chamber at Glen Parva. The gas smells of pear drops. The best day was when we went to the firing range at Kibworth. I was the best shot and I wanted to prove it but there was no ammo. Also we threw grenades and done bayonet charges but they weren't for real either There's no army trucks so we had to go in a furniture van. I asked the sarge why there was no ammo. I thought it was because they are saving it for when we really have to fight, but he said no, it's because there isn't any. He says the arsenal is called Leicester museum. Our rifles are called Enfields and they were used in the last war. They must have worked then because we won it.

I'll be home on leave in two weeks.

Love from Maurice

Leicester Football Ground Leicester Leicestershire

Sunday 9th March 1940

Dear Mum and Dad

I got paid my first wages last week. We get ten bob a week so me and Joe and Stan Mallinder went to the pub to celebrate. What with fags costing ten pence a pack and beer five pence a pint I didn't have much left by Wednesday. There's not much to do except smoke and play cards when we're not on duty. Mum, please can you send me a couple of pairs of socks. My boots are too small and after we did a route march to Wigston and back I got two big blisters on my heels. When we played a football match against some blokes from A company I couldn't run so they put me in goal. We lost 6-2 but two of the goals nobody couldn't have done nothing about. I could hardly walk to the pub. Also Joe said if we drink cider instead of bitter it's a lot cheaper, so we did and I drank too much (on account of my feet hurting so bad) so we got back to the barracks at five past twelve and they put us on a charge for being late and drunk. That meant I had to spend all of Sunday peeling spuds. By the time all the spuds were peeled I thought I had webbed fingers. All because we were six minutes late. The sarge said being six seconds late could mean the difference between life and death. I said in that case if I was six minutes late I'd miss my own funeral so I'd still be alive. You used to say, Maurice you'll miss your own funeral, Dad, do you remember? Anyway, it was only a joke but the sarge got really shirty and said he'd cancel my leave if I gave him any more of my lip. You used to say that as well, Dad. Can you come and pick me up next Friday at eight. I can show you the dressing rooms if you like.

Love from Maurice.

Sunday 17th March 1940

Dear Mum and Dad

It was great to come home for the weekend and I can come again in two weeks if Dad can pick me up again. Mum, you don't have to worry about me. I know I've lost a lot of weight but like I said, it's only because we've been doing so much PE and marching and digging those trenches was really hard work. I'm not ill, honest. I wish I could come home every night like the blokes who live in Leicester do but like you say Mum we can't have everything. The socks you knitted me are really good and I'm wearing them now. When I got back to barracks I got talking to a regular soldier who was in India for three years and he said you wouldn't believe how hot it was and he's right because it's freezing again and I can't remember the last time I was warm. He is called Davies and he shot a tiger once with an elephant gun. He says they're talking about sending some people to Norway but they wouldn't send the new recruits because we're all too young so you don't have to worry about me on that score. I don't even know where Norway is. He said it's a neutral country so personally I don't see the point of sending anyone.

I'll write again on Saturday

Your loving son

Maurice.

Chapter Twenty Seven

Reinhardt was feeling sorry for himself. He hadn't heard from Elizabeth for over a fortnight and was beginning to feel that he never would again. But the signs of her were all over the house, the way the furniture was rearranged to make the house more comfortable, her dressing gown hanging on the back of the bathroom door and the couple of dresses she'd left in his wardrobe. There were the records she'd left of Glenn Miller still on the gramophone turntable and her make up on the dressing table. It had begun to feel like their house, her kitchen, their bedroom, although the relationship had lasted only a short while. And though he had never had much confidence that her husband would inject some capital into his business, still, now that it was clear that he never would, it came as a blow to Reinhardt. He began to drink, at a loss to know what to do with himself. In his more depressed moments he wondered whether she had wanted to get out of the relationship altogether and had made up the story of her husband's arrest. At such times he picked up the phone to call her, and then hesitated, arguing with himself that if she was telling the truth it may well be the case that her phone was bugged. Then he would set down the receiver in its cradle again and pour himself another whisky.

He had never been good at being alone, so some evenings went to the pub, but there was never anyone there that he knew and he sat in the corner feeling more and more morose as he watched couples laughing and joking over their drinks before going out, arm in arm, which made him feel even worse.

One evening he had just come back from 'The Black Swan' and poured himself a large drink when there was a knock at the door. "It's her," he said aloud. He glanced in the mirror, ran his hand through his hair, which he noticed had grown too long, straightened his tie, and ran to the door. He had rehearsed this moment in his mind a dozen times, how he would take her in his arms, how she would say that she had finally left Coates for good and was going to move in with him immediately, how he would wind up the gramophone and they would drink whisky while they planned their future together before going to bed and how, in the morning, they would wake up wrapped around each other and start their new lives together.

He flung open the door. A short man in a tin hat was writing in a notebook. Reinhardt blinked at him in his shock of disappointment. The man finally stopped writing and looked up. "Blackout, sir," he said "You've got lights blazing all over the house and not one curtain even drawn."

"Well, I've just this second got in," said Reinhardt "I was about to draw them when you knocked."

The man made another note, whispering aloud as he wrote slowly, "Claims he just got in when I knocked." Then, drawing himself up as tall as he could, he said, "I'm afraid that is not the case, sir. I came by this way at," he flicked over a page in his notebook," nine forty-three and again at," he consulted his notebook again, "ten eleven. The lights were on then as well. Could I have your name please."

"Why?" said Reinhardt.

"Because I'm going to have to report you. You may well receive a summons to the magistrate's court."

Reinhardt's disappointment had given way to anger. "You really are an officious little sod, aren't you," he said.

The man was unmoved. "I'm only doing my duty. There's no call to get abusive. Your name, if you don't mind."

"Well," answered Reinhardt, leaning against the door frame," As it happens, I do mind. I'm going to close my curtains now and you're stopping me from doing it. And I'm not going to give you my name, so you can just fuck off." And he slammed the door. He drew the curtains violently and ran upstairs to the front bedroom where he had left the light on. Glancing down into the street, he saw the ARP was busily writing in his notebook. Reinhardt swore and pulled the curtains closed and went into the bathroom. He snatched Elizabeth's dressing gown down from the back of the door and took it into the bedroom where he pulled a suitcase from under the bed, and rolling up the dressing gown, flung it into the suitcase. Looking round for something into which he could put her make up, and failing to find anything, swept the lot into the suitcase. Then he went back downstairs and took the record off the turntable and hurrying back up, put it into the open case. He sat on his bed and put his head in his hands. He suddenly had a feeling of foreboding. He knew he shouldn't have sworn at the ARP, after all, the man was only doing his job, but he really hadn't wanted to give his name. Only that evening he had heard a couple in the pub talking about 'enemy aliens' and 'fifth columnists.' The young man who was chatting up a girl who was at least five years older than he was was saying how he'd heard that the country was full of spies and how the papers that wanted all 'foreigners' arrested were right, our politicians were far too innocent. "It stands to reason" he said, "Hitler's been planning this war for years. He's bound to have planted his spies all over the country. And the government knows it, else why would there be these posters everywhere that say 'Careless talk costs lives' and stuff like that?" The girl hadn't seemed very interested, either in the young man or what he was saying, but Reinhardt had felt worried. If people were beginning to think like that, then it was a short step to internment. It had been terrible during the last war. His wife had left him while he was away and he had never seen his daughter since. She would be thirty by now, no, thirty seven. He had no idea where she was. He could be a grandfather, he thought ruefully, in fact, he probably was.

He began to get undressed slowly. He would be summoned and at best fined. The penalty for not keeping to the blackout was five pounds, and he didn't have that kind of money. Anyway, he didn't want to stay here any more. In the morning he'd put the house on the market and move to a cheaper area, perhaps somewhere like Kilburn. That would release a bit of capital, especially if he rented. And if he moved out immediately, maybe they wouldn't bother to try and catch up with him. It was a forlorn hope, but it was worth a try.

The next morning Reinhardt got dressed, and feeling too delicate to want any breakfast, walked down to the estate agents. He listened glumly while Mr Parker, an elderly man in a shiny, threadbare suit flicked ash off his waistcoat and stubbed another cigarette into an overflowing ashtray. "We will do our very best, of course, Mr Reinhardt, but to be perfectly frank with you, the market is flat. Very flat, if you take my meaning. People are very short of money. There's a lot of activity on the black market, of course, but one can't sell a house on the black market." He chortled at his own joke until Reinhardt cut him off with a curt, "Quite."

"And of course," continued Mr Parker, "Those people who have money are tending to close their own houses and move into hotels. Folks are simply not willing or able to make long term investments. They're buying war bonds and suchlike, but by all means, I can pop round this afternoon, say at two if that would suit. Are you thinking of moving locally?"

"I thought I might rent for a while," said Reinhardt, "I want to release some capital."

"Ah, don't we all," sighed Mr Parker. He swivelled round and opened the top drawer of his filing cabinet. "These are all houses that we currently have on our books. Nothing's moving, you see. Still, we'll do what we can, I'll come round at two."

Reinhardt didn't feel like going home. He took a bus as far as Kilburn Park and wandered along the High Street looking in estate agents' windows, feeling determined to move, because he needed something to look forward to, and he needed to do something to get himself out of his present state of depressed apathy. One flat did catch his eye. It was in Beethoven Street, first floor with large rooms and very quiet. He went in to get the details. The price was also very reasonable and so, on the spur of the moment he made an appointment to go and visit it. The receptionist gave him a strange look, but having phoned the landlady, wrote the address and her name in large child like writing on a card.

"It's only ten minutes from here," she said, "Mrs Taylor's expecting you. She says to go straight away since she's just about to have her lunch.

Beethoven Street was ideally situated for him, being only a couple of minutes walk from the tube, so Reinhardt was feeling very optimistic about his plan. He knocked on the door and after a few seconds he could hear the bolts being pulled and the door unlocked. A tall, thin woman in an apron stood on the step above him. "Yes?" she said, "You're the gentleman who's come to see the flat."

"That's right," said Reinhardt.

"What's your name again? I didn't quite catch it when the girl was telling me."

"Reinhardt."

The woman narrowed her eyes and sniffed, then said, "What kind of name is that? It's not English."

"I've been in England for forty-five years," said Reinhardt, so I always think of myself as English."

"But where were you born?"

"In Germany." Reinhardt could see by the expression on her face that he wasn't going to get over the doorstep, let alone see the room.

Mrs Taylor half closed the door. "No, sorry," she said. My Sidney wouldn't stand for it. He's away in the army. Anyway, I told them at the estate agents, I won't have commercial travellers or Jews. I didn't think they'd be daft enough to send me a German." She shut the door, and Reinhardt stood waiting long enough to hear the bolts being slammed to.

He looked at his watch. It was ten to two. "Christ," he said, "I'm going to be late. When he reached home, panting from running from the tube, he discovered he had not one visitor, but two.

Chapter Twenty Eight

Niedermayer recovered from his flu slowly. He had written a long letter to his wife on the morning that he had received hers. He had sealed it and given it to Willi, who gave it to Lotte who, in turn, gave it to Mrs Rathbone who assured her that it would be sent to Geneva through the Czech Refugee Council.

A week later he was walking slowly along Westbourne Avenue to the Austrian Centre, surprised at how weak he felt but feeling that the thin spring sunshine was doing him good, and relieved to be out of the fetid air of his room. Doctor Schepke had told him that because he had bronchitis, he must stay in bed for a fortnight, otherwise it could easily turn into pneumonia, and he had prescribed aspirin. But he wasn't able to rest. Mrs Rathbone had come back a few days later with their landlord who protested weakly that the refugees paid so little rent that he couldn't afford to have the repairs done that were needed. Niedermayer was completely ignored as Mrs Rathbone pulled up the corner of the blanket that was against the wall and shouted at the landlord, "Look, just feel that. It's wringing wet. This man is very ill. And it's not surprising. This place is quite unfit for human habitation and unless you do something about it immediately, I shall have this establishment closed down."

It was the next morning that Niedermayer had got up for the first time. He dressed and put Ilse's letter in his breast pocket. He reflected as he went through the door of the Austrian Centre that he really wanted to write to her again. He'd felt so ill when he wrote the first letter that he had only said that he was fine and that he couldn't wait for them all to be together again. But he didn't think he could write again so soon. Still, he would compose a letter so that it could go the moment he heard from her. Now he went to find Lotte to see whether there was a reply. She was in the back room with Herr Richter who was repairing a pair of shoes.

She looked up when Niedermayer went in. "Hello Franz, are you better?" She smiled warmly at him, "Herr Richter is putting new soles on these shoes that belonged to Herr Jütte. He says the uppers are fine. What size do you take?" Herr

Richter peered down at Niedermayer's feet through thick steel framed spectacles. "The stitching's gone on those," he said, "I can mend them, but these are better quality. These were made in Italy, see, and they'd support your ankles better if they fit. Try them on gently."

Niedermayer took off his shoes, and to save his embarrassment Lotte looked away with a slight smile. His big toe had gone through the wool of one sock and half the sock was missing on the other.

"I could darn that one for you," he said, "but for the other nothing can be done."

Niedermayer pulled on a shoe. It was a little tight. He moved to stand up but Herr Richter put out a hand to stop him. "No, the glue is still too wet. Just tell me how it feels."

"It cuts across the top," said Niedermayer, but there seems to be plenty of room otherwise."

"I can see to that, here try the other one."

Niedermayer put on the other shoe. "Yes, that's fine. Can I really have them?"

"Sure. They'll be ready tomorrow. Bring me your old ones. Where did you get them?"

Niedermayer remembered how, when he had arrived from Austria, a lady from the Red Cross had come to the Centre shortly after he'd arrived and how she had gently taken off his old boots that were in such a state of disrepair that they had made him limp. His feet were swollen. She had said nothing but shaken her head sadly and having searched through a bag of old shoes, finally found a pair that fitted. She had left without saying a word, as if she were ashamed. He could clearly remember the look she had given him before she left. It had almost made Niedermayer feel sorry for himself.

"Thank you," he said to Herr Richter, "but you know I can't pay you. I haven't any money." Herr Richter waved him away. "None of us has, " he said. "Some day you'll do something for me, and then we'll be quits. See you tomorrow." Lotte and Niedermayer went through to the reading room.

A group of older men were sitting round reading the papers quietly, so they found a corner where they could talk.

"That woman, Mrs Hart came in looking for you a couple of days ago," said Lotte, " I told her you were ill and she said she'd come back next week. She said she wanted to try and get your 'B' changed to a 'C', so that's good news as well. She said she can't promise anything but she'll do her best, but I must admit, I don't really like her. Why couldn't she have made sure you got a 'C' in the first place?"

Niedermayer shrugged. "Perhaps it wasn't her decision. She didn't say anything at my tribunal, it was an older man who did all the talking, but as I told you, I didn't really understand what he was saying."

Lotte nodded, "I know. I still feel guilty about not being able to be there. But I think there's more chance of Mrs Rathbone getting it changed.

Niedermayer looked round and picked up a copy of 'Der Zeitspiegei' He glanced at the headline, which was about the Polish government in exile in France having issued a White Paper to the effect that from 1933 the German government had tried to persuade the Poles to join it in a joint declaration of war on the Soviet government, but that it had wanted nothing to do with the proposal.

"Poor Poland," said Lotte, "caught between two tyrants."

"I met a Polish Jew in Warsaw," said Niedermayer. He'd been a teacher in Krakow until he lost his job and told that Jews couldn't be civil servants. He knew nothing else. According to him, the Poles were just as anti-semitic as the Russians and the Germans. His family had fled Russia and now they were having to leave Poland as well. Where are we supposed to go? We're being driven out of every country in Europe. We're not wanted in France either. And if England receives many more refugees from Poland or Austria or Germany or Russia, don't you think we'll be equally unpopular here in a few years? In Poland we were accused of blood libel. The church, or at least the right wing elements of it, say that we slaughter Christian children to make our Passover bread. It's a lie of course, but one that's been about for centuries. People will believe what they want to believe to support their prejudices." He sighed. "If we ever come out of this alive I shall change my name and settle down here, but somehow I don't think that that's going to happen."

Lotte looked it him. He seemed to have shrunk inside his thin jacket, and his eyes had a glazed look of complete defeat.

She tried to cheer him up. "Come on Franz, look, things are looking better for you and your family than they have since you arrived here. You've heard from Ilse and you know that she is safe. You may well be able to finish your course and get a job and start earning money and be able to stay in this country where you'll be able to start a new life. You're so much more fortunate than the millions of people in Germany and Austria, and Poland for that matter... He seemed not to hear her, and then shook his head slowly. "No, he said, the English aren't ready to fight Hitler. He'll invade and then we'll be no better than if we'd stayed in Czechoslovakia."

She felt there was little point in arguing with him. She had never seen him so depressed before.

"Oh, well look," she said, "I've got things I need to do. As long as you think like that, then there is no hope, but I can't afford to, and I'm not going to allow myself to either. I refuse to believe that such evil can ever triumph in the end. Hitler will be defeated. One day Hitler and Stalin will be defeated. Look in the paper, see, about how a little country like Finland has fought off the Red Army. There are far more people in Europe who want to see Fascism destroyed..."

"Yes," said Niedermayer, with an animation that she hadn't seen before, "and when he is destroyed, it will be by Stalin, and he hates us Jews just as much as the Nazis. I was given a 'B' because I said I was a socialist, which I am. But don't try and tell me that there isn't anti-semitism in this country, and it'll get worse. No, the real reason why I was told that I couldn't get work here, or train to get a job was because I'm a Jew. And it'll get worse."

"Then," said Lotte, "fight it. Fight for what you believe in, not with arms and propaganda, but with all those people in this country, like Mrs Rathbone who believe in the important values that make us human."

She stood up, "I'm not even going to try and argue with you when you're like this," and she stormed off, wiping away tears of frustration.

Niedermayer went back to his paper and muttered, "She's not Jewish, she doesn't understand." He was angry, not so much with her, but with himself, for his feeling of hopelessness when he recognised that Lotte was doing everything she could to help him and at his frustration at not being able to help himself. He wanted to apologise to her, but his feelings were too complicated. There was nothing he could do for her in return and he knew he appeared completely ungrateful. He loathed himself for his self-pity but on the other hand he felt to receive any more help was simply demeaning which was why he had pushed her away.

He didn't want to stay in the centre, but he certainly didn't want to go back to his room. He wrapped his jacket round himself and went out. He still felt weak and a chill wind was blowing along the street as he turned towards Paddington Station. He turned down the steps and bought a platform ticket. He wanted the noise of the trains to drown out his thoughts and so he found a bench on the platform and looked down the track. A large engine pulled in, the steam hissing from around its wheels as the passengers, mostly soldiers, disembarked. A small group of them walked towards him, laughing and smoking, and then one of them broke away from the group and ran towards a young woman who had been waiting anxiously. The soldier caught her up in his arms and kissed her, and then, with his arm around her and his duffle bag swinging from his shoulder, he led her towards the exit. All around him Niedermayer watched people greeting each other. When they had finally gone he got up stiffly and followed them.

Chapter Twenty Nine

Busch awoke with a jerk. At first he couldn't make out where he was. There was a body lying across his chest. He rubbed his eyes and peered down, but the darkness was total. Only the hissing of the trains brakes and the soreness of his thighs reminded him that he was on a train and on a journey that had seemingly lasted for days. He pushed the body into an upright position and stood up to stretch his legs. Immediately a torch was shone into his eyes and a voice said, "Sit down." He sat down.

The voice beside him said, "I need a pee." Weiss stretched across Busch and tapped on the window. The compartment door slid open a couple of inches and the torch shone on the eight men who were either still asleep or who had just been woken by the train grinding to a stop. "Sorry old chap, but I am absolutely bursting for a pee," said Weiss, "Dreadfully sorry and all that."

The door closed again, there was a whispered conversation in the corridor and a moment later a pot was passed through the door.

Weiss stepped over to the window, undid his buttons and said in German, "I thought if I spoke to them nicely they'd at least let me use the lavatory."

When he had finished he stepped back and knocked again on the window. The door slid open once more and another man's voice said, "Anyone else, before I take this away?"

Weiss translated and when no one answered said to the guard, "Are we nearly there?"

"Where?" The voice was smiling.

"To wherever we're going," said Weiss.

"About another hour, I should think, as long as there's no more delays. That answer your question?"

"Thank you," said Weiss politely, "but it surely can't do any harm to tell us where we're being taken to."

Busch looked up as the torch was shone into Weiss's eyes which made him put his hand up to protect them.

Another voice said, "Camp thirteen. Any the wiser now?"

"Not really, where is that exactly?"

The pot was taken from his hand and the door slid shut. Weiss slumped back into his seat. "I don't know," he said, "I wish I knew where we are."

Busch lit a cigarette to muttered protests from the man opposite and passed it to Weiss. "Grunge Strasse," he said and those who were awake laughed. When they had boarded the train at Seaton, Busch had amused himself by pulling faces at the young guard who had been allocated to watch them from the corridor. He sat self-consciously with his rifle across his knee, staring fixedly at the floor as Busch made as if to shoot him. Meanwhile Weiss had kept up a commentary on where he thought they were as the train headed north eastwards. He was disappointed to find that all the road and station signs had been removed until Busch, leaning over his shoulder said, "There's one that they missed." But the train was going too fast at that point and he read it as Grunge St." Thereafter, whenever Weiss said he wished he knew where they were, the men in the compartment chorused "Grunge Strasse."

To begin with they had sung and told jokes and wolf whistled at any women they saw, but gradually they had slipped into a torpor. Busch and Weiss played a couple of games of chess which Weiss had won. During one lengthy stop they had been served with lukewarm potato soup served in tin mugs followed by sweet tea and in the evening bread and dripping. Eventually most of the men had fallen asleep and the train stopping for what seemed to Busch like the hundredth time had woken him.

Though it was still dark, the men were now all awake. Guards hurrying up and down the corridor alerted the men to the fact that they were approaching their destination. They all listened as the train stopped, and after a few minutes they could hear carriage doors being opened and then, minutes later, slammed shut again. The sound of compartment doors sliding open down the corridor and men shouting orders in English came closer. Eventually an older guard opened the door and nodded to the man sitting opposite Busch to get up, take his bag and get out. One by one they stood and stretched while the guard, his bayonet fixed waved them towards the open carriage door. The men were lined along the platform while the guards watched them suspiciously.

It was cold, with a frost on the ground. Above a line of distant hills the dawn was breaking. When the last carriage door was closed a man that Busch assumed was an officer moved down the line doing a head count.

"Sixty eight," he called when he had finished. Another man in uniform nodded and beckoned the two Germans at the head of the line to follow him. The group slowly left the station and walked down the middle of the road, with guards on either side of the line.

After a few hundred yards they turned into what looked like the high street of a small town. A sudden burst of laughter came from the men in front. A boy of about fifteen had been cycling down the road, and with the sudden shock of seeing more than sixty men walking towards him he had fallen off his bike and was now sitting against a wall, his flat cap lying on the pavement beside him and the rear wheel of his bike still spinning.

"Excuse me," said Weiss, "but we appear to be lost. Can you possibly tell me where w are?"

The boy stared at him mutely, and then jumped to his feet and pushed his bike off down the road.

After almost an hour they turned into a tree lined drive. In front of them was what appeared to be a stately home. "They've brought us to see the King," whispered Weiss to Busch. "He's got German family, perhaps he feels sorry for us and wants us to move in with him."

Busch looked at him. "Then perhaps he'll send us home," he said hopefully.

"I was joking," said Weiss. They walked behind the house, which, Busch thought, was the largest he had ever seen. It was a large encampment surrounded by high barbed wire fencing with four watch- towers in each corner.

The guards lined the men up and then waited. After a few minutes a tall officer approached from the house with a middle- aged man in civilian clothes. He looked at the line of men before speaking. Then in a loud voice he said, "Gentlemen, you are now at Camp 13. We will make your time here as comfortable as possible." He paused to allow the man standing next to him to translate. Then he continued. "Officers will sleep in the garden house, the large building to your left. Lower ranks will sleep in the large hall. There are recreation facilities at your disposal. There is also a chapel and a supervised exercise area. As you can see, armed guards are there," he waved towards the towers, "to ensure that there is no possibility of escape. You are a long way from the sea. Any attempts to escape will be punished by seven days in the detention centre. I strongly advise against it." He looked along the lines of men while they listened to the translation." Finally he turned and walked back to the main building.

A soldier stepped forward and began to call out names. Captain Burfeind and a dozen other men were led to the Garden House. Finally Busch and Weiss tailed the group that was following a guard to the hall. Rows of beds with thick brown woollen blankets were neatly arranged around the walls. Busch sat on the edge of his bed and looked around angrily.

"They can only put us in detention if they catch us trying to escape," he said. Weiss looked at him, smiling and said, "Tell me, Otto, do you think that we'll win the war?"

"Stupid question," replied Busch, "Of course."

"So you think we're going to invade soon?

"What's wrong with you. We'll overrun England just like we did Poland and Austria."

"So what's the point of trying to escape? When we invade, surely we'll be more use to the army if we're here and where there are lots of us than we will trying to escape back home and having to hide in some remote village somewhere where you're likely to be shot by some stupid farmer who's mistaken you for a rabbit."

Busch was about to reply when the doors of the hall opened and a dozen men marched towards them. The leader strode up to Weiss and gave the Hitler salute. "Heil Hitler," he said. Busch leapt to attention and returned the greeting, while Weiss waved his arm airily and smiled. The man pushed Weiss in the chest, which made him sit down on the bed with a startled expression. "Heil Hitler," he repeated. Weiss looked around. The group of men were standing round him wearing expressions that varied from curiosity to threatening. Weiss got slowly to his feet and raised his arm.

"This is a Nazi camp," said the leader. "if you don't know how to be a good German, we'll soon teach you." He nodded to two men standing behind him. They stepped forward, and taking Weiss by the arms dragged him backwards towards the door. Weiss, too shocked to protest, had gone red with anger. He wore a look of panic as he was pulled out through the door.

The leader turned to Busch. "Is he your friend?" he asked.

Busch shook his head, "But I'm a member of the party. Look I can show you my card."

The group of men stood aside to let another man through. He was older than the rest, and Busch recognised him immediately. "Where have you come from?" he said.

Misunderstanding the question, Busch said, "Bremerhaven, sir."

"No, I mean, which camp have you come from?"

Busch reddened. "Seaton."

The man nodded. "I thought so. Haven't I just seen your captain? What's his name?"

"Captain Burfeind."

"Well, you can tell your Captain Burleind that I am the camp leader here. We won't tolerate his communist social democratic ideas here. Tell him that from me." And he turned and left, followed by his henchmen.

Busch went over to a window to see what had happened to Weiss. There was no sign of him and he didn't feel that going to look for him would be a very wise thing to do. The rest of those who had come from Seaton were unpacking their bags and putting their things in lockers beside their beds.

A few minutes later a guard came in and beckoned them all to follow him. He led them along the path to a large dining room where there were still groups shifting round finishing their breakfast. Busch realised he was very hungry. Joining the queue to the serving counter, he took a mug of coffee and a large chunk of bread. He had just sat down when he saw Weiss come in. He was holding a handkerchief to his nose and there was the beginning of a bruise coming up on his forehead. He spotted Busch and came and sat beside him. "Initiation ceremony, they call it," he mumbled through his handkerchief. "The bastards," he added. "Can you get me some coffee, but I don't want anything to eat. I think I may have broken a tooth."

When Busch returned with his coffee, Weiss said, "But the worst of it is that on the way here I saw a guard who asked me if I'd walked into a door or something. When I said "Something like that" he laughed and said the doors have a habit of initiating people here. He said the camp commander always says it's no different than when boys start at public schools. It's nothing more than that. Can you believe it? Told me if I didn't know the words to the Horst Wessel song it might be a good idea to learn them."

Busch nodded sympathetically and looked round nervously. He wasn't sure that he wanted to be seen to be too close to Weiss.

"Look," he said, "The man who had you taken out is called Wirth. He was at Seaton and stood as camp leader for the Germans there, but the English didn't want him and pulled off some trick so he wasn't elected, though he must have got far more votes than Burfeind. Some people thought he was an SS spy. I don't believe it because he made himself much too conspicuous. But when the invasion does come it's men like him that'll lead the uprising and I'm all for that. If you've got any sense, you'll support him too."

Weiss shook his head. "So you want to be a bastard too, is that it?"

"If you like," said Busch, "But I'll tell you this. I'd much rather be giving out bloody noses than getting them."

He got up and walked out. By the periphery fence he saw Captain Burfeind and Müller standing next to a guard's tower and looking across the hills. He went up to them and gave the Hitler salute.

"Ah, Busch," smiled the captain, "I see you've settled in already. You should be more comfortable in this.. .what shall I call it? Atmosphere?"

"I've just seen Herr Wirth, sir," said Busch, "And he says to tell you that he is the leader in this camp. He's obviously still angry about what happened at Seaton."

Burfeind shrugged. "I've no wish to be the camp leader, it gives me no problem at all. I think we'll be here for some time and I've no wish to cause disruption. It seems to me that we all have to get on if life here isn't to be quite unbearable. But I will remind you, Busch, that I am still your captain. You heard what was said this morning about trying to escape, and I would add to that the situation here is the same as applied at Seaton. You will not do it and put us all in danger."

Chapter Thirty

It was a Saturday morning and unusually neither Franco nor Eugenio were working. Eugenio had wanted to have a lie in, but Julia had rapidly disabused him of the desire, saying that she needed some maternity clothes and that he was to go and buy them with her. The discussion had spilt over into the Baldini's flat, and was finally resolved when it was decided that Giovanna and Francesca would go with Julia to choose a dress.

"So you don't want to help me choose," said Julia angrily to her husband. Eugenio looked pained and shrugged his shoulders.

"Va bene," said Julia, "and you don't mind how much it costs?"

"Allora," sighed Eugenio, and he passed her a five pound note.

"I don't need your money," said Julia, "I've got the cheque book." Then she said to Giovanna, "I'm going to get my coat and scarf and I'll meet you outside."

Francesca had long since given up trying to be a go-between for her uncle and aunt ('Pandarus', Eric had called her) and had decided to try and be a role model for them instead, so, having put on her coat, she put her arms round Franco and said, "Papa, if you really want to understand why I love Eric, then read this. It's just so beautiful. Much better than Boccaccio," and she lay a book open on top of the paper that he had been trying to read at the kitchen table.

After the women had gone, Franco moved the book to one side, but Eugenio clicked his tongue, and took the paper, "No, no, you heard her, I'll take this," and licking his finger, he started flicking through the pages of 'La Stampa.'

Franco stared at the book and after a few minutes said, "What is this? I can't even understand the first line. What language is it? It's not in English." Eugenio laughed. "You didn't think understanding what she sees in Eric was going to be easy, did you? But she's given you the key. Try harder."

"No, but look, can you understand it?"

Eugenio shook his head and then suddenly stopped, "My God, Mussolini is going to declare war on France. He's signed an agreement with Hitler. We're going to war."

"Listen," said Franco, not listening, "Whan'- what does that mean? 'When' I suppose, but the man can't even spell. "When that Aprille. April doesn't have two l's, does it?"

Eugenio was exasperated. "Franco, put down that stupid book for a minute and listen. This is serious. Mussolini is going to declare war on France. Look here, it's been announced. That could be very bad for us."

Franco pushed the book away and looked at his brother. "Why?" he asked.

"Why? Britain's at war with Germany. That means that when we join the Germans, we'll be, what do they call them here? Enemy aliens. Then they'll send us back to Italy and we'll lose everything we've got. Can't you see that?"

Franco shook his head. "That won't happen. Look, I've been here for twenty three years. My children were born here. Francesca thinks she's English. We're no danger to the English. This is my country now. And you've been here, what, eighteen years. Why should the government worry about us? Anyway, they love us. We've shown them what food should taste like." Eugenio scratched his head. "They locked enemy aliens up in the last war. I was talking to an old German man only the other day. He said he spent four years on the Isle of Man as a prisoner. If Mussolini declares war on Britain, that's what they'll do to us."

Franco shook his head. "That's my point. This German customer of yours, he's free to go about as he likes. They haven't locked him up, have they? They did in the last war but they're not doing it in this one, or else he wouldn't be able to talk to you about it. There are thousands of Italians here, working hard, paying their taxes. Nobody could ever think that we're a danger to the country. So we're not in danger either. It's obvious."

Eugenio wasn't convinced. "I didn't say they'd lock us up. I said they'd send us home."

"What, all of us? Do you think they're stupid? They deport I don't know how many men, and the moment they get to Italy they all get recruited to fight against France. The French government would love the British for that. What you need is a bit of sense and a cup of coffee. I'll put it on."

"Well, I still think..." started Eugenio, but Franco wasn't going to let him finish.

"OK, lots of Italians here think Mussolini is great. He's the first leader to make the Italians here feel part of Italy, opening the Fascio club and all that. But most people couldn't give a damn about him. He's a puffed up little tyrant. Look, let's drink our coffee and go down there. The women won't be back for hours. But for God's sake don't tell Giovanna we've been. She hates me going down there."

They drank their coffee in silence, Eugenio, rereading the article and Franco shaking his head despairingly at the opening lines of 'The Canterbury Tales.' "No," he said after a while, "I give up." He drained his coffee cup. "Come on, let's go out, I can't stand any more of this rubbish."

The Casa del Littorlo was a ten minute bus ride from Clerkenwell. Franco had taken Francesca there for music and Italian lessons when she was younger and Giovanna had once taken their daughter for a free holiday back to Italy that had been funded by the Italian government. In spite of the fascist slogans that adorned the place, the Baldinis had always remained resolutely apolitical.

But the discussion that the two brothers had started in Franco's kitchen was being loudly argued in the lobby by an angry group of Italians. Four men were trying to usher two older men out of the door. Franco and Eugenio stood to one side as one of the two men wearing a pince- nez was pushed in the chest. His aggressor shouted, "You anti- fascists, you make me sick. You want to take advantage of everything the government does for us and then criticize it. You're not welcome here, just go and take your stupid communist ideas somewhere else."

The older man put up his hands as if to defend himself. "I'm not a communist. But do you really want Italy to go to war? Think what it'll mean for your wife and children. Do you want them never to be able to go home because your son will have to fight?"

Another man stepped forward and shouted him down." If you're not a communist you're a filthy Jew. That's why you're here, because you can't get a job back home. Il Duce was right to pass the race laws. Stops people like you from taking the jobs of real Italians, taking the wealth out of the country. Go on, tell us, how long have you been here anyway?"

"Two years, but..."

The group of men stood around him and laughed scornfully. "See," said one, "two years. I've been here fifteen. We all came to work and we work damned hard. We're proud to be Italian. Il Duce makes us feel like we still belong. What you lot don't understand is that the real enemy is the Communists. Hitler and Mussolini are saving Europe from the communists."

"Yes," said another, "and the Jews, now get out before we throw you out."

The two old men shook their heads. As the one with the pince-nez passed Franco, he looked up at him as if he were going to say something, but thought better of it and slowly went down the steps. Franco noticed he had tears in his eyes.

Inside the hall there were groups standing around arguing furiously. "Let's get a drink," suggested Eugenio, "I need something strong. You know, they shouldn't have treated those poor old men like that, even if they were Jews." Franco stopped and stared at his brother. "What have you got against Jews? I tell you, if it wasn't for rich Jews, I wouldn't have a job."

"Well," said Eugenio weakly, "You hear things."

"What kind of things? If you're stupid enough to believe everything you hear, well that's your problem. Haven't you heard people talking about greasy Italians and how they can't be trusted?"

"Of course," said Eugenio.

"And is it true?"

"It's true of that little crook Gino. I've told him, if he tries to fob me off with any more of his mouldy vegetables, I'm going to find another supplier."

"Eugenio, listen. Is it true that as a rule Italians can't be trusted?"

"Va bene," Eugenio held up his hands in mock surrender, "No, but I can always trust you to give me a lecture."

Groups were standing round fiercely discussing what the news meant. Franco and Eugenio bought their drinks and looked round. Sitting by himself at a table, Franco saw his friend Paolo. He was engrossed in what he was reading. When he saw them he laid the paper down and moved his chair back, as if he wanted to distance himself from it. He waved his arms towards it. "Allora, this is bad for us, Franco," he said, "Very bad."

Franco sat down and sipped his drink. "Why?"

Paolo looked at him in surprise. "Why? Don't you read the papers?"

"I've seen them," said Franco coolly, aware that Eugenio wanted to speak, and not wanting him to. He had great respect for Paolo's opinion, and very little for his brother's.

"How many reasons do you need?" asked Paolo. "Italy can't fight alongside Germany for a start. We don't have that kind of strength. We'd get smashed. English people have no problem with us now, but if we declare war on England, and things go well, they'll soon come to hate us. And if they go badly, they'll scorn us. Either way Italy will be ruined, either by the Germans, or by the French and the English. Look what they did to Germany after the last war. She was ruined, and she was a rich country before. We're a poor country and we'll be destroyed. You understand?"

"I don't think things are as bad as you're making out," said Franco.

"Well, we'll see, but I think they're even worse. Look at those boys over there." He nodded towards a particularly vociferous group. "What will they do? Maybe they want to show that they support this country, after all, they live here. And so maybe they join the army just to prove it. What about their mothers and fathers? Or maybe they don't. Then they're accused of being disloyal to the country that gives them a home and a living and they get conscripted. So can't you see that it'll finish up with brother fighting against brother and father against son. No, it's a terrible business."

Franco thought about the two men who they'd seen being abused as they'd come in, and then he thought about Eric. He looked around the room at the men shouting and gesticulating and nodded. "Maybe you're right Paolo. This is what it's like now, before we've even joined the war."

He no longer wanted to be there. "I'm going home," he said, "Eugenio, are you coming?"

But Eugenio was listening to the group standing next to them. "No, I'll come along later." There was excitement in his eyes.

Franco nodded. "I'll tell Julia. And I'll admire her new maternity dress as much as I can so she's less inclined to kill you when you get back."

"OK, thanks" said Eugenio, but he had already started to move away and wasn't really listening.

Chapter Thirty One

Esther Hart's Diary

Friday 22nd March 1940

The papers are full of the RAF's raid on Sylt, which was in revenge for the German's attacking Scapa Flow the other day. But we used thirty or so bombers to attack the island, which, we are assured is only a military base. No doubt there will be reprisals from the Luftwaffe and so the war will begin in earnest. Listening to two women talking in Boots, they seemed positively relieved that at last the war seems to be starting, as if the waiting were worse than the fighting. 'The sooner it begins, the sooner it'll be all over' said one of them and the other agreed. Perhaps it's because there have been so many false alarms over the last seven months that anything is better than nothing. But almost nobody carries their gas mask any more and we are all a lot more lax about the blackout, so in some strange way it's as if people want the war proper to start but somehow don't believe it ever will, and we all grow more apathetic by the day.

It's Good Friday. Sent the children some money for Easter eggs yesterday and then went out into the garden to start trying to get it nice for Sunday. We always had an Easter egg hunt and the clearing up of the garden after the winter was such a part of it. But without the children the garden seemed so bleak. Spent an hour cutting up the branch of the silver birch that had come down in the winter and felt a bit better. Douglas has take Charles out for lunch and is bringing him back for the afternoon. He's got terribly thin lately but is adamant that he is eating properly, but he obviously isn't.

Sunday 24th March - Easter Day

I just happened to mention that Paul Reynaud had succeeded Daladier as the French Prime Minister and it started the most extraordinary tirade from Charles, which Douglas joined in with. C said very haughtily, "Well of course, it's well known that the French change their PM more often than they change their underwear," a remark that he found so amusing that it caused him to have a prolonged coughing fit. Douglas said that was one of the things that make the French such unreliable allies, whereas Chamberlain's speech in the house on Finland was masterly and he completely silenced his critics by announcing that, as he spoke, bombers were attacking Sylt. And Chamberlain was of course absolutely right to say that the failure of the Finnish campaign was the responsibility of Norway and Sweden who wouldn't allow our troops across their territories. The two of them carried on with their speeches as if they were debating in the House of Commons themselves. I suppose it was nice that they found something to agree on for once.

I suddenly realised that the time when I assumed that Douglas was right about everything that goes on in the world has gone. He doesn't argue with people who don't agree with him, he simply ignores them. So Douglas and his father almost took it in turns to quote everything that we had apparently done to help the Finns- it was the same list that Mr Chamberlain gave in the House of Commons, as if that were the end of the story. Except that then Mr Macmillan, who has just come back from Finland, stood up and said that the Finns request for help from us had almost fallen on deaf ears, and what we had sent them was too little and too late. I didn't say that to Douglas- there would have been no point, and Charles would have been sneeringly condescending, as he always is when I express any view that isn't to do with food or the latest time-saving device for the home. But the French got rid of Daladier precisely because the Government hadn't done enough to help the Finns. I think there must be a lot more unhappiness about our government's conduct of the war within parliament than we get told about.

Tuesday 26th March

Douglas back at work, so went over to see Barbara at 11. Said she had no coffee, but had heard that roasted dandelion roots is a good substitute, so we went into the garden, dug up a couple of dandelions and put them in the oven for half an hour. When they were quite black, she crumbled them up and put them in a coffee pot, and poured boiling water on them. We agreed that it was quite the most revolting thing either of us had ever tasted. She said it was marginally improved by pouring a generous measure of Herbert's best cognac into the cups, so by lunchtime we were both quite tipsy. Still, the after-taste is still with me and perfectly horrible.

Wednesday 27th March

Barbara phoned to say that she hadn't got the recipe for dandelion coffee quite right- we should have dried the roots first, but we agreed that it had been an interesting experience and not necessarily one that we needed to pursue further. Talked about the government forbidding captured British soldiers from making broadcasts on behalf of the enemy. Barbara said apparently British soldiers that had been captured were being made to broadcast the fact that they were well, that they missed their families, but they were being very well cared for by their German captors who were playing games of football against them, etc etc. We joked about prisoners in Germany discovering that Mr Chamberlain had forbidden them to broadcast, and so their remonstrating with Hitler that, while they would love to reassure their families at home that they were alive and fine, they didn't feel they could as Mr Chamberlain had expressly asked them not to. Barbara suddenly went terribly quiet and said there were probably some things that were wiser not to discuss on the phone, and then she hung up.

Thursday 28th March

Barbara came round and said she was sorry if she had appeared very melodramatic when we spoke yesterday. Tried to jolly her up a bit by saying that I'd expect nothing less from someone who modelled herself on Hedy Lamarr, but she was awfully down, and not her usual self at all. She said the whole government had become very twitchy after Mr Macmillan's criticism of its handling of the Finnish affair. Herbert had come home depressed saying that civil servants were being scrutinised for their loyalty to the government and that he knew for a fact that there had been an order to tap a number of people's telephones, though he didn't know who was responsible for that. I said I knew that Douglas completely supported Mr Chamberlain, but that I wasn't sure myself. That did cheer Barbara up; she laughed and said that just proved that I've got a lot more sense than my husband. She said there's real fear in the Foreign Office that Chamberlain and Halifax want to reach some kind of truce with Hitler. That would effectively mean giving up our sovereignty and being ruled from Berlin.

She told me that because of the way that the Russians have treated the Finns, the French government has expelled the Soviet Ambassador and that has been a very popular move with the French people. It's terribly confusing. Half the time we seem to be told that it is the Soviets who are our true enemy and that Hitler is acting as a bulwark in protecting us from Communism. Then we remember that we are supposed to be at war with Germany, but we have actually done nothing to protect any of our allies or to protest at the lack of help given to them. To that extent I feel quite guilty at not doing anything but then I really don't know what I can do. Barbara says we can only do our bit on an individual level and that we're lucky we can be having the conversation at all; both in Russia and in Germany such criticism of the government would be viewed as acts of treason.

We listened to the news. We've agreed with France not to act independently in establishing a treaty with any other nation. I didn't really understand why that was necessary, but Barbara laughed and said it just proves how little the two countries trust each other. We don't trust France not to do a secret deal with Germany, and they don't trust us not to do the same. It probably means that the British have come up with some plan that the French don't like, and that they've come up with a plan that we don't like, so we've agreed to do nothing except put out a joint communique saying that neither will negotiate with any other country without the other's agreement, which they know that they certainly won't get.

Chapter Thirty Two

Reinhardt was fumbling with his keys when the door opened. He looked up, annoyed, expecting to see the estate agent standing there, and was about to ask how he had had the gall to enter his house, when he saw, not the estate agent, but a young policeman.

"Mr Reinhardt?" he said, stepping to one side.

"Yes," said Reinhardt.

Noticing the look of amazement on Reinhardt's face, the policeman explained, "It's all right, sir, your wife let me in."

"What?" Reinhardt couldn't hide his astonishment. He hadn't seen his wife (or was it ex-wife? He could never remember), for at least eight years. He certainly had no idea that she still had a key to the house. He sat down on the sofa and scratched his head in bewilderment.

"Are you all right, sir?" asked the young constable. He thought the old man looked as though he had just seen a ghost.

"Yes, thank you, I'm fine." There was a lengthy pause, and then he asked, "And where is my wife now?"

"The policeman nodded towards the stairs." She said she's got some things to sort out, and that I should wait for you until you got home. She said she was sure you wouldn't be long. And she was right," he added encouragingly, "I got here only a minute or two before you."

"Well, if it's all the same to you, constable, I'll just pop upstairs and have a word with her." Reinhardt had suddenly had an ugly premonition of his ex-wife rifling through his belongings. He had never sent her any alimony, and if she was now hard up, which most people he knew were, he would half expect her to come and claim what she saw as hers. In fact, for the first few years of their separation, he had often wondered why she had never come back to claim what she had always said he owed her.

Reinhardt stood up. "I'm just going to check that she's all right."

The policeman stepped in his way. "This won't take a minute, sir, and I think this had better be a private conversation."

"Oh, very well," said Reinhardt, "In that case I'll pour myself a drink. Would you like one?"

The policeman shook his head, "It's very kind of you, but I'm not allowed, not when I'm on duty."

He watched as Reinhardt poured himself a scotch. "The thing is, sir, we've received a complaint from the ARP warden about your failure to follow the blackout regulations. He also said you were extremely rude and abusive when he was only trying to do his duty. It is a serious matter, sir, not to follow the blackout regulations, and does carry a fine of five pounds for the first offence." He paused, as if not sure how to continue. Reinhardt thought he detected a certain amount of sympathy in the young man's face.

"Constable," he said, "I do appreciate your coming to warn me, and I do take the blackout very seriously. It has never happened before, and I assure you it won't happen again. And I was possibly unnecessarily curt with him, and for that I apologise. Are you sure you won't have a drink? No? Well, to be honest, when he knocked I was expecting someone else. You know how it is, I'd had a hell of a day, it was late, I was tired and I did find his attitude somewhat officious. But that's no excuse and I'm sorry. As I say, it won't happen again."

The policeman nodded. "To be frank, sir, we have had a few complaints that that particular warden is, how shall I put it, a little over-enthusiastic in carrying out his duties. Please be more careful in future, sir, and I think we can leave it at that."

Reinhardt smiled and held out his hand, 'Thank you, Constable, er.."

"Stevens, sir." He took Reinhardt's hand.

"I'm grateful for your understanding." Reinhardt opened the door for the policeman and once he'd left, turned as he heard a noise behind him. "See, you can be nice when you want to." Elizabeth was standing at the bottom of the stairs holding a bottle of perfume and a dressing gown. "But I don't think it was very nice the way you just shovelled all my things into a suitcase."

Reinhardt opened his mouth to speak but Elizabeth interrupted him, "And then there was that funny little man waiting when I arrived who said you are planning to move. I told him you are planning no such thing but he was quite adamant. Showed me the piece of paper with your name and address and everything and told me how you'd been in to see him and said you were moving to Kilburn. I said this is my home too and I have absolutely no intention of moving to Kilburn." She raised her eyebrows slightly and looked at Reinhardt quizzically. "Well?" she said, "You were going to say?"

Reinhardt struggled to find the words. He sat down heavily and then, looking up at her, said, "I don't understand. What are you saying?"

She sat down next to him and put her arm through his. "What I'm saying is that I'm moving in with you, if you want me to, that is."

"Well, of course, you've no idea how much I've missed you, but... I mean, what about your husband?"

She moved closer to him, squeezing his arm. "That last day that I was here and you said I ought to go because they had probably released him already and he'd be at home- well, you were right. But he didn't seem to think it odd that I wasn't there when he got back. In fact he hardly spoke to me for the next four or five days, he was completely preoccupied. Then he suddenly said he was going away and he didn't know how long he'd be. He came back about a week later, I don't know where he'd been, but by that time I had decided that I wasn't going to go on living like that any longer. I mean, we could all be dead in a year. All the time I was wondering if his strange behaviour was because he'd found out about us but in the end I decided that he was so completely tied up with his own preoccupations that it was nothing to do with me at all. I was just another piece of furniture in his life. But I knew that the time had come that I had to make a choice, because we couldn't go on as we were. If they were tapping our phone then sooner or later they would know about us and they could tell him, and I couldn't go on living in a cloud of doubt, so anyway, I decided to tell him that I was leaving him. I said that in time I would be wanting a divorce, but there was no rush for that, and that if he wished it he would be able to divorce me on the grounds of desertion. He just nodded. He didn't even ask me if there was anyone else. So I packed a suitcase and went and stayed with my sister for a few days. I told her everything. I didn't come here or phone you because I didn't want you influencing my decision. But also, I had to be clear in my head that I wasn't leaving him for you, but that I was leaving him, full stop. Then I could be with you. It means that I'm entirely responsible for leaving and that you have no part in that. Does that make sense? It also means that if you don't want me to live with you, you are free to say so. And you can, you know." She had been looking at the floor throughout, and now glanced up at him. He put his arm around her and held her tightly.

"God, of course I want you with me. That's why I was going to move. You had left such a mark on the place it that reminded me of you every time I came in, that I didn't want to be here any more if you weren't here. That's why I went to see the estate agent. I thought you were never coming back. In fact, I half thought that you had used the thing about your husband being arrested as the reason for giving me up, that you just couldn't bring yourself to tell me directly."

Elizabeth stared at him. "That's terrible that you should think that. I do think we have to be open and honest with each other. God, I've been living a lie for years in my marriage. We must be honest with each other if it's going to work, don't you agree?"

Reinhardt smiled at her and stroked her hair before answering. It was a novel concept and he wasn't sure that entire honesty wouldn't wreck a relationship as quickly as one based on a certain amount of duplicity. Still, as he had no experience of it he was willing to try.

"Yes," he said, "absolutely."

Chapter Thirty Three

Niedermayer had jumped at the chance when Lotte suggested that he should audition for the new production that the Austrian Centre were to put on at the Laterndl.'

Now he was more nervous, standing at the front of the stage, than he ever had been when he had acted in the last play in front of several hundred people. He felt a surge of relief when the director called out, "We'll take five minutes, Franz, I just want to hear you sing."

Niedermayer walked into the wings. "I can't sing," he whispered to the painter who was sketching a row of houses on a canvas curtain. The painter took his cigarette from his mouth and said, "So? I can't paint. I just pretend I can. Do the same with singing."

"But Erich really can sing, that was fantastic."

"Yes," said the painter, "that's why he'll get the biggest part. If you can't sing but pretend you can, you'll get a small part. If you can't sing and don't pretend, he'll give you the part of Filch."

"Who's Filch?"

The painter smiled. "The one who gets beaten up in the first act."

"Oh, thanks for your help."

The painter put down his brush and looked at Niedermayer searchingly.

"Did you come to the last things we put on- the Jura Soyfer pieces?" Niedermayer shook his head. "No, I've been ill."

"I worked with Jura in Vienna on a couple of his plays in at the ABC. That's where most of his stuff was put on. The thing I learned most from him was that the way to overcome fear is to let it out, to really express it. That way it becomes something like courage. It inspires people. When he was in Dachau, he wrote the Dachaulied. He died the day after he was let out of Buchenwald. He was 26. Don't you think it's a bit self-indulgent worrying whether or not you can sing?"

Niedermayer shrugged and returned to the front of the stage.

"Do you want an accompaniment?" asked the director.

Niedermayer shook his head and began to sing. After a couple of phrases the director shouted, "Good, OK, that's fine, that's enough, thank you. Right, I'm giving you the part of Filch- there's some singing in the part but we'll worry about that later."

Niedermayer turned to face the painter who was smiling broadly. He didn't know whether to feel hurt, or glad that he's got a reasonable part. The cast was beginning to find its way back onto the stage. An assistant was handing out well-used copies of 'The Threepenny Opera'. Niedermayer flicked through to see how much he'd have to learn.

"I want to read through the first act this morning," the director was saying, so if you're not in that, I don't need you till this afternoon. See you at two." No one left, and he went on, "Then clear the stage. We need Peachum, Filch and the two heavies. We won't do the opening song, but go straight to where Filch is captured and brought to the shop. Franz, you've been caught pickpocketing on Peachum's patch. In the eyes of the criminals, that's a crime, so in this scene you're going to be taught a lesson, trained to pickpocket properly and for the privilege you'll pay Peachum fifty per cent of your takings. Everybody got the place? Good, then let's begin, and I want to be able to hear you at the back of the theatre."

At the end of the reading Niedermayer felt quite daunted by how much he was going to have to learn. He was marking the passages when the painter came over. "I was working on Bauer's last production of this at the Kleinkunstbuhne" he said. "It was great, especially your entrance. He had the heavies throw Filch right across the stage so that he landed at Peachum's feet. They had to rehearse it for ages till it came out right. The trick is learning how to fall without hurting yourself." He smiled, "Of course, he might decide to do it differently this time."

"I hope so," said Niedermayer, "but thanks for the warning."

He took the bus back from Hampstead to Paddington, feeling buoyed at the prospect of having something constructive to look forward to. He'd get some lunch and then go to the reading room to start to learn his lines. Lotte grabbed him by the arm as he was about to join the queue. "Franz, there are two men who want to speak to you," she whispered, "They're waiting in the office."

"Who are they?"

Lotte shook her head, "I'm not sure. They could be from the police or... I really don't know. But they've been waiting a while. They did say I could interpret for you if you want me to."

She led the way to the office, a cramped room with a desk far too large for the space, three chairs, a filing cabinet and a shelf full of directories and files. A man in a double- breasted suit was sitting behind the desk scrutinising a document in a file. He didn't look up when they came in. His colleague was standing in the corner by the window and gave a brief nod when Niedermayer looked at him. The man at the desk continued to read, broke off only to examine the forefinger with which he had been scratching the inside of his ear, wipe it with his thumb and then he closed the file thoughtfully. Niedermayer felt a rising panic. How many times had he suffered this kind of experience in Austria before the war started? The summons, the lack of explanation, the interrogation that started with a long period of silence as if he weren't important enough to be even acknowledged, the pretence at friendliness which was somehow worse than being confronted, and worst of all, not having any idea what he was supposed to have done wrong. He stared at the seated man. He hated the way he stroked his moustache as he read, the way his eyebrows furrowed and his nodding, as if he had suddenly understood something that he was not going to reveal until he had made Niedermayer as uncomfortable as possible. Eventually the man looked up and pointed towards the empty chair. "Sit down, please." Niedermayer glanced at Lotte who nodded and pushed the chair behind him. "I'll stand," she said, "I'll be more comfortable standing." She moved behind the chair and gave Niedermayer a reassuring squeeze on the shoulder. The man noticed the gesture.

"As I understand it, this young lady is going to act as your interpreter, is that correct?" Niedermayer took some seconds to understand the question, and before he could reply, Lotte had answered, "Yes."

"Forgive me, but in that case I need to ascertain the nature of your relationship."

"I'm his teacher, I have a lot of men in my classes, and I translate for a lot of them, why, what are you getting at?" Lotte's voice was angry. Niedermayer felt that this was what the man was trying to do, to antagonise her, and that was dangerous.

The man looked at Niedermayer's shoulder and raised his eyebrows, "And are you as close to all your students?"

Lotte stiffened and folded her arms. "I don't understand what you're asking." The man looked at her steadily and then said slowly, "I'm asking about the precise nature of your relationship with Mr Niedermayer. If it is more important than you are telling me, you may be disposed to try and protect him, and this would not only be a mistake but would also get you into trouble. Is that clear?" Lotte could scarcely contain her fury.

"I have been his teacher, along with fourteen other students since last October. I have been trying to help him find the whereabouts of his wife and daughter, along with the help of Mrs Rathbone and I've translated for him, as I have for most of the men here. That is the nature of our relationship."

The man smiled thinly, "Ah, the redoubtable Mrs Rathbone," and wrote a note in his book. Then he put out his hand and said to Niedermayer, "Your papers." Niedermayer passed them across the table. The man copied the information from the permit and then asked, "Where were you this morning?"

"At the theatre," said Niedermayer.

"And where is that?"

"In Hampstead."

The man looked up to his colleague who passed him a map. He checked the distance from Paddington to Hampstead with dividers and nodded. "Just under four miles. And what were you doing there?" Lotte said, "He was auditioning for a part in a play."

"And did he get it?"

Niedermayer understood, "Yes, I am English thief. I steal money from men's pockets."

The man smiled, "You know that under the terms of your category B that you are not allowed to undertake any type of work, either voluntary or paid."

Lotte didn't bother to translate but said simply, "Acting in a play isn't working. If you decide it is, then you'd have to close the Austrian Centre. Nearly all the men are involved in music or acting or giving lectures or teaching. What else are they supposed to do with their time if they're not allowed to work?"

The man listened patiently and then said to Niedermayer, "In your file, it says that you are a socialist. Is that correct?"

"I am a socialist, yes." Niedermayer was at a loss to understand why he was being asked the question.

"And how do you feel about your country, Austria?"

"I love my country, but it is very bad there."

"So, if you love your country, why did you leave, why didn't you stay and fight?"

Lotte said angrily, "Because he would probably have been killed. He would definitely have been sent to a concentration camp, probably Dachau which is not far from the border."

The man ignored this and leaned forward. "You see, we think you are indeed a nationalist and a socialist, in other words, a national socialist, that is, a Nazi."

Niedermayer felt the threat in the voice but was having trouble making sense of them. Lotte laughed bitterly. "You're mad, "she said, "He's a Jew. He lost his job when Austria was invaded because he was a Jew, and now you're saying what? That he's a spy?"

The man reached down into his briefcase and took out a letter which he passed to Niedermayer. "This is addressed to you, isn't it?"

He recognised the handwriting on the envelope as Ilse's. Inside there was another envelope, addressed to her in Switzerland in a hand that he didn't recognise. The writing was small and neat and the letter was brief. It simply said that they were very concerned that they had received no news, would Franz write as soon as possible and tell them what they needed to know as the situation was becoming increasingly difficult. It should be much easier now that he could write to them addressing his letters to Geneva and they would then be sent on to Augsburg. The letter was simply signed 'Klaus'.

The man leant back in his chair and put his fingertips together, "So what exactly is it that Klaus needs to know from you, what have you promised him?"

Lotte was reading the letter and asked, "Who is Klaus, Franz? Do you know?"

"Of course," Niedermayer turned towards her, "He's my father-in-law."

"They want to know what information you promised to send him," Lotte translated.

Niedermayer shook his head, "I don't understand. All I said was that I would let them know where we were. I haven't seen him for over two years. I don't know what he can mean, unless..."

The man leant forward, "Yes?" He looked up at Lotte who translated.

"I left Austria because it was too dangerous, and being a Jew I had no choice. I was interviewed twice by the Gestapo and it was the second one that made me realise I had to go and we all went to Prague which is where I left Ilse. But I told them who my parents were and Ilse's parents too. The Gestapo obviously know that I'm in England, after all, I was given an exit visa, and they think I'll send my in-laws information to protect them from being threatened or worse by the Gestapo. What can I do?"

Lotte translated and added, "What can he do? He doesn't know anything. Anyway, if he was a spy, don't you think he would at least have mastered the language. His father-in-law is desperate. He's an old man who is being told to get his son-in-law to send information about I don't know what, and it's obviously an impossible situation for them both? Can't you see that?"

The man nodded and looked at his colleague. Then he scratched the back of his head and grimaced. "There are thousands of aliens here," he said, "and most of them have got close family in Austria or Germany. Of course they're going to want to protect their loved ones at home, so of course they'll send back important information if they can protect them from the SS or whoever.."

"Sure," said Lotte, "but first of all they have to have access to information. If this man," she put her hand defiantly on Niedermayer's shoulder," isn't allowed even a map or a radio and can't go more than five miles from his flat, how do you think he's going to get information that isn't readily available to the Germans anyway?"

"Networks," said the man, "there are cells that we are only just beginning to penetrate."

Lotte sighed, "But he doesn't know anybody, I can vouch for that."

The two men conferred briefly in whispers and then the first one said, "All right, that'll be all for now, but we'll be back."

Chapter Thirty Four

Weiss was lying on his bed reading when Busch returned from the lecture he'd been attending in the dining room. Swanwick suited Busch. The men were much more disciplined than they had been at Seaton. True, there were Jews here as well, but they kept out of the way and it was clear that the camp commander's sympathies was really with the true Germans. Also he was learning things that he had never really thought about before, like tonight. The lecturer had been a professor of Biology and had called his talk 'Germany and England- the Aryan alliance.' It had completely changed Busch's views of the English who he now felt were not so much the enemy as simply muddle- headed. If they could only see sense, then there would be no need for war; Germany and Britain could between them rule the world, which is actually what nature wanted. He wanted to explain his new understanding to Weiss who was obviously completely absorbed in his book.

"What are you reading?" asked Busch.

Weiss looked at the cover. "It's called 'Cause for Alarm'. It's by an English writer, Eric Ambler."

"Is it easy for you to be able to read English then?"

"It is when I'm not being interrupted," said Weiss.

Busch nodded, "Will you teach me English? I really want to learn."

Weiss threw his book down on the bed in mock despair. "What are you talking about? You've always refused to learn one word and were really rude about the men who are making an effort to talk to the guards in English. I even seem to remember you calling me a traitor for talking to the doctor in English. What's changed your mind?"

"Professor Senk's lecture tonight. It made so much sense. I mean, I always knew the Führer was right but I didn't know why. Now that I understand that we are the same racial type as the British and that we are natural allies we need to work together to establish a new world order. The professor is sure it's going to happen but the politicians who are not scientists are stopping it out of ignorance."

"I see," said Weiss, "and how does the professor know all this?"

"Well, he came to England last year to give a series of lectures for the British Eugenics Society and he said that they were very well received, in fact in some cases even better than at home. For example he said some of his views on sterilization didn't go down too well at home, but when he said here that it is ridiculous to allow the insane and the stupid, anti-socials and epileptics to breed, everyone agreed with him. In the same way British scientists have come to exactly the same conclusion as him. I made a note. Sir Julian Huxley, yes, he said every defective is a burden that the state has to feed and clothe and the trouble is that they are dragging down the whole country. The Führer has the courage to recognise this and to put into place policies of racial purity. The British know they have a problem but don't yet have the courage to do anything about it. That's right isn't it? I mean, he is right."

Weiss stroked his chin thoughtfully and asked, "Did the professor say why we have the courage and the British don't?"

"Yes," said Busch eagerly, "because we have one people, one country and one leader, so we all agree, but here they have a democracy, like we had under the Weimar republic and it's chaos. There's no one to make the decisions that have to be made. Also the British have been running their Empire for centuries and their best young men, the educated ones who are the pure Aryans have been working abroad so they've dissipated their strength across the globe and often been contaminated by inferior races. He says both us and the English lost a whole generation in the last war, but whereas we put proper policies in place to strengthen the race with our marriage laws, the English couldn't do that, so they've continued to decline whereas we've gone from strength to strength. Women at home know their place. Good Aryan marriages lead to having lots of children, girls who will grow up to be good mothers and have lots of children of their own and boys who will grow up to be soldiers and fight for the Fatherland. It all makes sense. It's why we've got to have England as an ally so that between us we can rule first Europe and then the rest of the world."

Weiss laughed and shook his head. "Why are you laughing?" asked Busch.

"Because," said Weiss, suddenly serious again," Women are not cows to have as many calves as they can before they're worn out. We had a neighbour whose husband persuaded her to go for a bronze medal, you know, have a fourth child so that he didn't have to get a job because they'd get enough benefit to feed his drinking habit, and then he wanted a silver medal, six children, and then the doctor told her it would be dangerous for her to have any more, but her husband said she had to have child number eight so he could show off their gold medal and then he wanted the tenth child to have the Führer as the godfather and they could call the child 'Adolf'. The mayor of our town presented them with the medal. They were model citizens who were showing the rest of the community the perfect example, except that when they applied for Winter Aid, they were told that they weren't eligible. The mother died when the youngest child was eighteen months old, worn out and the children were completely neglected. I know all this because my mother used to go round and take them food. Do you really think those children were going to grow up and be good citizens for the Fatherland?"

"One example doesn't show that the whole idea is wrong," protested Busch, "Lots of women have big families, they always have."

Weiss picked up his book and then put it down again. "Maybe, but I'd suggest that the majority of those families are Catholic. I don't imagine that Catholic families are much interested in bronze medals or silver medals or even gold medals. And if they do have a tenth child, I don't suppose they're much interested in the fact that they are entitled to call him, or her, 'Adolf'."

Busch clenched his fists in frustration. " I don't see why not. There's no higher honour than to serve your country."

"There is, though," said Weiss. "To serve your God."

Busch snorted dismissively, "This is the age of science. That's all just religious mumbo-jumbo and superstition, can't you see that?"

Weiss picked up his book again and turned to the passage he'd been reading, but he was too angry to concentrate. He looked up at Busch and said, "Look, all I'm saying is that you can't be a good Catholic and a good Nazi. That's why the Catholic Church keeps protesting at the way it is treated by the government in

Germany."

Busch laughed scornfully, "No, it doesn't like the fact that people are beginning to understand that they've been living under a lot of superstitious lies and are leaving the church because they can now see reason and are free of that tyranny."

Weiss shook his head. "Do you still want me to teach you English?" he asked.

"Yes, of course."

"OK, here's your first word." He smiled. "Bollocks," he said.

Busch looked confused, "What does that mean?"

"Eier," said Weiss.

Busch stood up, scarcely able to contain his anger, and then he laughed, "Oh, I get it, you're a Catholic. You're one of those people still living in the Dark Ages who believes all sorts of nonsense just because some priest tells you it's true. And I always thought you were educated."

"No," said Weiss, suddenly looking tired, "I'm not. I don't even know if I'm a Christian. But as far as I'm concerned the people who live in the Dark Ages are the ones who are so certain that they are right that they are prepared to go to war and kill for their beliefs. And I think what you call science is just another kind of religion, intolerant of anything that it doesn't agree with."

"You just won't see, will you," said Busch. "How can reason be a religion? It's obvious that the strongest are the fittest to rule. That's a fact of nature. The race that is strongest will rule. It's no good arguing with you, you'll see soon enough. And when we defeat England, I just hope for your sake that you have the sense to see reason."

Chapter Thirty Five

It was the last weekend in March. Franco had grown increasingly worried about what would happen when Italy joined the war. In his mind it was now definitely a question not of 'if', but 'when'. And although the English waiters at the Savoy had tried to reassure him that nothing would change, that he and his family would be perfectly safe, his concerns were shared by the other Italian waiters. Between serving customers they spoke in whispers. Some felt that when it came to it, the British government would not hesitate to put them all on a ship and pile them off to Italy. Others were of Paolo's opinion that they would be interned away from their families who would have no chance of surviving without them. Sometimes Franco reassured himself with the thought that because the head waiter was Italian and had worked in the Savoy for years, the rest of them would also be protected, but the thought of being sent back to Italy kept him awake at night. He didn't dare to discuss it with Giovanna - she would cry and ask what would become of them, and to that he had absolutely no answer.

It was on the Sunday morning that Eugenio knocked on the door of their flat and said he had made a decision. He was dressed in old overalls and was carrying a large leather bag.

"I've been thinking," he said, striding into the kitchen and putting the bag on the table, "There's only one thing for it. We've got to show that we're on the side of the British."

"What are you talking about?" Franco rubbed his eyes. It was early and he had only just got up, having been on the late shift the previous night.

"If we show the British that we are on their side, then we'll be safe, they'll ignore us and we'll be able to get on with our lives." Eugenio sat down heavily. "Let's get some coffee and I'll explain."

Giovanna appeared in her dressing gown. "What are you doing here so early on a Sunday?" she asked brusquely. Franco, worried about what his brother was about to say, picked up the kettle and put it on the hob.

"You go back to bed," he said to his wife, "I'll make some coffee and bring it through to you."

She ignored him and sat facing Eugenio. "What's up? What is it?"

Franco hovered uncomfortably by the kettle while Eugenio started to explain. "Everybody knows that Mussolini is soon going to join Hitler and declare war on England..."

Giovanna's hand shot to her mouth and she burst into tears. Franco rushed to console her. "We don't know that," he whispered, looking furiously at his brother, "We don't know that at all, and sometimes I can't believe how stupid you can be, Eugenio."

"What?" Eugenio held up his hands, "Well it's obvious isn't it. But I've got a solution. I've thought of a way that will make everything all right. Do you want to hear it or not?"

"No," said Franco emphatically, "We don't," and then he added as an after-thought, "unless it involves you going to Rome personally and explaining to II Duce that going to war with Britain would be a stupid idea, and then you staying in Rome to make sure he doesn't." He squeezed Giovanna's shoulder. She was staring wide-eyed in terror at Eugenio who smiled benignly.

"Very funny," he said, "but I'm serious. I'm going to change the name of my restaurant. I'm going to give it an English name- I haven't decided what to yet, that's why I came to get your advice."

"Why do you want to do that?" asked Giovanna, "What's the point. Everybody knows you're Italian, that's why they come to you."

Eugenio nodded. "I don't mean we'd start serving fish and chips. I mean if we change it to a really English name people will know that we are on the side of the English, that's all."

Franco thought for a second. "Well, there's no harm in it and it can't make things any worse. What do you want to call it?"

"Well, I thought something like 'The Great British Pizza Parlour' but that's too long. And maybe 'pizza' shouldn't be in the name.

Francesca came in. "Why's everyone up so early?" she asked, "What's happened?"

"I'm trying to think of a new name that sounds English for the restaurant," said Eugenio. "Look, I've bought a load of paint. I'm going to have a new name across the top and I'll do it all in red, white and blue. I just need a really English sounding name. Any ideas?"

Francesca frowned. "You're mad," she said, "I'm going back to bed." She stopped in the doorway, "What about 'Eugenio's Eatery'?" she said before closing her door.

"Sounds too Italian," said Eugenio, "unless I change my name as well. I could do that, I suppose, just for professional purposes. Something like 'Ricardo's British Restaurant.' It's got to have 'British' in the name."

"But not Ricardo," objected Franco, "that's Italian. You need an English name like Roger, or something like that."

"Va bene," said Eugenio excitedly, "That's it, 'Roger's British Restaurant'. Let's go and do it now. It won't take long. If you'll come and help me it'll be finished by lunch- time and when we get back I'll cook everyone a big lasagne. What do you say?"

Giovanna shook her head. "It's Franco's day off and I've got jobs for him here. The tap in the bathroom needs mending and I want him to see to the draught in the bedroom."

"OK," said Eugenio, "if you'll help me this morning, I'll help you this afternoon. And you can come as well, Giovanna. We need to take down the curtains in the window of the restaurant. It looks much too Italian, and I'll give them to you. They're in good condition, they just need a wash." He looked imploringly from Franco to Giovanna who eventually shrugged in agreement.

They put on their coats and hats and left the flat. At the bottom of the road the three of them caught the bus to Soho. On a Sunday morning the city looked drabber than ever. A cold fog had wrapped itself around the city; sandbags littered the pavements. The city was almost deserted. Eugenio opened the door of his restaurant. "I've got some ladders in the back. We'll just paint over the name. Giovanna, are you all right to stand on a table to get the curtains down."

He disappeared and came back with brushes and a ladder. Franco said, "We need to rub it all down first, this is going to take a long time. We can't possibly get it all done in one morning." Eugenio clicked his tongue.

"We don't have time, and anyway, I haven't got any sandpaper. Just paint over the top of it."

Franco protested that the new paint wouldn't grip but Eugenio tutted impatiently. "It will, it'll be fine, here, let me do it." He climbed up the ladder and began to daub white paint over the old. "Here," he said, pointing to the corners, we'll paint a union jack and you just write the new name across the middle. I'll paint the sill red and the edges blue. But we need to do it quickly."

"Well at least dry the wood down, have you got a cloth?" asked Franco. "It won't have a chance if it's all wet."

Eugenio disappeared into the restaurant and came out with a couple of table-cloths. He rubbed at the window frames and then suddenly stopped when he saw Giovanna watching him from inside the restaurant.

"Stand on a table to get the curtains down," he shouted, "Giovanna, hurry."

"She can't," said Franco, "She can't stand heights and she might fall. You do it and I'll finish drying the frames."

With a gesture of impatience, Eugenio stormed into the shop. "OK, I'll do it, Giovanna you go and make some coffee." He almost ripped the curtains from their rails and tossed them onto a table. Giovanna went outside to protest to Franco. "Are you going to let him speak to me like that?" she said. "If he's going to shout at me I'm going home. I won't put up with it."

Franco put his arm round his wife. "It's not you," he said soothingly, "he's frightened. I don't think there's any need to be but he is. If we do this for him he'll calm down and we'll get some peace again. It's best to go along with it. Why don't you go and make some coffee."

Muttering angrily under her breath Giovanna went back inside while Franco climbed the ladders and began to paint. They worked for a couple of hours with a quick break for coffee. Eugenio grumbled as he splashed paint on to the window pane and periodically berated Franco for working too slowly, but by lunch time the lettering was finished.

Franco stood back and looked at it critically. "It's not even in the middle," he said, "It's all too much on the left. It looks terrible with that big gap. Where Eugenio had painted a union jack the blue paint had run down the frame. He tried to wipe it off with a serviette but had only succeeded in smearing it, and painting over it with white had made it even worse. He viewed their handiwork from across the road and nodded. "It's not very good," he agreed, "but it'll have to do."

"Maybe we ought to write on the window, 'We can't paint, but we can cook" Eugenio looked at his brother to see if he was joking, decided he wasn't and said, "No, we'll leave it as it is. It's fine."

"We can't leave it with all the writing on the left hand side," said Franco, "It looks terrible."

"Then what do you suggest? It's not my fault if you did the writing too small. But people can still read it, it'll have to do."

"We'll add something. I know." Franco climbed the ladder again and carefully painted 'FINE DINNING'.

Then he climbed down and stood back to survey his work. "Good," agreed Eugenio. "Come on, let's go. I'll cook you lunch."

Chapter Thirty Six

It had been a very long day. Maurice and Joe were sitting in the mess complaining quietly at having had to march to Oadby and then come all the way back only to have to carry on digging the trench they'd been working on for the last fortnight. Maurice was watching Davies being served at the hatch. He'd written home about Davies, about his exploits in India, how he'd been asleep in his tent when he was attacked by a leopard and how he'd killed it with only a clasp knife. How he'd stopped an Indian princess from throwing herself on her husband's funeral fire and how they'd been chased by the entire village till, luckily for them, they'd found a temple where there were masks of demons hanging on the walls. They put them on and when it was getting dark rushed out and terrified the villagers. Then he had taken her back to his quarters which was actually a shack in the forest and he had got his batman who spoke the lingo to marry them and then he stood guard outside while his new wife performed a special nuptial rite on him that he was really too shy to talk about; just say that as special nuptial marriage rites go, it was the most special, and he should know, being something of an expert. Maurice hadn't liked to press him on what was involved, but he had spent many hours trying to imagine and deciding in the end that after the war he would join the regular army and get a posting to India. But he had wondered how Davies and the princess had communicated; presumably the princess didn't speak English so Davies must be able to speak whatever language they speak in India. He was mulling over these thoughts again when Davies and Clements sat opposite them. Maurice was flattered by the attention. Davies had never addressed a word to him directly, but always seemed to have a small crowd around him.

"All right boys?" he asked. He looked down at his plate, "Look at this, all jippo and no meat. An army's supposed to march on its stomach. I ask you. Tell you what though, when we get to France the grub'll be great."

Maurice started, "You think we're going to France?" Davies looked surprised and turned to Clement.

"He doesn't know. Perhaps I shouldn't have said anything." He leaned forward confidentially. "This is the griffin, yes ?"

Maurice wasn't always quite sure he understood what Davies was talking about so he gave a little nod to see if this was the right response and then shook his head when he decided it probably wasn't.

"Well don't look so fucking miserable about it," said Davies, "It's great news nesspa."

"Yeah, great nesspa," agreed Maurice.

"Eh," shouted Davies delightedly, "the boy parleys the lingo." He leant forward again and whispered, "You'll be all right, know what I mean. You speak French and you're home and dry. See, to French women we're very, how shall I put it, exotic and they don't speak English, so when you're exotic and can speak to them in their own language, they just love it. And they like to show their appreciation, I can tell you. So it's great you can talk French 'cos you'll have a great time."

A small crowd of soldiers had gathered round the table to listen. "So where did you learn French then?" Davies went on.

"Oh, you know, here and there," said Maurice, felling increasingly uncomfortable.

"Yeah? I learned it when I was posted to Normandy. Of course that'd be before your number was dry. I was about your age. Anyway it was a little village and this girl came and offered me some calvados, she called it. Nearly took my head off. I was working on guard duty every day and every day she'd come and offer me a drink and we got talking and then one day she said she wanted me to go back home with her because she'd cooked me a meal. So when I got there and I met her parents I wondered how they'd got such a beautiful daughter 'cos honest to god they were both pug ugly, but she was a real looker with raven black hair down over her shoulders. The old woman sat me down and served the biggest plate of frogs' legs and chips you can imagine and the old man was pouring the wine like it had gone out of fashion. And when I'd finished I said "Trez beans bombardier fritz" like you would, and I didn't want the old man to feel left out so I said "Trez beans vino." Well, the old man kissed me on both cheeks and the old woman cried and they said they wanted me to marry their daughter, just like that. "Tout sweet," they said, and I said, "The touter the sweeter." We had boko fun, me and Marie was her name. All 'cos I spoke French."

"Well, I'm not absolutely fluent," confessed Maurice.

"San Fairy Ann," said Davies dismissively, "You'll get the hang of it soon enough, I mean you've got the basics already, that's all that counts." He pushed the bench back and gave Maurice a friendly tap on the cheek before standing up. "Alley, alley, my son, don't put yourself down, napoo."

He walked away and the group of men followed him laughing. When they were all out of earshot Joe said, "What the fuck was he talking about?"

"French," said Maurice. "He was talking French. He's very good."

Joe said slowly, "You don't think that maybe he was winding you up, then?"

"No," said Maurice, "that was real French all right, otherwise how could the Frenchies have understood him. Anyway, I know enough to know real French when I hear it."

"Maybe," said Joe, "but that stuff about the Indian princess, I remember reading a book where a bloke saved a princess from throwing herself on a fire and everyone chased after him. It's a bit of a coincidence don't you think?"

"Yeah?" Maurice began to have an unpleasant sensation, "So who wrote this book?"

"We read it at school. A bloke has a bet that he can go right round the world in eighty days. That's what it's called and the bloke who wrote it was called Jules Verne. A French geezer."

"Well, there you are then," said Maurice, triumphantly and feeling suddenly relieved, "He must have got the story from Davies and put it in his book."

The following morning after parade, Maurice excused himself from playing football. He'd got two hours off and had things to do. Joe caught up with him as he was crossing the parade ground.

"Where are you off to, Mo?"

"Can't stand being cooped up in the barracks all day. Thought I'd go for a walk," he said, quickening his step.

"I'll come with you, didn't fancy playing much myself today. Where are we going?"

"Just thought I'd go into town and have a look round," said Maurice, wondering how he could either dissuade Joe or deter him from coming altogether, "Pretty boring really."

"We could go and have a couple of pints, we don't have to be back till one. Or we could catch a matinee."

"No, I'm skint. You go if you want, I don't fancy it anyway." He was walking as fast as he could towards the town centre.

Joe kept giving him sidelong glances, and eventually said, "Come on, spit it out, what's eating you?"

"No, nothing. Look, I didn't ask you to come. If you want to have a pint, go in. They were now standing outside the library and Maurice realised that he wasn't going to get rid of Joe. He looked up in surprise. "Oh, think I might just pop in here for a few minutes, catch you later."

Jo smiled, "No, that's OK. I like books, I'll help you find what you're looking for."

The assistant explained that he would need identity and that he could take out four books. "Can you tell me where the detective books are?" He wandered along the shelves and eventually took three at random. Then he saw what he was looking for. "Oh, Beginner's French" said Joe, taking it from his hand.

"Maurice blushed. "Mention this to a soul and I'll fucking swing for you," he said.

Chapter Thirty Seven

Esther Hart's Diary

Monday 1st April 1940

Terribly boring weekend. Douglas brought a whole pile of work home and sat doing it at the dining room table all day Saturday and Sunday and hardly said a word and just grunted when I asked him if he wanted anything. The only time he went out was to get the Sunday papers, and they were typically depressing. Big headlines in the 'Sunday Dispatch' about how the Home Office tribunals were adopting a 'kid-glove' policy towards the enemy aliens. It seems, though I find it hard to believe, that servant girls in rural areas have been reporting that German girls have been spending time around our airfields and sending information back to Germany about the movement of aircraft. I seem to remember the same paper saying how wonderful Hitler was before the war because he was protecting the West from Communism. Had a quick look at a memo that Douglas was writing while he was out which said how concerned he was at the popular press whipping up anti-alien feelings. Said to Douglas before he went off to work this morning that we really ought to have Barbara and Herbert round for a meal. He sighed and said, "If we must." I'll try and arrange it for next weekend- can't bear the thought of another like the one we've just had.

Tuesday 2nd April

'Daily Mail' headline today: "Aliens, Action at last." The Home Office has set up new committees which are to be much more stringent than the old ones, apparently. Sir John Anderson has told them to review cases of aliens, and when in doubt to restrict their freedoms or to intern them. I really wonder if the journalists who write these things can ever have visited places like the Austrian Centre. The majority of refugees, at least those from Germany and Austria are Jews who have lost everything, often been in concentration camps, speak little or no English and have made their way here completely alone. Those journalists must know this.

How can they possibly think these people could be spies. But they claim that 'the great British public' is very perturbed at all these aliens walking about free. I've never heard a single person express anything but sympathy for the aliens. Perhaps I just don't move in the right circles, but I doubt it's that. Rather it's the Kemsley and Rothermere papers, the very ones that were so pro-Hitler before the war, that are publishing this stuff. It makes me absolutely furious.

Phoned Barbara and invited them over for Saturday night and asked her what she thought about what the paper were saying. She agreed that 'The Mail 'is an absolute rag. I didn't see it at the time, but apparently they conducted a big campaign last month that had her hopping mad. One of Herbert's jobs is to monitor public opinion on the question of the aliens. They ran a piece at the beginning of March saying how millions of relatives of the men in the fighting forces are worried about the ease with which refugees can get into the country, and the article finished, "It's not good enough, Sir John." Then they claimed to have a massive postbag in support of their campaign, and published one letter saying that all the Germans should be put in a camp and have Poles guard them. None of the Germans would escape with their lives. She said one of the best ones was from 'Brigadier Eastbourne' who wrote in saying that all aliens should be forced to wear an armband showing their country of origin. No doubt he picked the idea up from the newsreels that show German Jews having to wear the Star of David. Anyway, she's been helping Herbert with his work by keeping a scrap- book of press cuttings and she's going to bring it over on Saturday, so that'll make for an interesting evening.

Suggested we might go to the Austrian Centre together and so it's agreed that we'll go on Thursday. She doesn't seem to be particularly concerned for the refugees because she says there are a lot of good people in Parliament like Victor Cazalet and Harold Nicolson who think that the right wing press is completely disgusting and aren't afraid to say so. But I'm worried because a lot more people read the 'Mail' than read 'The Spectator.'

Now the civilian population in Italy has been mobilised, so no doubt the press will start suggesting that we lock up all the Italians as well if ever it looks as if

Mussolini will join the war. It's all quite sickening.

Wednesday 3rd April

There's been a big ministerial reshuffle with Mr Churchill being the new Chairman for Ministerial Defence and Lord Woolton Minister for Food.

Last night the Luftwaffe made another attack on Scapa Flow. Went into town and I've never seen people looking so gloomy. You can overhear snatches of whispered conversation, mostly along the lines of how helpless people feel and why doesn't the government act. You also see a lot more men with sandwich boards proclaiming the end of the world and there was one standing on a soap box on the corner of Oxford Street shouting that we have to start bombing Berlin before the Germans start bombing us. I couldn't wait to get home.

Thursday 4th April

Barbara came round for coffee (ersatz, not dandelion) and then we went on to Paddington. She decided to drive which was an unnerving experience as she always looks at you intently when she's talking, and so keeps taking her eyes off the road. I was transfixed especially as she turns her whole body towards you as she speaks which means that we kept lurching to the left. I was quite flustered by the time we got to Westbourne Terrace and dreading the journey home. We met Lotte who said a lot of the men, including Herr Niedermayer were at the theatre in Hampstead rehearsing for the next production. She seemed very distracted until Barbara spoke to her in German, when she suddenly burst into tears. I didn't really understand what was being said, so went to find someone to make some tea for them both. By the time I got back she had calmed down a lot. Barbara explained that Lotte's flatmate had been arrested early that morning. She had been given a 'B' at an early tribunal which hadn't really been a problem because she was working as a translator for the BBC. The police said they'd most likely be taking her to Holloway. Lotte had immediately phoned the BBC and eventually got through to her friend's boss who said there had obviously been a mistake and they would get straight on to it. I wondered why she should have been given a 'B' and

Lotte said that Mitzi's (her friend's name) father was quite a well-known journalist who had been very critical of the Nazi regime. He'd been arrested shortly after Lotte and Mitzi came to England, and at her tribunal Mitzi had said that she was very concerned for her parents as her father was in gaol, though she didn't know where. The chairman seemed to be of the view that if he was in gaol he must be some kind of criminal- people don't get locked up for nothing, and so he was giving Mitzi a 'B'.

In the afternoon we went for a walk across St James's Park. It was the most glorious spring day, with the flowers in the park, hundreds of people out enjoying the weather and each other. Barbara said it was quite strange, like hearing a burst of birdsong in the middle of the night.

Sunday 7th April

Douglas has gone to work! The poor man, last night I almost felt sorry for him, though the feeling rapidly wore off this morning when the last thing he said to me before he went out was that he thought I should choose my friends more carefully, and that "That Mrs Radcliffe is a bad influence." The trouble was that Herbert being Douglas's boss means that Douglas doesn't feel he can disagree openly with him. He was obviously terribly uncomfortable when Herbert said he thought we would soon get a change of Prime Minister, "and not before time." Chamberlain had made a speech to his party saying that whereas we were not prepared for war when it broke out, he was now "ten times confident of victory," since we'd "made good the weaknesses in the armed forces" and he added that Hitler had "missed the bus." This didn't go down well with some members of his own party, especially the younger Tory MPs. As a big supporter of Mr Chamberlain, Douglas couldn't remain quiet and so just said that the last time the Prime Minister made a major speech he also announced the bombing of Sylt, which took the wind out of the sails of his critics. He thought that the Prime Minister was sure to have something up his sleeve. Barbara's suppressed guffaw created a frosty atmosphere which she tried to get around by producing her scrap-book. This only made matters worse because I hadn't told Douglas that we'd been to the Austrian Centre and met Lotte. But Herbert said he'd been onto the police at Islington and they'd confirmed that Mitzi had been taken to Holloway. Then he said that he'd heard that those women refugees who had been interned were having a difficult time with the English prisoners who were in prison for having committed crimes and it was good of Barbara and me to have agreed to try and get to the bottom of what had happened. So the meal was a bit of a disaster, though the bottle of wine they brought was delicious. I don't think Douglas approves of women who have Views. I think Herbert is right when he says that as the popular press have nothing much to report about the war they've latched on to the problem of the aliens and are talking it up for all they're worth.

Today's headline in 'The Dispatch': "The Great Aliens Scandal-Our Money for Communist Propaganda. Red Cells formed by Subsidized Refugees." The government has granted £2.5 million to Czech refugees who, it alleges are communists and are distributing leaflets.

Tomorrow I shall phone Barbara and see if we can't go and visit Mitzi in Holloway, which I know will absolutely infuriate Douglas, but that can't be helped. And then I shall write to the 'Sunday Dispatch' and point out in no uncertain terms that their reporter is simply wrong and how dangerous this kind of propaganda is. I don't think I've ever been quite so angry about anything, though how I'll be able to explain it to Douglas if they publish my letter, I don't know. They probably won't even bother to print it.

Haven't heard from the children for ages. Sometimes I wonder if they'll even remember what I look like. I try to console myself that their not writing is a good sign, meaning they are contented where they are, and that makes me feel very sad.

Wednesday 10th April

It's all very confusing, though one thing is clear. The Germans have captured Denmark. The papers seem to be divided into two camps- those who are all gung-ho and sure that we now have all out war and that the Germans will never be able to stand up to the Navy, which may or may not be true. Then there are others who are simply horrified at the terrible loss of life there will be. I sympathise with that, though like, I suspect the majority of people, I don't trust the news that's coming out of the Ministry of Information, such as it is. Mr Churchill gave a speech in Parliament in which he said it's not our fault if neutral countries turn down the help that is offered them, so reading between the lines, it would appear that things are also going badly in Norway.

Later. On the 9 o'clock news they've just said that Britain and France along with the Norwegians have retaken Bergen and Trondheim. Got out my old school atlas to see where these places are.

Thursday 11th April

In the queue at the baker's a crowd of women were surrounding a lady who said her son was in Norway. She obviously was very proud at being the centre of attraction and said that four German destroyers had been sunk, two of them by the cruiser that her son was on. Someone asked her if she'd spoken to him (a complete impossibility) and she said no, but she just felt it must have happened- she could feel it in her bones.

Friday 12th April

Phoned Barbara and have arranged to go to Holloway on Monday. Herbert quite happy about this, Douglas considerably less so. She's heard Harold Nicolson on the radio saying that a friend of his from a neutral country had had a long conversation with Hitler who had said that he wished he could meet an Englishman who had the same intelligence. He would say to him, "Give me Europe and I will give you the rest of the world."

The news is that we haven't taken Bergen and Trondheim at all. From what I can understand, the Germans have huge superiority in the air, and their navy seems to have managed to slip past our ships that were laying mines. Hard facts are impossible to come by.

People are going round in a state of a sort of wide-eyed euphoria, or are completely pessimistic.

The weather is absolutely lovely at the moment and the swallows are back. I stood watching them in the garden this afternoon and thinking that they've flown all the way from Africa, over countries that are preparing for the most terrible war imaginable and the birds are completely oblivious to all the suffering beneath them. This sounds ridiculous I know, but watching them made me forget the war and the low level dread that I've been feeling for days. Then a plane flew over and the feeling came flooding back.

Part of it is no doubt the fact that I've come to dread weekends when Douglas is like some ghastly disapproving shade. I really don't know what to do or to say that will make things better. And I won't give up my friendship with Barbara, although it makes him cross, because at least I can really talk to her.

Chapter Thirty Eight

A large gathering of men were sitting in the reading room of the Austrian Centre discussing the latest edition of 'Der Zeitspiegel', the digest of English newspapers that had been translated into German. Niedermayer and Willi were listening to the conversation as they prepared copies of the paper to be sent out by post.

"See, here it says the British have taken Trondheim and here it says they haven't," said an elderly man, throwing up his arms in despair. "What are we supposed to believe? Who knows what's going on?"

"No one, not even the British government," said another, "but I'll tell you what I think. I think the British wanted to protect the route out to the Atlantic to try and stop Hitler cutting of supplies from America. But Hitler actually wants Norway so he can protect the iron ore from Sweden that he needs. I think the navy was miles away when the German ships arrived. And Hitler's got the Luftwaffe. Norway doesn't stand a chance against him. It'll all be over in a few weeks and then he can turn on Britain because he'll have bases in Norway and Germany."

"What do we know?" said the man sitting next to him angrily. "Today it says they've captured Denmark, and tomorrow they'll deny it. Here, look at this piece. It says there were a thousand RAF planes against six hundred of the Luftwaffe. Do you believe that? I tell you, it's all propaganda and the Germans are a lot better at it than the English. You know, I come from Gleiwitz in Silesia. SS men dressed as civilians pretended to raid the radio station. They got two inmates from Sachsenhausen camp, killed them with injections and put them in the radio station and then got the photographers in. Then they got a prisoner who was a Polish supporter out of the town gaol, gave him an injection, put him in the radio station and shot him dead while he was still unconscious, and they broadcast this as evidence of Polish atrocities. No, the Germans do wicked things and make out it was 'the enemy'. The British do nothing and say nothing. You can't believe anyone any more."

Niedermayer packed up the pile of papers he's been addressing and stood up.

"I can't listen to any more of this," he whispered to Willi, "I'm getting the money from the office to post these off and then I'm going down to the post- office. Do you want to come?"

"Sure," said Willi, and then keen to change the conversation about the war, asked, "How's the play going?"

"I can't really get into the part, I don't know why. Every time I've finished rehearsing I feel really depressed. Bauer's a really good director and I know what he wants me to do, I just can't bring myself to do it. When we did 'Schweik' in January I had no problem, but that character was so different from me. With the part of Filch, I don't know, sometimes I think I'm too close to him. Do you know what I mean?"

He left the question hanging in the air while he went into the office and got the money for the stamps. They went out of the Centre and turned towards the main road.

"So what's this character like that you're afraid is too close to you?"

"Filch?" Well, first of all he's a beggar, and he starts begging on a patch that's run by a criminal gang. They capture him and take him to Peachum, the leader of the gang. They beat him up first. Peachum says he's got to join the gang, train as a pickpocket and hand over fifty per cent of his takings."

"Is that it?" asked Willi

"I only really appear in the first scene, so yes, it's not much of a part, I suppose."

Willi thought for a moment. I don't really understand your problem. What are you saying? You identify with a beggar? Is there something I should know about you that you haven't told me?"

Niedermayer smiled, "No, it's not that."

"What then? That you're a criminal, working for a vicious gangster?"

"No, you don't understand. I said I don't know why he depresses me. No one else has this problem. Let's forget it."

"You feel you're a victim, then, is that it?"

Niedermayer turned angrily towards him, "I said forget it. I don't know why and let's just leave it at that." He quickened his step and shook his head. Willi caught up with him and put a hand on Niedermayer's shoulder. "So that's it. You feel like a victim, you've been beaten up in a way by a gang of criminals led by the biggest criminal in the world who goes round beating everybody up. The only difference is that you're not allowed to join his gang. Do you want to?"

Niedermayer felt his fists clench. "Don't be ridiculous. Look, I don't want to talk about it."

"OK," said Willi, "If you don't mind getting more and more depressed the more rehearsals go on, it's no skin off my nose." He gave Niedermayer a sideways glance as they moved on. After a while Niedermayer slowed and turned to Willi and looked at him searchingly. "Don't you ever feel like a victim?" he asked quietly.

Willi shook his head, "Remind me what happens in the end."

"Well, Peachum is going to have Macheath hanged because Macheath has secretly married his daughter, so Peachum hates him for that. Macheath's in prison, he can't raise the money to bribe his way out but just before he's about to die, the queen sends a letter of pardon, grants him a pension and makes him a lord and gives him a castle. Then there's a song at the end that says criminals shouldn't be treated too badly because life is tough. The ending is really stupid I think."

Willi feigned a look of shock. "What, you a socialist dare criticise the greatest socialist playwright who's ever lived? Has it even occurred to you that maybe you don't get what Brecht is driving at?"

Niedermayer shrugged his shoulders.

Willi went on, "So how does Bauer want you to play the part?"

"He wants me to put more energy into it, to play it less like a... a..." Niedermayer couldn't bring himself to say the word. Willi said it for him. "Like a victim? But you're not a victim. Look, if you were still in Austria we couldn't even be having this conversation. You know as well as I do that Brecht's plays are banned. I couldn't say that Hitler is one of the greatest criminals the world has ever seen, not without getting sent to a camp or something even worse. No, Franz, think about it. You're more like MacHeath, saved from the gallows at the last moment, and given a pension. Think about it."

"Maybe that's why I find the part so hard," said Niedermayer, "I really am a beggar. I'm not even allowed to work for my living. I depend on charity, we all do. You might be able to stand that, but I can't."

Willi laughed, "Oh, stop being so bloody morally superior and just be thankful. OK, so it's hard for all of us. We've been given somewhere to live, clothes, food and we are grateful to the English government for saving us from the Nazis. But it seems to me that it's a good idea to remember what Meister Eckhart says about beggars. I can't remember exactly but it's along the lines that everybody admires the person who gives to a beggar. He gives money and receives honour which is much more important. But the beggar gives his soul, which is more important still."

Niedermayer grunted, feeling that he'd lost the argument, but didn't want to concede the fact.

"Well," he said, changing the subject, it's true that I get beaten up off stage, so that's not real, but when I do appear, Bauer wants my appearance to be as dramatic as possible. It bloody well hurts when I get flung across the stage to Peachum's feet. We've done it about thirty times in rehearsal and it doesn't get any easier. I've got bruises all the way up from my shins to my thighs and a splinter on my hand from the stage floor."

"Good," said Willi, "the way you've been whingeing it serves you right. I suggest you start putting more of yourself into the part and less of the victim, which you are not."

They had reached the post office. Willi waited outside while Niedermayer went in and sent off the copies of the newspapers. He sighed, "I think you're right," he said, "I'll try."

Chapter Thirty Nine

By early April Busch was beginning to get cabin fever. He was feeling keenly the isolation which he had felt at periods throughout his life. The enthusiastic Nazis in the camp were making life difficult for those who wouldn't openly join them in singing Nazi songs, and Busch looked at them with a strong desire to join in, but he had been warned off by Captain Burfeind, whom he still regarded as his superior officer. Also, though he didn't agree with his politics, Weiss was the only person who he felt he could really confide in. They spent hours together walking around the perimeter fence discussing the war, their families and their hopes for the future.

Weiss was teaching him English and he was making slow progress, and he also knew that the Nazis would strongly disapprove if they found out. Some of the guards were sympathetic and he practised his English on them, especially a young soldier called Jones who he took to be about the same age as himself.

Occasionally he got news of the outside world, although newspapers were banned, but there was the short wave radio and he celebrated when he heard that German troops had taken Denmark with a minimum of resistance. "Twelve hours it took to overrun the whole country," he announced triumphantly to Weiss, "Twelve hours, can you imagine. Next it'll be Norway and then Sweden and then England. We'll be out by the end of next month." "All the more reason not to get mixed up with the Nazis then," said Weiss. Busch looked at him, confused. "Why?"

They were looking through the fence at the lake and beyond at the hills of the Peak district. Weiss nodded towards the guard's tower fifty yards away.

"How do you think they'll come?" he asked.

"I don't know, I suppose the Luftwaffe will come first and when they've taken out the RAF then they'll bring over the army."

"So how are we going to be released?"

Busch knew Weiss well enough by now to know that a trap was being laid for him. He thought carefully before replying. "They'll drop parachutists, probably at night, right into the camp, and then we'll set on the guards and get out. It's obvious when you think about it."

"So, OK, if you were the English camp commander, and you knew that the invasion was about to happen, how would you stop the internees helping the parachutists?"

"Well, I'd separate the ones that were obviously going to help the parachutists from the rest."

"Right, and then?"

"You mean if they were actually beginning to drop parachutists into the camp?"

"Yes."

"I'd have them shot, you couldn't do anything else."

"Precisely, so as I say, all the more reason not to get mixed up with the Nazis. Except it won't happen like that because I very much doubt that anyone in Germany knows we're here. That's why they keep moving people about." Weiss looked on Busch as a younger brother that needed looking after, though by now he knew him well enough always to change the subject once he had won an argument. "But they must be fairly confident that this camp isn't known about or I think they'd have moved us by now."

"So we just have to wait, do we, and in your opinion when we do invade, we're all going to get shot anyway."

"Who knows?" It was one of Weiss's favourite sayings which never failed to rile Busch, "but in the meantime, I think you need a project."

"What kind of a project can you have in a place like this where there's nothing to do except go to a few lectures, or play chess- you can't do that all the time." "My project is to read all the detective books in the library, "said Weiss, "It keeps me busy and my mind off things."

Busch grimaced, "You know I can't read well enough to do that, in fact, there's nothing I can do that's any use here."

Weiss said, "Look, you made a chess set, you're good with your hands. You're always saying that the happiest time in your life was when you were at sea. Why don't you make a model of your ship, what was she called?"

"The Adolf Woermann." Busch nodded, "She was a great ship. She didn't deserve to go down. It was all because of the bloody Portuguese. They kept us holed up in Lobito when we were on our way home. We worked like slaves to disguise her as a Portuguese ship, what was her name, the Nyassa, and then we made a run for it to try and get to South America, but the Neptune caught up with us and we had to scuttle her- orders from Berlin. One of their sailors got injured trying to close the valves we'd opened, the stupid idiot, but yeah, she was a great ship. I remember being in port at night when I was on duty. It was about thirty degrees and the only sights were the stars, millions and millions of them and the only sounds were the waves lapping on the bows and the strange noises coming from the forest. I knew it was going to be bad but I just couldn't bring myself to believe it because everything was so peaceful. It was as if there was nobody else in the whole world except me and her, because she always seemed to me like a great gentle animal. I've never told this to anyone else, but I couldn't watch when she went down. I had to go below decks because I couldn't let anyone see how upset I was. Except there was a British crewman down there. I thought he was going to shout at me, but he just came over and put his hand on my shoulder for a second and then went up on deck. I'll never forget that gesture. It was as if he knew exactly how I felt."

He turned away and wiped his eyes with his sleeve. Weiss heard voices coming towards them and whispered in Busch's ear, "Müller's coming over to talk to us." Müller and three other members of the ship's company were talking animatedly as they strode along the path towards them, "Have you heard the news? It's brilliant." He was laughing. "The British press was full of how the navy was laying mines along the Norwegian coast. The Norwegians were worried that the British were going to violate their neutrality and were so busy watching what the British were doing that they didn't even see our Navy slip past the British and take Trondheim and Narvik without any resistance at all. And we've got Oslo. The old government has gone and the Führer's put his own man in charge. We've got Norway."

"In order to protect her neutrality," said Weiss.

Müller looked at him quizzically, "Precisely."

"And presumably we'll have to leave an army there to make sure the British don't violate Norway's neutrality at some future date," went on Weiss. "Obviously," said Müller, "What are you getting at?"

"No, nothing. It's just that if I were Norwegian I wonder if I would care whether the occupying army that is there to protect my neutrality was German or British."

Müller frowned, "The British were laying mines in Norwegian waters. They were violating Norwegian neutrality. We had to protect Norway. Anyway, we have to protect our interests, the iron ore shipments from Sweden. What are you, some sort of communist British sympathiser? You need to be really careful what you say in this place, Weiss. You can get yourself in a lot of trouble talking like that."

"Yes, "agreed Weiss, "I already have - the day we got here." He cast his mind back to the beating he took from Wirth's group on the evening after they arrived.

Busch took him by the arm. "Come on, don't start an argument, it's not worth it."

Weiss pulled away, "I'm not. But it's seems to me that kicking out the old government, putting your own supporter in its place and landing troops all over the country is a strange way to protect Norway's neutrality. It's a philosophical point really." He smiled.

Müller jabbed him in the ribs with his forefinger. "That's the only kind of philosophical point that counts these days, so just be glad that you're a German and not Norwegian. I thought Busch was a bit mad, but at least he knows which side he's on."

Busch took Weiss's arm again, "Come on," he said, "Let's leave it. He's right, you know he is. We're at war. We're going to win. Then you can argue about philosophy if you have to." Weiss nodded, "Fine," he said, and shrugged. The two men walked back to their quarters.

Chapter Forty

"I don't know why I bothered," sighed Eugenio, slumping down next to Francesca at the dining room table, "I buy all that paint, I make my restaurant look more British than Fortnum and Mason's and then my customers come in and say, "Hey, Eugenio, who did that to your nice restaurant? Who made that mess? You should see them in court, that's vandalism," and they laugh and say if my food is as bad as my window looks, they wouldn't feed it to their dog. So I say, "It's important. We need to show we're on the side of the British, and then the British say, "We know that. I'll have one of your British pizzas, but not if it's red white and blue. What do you think I should do, Francesca?"

Francesca looked up from her book. "Sorry, Uncle Eugenio, what did you say? I wasn't listening."

Eugenio sighed again. "I was saying….oh, never mind. How's your young man, anyway?"

"He's picking me up in twenty minutes, we're going to the pictures."

"Oh," said Eugenio, "I love the pictures, but I can never get Julia to go. What are you going to see?"

Francesca stood up in front of the mirror and started putting on some make up. "We haven't decided, but I want to see 'Gone with the Wind' but Eric is dying to see 'Dodge City.' The trouble is whenever he sees an Errol Flynn movie he starts talking in a strange accent and walking funny. It's really annoying."

Eugenio stood and watched attentively as she put on her lipstick.

"Why don't you think Julia ever wants to come out?" he asked.

Francesca paused and looked at him in the mirror. "Perhaps she doesn't feel very good about herself," she said, "You should make more effort with her. When was the last time you told her how attractive she is, for example?"

Eugenio grimaced, "Well she's not very attractive at the moment, so there's no point in telling her she is. Anyway, we're married. It's different for you two, you're courting."

"Or the last time you bought her flowers, for example," Francesca went on.

Eric always brings me flowers or even a bar of chocolate. He makes me feel cared for. It's important. You'll see when he arrives."

"You've smudged your lipstick," said Eugenio and sat down again. The idea of an Englishman giving him, an Italian, lessons in how to be romantic, hurt his pride.

A few minutes later there was a knock at the door. Francesca ran to open it and kissed Eric on the cheek. Somewhat embarrassed in front of Eugenio, he was holding out a small bunch of anemones.

"Come in and talk to Uncle Eugenio while I finish getting ready," said Francesca, "we've got plenty of time. I thought we could go and see 'Gone with the Wind."

Eric frowned, "But we've seen it twice already. Isn't there anything else? Like Dodge City, for example."

"No, Eric, there's a war on. There's enough violence in the world without having to pay to go and see more of it."

Eric sat down at the table. "And that Scarlet O'Hara is just horrible."

Francesca blew him a kiss from the door to her bedroom. "Frankly, my dear, I don't give a damn," she said, before closing the door.

"So," said Eugenio, turning his chair to face Eric, "what are you going to see at the pictures, do you think? Will it be 'Dodge City' or the other one?" He smiled.

Eric shuffled uncomfortably, "We'll just have to see." And then, to change the subject," How is Mrs Baldini?"

"Which one?" Eugenio was still feeling riled at the thought that this gangly Englishman with his habit of glancing at people rather than looking at them directly and yes, now he came to look more closely, the unpleasant spot on his chin, could be thought of as being more romantic than he.

"Your wife, Mrs Baldini," said Eric.

"She's pregnant, which makes her fat which makes her unhappy so she tries to eat everybody's chocolate rations which make her fatter, which makes her unhappier and very bad-tempered. Do you think all women become like their mothers?"

"I really don't know that I've ever thought about it."

"They do, let me tell you," said Eugenio, "You look at Francesca. She's a beautiful girl, very lively and interested in everything." He nodded towards her bedroom door and dropped his voice, "She's going to become just like Giovanna, I can see it already. Giovanna tells Franco what to do all the time, and he's so worn out that he always does it. He never stood up to her in the beginning, that's his problem and now it's too late. You've got to tell Francesca what's what and show her who's boss or she'll ruin your life."

Eric was about to comment when Francesca came back.

"I think we will go and see 'Dodge City'," said Eric, standing up, "it's got great reviews and I think you'll like it. I mean, it's not all violent you know and it's supposed to be very exciting."

Francesca threw a glance at Eugenio and smiled knowingly, then she tucked her arm into Eric's and said, "Well, we'll see. I expect you've been having a nice chat with Uncle Eugenio. Come on, let's go."

Eugenio sat deep in thought for a long time, not wanting to go and face Julia's temper and hoping that Franco and Giovanna would come back soon. Then he picked up the anemones and went back to his flat.

Giovanna was preparing supper when Francesca came home some hours later. "Mama," she said as she checked herself in the mirror, "If I wasn't going to marry Eric I'd want to marry Clark Gable."

"Lay the table," said her mother, "and your father's getting changed. I don't want you talking like that in front of him, you know it upsets him."

Francesca stopped, "What did you do with my flowers? Did you put them in water?"

Giovanna shook her head, "I haven't seen any flowers. And will you please lay the table properly."

Franco came in and kissed Francesca on the cheek. "What's the matter?" he asked.

Francesca put on her Scarlett O'Hara accent, "Tara! Home. I'll go home. And

I'll think of some way to get him back. After all, tomorrow's another day."

Giovanna shook her head again. "That boy's a bad influence," she said.

Chapter Forty One

"You sure you've driven one of these things before?" yelped Maurice as the army truck swung through the gates of the yard. "You've scraped this side on the wall." Joe turned off the engine, "Yeah, like I said, once or twice. It'll only be a little scratch. There's the old geezer, I'd better back up a bit."

A stooped figure in a brown coat was limping towards them. Joe watched him in the wing mirror. Maurice leaned across and took the keys out of the ignition.

"You're not going to back this thing with me in it," he said, "The way you drive we'll be straight through that wall."

The old man put his head through the driver's window. A roll-up cigarette was stuck to his bottom lip, and a facial tic made him twitch his nose as he spoke.

"All right lads? You want to be further back. They're all under that tarpaulin, all ready for you."

Maurice climbed down from the cab and went round to the driver's side. "Can you drive?"

The old man's eyes lit up "Can I drive? I only drove for the Tigers in the last war. All over France. Give us the keys and I'll show you."

"We need a slash," said Maurice. "Park her up, and we'll be back in a jiffy."

"I don't need a pee," protested Joe on their way to the lavatory. "And what if he crashes it?"

"Listen," Maurice said, "I nearly wet myself three times with you driving, so I'm taking over from now on. And I've never driven one of them things. Have a pee, you'll need it."

The lorry had been backed up to within a few feet of the tarpaulin. "Now, lads, as one old soldier to a couple of mates I'm going to do you a favour. They're in mint condition, but because we're comrades, like, I can let you have the lot for fifty quid. There's twenty five of 'em, not twenty as was ordered, so I'm throwing in five buckshee. I've even written out a receipt."

Joe shook his head. "What are you talking about? The ruddy things have been requisitioned. Let's just get on with it," and he went to pull the tarpaulin off the mound that it was covering.

The man put his arm on Joe's, "Just hear me out, son. I'm doing you both a big favour. You'll like it or my names not Fred Jones." He carefully removed the cigarette end from his lower lip, licked carefully where some skin had come away and then said, "I know they've been requisitioned. But what happens to them afterwards? You tell me that."

"You'll get them back," said Maurice.

Mr Jones threw up his arms in despair, "What bleedin' use they going to be to me after the army's had them for Christ knows how long? They'll be ruined. But, see, you two boys buy them as an investment. Right, when the bombs start to drop, and you mark my words, they will drop, smashing houses into ruins, people will be queuing up for these when they're rebuilding. You'll get a fiver each for them no problem. That's a thousand per cent profit. All right, I really shouldn't, but as I like you, thirty quid."

"Sorry," said Maurice pulling at the tarpaulin and revealing a pile of old and battered looking baths. Mr Jones looked at them fondly, "I don't know how you could turn down an offer like that. Not businessmen, that's obvious. What does the army want them for, anyway?"

Joe winked at Maurice, "Sorry, mate, military secret. Where's the plugs then? There's no plugs."

Mr Jones brightened, "Your commanding officer didn't say nothing about no plugs. Plugs'll cost you extra. Tanner each and ones with chains on, ninepence."

"No," it's OK," said Maurice, peering down at a bath that was covered in a green slime. This one's got a plug. One'll be enough."

"This one's got a bloody great crack down it," said Joe," You could stick your finger in it except you'd probably get the pox."

"No, that's nothing, that'll patch beautiful with a bit of weld and a lick of enamel paint," protested Mr Jones.

"OK," said Maurice finally, "let's get them loaded up, give us your docket to sign and we'll be on our way."

Mr Jones produced a slip of paper. Maurice read it, took the pencil from behind

Mr Jones's ear and said, "I'm changing this. It's not twenty five baths in mint condition, it's nineteen baths in crap condition."

Mr Jones looked astonished. "I counted them meself this morning. My son must have had the others. He is what you'd call a businessman. He'll make his fortune out of this war, you want to meet him."

"Another time, perhaps." Maurice dropped the backboard and they began to lift the baths into the rear of the truck. To begin with they tried to stack them neatly but finally they were throwing them in the back with abandon. When Maurice turned on the ignition, the things clattered around so that the boys couldn't hear themselves speak. The lorry stalled, kangaroo hopped out through the gates and then stalled again.

"Where are we supposed to be going?"

Joe took a piece of paper out of his breast pocket, "Market Harborough Golf Club. Don't ask me where it is. Oh, hang on, it says take A6 south and follow signs."

Maurice turned to face him, "I thought you knew where we were going. You got the information from the sergeant."

"Yeah, that's what he said. That's what he's written."

Maurice put his head on the steering wheel, "You stupid prat. It's a bloody wind-up. There are no signs, remember? They've all been removed. Who phoned to requisition the baths?"

"No, that was Major Turnbull. I was there when he made the call to clear it with the club. No, they're expecting us all right."

"OK," Maurice nodded, "but we still have no idea how to get there."

"Tell you what," Joe said, "drive to the station, someone there's bound to know the way and we know the way to the station.

Maurice gradually got used to the gears and the weight of the steering, though he found the constant crashing from the back worrying and twice had to stop and check that none of the baths had fallen out of the back.

"It's dead easy," Joe smiled when came back from the station office, "we just keep on this road for about ten miles and it takes us straight there. "

Once they were out of the city, Maurice began to enjoy himself. The day was warm and the countryside reminded him of home. He watched a kestrel hovering over the verge ahead and smiled as it turned into the wind, allowed itself to be lifted on a current of air and then seemed to stall again over a hedge. After twenty minutes or so they came to a village and Joe gave a shout, "Look, that's it. Golf Club. They've left a sign up for us. "

"Or put it back," thought Maurice, "that was really nice of them."

He followed the road and eventually stopped in front of the club house. There was nobody around that they could see.

"We can't take this thing on the golf course, can we?" Maurice looked out at the manicured fairway of the first hole, "They'd kill us if we scuffed up their grass."

They manhandled a bath out of the lorry and started carrying it up the first fairway. It was heavy and Maurice wished he'd thought to bring some gloves as it cut into the palms of his hands. They kept putting it down until Joe said, "I reckon this is about halfway. Make sure it's right in the middle, that'll do."

They were exhausted by lunch time, having carefully placed seven baths in the middle of each fairway and Maurice was admiring the lion's feet on the one they had just set down when a ball clattered into the trees on the right of them, followed by a roar of outrage.

An elderly man in plus fours was marching towards them angrily waving a golf club above his head. Behind him a younger man was sauntering along with an amused expression on his face. The older man was still shouting when he reached them, "What the bloody hell is the meaning of this?" he demanded, "Is this some idea of a joke? Get these damned things off our course now, or I'll report you to your senior officer."

Joe stood to attention, "It was our senior officer who told us to put them here, sir."

"What? Rubbish, what's his name. I've got connections with the army. What's his name, I said?"

"Major Turnbull, sir."

The younger man smiled, "You know Chris Turnbull, father, plays off five. We'll give him a ring and get this sorted out."

"Damn right," said the father, "and I'll give him a piece of my mind. Come on, you two, you can explain yourselves to him."

They made their way along an avenue of trees back towards the clubhouse. The young man paused to light his pipe and then said to Maurice, "Did he say why he wanted these baths to be placed all over our course?"

"Yes, sir, he said that the Germans could easily use golf courses as runways to land their gliders when they invade. They used a lot of gliders when they invaded Norway. The baths would stop them."

The young man nodded, "Makes sense. Did you hear that, father?"

The old man shook his head, "Well, in that case they should have bloody well warned us. We needed time to sort out rulings."

Joe said, "I was in his office when Major Turnbull phoned the club, sir."

The club house office was empty. The old man took a note book out of his pocket, checked the number and dialled. "Chris? George Riley here. Listen, I've got a couple of your chaps here dropping old baths all over our ruddy golf course. Said you told them to do it." There was a lengthy pause, a muffled reply and then he handed the receiver to Maurice.

"Hickey," said Major Turnbull, "where did I say to deliver those baths?"

"Market Harborough golf course, sir."

"Correct. And where are you now?"

"Market Harborough golf course, sir."

Maurice had to hold the receiver away from his ear, "No, you bloody idiots. You're at Kibworth golf course. Where I've got a match on Saturday." There was a pause. "Your leave this weekend is cancelled. You'll be caddying for me and you and Harper will be moving those things off the fairways and replacing them when each hole has been played. Is that clear?"

George Riley took the receiver, and was about to replace it when a thought crossed his mind. "Chris? George again. Here's a conundrum for you to sort out. We'll need local rulings on this one, but if a ball rolls underneath a bath, does it count as a moveable obstruction or an immoveable hazard? The chaps'll want to know. It happened to me on the fourth and Ralph and I had an argument about it. I think I was entitled to a free drop but my boy insisted it was a penalty drop. Cost me the hole. What do you think?"

He put back the receiver. "He says it's a free drop. That makes me one up, I believe." They were still arguing about the rules when they reached the door. Ralph turned round.

"You can finish off, but I strongly suggest you go on the eighteenth and work backwards. Then you'll be keeping out of our way."

"I didn't want to go home anyway," said Joe, "I think I'd kill my old man if I had to go home. Saturday night we'll go out and get rat-arsed."

"Yeah," said Maurice, who had been looking forward to going home, "and then spend Sunday peeling spuds. No thanks."

Chapter Forty Two

Reinhardt opened his eyes and stared at the ceiling. He hadn't been sleeping well. For some reason he'd been kept awake by the memory of the night they'd left Berlin sixteen years earlier. It had been his sister's twentieth wedding anniversary. They'd hired the ballroom at the Grand Central in Charlottenburg, invited over two hundred guests and everyone had dressed up in their best finery. He had been completely carefree, until at the end of the evening, when he had gone to congratulate his brother-in-law for putting on such a great evening, Kurt said to him, "We invited you only to say good-bye. So good-bye."

Not knowing what he was talking about, Reinhardt had gone off to find his sister who was talking to their mother. In that supercilious tone that she always used with him, she said, "We have placed a substantial amount in your English account. You must leave Berlin. You've run up debts that you can't possibly pay, we get complaints almost daily about your behaviour. We've told your wife that if she'll take you back to England there's enough for you to live comfortably for a long time, and to support your children. In fact there's enough for you to maintain the extravagant lifestyle you've been living here. But you have to go, " and she had burst into tears.

His mother had looked up at him and shaken her head. "It's what you want, isn't it? I'll come and see you when you're settled." He had turned away and got a taxi to the dingy flat that he had set up for his wife and the boys. He'd explained their sudden departure by saying that business was calling him back to London. From her expression it was clear that she hadn't believed him.

He propped himself up on an elbow and looked down at Elizabeth who was sleeping beside him. He loved her vulnerability when she was asleep, the gentle rise and fall of her breath, the little snuffling noises he made as she stirred. He'd felt the same way about his second wife once. She'd come back from the last war where she'd been nursing soldiers near the front. That was in 1918. He'd been staying with her parents in Scarborough after he'd returned from being interned and given up his room to her which overlooked the sea. He'd spent hours with her as she recovered from the things she'd experienced and often sat by her bedside and watched her sleep. As she grew stronger they went for walks along the cliff tops and he told her about his upbringing on the estates in Silesia, how one day he would inherit, and if she would marry him, how she would spend the rest of her days in luxury. He taught her a few words of German, they planned their future, and then he went back to Germany to sort things out. But they had got carried away with the dream. When he wrote to her to join him in Berlin, they married in a register office with two cleaners as witnesses, his mother and his sister having refused to attend. And when the two boys were born she stopped being vulnerable and became simply needy. He took to saying that he had to go and sort things out in Silesia and stayed away for weeks. It wasn't until that night in the ballroom, when his sister said , "We've told your wife..." that he realised that his wife had probably known for ages that his staying away had nothing to do with his sorting out the estates in Silesia. Yet she had never berated him. Maybe things would have been different if she had. Reinhardt shook his head as he looked down at Elizabeth. No, he decided, she had devoted herself entirely to the babies. There was no room for him in her affections and there wouldn't have been, no matter what he'd done. It was different with Elizabeth. She didn't have children. If anything, he needed her.

The feeling made him uncomfortable. He slid out of bed, reached for his dressing gown and monocle, shut the bedroom door so as not to wake her and went downstairs. Then he closed the living room door so as not to be heard and searched through his address book and dialled a number.

"Mortimer? Reinhardt here. Look, old chap, if you still want her, I'm ready to sell. But you'd better make it quick, there's been a lot of interest. But I promised you first refusal and I'd never break my word. What d'you say? Cash in hand, of course."

He smiled, "Good, then if you can arrange that, I'll run her over later, in time for a bite to eat."

He replaced the receiver and then dialled another number. "Eddie, Mr Reinhardt here. Could you be a good chap, give her a spot of polish, you know spruce her up a bit and run her over here for about eleven. Same address, yes, number twenty-eight."

He went into the kitchen and put the kettle on the hob. It wasn't that long ago that he had learnt to make tea, he reflected, but lately the ghosts had become more pressing. This had been the cook's domain, what was now his dressing room had been the boys' governess's room, what had been the nursery was full of boxes.

He took a pot of tea up to Elizabeth. "I've got a surprise – no two surprises for you today," he said. "Make sure you put on extra warm clothes."

At eleven o'clock there was a hoot outside the front door. Reinhardt beckoned to Elizabeth. "We're going for a spin," he said, "What d'you think?"

"My God," said Elizabeth, "Is that really yours. You never said anything about having a car. What is it?"

"She a Delage D8-105, one of the last ones made. I bought her in '35, but it's time to let her go. Friend down in Henley's buying her. Then this evening we're going to celebrate by having dinner at the Savoy."

He went down and spoke to the driver, "Thanks Eddy, old man. Look, I'm a bit strapped at present, but I'll give you my petrol ration book and I'll square with you when I've sold her, how does that sound?"

Eddy looked doubtful but took the ration book. "There's no problem," Reinhardt reassured him, "I'll run round what I owe you in the morning."

Eddy went off looking dubious. He'd had dealings with Mr Reinhardt before. He usually had managed to get his money in the end, but the man was more slippery than an eel.

Reinhardt opened the passenger door for Elizabeth and then climbed into the driver's seat. He caressed the steering wheel, "Isn't she beautiful?"

"Why are you selling it then?" asked Elizabeth. He turned on the engine which gave a roar. Over the noise he shouted, "It was something you said, about the fact that we could all be dead in a year."

He pulled slowly out of Mecklenburgh Square, "So I thought, what's the expression? Let's drink and be merry for tomorrow we die?"

Chapter Forty Three

Esther Hart's Diary

Monday 15th April 1940

Walking back from the shops this morning a woman was coming towards me dragging a screaming little boy in tow. I don't know what he was so upset about, but she was grim faced and obviously furious with him about something. Behind her was a girl- presumably her daughter, seemingly oblivious to her screaming brother. She was pushing a hoop in front of her, and every time she gave it a shove she chanted, in rhythm,

'Underneath the spreading chestnut tree

Hitler dropped a bomb on me,

Now I'm a blinking refugee

Underneath the spreading chestnut tree'

Every time the hoop fell over she sighed and picked it up and began her song again, and then finally picked it up and ran after her mother. She can't have been more than seven or eight. She wore an old threadbare coat that was several sizes too big and a rather severe hair clip. I suddenly felt a great pang of longing for my children. I know it's impossible to bring them back to London now because the whole situation is far too dangerous, but when I got home I went and lay on the bed and couldn't stop crying for a long time.

I know it's partly to do with how things are between Douglas and me at the moment.

Went with Barbara to visit Herr Niedermayer but were told that he was rehearsing a play at Hampstead, so that was a wasted journey, except we agreed to go and see the production which is 'The Threepenny Opera,' apparently.

Douglas came home early for a change and gave me the news that he has persuaded his father to move in with us. Oh joy.

Tuesday 16th April

Spent the morning sorting out the children's bedroom to make it inhabitable for Charles when he moves in at the weekend. Last few days of freedom, I suspect. Found Gordon's old teddy bear stuffed down the side of his bed. I clutched it and held it for a long time, remembering how he'd said he was too old for teddy bears on his eleventh birthday, but it seems he wasn't. Then I wondered if I should send it to him, and decided against.

I wonder whether Douglas suddenly announcing that his father is moving in with us is his way of curbing my friendship with Barbara. I fear it may be. After all, whenever I mention her name he just grunts, and his remark that she was a 'bad influence' left me speechless. But lately he's been treating me more like a rather wayward daughter than his wife, which makes me both resentful and more determined than ever to live my own life.

The situation in Norway sounds more and more desperate. I've taken to listening to Lord Haw-haw, much to Douglas's disapproval, and it is difficult to tell who, if anyone, is telling the truth. But anyway, German propaganda is much more interesting than ours.

Wednesday 17th April

There'a been a lot of discussion about Goering complaining that the RAF has been bombing German towns. I seem to remember at the outset of the war that he had been saying that the Luftwaffe is invincible and that that it would be quite impossible for that to ever happen. It seems to me that it is highly unlikely that any Prime Minister would sanction the bombing of German civilians though God knows there have been enough preparations with barrage balloons, sandbags and the wretched blackout to protect people in the towns and cities here. Rather it seems to me that Goering's statement is a prelude to the Luftwaffe bombing London in 'revenge', a thought that makes my blood run cold. I wonder if they've been making the same preparations in Berlin, with air raid wardens, drills and civilians being inundated with information about the importance of wearing their gas masks and where to find their nearest bomb shelters etc etc.

Thursday 18th April

Douglas had a long phone conversation with his father last night reassuring him that there was nothing we wanted more than for him to come and live with us and that we would be delighted to have his incontinent cat as well. Douglas would never let the children have a pet- not even a goldfish, no matter how much they pleaded. I bit my tongue.

Then they were discussing the war in a way that he would never dream of discussing it with me. I overheard him say that some troops have landed in Norway at Namsos, which apparently is good news, but their equipment was found to be faulty. Their skis lack the proper binding so that they are useless. Southern Norway has now been completely occupied by the German army and he said his colleagues in the Foreign Office are very pessimistic about the outcome. Before ringing off I heard him say, "You're probably right, Father," which I'm sure was in response to his father saying that Chamberlain would sort it all out. I get the feeling that even Douglas is losing faith in Mr Chamberlain.

Friday 19th April

Last day of freedom. Charles is moving in tomorrow. I'm trying my hardest to be positive about it and went out for lunch with Barbara to get her to give me some moral support. She was very sympathetic but said it was ridiculous for me to say that I wouldn't be able to leave the old man. After all, he's been living on his own with no one to care for him ever since his wife died, which is true enough. I suppose it might just be that I don't like the idea of his being alone in my house. It's awful, but I wouldn't put it past him to go through our things, and the idea of his fiddling around in my kitchen infuriates me. It's not that I particularly dislike him, it's more that I don't really have any ways of dealing with him that don't make me feel like a complete hypocrite. He is so condescending and has always treated me like a scullery maid. I shouldn't take it personally, because that's also exactly how he treated his wife when she was alive. Come to think of it, that's how Douglas treats me too, lately.

Saturday 20th April

I'm writing this in bed while Douglas and his father discuss the war. Charles moved in this morning, saying he doesn't want to be a burden, but wondered whether I could do some washing for him and get his suit cleaned. He brought with him two suitcases full of dirty washing. The lady who had been cleaning and doing his washing handed in her notice two weeks ago when she heard that her services would no longer be needed, so obviously I wasn't kept up to date with their plans, since Douglas only told me on Monday that his father was coming to live with us as from today. I thought it would be a good idea if we all went for a walk and suggested Hyde Park. They reluctantly agreed but it was a glorious day. They ignored me throughout, and I stood by the bridle path and watched as a rider on a huge great horse came galloping towards me. I had a fleeting dream of his scooping me up onto the saddle behind him and of us galloping off together. I was wonderfully surprised when the rider lifted his hat to me, and I smiled and waved, only to see, when I turned around, that he was actually waving to another woman who was taking his photograph. Feeling rather embarrassed, I rejoined Douglas and his father who were deep in conversation with a gun crew which was manning an anti-aircraft gun. Douglas's father was carefully explaining to the bewildered soldiers that war is like a football match- that you concede territory only to strike on the counter-attack. "That's Chamberlain's plan, don't you see, to lull Hitler into a false sense of security and then to strike when he's least expecting it." As we were moving away, one of the soldiers laughed and said to his friend, "Trouble is, it's nearly full time and we're four nil down- they've got Poland, Czechoslovakia, Austria and now Norway." "Five nil," said his friend, "Don't forget Denmark."

Over supper Douglas said, I thought really spitefully, "Esther been doing good works with a refugee friend," which set his father off on a long tirade about how he's read that there were possibly thousands of refugees who were really fifth columnists and who were busily sending messages back to Germany about our military capability. Stupidly I rose to the bait and said I really couldn't understand how an Austrian Jew who is living in a squalid flat in Paddington and who hardly speaks any English could possibly have access to anything of any interest to the German government. He had fled the country precisely because his life was in danger in Austria. Charles said of course these people had completely believable alibis and new identities created for them, it was just such people who appear to be totally harmless who pose the greatest danger. In his view, all aliens should be put out of harm's way.

I was so angry that I excused myself, went and washed up and then came to bed. I can see that the foreseeable future is going to be unutterably grim. And what was even worse was that Douglas agreed with his father that the government is being very naive in not taking the alien threat more seriously.

I have to admit that I smiled to myself when the loathsome cat that has moved in with us was sick on the living room carpet. I could hear the two searching for the cloths and disinfectant, and was very pleased that they thought better of coming to ask me to help them out.

Sunday 21st April

Over breakfast Charles wanted to placate me by saying how it had been such a good idea of mine to suggest he got a cat. Felix has been his 'boon companion' for fourteen years. He could tell the difference between enemy and friendly aircraft. Whenever a German plane flew over he would run and hide under the bed, whereas if it was an RAF plane he simply went on washing himself. As there haven't been enemy aircraft over London yet, his owner also obviously has second sight. It only reminded me of poor Mrs Cunningham next door who pleaded with her husband not to have their cat put down last September. She was sobbing in the street as he marched down the road and shouted after him, "At least let me carry him." When she came back she seemed reconciled and told me that the vet had said that since the outbreak of war his main job had been putting down cats and dogs. People thought they would no longer be able to afford to feed them. As a result there has been a plague of rats and mice in lots of places. Still, Felix doesn't strike me as being much of a ratter since he's blind in one eye and quite arthritic.

Monday 22nd April

Had a brainwave this morning and don't know why I didn't think of it before. The weekend having been quite as horrible as I feared it would be, I was listening to one of the many gardening programmes that get broadcast during the week, and I thought why not give over the garden entirely to vegetables? I don't know why this should have come as such a revelation, after all, as Barbara says, you can't move in public parks for anti-aircraft guns and artichokes. People are using their Anderson shelters to grow vegetables on. Perhaps it didn't occur to me before because I didn't really want to acknowledge we are at war. In fact, were it not for the fact that Charles has come to live with us, it probably still wouldn't have occurred to me. After breakfast I put on a head scarf and my wellingtons and set about digging up Douglas's rose bed with a will. I wrapped the roots in bags and put them in the shed, so he shouldn't be too cross.

Charles pottered down to the paper shop and came back with a copy of yesterday's Sunday Chronicle which he insisted on reading to me while I dug. He prefaced his reading by saying, "You see, the thing is my dear, your husband and I really do appreciate the menace that the aliens pose for the country, it's all here in black and white.' He went on to read me a long piece by Beverley Nichols to the effect that many aliens know that in spirit they are as good Englishmen as anybody and for that reason should be glad to be interned as they know that there are traitors among them, and that only in wholesale internment will safety be found.

I preferred to reply by batting the head off a red rose that soared away like a well struck cricket ball. He failed to notice and went on reading. According to Mr Nichols 'hardly a day goes by without someone being fined five shillings for a blackout offence. The person is a keen supporter of the war effort, has escaped from Berlin but because of ill health has moved to the east coast of England where he lights up the top floor of his house for ten minutes every night.' My spade slipped and I cut off the next rose at the roots. He finished the last bit of the article which said that 'even if there's no evidence, which there must be, why would Hitler neglect his most powerful weapon against his most powerful enemy?'

I said that actually just at the moment I was far more interested in Mr Nichols' gardening books than in his political ideas and that hadn't he been proved quite wrong in saying, as he had, that the German mistreatment of Jews had been greatly exaggerated. But he certainly could help me with his knowledge of vegetables. Charles looked slightly confused for a second, and then said, "Flowers, my dear. The man's an absolute authority on winter flowers." Then he added," Of course the chap's as queer as a coot, if you'll pardon the expression."

I finished digging my row while he watched me and then went to the ironmongers to buy some potatoes and carrots.

Tuesday 23rd April

As I thought, Douglas wasn't delighted that his rose bed is now full of potatoes and carrots, but I said I'd noticed the government had lifted the restrictions on the number of chickens that can be kept in town gardens, so we could give over the area beyond the shed to a dozen or so and I'd picked up a leaflet on how to build a chicken coop. This upset Douglas even further but got him off the subject of his roses. Charles helpfully said that as a child in Barnes they'd kept a goat. I said it would be lovely to have a goat as well, but Douglas said he wasn't going to have his home turned into a damned zoo. When he came to bed last night he took the tissue with my cress on it off the window sill and flushed it down the lavatory. My husband isn't very keen on nature.

Wednesday 24th April

I caused further dissension over the breakfast table by commenting that I thought it a dreadful shame that the government was putting up the price of stamps. It was very hard on soldiers writing home and on children who have been evacuated. Tuppence for a stamp on a postcard is very expensive. Douglas, who takes every tiny criticism of the government as a personal sleight and as being tantamount to treason, said that wars are very expensive to run, and then fell back on his usual saw, which is that "You don't understand these things."

Charles came out as an unlikely ally, complaining that the price of his cigarettes has now gone up three times in as many months. Perhaps it will stop him from being able to smoke at the breakfast table. Spent the morning in the garden and planted sprouts and cauliflowers.

While Charles was having his afternoon nap, I phoned Barbara for a chat and to hear a sane voice. She always cheers me up. She said that members of The Link were being arrested which she was really happy about- all those far right people who were Nazi sympathisers and that they were far more of a danger to national security than any aliens.

She had also read the article in the Chronicle and we laughed at the idea of refugee Nazis taking the sea air for their health and all of them frantically rushing around turning on all the lights in their B&B's at midnight every night.

Thursday 25th April

There was a long queue in the bakers which gave everyone a chance to talk about everything from the price of matches to the wisdom or otherwise of the Prime Minister. One lady said that she thought Mr Chamberlain was doing a wonderful job and that we certainly would have had German bombers over London were it not for his threat to bomb German cities. A much younger woman clutching a baby said her husband in Norway thought that the whole campaign was a complete disaster- they hadn't got the right equipment, the maps were either out of date or non-existent, that the supply ships had got completely separated from the main force so that the troops had none of the right things and when he was unloading what little there was in the hold, he'd found ten bicycles, which were useless in five feet of snow and a map of Belgium, so he asked himself if they hadn't come to altogether the wrong country. The first lady said rather crossly that she supposed the husband in Norway had written all this in a letter, and she thought that was disgusting and should have been censored- such talk was very bad for morale. The younger woman said he didn't have to write it all down, he just sent her the map of Belgium with a comment in the margin. She knew what he meant. Anyway, it was common knowledge that the Germans had completely outwitted the British. She thought that the troops would have to be brought back from Norway in order to protect the Scottish ports. There was a long uncomfortable silence which was only broken by an elderly gentleman saying that he'd been listening to Lord Haw-haw last night who had said that the church clock at Steeple Morden had stopped at twenty-five to two. "What I want to know is, how did he know that if one of these aliens that's living here among us hadn't told him?" I couldn't suppress a giggle which got me a very dirty look from the cross lady who said, "I don't see what's funny. There are aliens everywhere and they're just so cunning they haven't been caught yet." Everyone looked round as if expecting to see a bug-eyed monster with a green head at the back of the queue. I imagined it on the phone to Lord Haw-haw, whispering, " A piece of important intelligence- the church clock at Steeple Morden has stopped at twenty-five to two, I repeat...."

The lady with the baby said angrily, "Have you been to Steeple Morden to find out if it's true? It's all just propaganda. But it works on stupid people." Luckily she was next in line to be served.

Friday 26th April

The evenings are so light now and I am so tired of going to bed early that I've decided to stay up and either read quietly under the standard lamp in the corner, or knit mittens for the troops in Norway. It has the additional advantage of showing Douglas that I'm doing my bit. They sit in front of the electric fire talking sotto voce, but because Charles is really quite deaf, it's impossible not to hear what they are saying, and they are completely oblivious to my presence.

Douglas is having a horrible time in the department, which explains why he is being quite intolerable at home. He said he couldn't understand why Sir John Anderson, who is ultimately his boss in the Home Office, was persisting in ignoring the public's clamour for the internment of more aliens. Every other department, especially the War Office was arguing for greater internment and there was a feeling that the longer it went on the more time was being given to Hitler to get his fifth column in place. That's what happened in Norway. He'd had quite a heated discussion with Herbert, his boss about it, but he was more interested in trying to refute the stories in the press and said that if anyone could produce a shred of evidence that refugees were actually working for the German government, then he would take it higher. "By which time it'll be too late," added Charles, "I know, as I tried to explain to Esther..." and they both looked at me, suddenly remembering that I was there.

I said I was coming to bed, and so I've been writing my diary, feeling a bit like a spy. It seems to me, but what do I know about it? that Sir John Anderson has done exactly the right thing in locking up members of The Link who are dangerous and leaving poor refugees like Herr Niedermayer alone.

Saturday 27th April

Lots in the papers today about how the troops in Norway have weapons that are either completely useless or are so ill-equipped that they can't possibly fight. Had a quick conversation with Barbara who said a friend in the Foreign Office had told Herbert that at one stage early in the campaign they'd had to phone a journalist in Sweden to ask him if he knew where the British troops were! One of the problems is that the French don't trust us, we don't trust the French, and nobody thinks to tell the Norwegian army anything.

Charles seemed to find the articles very entertaining and said it just proved that Chamberlain is 'a cunning old devil'. "Lulling Hitler into a false sense of security, don't you see? Waiting till he can see the whites of his eyes, then counter-attack. The Germans won't know what's hit them."

I pointed out that even the papers most sympathetic to Mr Chamberlain were now criticising the way the campaign was being conducted and he said that of course- that was all part of the Grand Plan. By suggesting that we were losing, under-equipped and on the point of giving up, the Germans will over-reach themselves and the war will be over. "We'll win the war after losing the battle," he said triumphantly as if a surfeit of clichés won the argument as convincingly as we were about to win the war. I wondered why the refugees all needed locking up in that case, but thought better than to ask and went and made a cup of tea instead.

Sunday 28th April

Yesterday was the most beautiful spring day and Douglas was at home. He even joined me in the garden just long enough to dig a new bed at the far end, beyond the shed, and replant his roses. Meanwhile I planted peas and shallots which involved taking up a few feet of lawn. That didn't go down very well either.

Now Charles has dragged Douglas off to church. I said I'd stay behind to cook lunch. The butcher offered me a cow's hoof yesterday. I haven't the faintest idea what to do with it. Writing this makes me realise why Douglas thinks that Barbara is 'a bad influence.' Funnily enough, I think she's been a far worse influence since I've stopped seeing her so regularly, probably because I find myself wondering what she would do in certain situations and then doing them myself. Life has become a lot more relaxed since I've distanced myself from Douglas's disapproval, something that I was quite incapable of only a matter of months ago.

The Sunday papers are terribly thin because of the problem of importing wood from Norway. It's very easy to understand why there is such widespread apathy about the war- people are sick and tired of being subject to so many petty irritations from the government, while at the same time getting a barrage of propaganda and no real news about what is really happening. So much confusion is bound to make people disengage and find some kind of security in their ordinary everyday lives.

Tuesday 30th April.

It's being rumoured that the Germans have captured Stören and this means that Norway is lost. Douglas let slip last night to his father that British troops are starting to withdraw from Norway, since they'll be needed to help out in Belgium and Holland. Charles went quite white at the news and I felt very sorry for him. He'd completely convinced himself that the government's master plan was to wait until the last possible moment and then 'snatch victory from the jaws of defeat' as he put it. Several times.

For the first time since Charles has been with us, the men went to bed before me. Had to find a temporary new hiding place for my diary. I put it in the saucepan I'd used to cook the cow's hoof. Now it smells of glue, which is most unpleasant, but expect it'll wear off.

Chapter Forty Four

It was the opening night of 'The Threepenny Opera' at *Das Laternd*. They had been rehearsing all afternoon. Niedermayer examined himself in the dressing room mirror and smiled. His battered hat was at a raffish angle, with the grey wig sticking out under the sides; he'd applied another layer of make up to give himself heavy wrinkles and the suggestion of a badly shaved moustache, and his jacket, with a hole in the right shoulder made him resemble an eighteenth century beggar, which, after all, was what he was supposed to look like.

Herr Bauer had been pleased. At the last few rehearsals he's been shouting at the cast, saying that he couldn't hear them from the back, or telling the singer that he had to come in right on cue. But today he'd been all smiles, and said to Niedermayer that his afternoon performance was much more what he was looking for. "It's not a big part, I know," he'd said, "but you set the scene with your entrance. You've got to make the audience sit up in their seats and make them stay there. I want them to forget that the thing is in a language they don't understand, or most of them anyway. I want them to get the meaning from the action, and since your coming on stage is the beginning of the action, it makes or breaks the rest of the play." And when Niedermayer had left the stage after the last dress rehearsal, Bauer had applauded and shouted, "Bravo!"

Fifteen minutes before the curtain was due to go up he could hear people taking their seats and chattering as they flicked through their programmes. Behind him in the corridor members of the orchestra were unpacking their instruments. He felt a thrill of anticipation as each instrumentalist started to tune up, each quite oblivious of the mounting din.

This moment always reminded him of the first concert he went to as a child. He and his father had taken the train from Graz to Vienna. He had never seen anything like the Musikverein with its gold ceiling, massive golden statues and the crystal chandeliers. But then he had grasped his father's sleeve when the orchestra started. He had thought that that their tuning up was the beginning of the concert and couldn't believe that anyone would actually pay to come and hear this hideous cacophony of bellowing, screeching and trumpeting. Then suddenly they all fell silent and the audience applauded loudly, he couldn't understand why, until the conductor stood on the rostrum, bowed to the audience, turned to the orchestra and the opening bars of 'The Jupiter' Symphony took his breath away.

With five minutes to go until the curtain was due to rise, this much smaller group of musicians filed out to the orchestra pit. He slid the curtain to one side and looked out at the audience. he was really hoping that Mrs Hart would be there. He'd heard that she had come to the Centre when he was rehearsing last week and left a message to say that she was looking forward to seeing the production. He would invite her backstage and show her how much his English had improved. But scanning the rows from the back, there was no sign of her, but he did recognise the two men sitting stone-faced in the front row. It was the policemen who had interviewed him at the Centre a couple of weeks ago. He drew back as the curtain was raised and the orchestra struck up. The singer stepped forward in his beggar's clothes and began

'Und der Haifisch, der hat Zähne
Und die trägt er im Gesicht
Und MacHeath, der hat ein Messer
Doch das Messer sieht man nicht'

Lotte had set him to translate the song into English for homework last week, but he could never quite get it to sound right.

'And the shark, he has big teeth
And he wears them, in his face
And MacHeath too, has a big knife
But the big knife, you don't see'

Now the sharks were sitting in the front row. He felt a stab of panic and then the song was coming to an end. Herr Bauer was standing at his shoulder. "Good luck, Franz," he whispered, "Listen, I've got a letter for you. I forgot to give it to you earlier, I'll slip it into your pocket, ready?"

The applause for the singer was dying down. Franz felt himself being pulled back and then violently thrown forward across the stage. The lights momentarily blinded him as he stumbled and then fell at the feet of Mr Peachum who put a heavy foot on his chest. The audience laughed and applauded. Peachum started taking it much more slowly than he had done in rehearsal, looked down at him with exaggerated disapproval while it was explained that this man had been found pick-pocketing on Mr Peachum's territory. Peachum removed his foot and ordered him to stand.

"Empty your pockets," shouted Peachum.

He dutifully pulled out the linings of his pockets that sent a cascade of pennies rolling across the floor. "And your jacket." He fumbled in his inside breast pocket and pulled out a sheaf of papers and a piece of carrot. Then he plunged his hands into the side pockets which contained nothing but the letter that Bauer had slipped into it. "What is this?" said Peachum, with a toothless grin.

This wasn't scripted. Niedermayer glanced at the envelope and immediately recognised the writing. It was from his wife. He looked at Peachum, who was advancing towards him with his hand out, with an expression of horror. He wouldn't give up the letter - Peachum was on stage until the interval and the play had only just begun. He backed away, while Peachum feigned fury and continued to demand the letter. Niedermayer glanced down at the audience; one of the policemen was busily scribbling in his notebook. Niedermayer took the sheaf of papers and threw on the floor at Peachum's feet, then holding the letter aloft, he marched from the stage.

Bauer was agitating in the wings. "What the hell as that about? What's going on? he demanded. Niedermayer brushed past him without answering and rushed to the dressing room where he ripped the envelope open.

"Dear Franz," it read, "It was wonderful to get your letter, and I am so glad that you are safe. You won't believe this, but I have saved enough money to buy us tickets for England! We are getting a flight to Lisbon in a week's time and from there a boat which will be arriving in London on the 13th June. I'll explain all the details when we see each other. I have been assured that it will be possible to get work in London as a translator. Clara is very excited about going on a plane and a ship and has already packed. How all this has come about is too complicated to explain, but I wanted to let you know as soon as I was certain it was possible. With much love, Ilse and Clara."

Niedermayer stared at the letter and then read it through a second time. He couldn't believe it. Why did they have to go to Lisbon, of all places? The vague dread that had been at the back of his mind since he had arrived in England - the thought that he would never see his wife and daughter again suddenly crystallised into a series of terrible images. They'd be flying over German and Spanish air space where German planes would be patrolling. And what about U boats? Only last week he had read an article about the numbers of British ships sunk by the German navy, including merchant ships. Would all this have been reported in the Swiss papers. Would they even have known about it? But Ilse was always careful and she wouldn't take any risks with her and Clara's lives, especially as they were quite safe where they were. He read the letter a third time, looking for some clue as to how all this could have happened, but there just wasn't enough information. Maybe she felt she couldn't say more as the letter might have fallen into the hands of the censor and the scheme would have to be cancelled. There had been discussion at the Centre about just how neutral the Swiss inspectors really were. Some had argued that the Germans could make it impossible for the Swiss authorities to keep the whereabouts of refugees secret in England. After all, it had been rumoured that Hitler had threatened to invade Switzerland. He might well have agreed not to as long as the Swiss government agreed to pass over information in return for being promised their neutrality.

He was still thinking this over when he heard the applause for the ending of the first act. Peachum came in mopping his brow and slumped down next to him on the bench.

"What the hell was all that about?" he asked, "One minute you were there right with me and the next ... I had no idea what was going on. Don't ever pull a stunt like that again."

He turned to face Niedermayer, "Are you all right?"

Niedermayer had tears streaming down his cheeks. "It's a letter I got," he said, "I'm sorry. And then I saw a couple of men in the audience - I think they're police or something and they came to the centre a few days ago . They threw me. I'm sure they were checking up on me."

"But that's not what you're upset about, is it?"

Behind the mask of heavy stage make up, Niedermayer could see the look of concern in Peachum's eyes. It was too confusing. This man that he hardly knew, who was his tormentor on stage and who had been so angry a couple of minutes before, was now offering a kindness that Niedermayer couldn't deal with. He shook his head and went out onto the stage. He peeked through the curtains. There were two empty seats where the men had been sitting. Still, that didn't necessarily mean anything. Lots of people had got up to stretch their legs or go out for a cigarette in the interval. He just felt that he didn't want to be alone. He was scared. On the other hand he didn't want to speak to anybody either. A small huddle of stage hands were talking to Bauer about the props for the second act. He sat on a stool and listened as they discussed the precise positioning of the props. Suddenly he felt a hand on his shoulder.

"That was great, Hans." Lotte was smiling down at him. He sighed heavily and put his head on her breast and then withdrew as if shocked by what he'd done.

"Sorry," he said, "I've just heard from Ilse. I can't decide whether it's good news or not."

Chapter Forty Five

Weiss had been right. Busch had needed a project. He drew a picture of the SS Woermann as nearly to scale as he could and then showed it to Captain Burfeind. They spent some time discussing the precise positioning of the smoke stack and the angle it sat at, the way she lay in the water and the relative size of the bridge to the breadth of the ship. He was determined to get it exactly right, but was surprised at what he couldn't remember. They consulted Müller and other members of the crew who pored over the drawing, arguing about the locations of the lifeboats until Stieglitz said, "Hang on a minute, I'm sure I've got a photograph somewhere." He came back a few minutes later with an over-exposed picture which had been taken in Hamburg.

"Can I borrow it?" said Busch.

Stieglitz shrugged, "Keep it."

Busch spent hours studying the photograph and finally started the drawing again. After a week he was ready to start making the model. In the dormitory there was a table at the far end from the door. While he worked, Weiss lay on the bed and watched him or read. Jones, the young English guard offered to try and get him the materials he needed. Having struggled to explain himself at all in spite of the lessons he'd been getting from Weiss, Busch suddenly developed a wide vocabulary for the things he needed.

"I need wood, please, for my ship."

And Jones began to pick up some German, as he heard Busch ask Weiss, "Wie sagt man Schnur auf Englisch?" He heard the expression 'Wie sagt man...?' so many times that he started asking 'Wie sagt man 'ship' auf German?"

Weiss decided that if he wasn't going to be interrupted from his book every five minutes he'd better give them both lessons, and he wrote out a basic vocabulary, so that Jones practiced his pronunciation while Busch worked and laughed at his accent.

Having watched Busch for a few days, he appeared one afternoon with a small bag containing tools from his father's shed.

"My old man won't need them for a while," he said, "he's too busy with the Home Guard, so you can keep them for as long as you like. There's some little screw drivers, a hammer, a plane and a chisel, but for Christ's sake don't tell anyone where you got them from or I'll be in dead trouble.'

Starting with the hull, Busch painted each small piece of wood before putting it in place and securing it with glue that he had managed to persuade the camp's handyman to give him. As he worked he talked to Weiss about the trips he had made ever since he had joined the crew in '36. Most of the time Weiss merely grunted - he was too wrapped up in his book to take notice, but when Jones was there he would listen and translate.

"I've never even seen the sea," said Jones. We were supposed to go to Skegness for a holiday when I was twelve, but I got chicken pox and my Dad took my sisters and my Mum stayed at home to look after me. I can't really imagine it, though I've seen pictures of course. It must be great."

Weiss shrugged. "It's not for me. I get sea sick. When you're inside the smell of the oil makes you feel worse so you go out on deck to get away from the smell and then get freezing cold and wet."

"Yes, but it must be exciting to go to all different countries and see different people and that. I'd give anything to do it, I would."

Weiss smiled. "Where would you like to go?"

"I dunno. And it's never like you imagine it anyway, is it? It's like you lot. When I was called up and told that I was going to be guarding German prisoners, I don't mind telling you now and it'll probably make you laugh, but I was shit scared. The things we got told and the things you hear on the wireless, I mean you're nothing like what I imagined."

Weiss laughed and translated for Busch. "What did you imagine?"

Jones reddened slightly and shrugged. "It sounds stupid now, but I thought you... well, to be honest, we all did, we thought you'd be really tall and be blonde with great big muscles and scars from fighting and little slitty eyes. But I was really surprised. I mean really, you're just like us. The ones who go round singing and chanting their Nazi songs, I don't like them, none of us does, but mostly, like you, you could be one of us. Don't you think?"

Weiss laughed. "Or you could be one of us."

Jones thought about this and then shook his head. "Nah, you couldn't ever get a bloke like Hitler running the country. The people wouldn't stand for it. He'd never get elected anyway."

Weiss looked at him for a while, as if wondering whether or not to give him a lesson in German history, and then decided against. Instead he went back to his book. He was fairly sure that the gamekeeper had shot the lord in the library. After all he had both the means and the motivation, but that solution seemed a little too obvious. But then, he had found the body and raised the alarm and then tried to pin the blame on the butler, but it was also true that the butler was having an affair with the lord's wife, so he had the motivation as well.

"No," he said, putting the book down again, "we're not really all that alike. I can't imagine any German writing a detective novel, it just wouldn't happen."

"Why not?"

"Well for one thing, the government wouldn't allow a novel to be published that made the police look so stupid. So they're very happy for people to read English detective novels in translation, because they make the British police look stupid. And for another our minds just don't work like that. I can't explain it."

During the day, the dormitory became a quiet haven for Busch and Weiss. Outside there were frequent outbreaks of violence, especially among the Nazis who were furiously resentful at having to share the camp with Jews. Jones confided that he'd been warned about spending time with the prisoners, but that he didn't really get on with the other guards. They teased him because of his height and his nickname was 'Squirt.' Most of the time they ignored him, or gave him jobs to do that he felt were no part of his duties, especially Jenkins, who was six months younger than him and who had joined up three weeks after he had. But Jenkins was taller by several inches and popular amongst the other guards.

Jones had no one to complain to, so he complained to Weiss. "It's not fair. Jenkins told me to go and scrub out the laundry. I heard the sergeant telling him to do it, and he just turned round and ordered me to, and when I said that was his job, he threatened me, and the sergeant didn't say a word. But I don't see why I should, do you?"

Weiss made a sympathetic noise and translated for Busch, who laughed. "If all the British soldiers are like him, we'll win this war by Christmas," he said.

Jones asked Weiss to translate. "He agrees with you, it's not right. He laughed at the cheek of it."

"Please can I have some paint," said Busch to Jones.

"What colour do you need?"

"Hunh?"

Weiss translated and explained that the hull of the ship was grey.

"I'll see what I can do, I'd better go. I'll see you tomorrow."

Busch looked up and watched him go. "It's a funny thing, but until I started this I thought I'd go mad. And now I'm doing it, I only hope that they don't move us again before I get a chance to finish it. It reminds me of all the trips we had on her, things I'd forgotten. I was on watch one evening as a storm was beginning to blow up. The sky was grey and there were waves breaking over the bows, and I looked down and saw what I thought was a bat under the lee of the ship. I called over to Captain Burfeind and pointed it out. It was a tiny thing. I kept expecting it to be swallowed up by a wave, but it kept darting out from under the crests. We were a hundred kilometres or so from the nearest land and I thought it must have come onto the ship and then flown out from the hold, but Captain Burfeind said it wasn't a bat and it hadn't been on the ship with us. It was a bird. He'd seen them before. He said French sailors say they're the souls of dead captains who were cruel to their crew and who are condemned to fly over the waves for all eternity."

He looked at Weiss. "It stuck in my mind for ages, that. I don't mean the nonsense about the souls of dead captains, I mean the way it hovered and dived under the breaking waves and then suddenly reappeared just when you thought it must have drowned. You could see why they saw something human about it and you couldn't help admiring the way something so tiny and so far from land was riding the elements so easily, though it could have been drowned at any second."

"Is that why you like being a sailor?"

Busch nodded, "I suppose so. It is like being outside the world. Everything has to be ordered and organised perfectly, because the sea is so dangerous, so disorganised, so chaotic. And then you suddenly see an unexpected sight like that that you could never have imagined. Life on land is so messy. There's no discipline, no order."

Weiss recognised the mood change in Busch and didn't want to hear another diatribe about how the Führer was bringing back self respect and dignity to the German people through imposing a badly needed discipline, so he climbed off the bed, stretched his arms out and said, "Come on, you can't do anything more to that now, let's go and watch the football."

It was bright outside. Beyond the footballers and the high barbed wire fencing the Derbyshire hills rolled away into the distance. Weiss thought that being in the camp must be a bit like being on a ship. the countryside was unapproachable, like the sea. He stood watching a thrush that was sitting on a tree just beyond the fence. It was singing for a mate, or threatening other males, saying this was his territory - Weiss wasn't sure which, but he had a feeling that this peaceful scene wouldn't last long.

He sighed and looked at Busch who was walking towards the footballers. Some lines from Goethe's 'Faust' came back to him.

'Des Hasses Kraft, die Macht der Liebe,
Gib meine Jugend mir zurück!'

'The strength of hate, the force of love
give me back my youth again!'

Chapter Forty Six

Franco left by the back exit of the hotel. He didn't want to go with the others to a café and discuss what they could do. He didn't want to be with anyone, and he felt sick. His head was swimming. He couldn't go home, although it was only eight o'clock. He leaned against the palings and stared at a heap of sandbags. Without thinking about where he was going he drifted along the Strand towards Lancaster Place and then stopped. A newspaper seller was standing on the corner.

"You all right mate?" he asked Franco, "You look all in. Buy yourself a paper and cheer yourself up, it can't be that bad." He thrust a copy of 'The Daily Mirror' towards Franco.

Franco took it and fumbled for a couple of coppers and shoving the paper into his mac pocket he turned towards Waterloo Bridge. The dirty brown river seemed to be pulling him.

Suppose he fell in. Giovanna would think it was an accident, though she would wonder what he was doing on the bridge when he should have been at work, and anyway, she'd find out soon enough the real reason. In any case, it was a mortal sin to take your own life. He would go to hell. He looked round. People were hurrying to work all around him. A man jostled him and then apologised. Franco shook his head. Maybe it was all a big mistake and he had misunderstood. It was only temporary, while the present situation lasted and then he'd be able to go back.

He reached into the inside pocket of his jacket. But if it was a mistake, why had he got four weeks' wages in an envelope? He flushed with embarrassment at the memory of saying to the wages clerk that he would rather stay on in his current position than take all this money and have to go. The wages clerk hadn't even bothered to reply, but simply looked past him to the next man in the queue.

They'd been told it was because of all the anti-British feeling in the Italian press. They also said that customers had objected to being served by people who were supporting Mussolini. Most people assumed that the two countries would be at war within weeks, if not days. "It is nothing personal," Mr Hore had said, but it felt very personal to Franco. And he just did not believe it about the customers.

Only two evenings ago Mr Churchill had come in with a few of his colleagues and ordered a 'pre-prandial snifter, please Franco.' Franco had fetched a large double from Mr Churchill's private bottle that was kept under the bar and Mr Churchill had dropped a sixpenny piece onto the silver tray before swigging the whisky and replacing the glass with a nod for a refill. If Mr Churchill had been Prime Minister, they'd have all kept their jobs.

Something at the back of his mind said that that wasn't true. Cochis, the manager at Claridge's had been sacked a couple of days previously. Everyone had got to hear of it, and he had lost his flat in the hotel as well, but it was generally assumed that it must have been for something he'd done wrong. Now they knew. It was because he's Italian.

Franco dragged himself away from the bridge and started back up Lancaster Place. He couldn't go home, anyway, not until he'd thought of how to tell Giovanna and she wouldn't be expecting him until seven tonight at the earliest.

He wandered towards St Paul's and then turned into Garrick Street. This was where, only a couple of months ago a woman had asked him to take a picture of her son who was in the parade welcoming the heroes back from the Ajax when all those sailors had been rescued from the German ship. He remembered her giving a Union Jack to Giovanna to wave, but she had walked away from the crowd and dropped the thing in the gutter.

He sighed. They weren't British after all, but they certainly didn't support Mussolini, and he'd been working in the Savoy for as long as Cochis had been at Claridge's - twenty one years come July.

Suddenly he felt the need to be off the streets. People kept looking at him which made him feel ashamed, as if they knew that now he was out of work. It wasn't that far to Eugenio's restaurant. He'd go there and sit in the kitchen and ask his brother's advice about what he should do, though Eugenio's advice was nearly always about as unhelpful as it could be.

The bell tinkled as he entered the restaurant. Eugenio came out smiling and wiping his hands on his apron, but when he saw the expression on Franco's face, he stopped and said, "Hey, what's wrong? What are you doing here? Shouldn't you be at work? Are you ill?"

Franco brushed past him and went into the kitchen. He slumped down at the table and said, "I've been sacked. We all have. All the cooks, waiters, barmen at the hotel, all gone."

"What d'you mean all? They're closing the place down?"

"Stupido, all the Italians. And you know, I'll never find another job. Who's going to take any of us on now? And I'm older than most of the others, nobody'll want me."

Eugenio sat down opposite him and clapped his arms across Franco's shoulders.

"Si, you are older and so you're more experienced. They gave you a good reference, no?"

Franco opened his palms and sighed. "They gave us all a month's pay and that was it. How am I going to tell Giovanna? It'll kill her."

"I'll tell you what," said Eugenio, "Why don't you come and work with me? I could do with an experienced waiter. Now I've got a really English restaurant we'll get more customers and build up the business. You'll be my partner."

"But you were complaining only last week about how business has gone down. This place won't support two families."

Eugenio was determined to be upbeat. "I know, but this feeling against the Italians won't last. They'll forget about it once the Germans get closer, you'll see. It's true, some customer wanted to show me something in the paper this morning about how we're not to be trusted, how we're all secret spies, or some nonsense like that, but no one believes it. Hang on, there's a customer, I'll be back." He turned back as he lifted the plastic curtain to the restaurant, "He said it's a shame the stuff they're publishing about us, and he's English."

Franco pulled the paper out of his pocket and, licking his finger, began to flick through the pages of the 'Daily Mirror'.

In an article by John Boswell he read, 'There are more than twenty thousand Italians in Great Britain. London alone shelters more than eleven thousand of them. The London Italian is an indigestible unit of population.'

Franco didn't feel he was being 'sheltered', in fact just the opposite. He had always prided himself on how hard he had worked. He glanced down the page. 'He often avoids employing British labour. It is much cheaper to bring a few relations in from the old home town. And so the boats unloaded all kinds of brown-eyed Francescas and Marias, beetle-browed Ginos, Titos and Marios...'

The mention of Francesca made him wince. She hadn't come off a boat - she was born here. Most of her friends were English. What was this man suggesting? That his daughter should be locked up? He went on with an increasing sense of outrage.

'Now every Italian colony in Great Britain and America is a seething cauldron of smoking Italian politics.

Black fascism. Hot as hell.'

Franco closed the paper and pushed it away in disgust. How could anyone write such stuff? Had this person ever met an Italian? Everyone he knew thought Mussolini was a crazy man. Sure, lots of his friends went to the Fascio, but that was just that it was a nice place to meet, to reminisce and to discuss what was going on in the world. He opened the paper again.

'Even the peaceful, law-abiding proprietor of the back-street coffee shop bounces into a fine patriotic frenzy at the sound of Mussolini's name...

We are nicely honeycombed with little cells of potential betrayal.

A storm is brewing in the Mediterranean.

And we, in our droning, silly tolerance are helping it to gather force.'

It was too depressing. Eugenio was the kind of man that this writer was talking about, with his 'back street coffee shop.' But Eugenio was far too busy running the place and trying to look after his pregnant wife to even give a thought to what Mussolini was up to most of the time, and when he did think about it, it was to wish that the Italians at home would get rid of him.

He got up and poured himself a cup of coffee. Eugenio came in shouting an order for 'two baked beans and tea for table six.'

Franco said, "I've read the article and it explains why we've been sacked."

"Why?"

"They think Mussolini's going to declare war. It would be embarrassing if we were arrested while we were on duty. Better get rid of us before it comes to that." He pushed the paper across the table where Eugenio glanced at the opening paragraph.

"What's indigestible mean?" he asked.

"You know, you can't swallow it, you can't get it down because it's so disgusting."

"Ha!" laughed Eugenio, "The only indigestible thing around here is their food. I've had to change to a British supplier and you've never seen anything like the rubbish I'm getting delivered. Anyway, like it says, there are eleven thousand Italians in London. What are they going to do? Arrest us all? They'd have to put up a massive barbed wire fence all round Clerkenwell. There aren't enough places in the prisons for all the Italians in the city, let alone the country. Anyway, I've been thinking. The shop next door is empty. It's been empty for months. You could open up an ice-cream parlour. Giovanna makes great ice cream, and while we're doing up the shop you can come and work with me. And the rent on the place won't be very much. We'll go and have a look at it after work if you like, I know who's got the key."

He took out the beans that he ladled out of a vat on the cooker and looked at the plates in disgust. "This is what I call indigestible" he said, before putting on his best waiter's smile and disappearing through the curtains.

Franco had to admit it wasn't a bad idea. If he could go home and tell Giovanna they'd got a plan and that his being sacked did not mean that they would be out on the streets with only the clothes they stood up in, then she might not have hysterics and threaten to... he wasn't sure what. The last time she had threatened to go back to her mother in Lucca. That was four years ago and Franco thought it would be too unkind at that moment to point out that her mother had been dead for five years. Still, he would have to handle the situation delicately. It would mean spending the money they had saved up to bring her cousin over on doing up the shop next door instead and she wouldn't like that. But now there was no chance of anyone moving to England from Italy - so there was no point in keeping the money for that.

The bell at the front of the restaurant rang again. Eugenio hurried back into the kitchen. "Give us a hand, Franco. Two breakfasts and a pot of tea for four."

Franco looked around at the gloomy kitchen as if seeing it for the first time. The kettle was charred black on the gas ring. He washed his hands in the sink that was full of crockery, and his spirits began to lift a little. He could get this place cleaned up if Eugenio would let him and the idea of running an ice-cream parlour appealed to him. It would be strange being his own boss and not having to run around after the head waiter at the Savoy any longer. He'd miss all the important people who came in every day and listening in to their conversations about who had left whom, who was meeting whom to try and get rid of Mr Chamberlain. Only last week he had been serving Mrs Pritchard afternoon tea when Mr Pritchard suddenly appeared with a young lady on his arm and it was clear from the expression on his face that afternoon tea was the last thing he had on his mind. Franco had moved quickly to block Mrs Pritchard's view. She had looked up at him languidly and smiled and said, "It's quite all right, Franco, I'm not going to make a scene. My husband is one of those men who keeps his brains in his trousers."

Franco had been embarrassed and gone off to fetch the Swami so that Mrs Pritchard could be distracted by having her palm read. Now he found himself serving a young soldier and a woman he took to be the boy's mother. She was wearing a threadbare grey coat and the kind of hat that had gone out of fashion ten years earlier. She was holding the young man's hand and saying, "But you can't blame me for worrying about you, it all sounds so dangerous. They say that the Germans are going to invade France soon. Do be careful, I pray every night that you'll come home safely."

Franco took their order and went back into the kitchen. Everyone has their worries, he thought to himself. At least he wasn't going to have to go off and fight. What was the worst that they could do to him? Perhaps Eugenio was right, he would start up a new business and then he wouldn't have to worry about losing his job.

Chapter Forty Seven

In the yard the lorries were rumbling, the smell of exhaust making the night thick with fumes. Orders were being shouted, doors slammed and men were stumbling out of the quarters, hoisting their knapsacks onto their backs, bleary-eyed and confused. Maurice was one of the last out. He had packed the night before feeling a mixture of excitement and trepidation. He felt slightly sick, and wasn't sure if that was the effects of the cider he'd drunk, the fact that it was four o'clock in the morning, or the lack of sleep he'd had once he'd learnt that they would be going to France. He clambered into the back of the lorry and closed his eyes. Once he was on the train he'd be able to sleep. He also felt somewhat guilty. He'd left two of the three library books he'd taken out on top of his pillow with a note asking that they should be returned, but the French phrase book was hidden at the bottom of his bag. He hadn't got very far with it - he just couldn't get past 'Comment vous appelez-vous?', a phrase that he had repeated to himself a hundred times a day, in his mind's eye always addressed to a beautiful French girl of his own age.

The other question, which was easier to answer was, "Will we be fighting?"

"No, lad," the sergeant-major had said, "We're not even taking any weapons. Pioneer work's what you'll be doing."

Maurice wasn't sure what pioneer work was, he just prayed it wasn't digging more tank trenches. The lorries drove in convoy to Leicester station. The streets were deserted and dark. The rocking motion of the lorry made him feel queasier than ever and he had a sharp pain above his right eye. With relief he climbed gingerly out of the back of the lorry and went down the steps to where the train was waiting to take them to Southampton.

He slept for a couple of hours and when he woke up the crowded compartment was full of cigarette smoke and he was being nudged to take a tin cup of hot, sweet tea. He looked out of the window. In the east the sun was coming up over the fields. Joe was still asleep next to him. He stretched and stepped out into the corridor. He needed to pee. There were soldiers sitting on their kitbags in the corridor slumped against the window. Climbing carefully over them he eventually found the lavatory and had to steady himself as the train swayed along over the tracks.

They arrived at Southampton Water in the early evening. A chill wind was blowing off the sea. Maurice was surprised at how calm it was - all the pictures he had seen were either of a tropical paradise kind of a sea, a deep blue faraway place, or a ship-tossing turbulent sea surrounding the British Isles. This wasn't either of those. And there wasn't a ship in sight. He was hot in his uniform and having wandered down to the end of the quay, he put his kit-bag down against a wall and slumped down with his back against it. There seemed to be about two hundred men sitting around listlessly until the news came through that they wouldn't be sailing that night, in fact it probably would be early the next evening before they got away.

The older soldier next to him said resignedly, "War's not about fighting, it's about hanging around for bloody days on end." He didn't seem to be addressing anyone in particular, and Maurice decided to try and find Joe and to stake out their place to spend the night. It wasn't at all as he had expected. There didn't seem to be anyone who knew what was going on, but there were lots of rumours. They would be going to Paris; anyone who thought they weren't going to the front was stupid. Why would they be taking all these soldiers to France if it wasn't to go and defend the Maginot line? The reason the army wasn't telling them was because they didn't want men to desert. There were no ships because they'd left port the day before to transport the weapons to France. There were no weapons. They were still being shipped from the armament factories.

"Who the fuck knows what's going on?" said Joe, "I need a drink, let's go and have a last couple of pints. They might be the last we ever have."

But when they reached the gates leading out of the port, two guards with rifles over their shoulders turned them back. "Sorry, lads," they were told, "Town's out of bounds."

Reluctantly they returned to the sheds by the quayside where they were billeted, Maurice beginning to feel for the first time that it was all for real, that tomorrow they'd be in France.

The following day dragged slowly, the only interest being the large ship that moored in the early afternoon. By the time the men had embarked it was growing dark, and Maurice and Joe, weary from waiting, found a corner where they could bed down and went to sleep. Maurice woke in the middle of the night, the gently rolling sea and the strange creaking sounds as well as the murmuring voices of men unable to sleep made him feel uneasy. He went out on deck and lit a cigarette. He watched the mares' tails that shimmered under a full moon as the ship rolled gently. He flicked the cigarette end overboard and watched it disappear into the darkness and sighing heavily, went back to his sleeping bag.

He was woken by the droning sound of a plane above the ship. It was dawn and already a number of men had collected on deck.

"Is it one of ours?" he asked anxiously.

"No, mate, that's a Froggy plane, someone said, "Come to show us the way in. There's the harbour."

In the distance, through a haze, he could just make out the grey outline of a town on the horizon. The wind was chilly and he shivered, not sure whether it was with cold or apprehension. The men all around him seemed nonchalant, joking about the breakfast of frog legs and red wine they'd be having when they arrived. He went back inside and rolled up his sleeping bag and nudged Joe, who was still asleep.

"We're nearly there," he said, "You'd better get up, we can see France."

"What's it look like?" asked Joe, rubbing his eyes and reaching for a cigarette.

Maurice shrugged. "I dunno. France I guess. Why don't you come and see for yourself?"

An hour later the ship docked and the men filed down the gangway. It was a twenty minute walk to Calais Station where an old steam train was making a strange rattling sound and belching steam into the air. Maurice read on the side of the carriage '8 chevaux ou 40 hommes.'

"What's it say?" asked Joe, "You're the French expert."

"40 men in 8 carriages," whispered Maurice, "and just shut up, will you. I'm not an expert."

"Don't be daft. There's fifty of us in this carriage, if you can call it that." Joe shook his head. "My old man told me about French trains. These wooden benches that give you a numb bum after ten minutes. And it stinks of horses or cows or something like that."

As the train pulled slowly out of the station he added, "Well, at least we're not going towards Germany. We're going south west. And I didn't see any armaments being unloaded, did you?"

Maurice shook his head and gazed out of the window. The houses looked different from those at home, and he couldn't put his finger on why, but the countryside wasn't the same either.

For most of the journey there was silence as the men either dozed or slept. The crossing had been tiring and after another long and tedious train trip there was little conversation until they finally came to a stop near Rennes. It was almost four o'clock when they reached their destination, an encampment of tents already put up for them.

"Right, men, this will be our home for the next month or so. Our task is to build a siding so that ammunition can be taken from here to the front. The mess is over there, and your quarters are behind me. You have this afternoon and evening to get your bearings and everyman will report for duty at 0700 hours when you'll receive your work schedule. Every man will be back in their own quarters by 22 hundred hours. Dismissed."

Having found a tent and unpacked, Maurice and Joe decided to explore the area. They crossed the railway line and followed a sign to L'Hermitage, a small village twenty minutes walk from the camp. Though it was early evening the sun was still hot and the buildings gave off a glare that hurt their eyes. The place seemed to be almost entirely deserted until they reached a bar in the town square where a couple of old men were sitting at a table. They didn't look up as Maurice and Joe passed them. Maurice had been practising how to order two beers under his breath ever since they'd left the camp.

The barman looked up from from the door behind the bar and called through it, "Anaïs."

Then he went back to polishing his glass without giving them another glance. Unsure what to do, they looked around. Some older men were sitting in the corner deep in conversation, and Maurice was disappointed to find that he couldn't make out a single word of what was being said. After a few minutes a girl of about their age came in smiling.

"Can I help you?" she asked in English. Maurice was taken aback, but having worked so hard on it, he was determined to use it.

"Deux beers, silver plate," he said.

The girl smiled and pulled the beers. "Four francs, please."

Maurice blushed, "Shit, they don't take English money, I'd completely forgotten." he looked helplessly at Joe.

"Don't look at me, mate, you're the expert." He picked up his beer and walked outside.

"It's all right," said the barmaid, "I can take your English money this time. Many soldiers do the same."

Maurice handed her a sixpenny piece which she put in the pocket of her apron. He had been expecting some change, but when none was offered, he thought it must be something to do with the high price of beer in France. And it wasn't beer either, but a kind of rather warm lager that didn't taste right at all. She was looking at him with an expression of faint amusement.

"You don't like our beer?" she said.

"Um, well, it's not what I'm used to." He took another sip, put the glass on the counter and then asked, "How did you learn to speak such good English?"

"Most men who come in are English soldiers now. It is like that since more than one year."

He wanted to ask her if she would help him with his French, but before he could, she gave a little laugh. "I'm not a teacher," she said, "I don't give French lessons."

Maurice looked embarrassed. "I wasn't going to ..." But she interrupted,

"Oh? Nearly all soldier who comes in and talks with me asks me to give him lessons. You don't want lessons?"

"Well, of course I'd like lessons, but that's not what I was going to say." Maurice swigged his glass quickly and put it back on the counter.

"Another one?" he liked the way she pronounced the 'th' as if she had a slight lisp, and the way she rolled rolled the 'r'. He nodded and put a threepenny piece on the counter.

"So what were you going to say?" She glanced up at him as she pulled the beer. He was aware of being teased, and didn't know how to react at all.

"Nothing really. I was going to ask...oh, it doesn't matter."

A boisterous group of English soldiers came into the bar. Maurice took his beer outside to join Joe who was talking to another soldier and who followed the others into the bar as Maurice sat down.

"Works bloody hard they say," said Joe gloomily, "Laying railway sleepers and shoveling gravel. And the beer's crap. And he says what you get on the French news is a lot more than what we get in England. He says the French reckon it's our fault that Norway is such a balls up. They don't reckon that our politicians have got a clue. Not one of them. They don't like us very much. Shall we go?"

He stood up and looked at his beer before setting it back down on the table. "I won't be having that piss again. Try the old vino next time."

They walked back towards the camp. "What's biting you?" asked Maurice.

"Don't know why you have to ask. Holed up in a god forsaken dump with nothing to drink and nowhere to go."

"Doesn't seem too bad to me, said Maurice. "Nice weather, spring's here. It's OK."

"That's because you think you'll be able to shag that barmaid," said Joe. "You won't."

Chapter Forty Eight

Reinhardt sat back and looked around. Something was different, but he couldn't quite make out what it was. While Elizabeth went to 'powder her nose', he glanced at the menu, opened the paper and flicked through it, not sure what he was looking for, but feeling that something was wrong. A waiter came to take his order. Reinhardt glanced up at him.

"Hullo, you're new, aren't you?"

The waiter gave the slightest nod, "Yes sir, we started last week."

"We?" repeated Reinhardt, wondering whether waiters had suddenly assumed the status of royalty.

"Fourteen of us, sir, we started on the same day."

"Ah," said Reinhardt, looking around at the other waiters who were serving some of the other tables, "I hadn't realised that the Savoy was doing so well."

"I believe some members of staff left," said the waiter, "Can I take your order, sir?"

Reinhardt suddenly understood and felt a sharp spasm of fear. "Bring me a large whisky and a sherry, please."

He was so preoccupied by his thoughts that he scarcely noticed Elizabeth sit down next to him and slip her arm through his.

"What is it?" she asked quietly, "You look as if you've seen a ghost."

He smiled thinly and withdrew his arm. "It's probably not important," he said, shaking his head.

"What isn't? You're being very mysterious."

He turned to face her. "Do you notice anything different about this place. Just look around for a second."

Elizabeth turned and shrugged, "I don't know what I'm supposed to be looking for."

"The Italian waiters," said Reinhardt, "They've all gone. They've been sacked."

"Well," said Elizabeth, "That's terrible for them, of course, but I don't see how that affects us." She took a sip of her sherry.

Reinhardt looked around before answering, "Italy is about to join the war, so they've got rid of the Italian staff. The right wing press has been talking about the need to intern Germans for ages and the more time goes on, the worse it's going to get. The Home Office up till now has been very reasonable. Interning all Germans at the outbreak of the last war was a disaster and they don't want to repeat the mistake. But the fact that they've suddenly got rid of the waiters here means they've been leant on, and I think it'll be by Tory MP's. After all, they come here enough and the management wouldn't want to upset them."

"But I still don't see what you're so worried about. I mean, no one can really think that those poor waiters are spies, any more than they could believe that you're one."

"Don't you see?" Reinhardt was whispering, "The fact is that under pressure they've sacked a lot of staff. That pressure comes from the press and from from Tory back-benchers who need to be seen as patriotic Englishmen, especially as most of them thought Hitler was a jolly good thing until it was proved that he wasn't. Now they think all Germans are fifth columnists. It's going to end badly, I'm afraid, and that's the first time I've really thought that."

Elizabeth stared at him, "I do think you're being a wee bit paranoid, darling. I mean I hate to remind you of the fact, but you are over sixty. With a little less hair and an appalling taste in suits you could pass for a Tory MP yourself. And what do you think they could do to you?"

He smiled. "I really don't want to be interned again. After the first few weeks it wasn't too grim, last time." He put out his hand to Elizabeth. "But it did cost me my marriage. I mean, a relationship has to be incredibly strong to survive four years of separation and I couldn't bear to lose you.

Elizabeth feigned a shocked expression, "I thought you told me your first marriage was one of, what did you call it? Convenience? You said you were not unhappy when she divorced you."

Reinhardt shook his head, "It's not the same, and anyway, we were both too young and that was about, you know, money and carrying on the family name and all that nonsense."

"Links, darling, if you are interned, I promise I'll be here for you when you come out, but I don't think for a minute you will be, so let's eat. Can you get a waiter?"

He hesitated, "But it won't be the same as last time. There are thousands of refugees and add those to the thousands of Italians and the people like me who have been here for ever, whatever will they do with us all?"

Elizabeth gave him a gentle slap on the leg, "Whatever are you talking about? All right, listen. If you really are worried, we'll order lunch and then we'll discuss what we can do. But can we please eat now, I'm starving."

Reinhardt looked around. There was a heated discussion going on in the far corner of the room where a waiter was trying to placate an angry woman who was saying that she didn't know what had happened to the hotel, but she had never before been served a gin and it in a warm glass and really didn't see why the service had to be quite so appalling even if there was a war on. The waiter rushed off with the offending glass and nodded towards Reinhardt, "I'll be with you in a second, sir," he said.

Elizabeth sighed and picked up the paper. "If they've got rid of the Italians, you do have to wonder where they got the new ones from, don't you? I mean, why haven't they been called up, or joined the air raid people, or something. I must say, the service certainly isn't as good as it was." She found the fashion page and shook her head, " Do you think the latest fashion for every one to dress like seventy year old spinsters is so that when the Germans see our attempts to look glamorous they'll say, "Why on earth would we ever want to invade England?""

Reinhardt often wondered at Elizabeth's absolute refusal to engage with any information that she found disagreeable. For a while he'd found it amusing. As long as it didn't impinge on her life directly she could ignore it, and even when something threatened to upset her equanimity, she would simply behave as if it wasn't there. He had asked her about it once, but she has laughed and said, "Really, Links, you do say the funniest things sometimes. I have no idea what you can possibly mean, but there's no point in getting worked up about things you can't do anything about, is there?"

In the end he had decided that being stuck in a meaningless marriage for fifteen or so years had taught her first of all to ignore what she didn't want to hear, and then, later, not to hear it at all. But he felt that this was really important, that they must make a decision about what to do. He put his hand in hers.

"Elizabeth, listen to me. Things are moving very fast now. Like I said, if they are getting rid of the Italian staff, then it won't be long before there's a really big campaign to intern people like me, don't you see that?"

Elizabeth took a menu from the waiter, "At last," she said, "Now, I'm starving, what shall we have?' and she began to study the hors d'oeuvres.

Reinhardt knew there was no point in trying to continue the conversation, at least until she had ordered, so he was surprised when she said, without looking up, "Then I think we should go to America. I don't think you can be right, but it's obviously bothering you a lot, so I've been thinking for some time that a move would do us good. You've got the money, we could start a new life away from all this dreariness. It's browning everybody off. I'll have the oysters followed by the beef." She put down the menu and smiled at him. "You see, I'm not just a scatter-brain, I do think about things and I do read the papers. I can't believe any government would be so wicked as to lock up perfectly innocent people, not in this day and age, especially after the last time but that's not the point, is it?"

"Sorry," said Reinhardt, taken aback by this completely unexpected turn of events, "What is the point, then?"

"Silly," said Elizabeth, squeezing his hand, "The point is that you're worried about being locked up again in some frightful place and that while you're away some beau is going to come and sweep me off my feet. I don't think for a single minute any of that is going to happen, but I don't want you to worry and it seems that the only thing that's going to reassure you is if we go far away, and the only place I can think of is America."

The waiter brought their drinks and Elizabeth and Reinhardt touched glasses.

"I don't know," said Reinhardt slowly, "I don't even know if it would be possible. I mean, we'd need visas, and how would we get there? So many ships are being sunk by U-boats. I know the Queen Mary got across to New York, but that was weeks ago. Are passenger liners still going to America? And where would we live once we got there?" He sighed. "I don't think it would be possible, but I love you for thinking of it." And he kissed her on the cheek.

"Well, if we can't, we can't, but then you've got to start being realistic and accept the fact that even you are not so important as to be seen as a danger to national security. So perhaps we can talk about something else now." She opened the paper and began to read about a murder on Barnes Common.

Reinhardt looked out of the window while he absentmindedly shook his whisky. Perhaps she was right, he wouldn't be seen as a risk. After all, at his hearing back in January, the tribunal gave him a 'C' without a second thought. But that was over four months ago and a lot had changed in the meantime. We had effectively lost Norway, Scapa Flow had been bombed, the war was going badly and the popular press was turning against refugees. He shook his head. But that's why he had sold the car, so that they could have a really good binge, but it was only now that he really felt that his situation was hopeless. 'Let's drink and be merry for tomorrow we....' he swallowed down the last drop of whisky and called for another.

Elizabeth was pointing out an article about how many people had been prosecuted for not following the rules about the blackout. "I can't believe they're as strict about it in other cities," she said. "If we can't move to America perhaps we could go to Bristol or somewhere like that. I'm sure they would never catch up with you, even if they did want to intern you."

Reinhardt looked at her fondly, but he was no longer hungry.

Chapter Forty Nine

Esther Hart's Diary

Thursday 2nd May 1940

It does seem as if Norway will be lost, though the whole situation has no reality for me at the moment. Spent the whole day yesterday in the garden to escape Charles and his increasingly incontinent cat. Where the branch from the silver birch came down in the winter I noticed a woodpecker, a black and white one and not one I've ever seen before. It was pecking furiously in the wound on the tree and only flew off when I went into the greenhouse. While I dug I kept thinking about those young men, hundreds of miles away trying to manage in the freezing cold, wrestling with skis that they can't have ever learned to use properly while German aircraft swooped down on them. And here I was, in the summer sunshine under a clear blue sky with only the barrage balloons to say that there was anything out of the ordinary. Perhaps that's why the politicians who are in charge of the war seem to be completely unable to make a decision that would retrieve the situation; they just can't imagine what is going on. Churchill is the only one who has ever been in the front line and he isn't trusted by his own party.

Friday 3rd May

Yesterday the Prime Minister announced that our troops in Andalsnes and Namsos had been forced to retreat and were being evacuated. I watched Charles as he read the article. For a long time he didn't move, and then he surreptitiously wiped his eyes with his napkin and said, "Bloody Churchill, excuse my language, but the man's a bloody liability. It's the Dardanelles all over again."

I couldn't argue with him. I didn't even want to, in fact I felt sorry for him, but at the same time I felt very frightened. Somewhere at the back of my mind I did believe that over the last few months we had been building up a much stronger army and navy which were properly equipped. But then it turns out that we are spending less than half of what the Germans are spending on the war effort.

Maybe it is in part Mr Churchill's fault. After all, he is responsible for the Admiralty. But Mr Chamberlain has lost all credibility. He seems completely unable to understand the danger we're in. He is the same age as Charles. Perhaps when men reach that age they become so fixed in their ideas that it is impossible for them to see the reality. Anyway, there were lots of politicians on the news saying that no one who didn't have all the facts was in a position to judge, but it's difficult to believe that the Prime Minister can survive. There is so much anger amongst people. It is also clear that the BBC is simply a mouthpiece for the government. It's not knowing what is happening that is the most frightening thing of all.

Still, one good thing has come out of it. Douglas and Charles didn't discuss it last night for the first time.

Monday 6th May

Another weekend survived.

"When the world wearies and society ceases to satisfy, there is always the garden." - Minnie Aumonier. I don't know who she is, but I think she must be a wise woman.

Tuesday 7th May

There's a big debate in the House of Commons today. Last night Mr Chamberlain was on the radio. He kept saying things like, "The people of this country don't realise what they're up against." Last month he said that Hitler had "missed the bus." Anyway Charles kept nodding with his face pressed up against wireless. When Mr Chamberlain had finished his broadcast, Charles clapped his hands together and said, "There, what did I tell you?" which even made Douglas look at his father rather oddly. Charles went off to bed looking much more chipper than he has recently.

The debate in Parliament is scheduled to last for two days. There doesn't seem to be any real opposition to the government from the Labour party which means the government will win the debate and Mr Chamberlain will carry on and that will be terrible for the country as we will certainly lose the war. Barbara phoned from a call box near Parliament Square. She said I should go down and join her, there's so much excitement with thousands of people waiting for the outcome. She had to shout and said that she was sure that something momentous was going to happen and that Chamberlain would soon be out. I wish I had her confidence.

Wednesday 8th May

I don't think anybody had any idea how many Conservative MP's want to see the back of Mr Chamberlain, and it seems he might be forced to resign after all. What must have really wounded him was Admiral Keyes, dressed in full naval uniform saying that the government lacked nerve and that he had been assured that it would have been easy to attack Trondheim but unnecessary because the army was being successful. But the worst attack of all came late into the night from Leo Amery who stood behind the Front bench and finished by quoting Oliver Cromwell's speech to the Long Parliament. "You have sat too long here for any good you have been doing! Depart, I say, and let us have done with you! In the name of God, go!" The paper this morning said it was 'the most damaging assault since the war."

Charles was predictably outraged when he saw the report and said Amery should be hanged for treason, but he's a great admirer of Lord Keyes, who was, after all, one of the heroes of the last war and so confined himself to saying that Keyes was a great admiral but his political judgement wasn't up to much. Spent the afternoon in the garden to avoid any more lectures, and am writing this outside in glorious sunshine before Douglas gets back from work and the whole conversation starts up again.

Thursday 9th May

Men born since May 10th 1903 are being called up. It's being said that Mr Chamberlain has asked to see the King, but there's been no announcement of it on the wireless, which Charles has completely commandeered. Anyway, in the greengrocer's a group of women were saying that the government wants to form a coalition with a war cabinet but that the Labour party is only willing to discuss it as long as Chamberlain steps down. At the same time as the politicians argue about who should be Prime Minister, there are increasing reports that Germany is about to attack Holland and Belgium. I have an image of two children squabbling in the middle of the street, so intent on their fighting that they don't notice the steam roller bearing down on them which is about to squash them both flat.

I sometimes find myself more concerned about my beans than I am about the war, which shows how, after a while, war makes our values all go to pot. I worry constantly about the children and write to them, but I also think that people who say the bombing will begin soon must be right. I suppose what I'm saying is that I'm just as bad as the politicians. Sometimes I look at all the work I've done in the garden and think hat in a few short weeks, before things have come up properly, this could just be a bomb crater.

It doesn't help me at all to write down depressing thoughts. I thought it might, but it doesn't. I must stop doing it.

Friday 10th May

The news is everywhere that Holland and Belgium have been bombed by Germany. Douglas had a phone call and rushed off at six this morning. Charles woke up and insisted on going down to the shop to get the papers, but he has become quite unsteady on his feet, especially early in the morning so I went with him. He bought every available newspaper and seemed to take a grim satisfaction in the news. French cities have been attacked, including Calais, and that surely means that we'll be next. In some ways it has come as a relief after so much waiting. There is talk of implementing the evacuation plan, but then all the available transport is needed for troops. Anyway, I've got the gas masks out of the cupboard and made Charles try his on. They were very dusty and it took me a while to remember where I'd put them.

There was an awful lot about how German parachutists dressed as Dutch soldiers had captured Dutch aerodromes very quickly and then been supported by the Luftwaffe.

Charles said that it would be madness to get rid of Chamberlain now, that was why the enemy had attacked when it did, what was needed was a strong prime minister with the whole country behind him.

Douglas phoned at eight to say he wouldn't be home tonight, there were some urgent things to deal with, so Charles an I listened to the nine o'clock news. When the pips sounded and the announcer said 'This is the Home Service. Here is the Right Honourable Neville Chamberlain MP who will make a statement", my heart sank, but then he announced his resignation. He said it had become clear that the country wants a coalition government and that the obstacle to one being formed was himself. He had therefore tendered his resignation and Mr Churchill is Prime Minister.

I felt quite sorry for him. He has not been an effective leader since war broke out, but his thin reedy voice made him sound so vulnerable. Surprisingly Charles said nothing, but shook his head and went to bed.

I went out into the garden. It was a beautiful evening. The blackout means that the stars are so clear in a way that they never are in London normally. I sat until it grew dark and wondered how many more times that will be possible. The fear is palpable everywhere, in peoples' voices and in their eyes. Only sixty miles away towns are being bombed, and people are dying.

Saturday 11th May

Hardly slept at all last night worrying about the children and wondering whether I'll ever see them again. Bombs dropped somewhere in Kent. Lay awake thinking our time could come at any minute and wished Douglas were here. He came back at seven this morning for a change of clothes and some breakfast but was very tight lipped and wouldn't say very much at all. Barbara phoned before Charles was up . She said there were real concerns that the reason that Norway and Holland were so easily overrun was that the Germans had trained thousands of fifth columnists who all knew of Hitler's plans and so sabotaged their own armies. She also said that Douglas isn't working with Herbert any more! He was called away yesterday, cleared his desk at 5 o'clock, wouldn't say what was going on and hasn't been seen since. I said I had no idea, that he's been back briefly this morning but hadn't said why he was away all night and I don't know when to expect him back. He never tells me anything anyway.

Barbara said it would be a really good idea to meet. Scribbling this while Charles goes and gets the papers. Seeing Barbara at Lyons at three.

Evening.

Though it's a Saturday there's still no news of Douglas. Barbara said that with Mr Churchill becoming Prime Minister but especially the German invasion of the Low countries, everything has changed. Herbert told her that the Home Office has been bombarded by demands from the military authorities to have all alien men in east and south east England interned. Don't know if that includes men in London or not. Agreed to visit the Austrian Centre on Monday to find out, though it's surely not possible that they would intern the men there.

Sunday 12th May

When Douglas got home I told him how worried I'd been and how I really thought he might have phoned. He did apologise for that, but said that everything at the Home Office had been completely frantic. It wasn't just the change of government, it was also the increased threat to the country's security. He said he thought it would be a good idea for Charles and me to move out of London. He would stay in a hotel. I asked him how we could possibly afford it. He thought about this and then said that I was absolutely not to breathe a word of this to anyone, but that he has been given a new job within the Home Office. He wouldn't say any more than that but that his hotel bill would be paid for. For the next few weeks his hours were going to be completely unpredictable. Then he said it would be best if I went to stay with the children and his sister. I need time to think about this. I really feel my duty is to stay here. The children are safe where they are, and though I ache to see them, the idea of living with Ada is too awful to contemplate. She wouldn't be too keen to have me under her roof, either. I suggested that Charles might agree to go, but when it was put to him his reply was, "Good God. The idea's preposterous. The woman may be my daughter but she's also a bloody harpy. We'd end up killing each other." I couldn't have put it better myself.

The papers say the Expeditionary Force in France has moved into Belgium, "as smoothly as a machine." My heart sank when I saw that. There was the same kind of propaganda over Norway only a couple of months ago. Tomorrow is the Whit Bank Holiday. It's been cancelled.

Monday 13th May

Went to the Austrian Centre with Barbara who was dying to know what Douglas's new job is. I couldn't tell her even if I knew. She said she really fears for the refugees. Word got around the Home Office that Sir John Anderson found the Cabinet Meeting very difficult and is being heavily leant on to intern more aliens. Herbert thinks it's all a great deal of hysteria on the part of the Joint Intelligence Committee but he is frightened that as war over England may break out at any time, the Austrians and Germans in particular will be in danger from people accusing them of being spies or fifth columnists, so it may be safer for them to intern them.

The atmosphere at the Austrian Centre was very depressed. There are no more plans to do plays or put on concerts. Herr Niedermayer hasn't had any more news from his wife and is worried sick. She is due to be here in ten days or so, but Lotte said that it has been impossible to receive any letters from Austria for the last few days. We didn't stay long.

We both feel we've failed in some way. We haven't been able to help Lotte's friend, and we haven't been able to help Herr Niedermayer. The people at the Centre seemed resigned. Lotte said that no one thinks we can win the war against Hitler and that most of them will end up in camps after the invasion, or before the invasion if the cheap papers get their way.

Got home in time for the six o'clock news when the announcer warned us against having 'an optimistic outlook'!

Tuesday 14th May

Everyone's talking about the German parachutists and the way they are infiltrating local populations in Holland, apparently disguised as peasants and clergymen, or wearing Dutch uniforms. Charles is absolutely refusing to leave London. Douglas looks exhausted and is very monosyllabic.

Wednesday 15th May

Eden broadcast a call for people to join a volunteer defence corps. The Dutch army in the north of the country has surrendered. Charles and Douglas have taken to muttering in corners again. Makes me feel unutterably bleak and alone.

Chapter Fifty

When Franco told Giovanna that all the Italians in all the big restaurants and hotels had lost their jobs, she reacted in a way that was only partly predictable. First of all she refused to believe it and accused Franco of having got himself dismissed for being idle. Then she demanded to know exactly when he was told that he had been sacked. When he said, "Today," she wanted to know at what time. He admitted that it was at seven thirty that morning. "So where have you been for the past twelve hours?"

He explained that he had been helping Eugenio and they had a plan to rent the next door shop and open an ice cream parlour.

She gave a little scream and hurled the piece of dough that she had been rolling out towards him. It hit the calendar with the picture of the Virgin and calendar and dough fell to the floor.

"So you think it's better to go and tell your stupid brother about it than come home and tell your wife and keep her in the dark for the whole day, do you? Well, in that case you can go and live with him." Then she burst in to tears and went off into the bedroom. Franco was hanging up the calendar when she reappeared a minute later.

"Pazzo, Franco, you're both mad. Eugenio goes to all the trouble of turning his restaurant into an English one and then you think it's a good idea to open an Italian ice cream parlour right next door. You're mad." She pressed a forefinger against her temple. "Pazzo, completamente pazzo."

Then she burst into tears again and rushed off to their bedroom. Franco was sitting staring into space when Francesca came home an hour later. She put her arms round him and asked him what was wrong.

"I've been sacked," he said bluntly, "Just like that, with no warning."

Francesca sat down next to him and squeezed his arm. " I don't suppose Mama has taken it very well," she said.

He nodded, "Eugenio says I can go and work with him and we could set up an ice cream parlour in the empty shop next door. But your mother thinks that's a mad idea."

"I think it's a great idea, and I'll help. I've got back together again with Eric. He's joining some new thing the government has just set up, something to do with local defence. Eric says now that Mr Churchill's the Prime Minister England has a much better chance of winning the war and he doesn't think Italy will join in. He says Mr Churchill is a great admirer of Italy."

Franco sighed. "I hope he's right."

"But can we afford to open a new shop?" Francesca asked.

Franco shrugged, " We've got nearly two hundred pounds saved to bring your cousin over and get them a flat. That's not going to happen now, at least until the war is over, so we can use that, though your mother thinks that's a really terrible idea as well. What she doesn't seem to understand is that I must work, not just for the money, but for myself. What kind of man can't even support his family? He's not a man at all, he's better off dead and they're better off without him."

Francesca put her arm round round her father's shoulders. "You shouldn't talk like that. Nobody blames you. I'll talk to Mama. She's cross because she's frightened, but I'm sure she'll help. She thought converting Eugenio's restaurant was a crazy idea but she still came and helped."

Franco shook his head. "I don't know. She might be right this time. Perhaps it is crazy to open an ice-cream parlour right next to a café that we've just tried to make look English."

Francesca smiled. "Does Eugenio have any more customers now that he's painted his place red white and blue? Were people really boycotting it before? I don't think so. Do you really think that people are going to say that they're not going to eat ice cream because it's made by Italians? That is crazy. They eat our ice cream because it's the best and they know that Italians make the best ice cream in the world. Are we eating tonight or have we decided to starve ourselves to death?"

She got up and started to prepare the evening meal. "Go and talk to Eugenio. Tell him we'll help and I'll got and talk to Mama. She'll come round."

Franco crossed the landing and found Julia and his brother sitting at the table over supper and not speaking to each other. Eugenio looked relieved to see him and jumped up. "Hey, Franco, come and tell my miserable wife how everything's going to be all right. In a month's time we'll be selling the best ice cream in London and she won't have to lift a finger to help.'

"Shut up," Julia hissed, "you don't understand anything. I don't mind helping, it's not that, and I can make great ice cream. I use my grandmother's recipe, and she made the best ice cream in Lucca. Everyone said so. But don't you know there's rationing? Where are you going to get the ingredients from?"

Eugenio waved his arms in exasperation. "Do you think I've ever been able to get the best ingredients for my restaurant? Have you ever been able to buy decent tomatoes in this country or truffles or anything to make proper food? Has that stopped people coming? Of course not, because they don't know any better. It'll be the same with the ice cream. It's Italian so it's good. The English don't know what their missing, so there's no problem. Tell her Franco. She's cross because the baby keeps kicking and she's tired because she can't get comfortable."

Julia snorted. "It's nothing to do with the baby. You need a good kicking, Eugenio. Look, I'm sorry to have to say this in front of Franco, but at least he'll understand. The restaurant is hardly making enough to keep us, what with the rent and the cost of food going up, we can hardly keep ourselves. We can't pay you, Franco for working in the restaurant."

Franco sat down, "I know that and I don't need you to. I've been paid a month's wages. What we need is help getting the new place ready. We don't even know whether we can rent it, or how much rent would be, but I think we must try."

Eugenio stood up, "I know who owns it. We'll go and see him now. It can't be much, it's been empty for over a year."

Franco stuck his head around the door of his flat but the kitchen was empty. He could hear Francesca trying to soothe her mother while Giovanna protested between sobs that Franco couldn't possibly run a business, he was terrible with money and they were all going to starve to death. He closed the door gently and joined his brother on the street.

"It belongs to someone called Mr Shaw. I phoned him after you'd gone," said

Eugenio. "I got his number from the bookies opposite. He told me that he's a good landlord. I didn't know it before, but he owns half the shops in the street. Anyway, I phoned him and said we were interested and he's going to give us the key so we can have a look."

Mr Shaw's 'business acquaintance' was waiting for them outside the shop. He was brandishing a large torch and a bunch of keys.

"Thing is lads," he said, "It's been empty a few months now, so there's no electricity. Course, it'll need a lick of paint and be spruced up a bit, so Mr Shaw is willing to be very generous over the rent, though of course it is in a prime location. All the businesses here are doing very well. Very well indeed."

"I've got this restaurant....." said Eugenio pointing to his door.

"So you'll know that I'm right, and that'll be nice for you both won't it, working next door to each other, like."

He unlocked the door and shone the torch into the darkness. It smelled terribly of damp.

A shelf running the length of the shop had come away from the wall and there was a large pile of plasterboard where part of the ceiling had collapsed.

"So we've got a kitchen at the back. When the boarding's been taken off the window you'll see it'll look a lot bigger."

Eugenio went to remove it but the man put his hand on Eugenio's arm.

"No, don't jump the gun, son. Mr Shaw was very particular. Nothing's to be touched until terms are agreed. We don't want you liable for damages before you've even moved in, do we?"

Franco peered into the darkness. "Can we see the kitchen?"

They climbed over the collapsed ceiling and felt their way into a narrow space that had a couple of loose shelves and a sink.

"See, this'll come up lovely with a bit of work. And the fact that it does need a bit of sprucing up here and there is obviously reflected in the price." He shone the torch around the floor. Franco thought he heard scuttling behind the skirting boards.

"I don't know," he said doubtfully, "it needs a lot of work doing on it."

The man shook his head, "Two days work at most. Look, I'll tell you what I'll do. I'll see if Mr Shaw will agree to two, no three days rent free while you do it up. You know, fix the ceiling, well that's nothing, put up the shelves, get the electric connected and Bob's your uncle. I'm not promising mind."

"How much is the rent?" said Eugenio.

"Twelve pounds a week, payable in advance with a two month deposit. Then there's a couple of little extras that aren't worth bothering about, you know, rates and ground rent but they're nothing."

Eugenio shook his head, "That's a lot more than I'm paying and this is half the size.

I think it's too much. Don't you, Franco?"

Franco hesitated. He'd built all his hopes on this place and without it he couldn't imagine any kind of future at all. but he was worried that he simply wouldn't be able to manage the renovation on the money he'd got, and simply dreaded Giovanna seeing it. He had already persuaded himself that she wouldn't see it until it was all fixed up.

"Is that Mr Shaw's best offer?" he said.

"There's a lot of other people interested,"said the man, stroking his moustache thoughtfully. "Let's get outside and we'll think about a way around this. I can see you're hard working lads and I'm sure Mr shaw would be pleased to have you as his tenants, so let me think a minute."

Franco was pleased to get out into the comparatively fresh air. The outside needed a lot of work as well; the window frames were rotten and it was clear that with a decent push the door would open without a key.

"Right, this is what I'll do. I'll go and see Mr Shaw right now He's a very busy man, but as a favour to you I'll put it to him that it would be a good investment to drop the rent to say, eight pounds a week in return for a cut of your weekly takings. That way everyone wins. You've got a knock down rent and just pay, say twenty per cent of your income. Gross, of course.

"I don't know,' said Franco, "We'll have to discuss it. It still seems a lot."

The man looked at him pityingly. 'I can give you till tomorrow at noon. I've got two other geezers interested at the going price, but like I say, I like you lads, and I'm partial to a bit of Italian ice cream myself. You won't get a better offer I promise you. Phone me in the morning. Here's my number."

He pulled out an old betting slip from his back pocket and the stub of a pencil from behind his ear. " My name's Mr Harper. You can get me on this number. Mr Shaw's in meetings all day tomorrow, but I'll let him know your decision."

Franco and Eugenio walked slowly to the bus stop. It was beginning to get dark and people were blacking out their windows.

"I couldn't see how much work it needed," said Franco, "but there's a lot more than two days. On the other hand, if we agreed to pay some of the income, that might mean that I wouldn't have to spend so much of the money we'd saved for Giovanna's cousin to come over. She might be happier about that. But she mustn't see the place as it is. She'd go crazy."

"It sounds like you've decided to do it, then," said Eugenio.

Franco grimaced. "It's a stinking expensive hole but I've got no choice. If I don't do that, then what will I do? Somehow I'm glad it was such a mess because it means I'll have to work really hard at it and that'll mean I can start to feel useful again."

Eugenio clapped his arm round his brother's shoulder.

"Let's celebrate and have a drink," he said, "I've got a bottle of Barolo I've been saving for when the baby's born but I think we should drink it now. But we'll have to take it to your place. Julia'll be in bed." he sighed. "She's nicer when I've had a decent glass."

Chapter Fifty One

Reinhardt was asleep when the knocking on the door started. He was dreaming that a group of men was taking a sledge hammer to his house and he was too afraid to go and stop them. He opened his eyes and peered at the alarm next to the bed. The hammering started up again. Reinhardt slipped out of bed and took his dressing-gown from the back of the door and ran downstairs.

"All right, I'm coming," he said, and opened the front door. Two policemen were standing in front of him. He recognised the younger one. He had come a few weeks earlier to tell Reinhardt that the local warden had complained that Reinhardt had been rude when warned about not obeying the blackout regulations. He breathed a sigh of relief.

"Hello, Constable," he said, "if this is about the blackout, I have been very careful...."

"It's not, sir," said the older one, "I'm afraid you're going to have to come with us. It won't be for too long, I'm sure. We'll wait while you get some effects together," and he pushed past Reinhardt into the living room.

Reinhardt looked at the younger policeman, "It's Constable Stevens, isn't it? Look here, my dear chap, can't you tell me what's going on?"

Constable Stevens lowered his eyes and followed his colleague into the living room. Reinhardt knew very well what was coming but he didn't feel inclined to make their job any easier.

"Well," he said, "I'll go and get dressed once I'm clear about why I should come with you. Am I suspected of having committed a crime of some sort? Am I under arrest? Do you have a warrant?"

The older man stood stiffly and took out his notebook, glanced at it, and then began to intone,

'Under Regulation 18B of the Defence, in brackets, General, Regulations 1939," he then read haltingly, "Item 1. If the Secretary of State has reasonable cause to believe that any person to be of hostile origin or associations or to have been recently concerned in acts prejudicial to the public safety or the defence of the realm or in the preparation or instigation of such acts and that by reason thereof it is necessary to exercise control over him, he may make an order against that person directing that he be detained. Item 1A..."

Reinhardt interrupted, "Excuse me, but is there much more of this?"

The policeman shuffled through his notebook. "Four more pages, sir."

"Well, I think I'd rather spend the time packing and saying good-bye to my wife, if it's all the same to you. She's still in bed. I really don't want her alarmed, so would you be decent fellows, make yourselves at home and I'll be down in a jiffy. What do you suggest I say to her?"

The two policemen looked at each other uneasily and shuffled their feet. "It should only be a matter of a few days."

Reinhardt paused on the stairs and turned back towards them. "Do you know, those were the exact words used last time. In 1914. "Just a few days." It was four years. But don't worry, officers I won't do anything stupid, like trying to escape through the bathroom window, I give you my word, as an Englishman."

Elizabeth was sitting up in bed with her side light on. "What's happening? Who's downstairs?"

Reinhardt sat on the edge of the bed and put his hand in hers, "The police. They've come. They say it'll only be for a few days."

"But you don't believe them, do you?"

Reinhardt shrugged his shoulders, "I just don't know, but in case it is longer, look, you need money. I'll write you some blank cheques. There's quite a bit left from the sale of the car, but, I know you wouldn't go mad, but be careful with it because I don't know how long I'll be gone. Why don't you go down and make them a cup of tea while I dress and pack."

Elizabeth shook her head and got up, " If I don't know when I'll see you again I'm buggered if I'm going to go and talk to them. I want to be with you."

Reinhardt took a suitcase from the top of the wardrobe and began to pack. Then he hung his dressing gown on the back of the bedroom door and began to dress hurriedly while Elizabeth watched.

"Do you think this is anything to do with my husband?" she asked, "Do you think they've been tapping our phone? I feel terrible, as if I've got you into this mess. Suppose they think you've been tied up with his madness."

Reinhardt sat down and pulled her down beside him. "No, it's nothing like that. If it was, they'd have come ages ago. They'll be after all the Germans, it's not just me."

A voice came up the stairs, "Mr Reinhardt, sir, we're waiting."

"Coming," he called, "Just give me two more minutes."

He took his cheque book out of his suit pocket and started signing cheques. Then he ran downstairs where the policemen were waiting impatiently. "Just let me put my affairs in order, it won't take a minute."

He took some writing paper from the cabinet and ran back upstairs and scribbled a letter to his bank manager to the effect that the bank should honour any cheques in his name that were presented by Mrs Elizabeth Coates. He put it in an envelope and held her.

"Don't come down," he said and he kissed her on the forehead. "I'll write as soon as I can and let you know where I am. Perhaps you'll be able to visit."

He felt empty as the police car crawled along Grays Inn Road. He'd often wondered about this moment, when he would be about to be imprisoned again. The last time he's felt a mixture of emotions- fear, anger, embitterment, but now he felt a strange numbness, as though he was removed from himself and curious about what was going to happen to him.

Scotland Yard smelt of disinfectant. He was right, there had obviously been a round up of Germans, and there were men of every age standing in small groups being watched by suspicious policemen. An elderly rabbi was watching as the person that Reinhardt took to be his son was remonstrating with a desk sergeant. "I wish to complain in the strongest possible terms," he was saying, "We have been brought here without explanation and what are we supposed to have done? This is as bad as Germany. When we came here we thought we were coming to a civilized country."

The rabbi put his hand on his son's arm and led him over to one of the groups. The desk sergeant shook his head and scratched the back of his head with the blunt end of his pencil and made a note in report book.

Constable Stevens led Reinhardt over to the desk. Without looking up, the desk sergeant asked in a bored voice, "Name?"

Reinhardt gave his name. "Address?"

"Age?"

"Sixty."

The two policemen glanced at each other. "And what's your nationality, sir, and how long have you been resident in this country?"

"I came here in 1901. I was born in Silesia, so technically I'm German, I suppose, though I've always regarded myself as English. My wife is English, and my sons are English."

The desk sergeant thought about this for a while, and then, in the box, wrote, 'stateless'.

"I'm not stateless," protested Reinhardt, "I've been here for forty years. As far as I'm concerned, I'm English."

"Do you have your naturalisation papers?" asked the policemen.

"No, but..."

"Then, if you don't mind me pointing out, you're not English, and you're not German, according to you, so that means that your stateless."

"That's ridiculous," said Reinhardt, but the policeman was not to be interrupted.

"You've been told why you've been arrested. You'll being staying here overnight and then transferred to a camp. And before you ask, you are not entitled to consult a lawyer. Have you had any breakfast?"

Reinhardt shook his head. "Then the constable will show you the dining room."

Though full of men queuing for breakfast and others sitting at the long trestles, the room was almost silent. Around the walls soldiers were watching as the queue slowly shuffled round. Some had pushed their food away from themselves, unable to bring themselves to eat more than a few mouthfuls. Others were eating as if it was to be their last meal, hunched over their plates and looking round as if they couldn't believe their luck at having suddenly been presented with so much food.

Behind him an old man with a strong german accent was remonstrating with a bemused guard. He was holding his plate up to the guard's face, as if he were responsible for the outrage that had been perpetrated on him. "Look," he was saying, "See this? What insult are you wanting me to eat now? This is pig meat, nicht wahr? You know I am Jew and you give me pig meat to eat. You lock me up here because I am Jew and then you give me pig meat. And this," he pointed at at a piece of fried bread that was lying in a small pool of lard, "this is..." he searched for the word in English, and failing to find it, spat, "Schmutzig, ja, schmutzig." And then, as an afterthought, added plaintively, "Es ist unrein."

The guard stared unblinking ahead as if the old man wasn't there and caught Reinhardt's eye.

"He can't eat it. He says it's taboo, unclean," explained Reinhardt.

The guard looked offended, "But it's nothing to do with me, I don't care if he eats it or not."

Deciding there was nothing more to be said, Reinhardt joined the queue. Unsure when he would be eating again, he ordered everything - burnt toast and margarine, bacon and egg swimming in fat and a large mug of tea. He took his tray over to a table that had just been vacated by a group of men who were being led away at the far end of the dining room and forced himself to eat. "Still as awful as last time," he muttered under his breath. The grease left an aftertaste on the roof of his mouth and he shivered in disgust.

Once he had finished he looked around. The silence was unnerving. Two policemen approached him, one holding a clip-board. "What's your name?" he asked slowly. "Do you speak English?"

Reinhardt gave his name and then said, equally slowly, "Yes, thank you, I speak English very well. In fact I was brought up speaking English."

The policeman made a tick on the clip-board and said to his colleague. "Cell six, and watch him. We've got a right clever bastard here."

"Tell me," said Reinhardt as he was being led down the stairs, "Have you really got enough cells for all the people here?"

"Most are being moved out this morning. Don't ask me where because I don't know, and I couldn't tell you if I did. You're in here."

He unlocked the door and pushed it open. Between the two bunks in the narrow space a man was lying on the floor while another bent over him, lifting his head and holding a plastic beaker to his mouth. He looked up and said to the policeman, "This man needs to get to a hospital now."

The policeman waved Reinhardt into the cell. "Why, what's wrong with him?"

"For God's sake, look at him, man." He looked down and lifted the mug to the other's mouth again, "Come on, you must drink."

The policeman hesitated. "I'll see if I can get the doctor down. I bet he's swinging the lead."

"Listen. I am a doctor. This man is almost comatose. If he doesn't get to a hospital now he's going to die. Smell his breath. He's diabetic and he's got no insulin with him. For God's sake go and phone for an ambulance."

The policeman still hesitated.

The doctor lay the man's head gently on a pillow and stood up and advanced on the policeman. "If he's not treated quickly he is going to die. Tell the hospital he is diabetic, and has ketoacidosis. If he dies because you haven't done the right thing, his death will be on your conscience. Now go. And tell them to bring insulin."

"All right," the policeman had gone pale, "but I'll have to lock you in."

Reinhardt heard the key turn in the lock and the sound of footsteps rapidly disappearing.

"Bloody police," said the doctor, "I bet they didn't give him time to remember his insulin."

He knelt down beside the man who now lay completely motionless and felt the pulse on his neck. "God, what a mess," he sighed.

Reinhardt looked down at the gaunt face. The man's breathing was coming in deep and laboured gasps and a dark patch was forming around his groin.

"Help me move him into the recovery position," said the doctor. "I don't want him to choke if he vomits. You take his arm and I'll move him by the shoulders, but do it carefully."

Reinhardt knelt down. He reflected that he wasn't very good at this sort of thing. Between them they managed to roll the man onto his side and the doctor adjusted the pillow. The man gave a belch and moaned.

"I can't get him to drink, but all we can do is pray that they get here quickly." The doctor looked at his watch, and ran his fingers through his hair. Then he sat back on the lower bunk and looked at Reinhardt through steel rimmed glasses.

"Have you just arrived?" he asked. He spoke with a slight German accent.

Reinhardt nodded, "They came for me at about seven o'clock this morning. And you?"

"Yesterday. They arrested me in my surgery would you believe. Marched me out in front of a queue of patients, took me home and gave me twenty minutes to get my things. I couldn't even say good-bye to my wife and children. She'd taken the little one down to the beach. The others were at school. They did let me leave a note, but I couldn't let her know where I'd be since the police couldn't tell me where I would be taken. Spent the whole of yesterday on a train and arrived last night at about eleven."

"The beach?" queried Reinhardt. "Where d'you live?"

"Devon," said the doctor. "A little town called Seaton. It's ironic, really. Until yesterday I was treating internees in a camp there, and now suddenly I find myself one of them. It never occurred to me that this could happen."

The man on the floor suddenly convulsed and the doctor quickly knelt down by his side and put his head to the man's chest.

"For God's sake hurry up," he whispered, and then to Reinhardt, "I don't understand why they don't have a doctor on the premises. Did you see the average age of the men in the canteen? It must be over fifty. They seem to think that the refugees are going to be as healthy as the rest of the population. It's craziness."

Reinhardt nodded. "I'm over sixty."

"Precisely."

"In fact, I was interned during the last war. A place just outside York. It wasn't too bad, actually."

Dobel nodded, "But I thought they sent most Germans back home. I couldn't stand that, but it wouldn't be as bad for me as for the Jews, I suppose. Maybe they've stopped doing that."

The shutter on the door slid open and a voice said, "Move back. Stand against the wall where I can see you."

Then the sound of the key turning and an elderly doctor with a goatee beard who was skirted by two policemen peered in. The doctor entered and then with difficulty stooped to the figure on the ground. He looked up at Dobel.

"They say you're a doctor. So what's your diagnosis, doctor? There was sarcasm in his voice.

"I am a doctor and from the fruity smell of his breath, the dryness of his skin, and his breathing all suggest to me that he is suffering from ketoacidosos. And the fact that he is now in a coma also suggests that unless he is rehydrated very quickly and receives insulin he will die if we stand here talking for much longer."

The old doctor grunted. "Lucky I'm here then." He reached into his bag and took out a syringe.

When he had injected the man on the floor he turned to the policemen. "Get that stretcher. We'll have to get him to the hospital and onto a drip."

Dobel and Reinhardt watched as they struggled to lift the patient onto the stretcher. As they left and began to close the door, the doctor turned to Dobel. "You might be right. More likely to be hyperglycemia in my professional opinion." He lay stress on 'professional'.

Dobel sighed.

"Is he right?" asked Reinhardt.

Dobel shrugged. "I don't think so. Both are fatal if not treated quickly so points scoring seems a bit irrelevant really. There was a doctor at the camp at Seaton who used to do the same. So," he sat down on the bed, "you don't think we need to be unduly worried about where we're going to be sent. I mean, they can't keep us here for long."

Reinhardt smiled. "Well, if last time is anything to go by, I got letters and money from my wife. I remember she even sent me some oil paints and canvas so

I didn't get bored. That was on the plus side. On the minus side, it was four years. Oh, and she divorced me, but on the whole I'd put that among the plusses."

Dobel shook his head. "It wouldn't be a plus for me. Did you have children?"

"One, a daughter. But it was never a particularly happy marriage, more one of convenience. I had two boys by my second marriage, but that didn't last either. I'm not very good at marriage, I don't think. It sounds as if you are."

Dobel thought for a moment. "We are happy, I think. We've got three children as well, two girls and a boy. I think we'll be all right as long as we can write to each other and perhaps they can visit. But obviously, I don't know. She's a nurse so she'll be able to support them and, well, perhaps like they said, it'll just be a few days. I mean, who in their right mind could possibly think that either of us could be a danger to the state?"

Reinhardt nodded. "But on the other hand there's no one madder than a politician in time of war. So let's hope they're right. That it is only a few days."

Chapter Fifty Two

It was Weiss who thought up the game, though Busch was better at it. When new internees were brought to Swanwick Camp they ran to the edge of the compound so that they could see the new men climbing out of the trucks or marching through the gates. The game was to guess where each man came from, his profession and his age. It was difficult with the refugees because they had invariably been given their clothes rather than having chosen them, so a man who had been a wealthy lawyer in, say Berlin, could be reduced to penury within a matter of days. And guessing ages was also tricky. Weiss was by nature more optimistic and invariably misjudged ages by as much as fifteen years. So for each new internee there were a possible three points to be gained.

At first they were both wildly wrong, but then amended the game so that whoever's guess was closest got the points.

It was a beautiful morning in May when they heard an army lorry rumbling up the road and saw the gates swing open. The lorry crunched over the dry gravel and a couple of guards ran over to lower the tailgate and then stood back. After a few seconds the canvas was lifted and a tall gangly figure gingerly climbed down, took off his glasses, wiped them on his sleeve and looked round with the air of someone who had just woken up and was trying to identify his surroundings. With a look of surprise he stood aside while the next man clambered down.

"I'd say fifty three or four, from Tübingen, so a lecturer at the University. Probably in chemistry, anyway, one of the sciences," opined Weiss.

Busch shook his head. "Forty eight and from Leipzig. He's a journalist, one of those socialist rags. Anyway, you can check him out because I'm not going to." He turned away.

Weiss glanced at him , "Why not, it's your turn."

"It's obvious, isn't it? He's a Jew boy. I don't talk to Jews. You know that. They shouldn't be sent here. This should be an 'Aryan only' camp. It's asking for trouble."

Weiss remembered the expression on the face of the jewish internees the first and probably only time they had walked into the room which had been the chapel but now was used for the men to play cards in or simply sit and talk or read. It was known as the recreation room. The pews and altar had been removed and replaced with tables with attractive cloths on them and comfortable chairs. Weiss had watched the newcomers as they looked round with approval at the flowers on the table, the wooden chandeliers hanging from the oak beams and the model galleon that one of the internees had made and which was suspended from one of the rafters. And then Weiss recalled how the men's expressions had changed when they caught sight of the German eagle which had replaced the crucifix, and the swastika just below it. Below that, and just above the oak panelling there was a large framed photograph of Hitler in three quarter profile wearing his cap. The men had turned abruptly and left to the hoots of derision from the dozen or so men who were in the room. Weiss had felt guilty at having taken them there. He'd felt pleased because he had won his bet with Busch over one man who was from Munich, or at least Bavaria, and was thirty three, which was a lot closer than Busch's guess. But, he reflected, perhaps it was better that the Jews should find out the no go areas than to get beaten up as he had been the day that he arrived.

"OK," he said, now turning to Busch, "what about the next one?" It was a boy of perhaps eighteen, tall and fair-haired who was looking up at the building with an air of casual indifference. It was an expression that Weiss recognised in Busch, a front to hide his fear and one that was often followed by an outburst of fury.

Busch shook his head. "I'm not playing any more. I'm going to fix the funnels on my ship and he walked off.

Weiss watched the remaining men climb out of the back of the lorry, line up with their suitcases on the ground in front of them and listen to the same talk that was repeated to all the newcomers.

Behind him tents were being put up in front of the recreation hut to accommodate the new internees. He wandered off to the library to see if he could find another thriller by Eric Ambler. Busch's attitude disturbed him; he wanted to tell him that his best friend at university had been a Jew who was suddenly ejected from the course without explanation. The tutors on the faculty had all said his friend would be a brilliant criminal lawyer one day. He and Weiss had been studying in the library when the SS had arrived, told him to collect his books and to go with them. After his last lecture of the day Weiss had gone round to his house and found it empty. He had asked the tutors if he knew of his whereabouts but it was if a wall of silence had descended and one of them even had the nerve to say that he had been expelled for being 'a subversive influence.'

It wasn't only the fact that his friend seemed to have to have disappeared without trace; it was the fact that no one seemed at all concerned. When Weiss remonstrated with the head of the faculty that he saw little point in learning law if people could be sent down with no explanation, an act that was contrary to all principles of natural justice, he was told that he needed to be very careful himself, that the needs of the nation were above the needs of the individual.

Weiss remembered how he had been too angry to speak. When he told his father about the incident, his father immediately contacted friends in England and through their influence arranged for him to continue his studies at Oxford. Later he wrote several times imploring his son not to return to Germany. If he came back he would certainly be called up and knowing well his son's ability to challenge authority when he felt an injustice had been done, he described in detail the febrile atmosphere that was everywhere in the country.

Then, about a year ago, the letters suddenly stopped. Ever since that time Weiss had worried that his own replies to his parents had got them into trouble. Now he shook his head as if trying to dismiss the thought and went into the library. There was now a section of German novels, but nothing by his favourite authors - Thomas Mann, Robert Musil and Herman Broch. There was nothing by Eric Ambler he hadn't read either. Feeling depressed and listless he went outside again. A soldier came over to him.

"Don't you want to earn a few bob?" he asked. "Give a hand with the tents and you'll get half a crown a week. Keep you in fags, anyway."

"I don't smoke," said Weiss.

"It'd still be better than drooping about about like a tit in a trance. You look like you could do with something to get you out of yourself."

"Thanks," said Weiss, "I'll think about it."

Walking over to the perimeter fence, he caught sight of the newcomer who he had had the bet over with Busch earlier. He was standing alone beneath the watch tower looking up at the hills in the distance. Weiss approached him and said in German, "It's a beautiful view, isn't it? Where are you from?"

The man turned quickly towards him and answered reluctantly, "From London. I was in London."

"No, I mean originally, where are you from?"

"I'm from Krems. In Austria."

Weiss smiled, nodded and said to himself, "That's one to me."

He studied the man before speaking again. " You've just arrived, haven't you. I saw you getting off the truck. Have you got any friends who came with you?"

It was as if he had opened a flood-gate. "No, I don't know why they brought me here. I don't know what this place is. The police came to my place where I was working. They took five of us and put us in a school for two nights and then they took the others away, I don't know where to and brought me here with a lot of other people that I'd never seen before. We're all German or Austrian, but I don't know what we're supposed to have done. If they told me I didn't understand. " He finished as an afterthought, "My English isn't very good. And I don't even know where I am." Weiss thought he was on the verge of tears and said quickly, "It's all right, and it isn't too bad here and if you're interested there are English lessons in the evening." He held out his hand, "My name is Weiss."

The man looked down and took it, "Niedermayer," he said.

"Well," said Weiss, let's walk and I'll tell you what I know. The British call it an internment camp, which I suppose it is but it's also a prisoner of war camp. Some people like me just happened to be here when war started. Others, like you, I think, came to get away from the Nazis or were driven out of Germany. There's a third group who are prisoners of war, and if I were you I'd stay away from them. They are mostly - look, I don't want to frighten you, but it's best to be warned, they are often Nazis. They've taken over some of the best places, like the recreation room. They stick together, but it's best to stay out of their way. There are enough decent people here. Are you jewish?"

Niedermayer nodded.

"Then keep quiet about it."

"But why do they put us in the same camp?"

Weiss shrugged, "No idea. I suppose they suddenly found they wanted to round up far more men than they had room for. As far as they're concerned every German or Austrian is a potential enemy, so they just lump us all together. Do you know where you'll be sleeping yet?"

Niedermayer nodded towards the row of tents that had been put up. "They said they're putting the older men in the big building over there. I'm forty-two, so I'd have thought that I was one of them, but it appears not."

Weiss grimaced - that was one for Busch. He began to say that it would be all right as long as the weather was warm, but it would be insufferable by the winter, but then he thought better of it.

"I expect they'll move us before too long, at least they will if they've got any sense." He looked around to check that they couldn't be overheard. " There's a radio hidden in one of the bedrooms which is obviously forbidden. It's possible to send messages to Germany to give our whereabouts so that when the bombing starts we can be avoided. The British make searches every week but haven't found it yet, but I think they'll keep moving us around so that the news about where we are is quickly out of date."

"So we can't send letters out?" Niedermayer was horrified.

"Oh, sure, but there's no guarantee that they'll arrive, and they'll be censored. Come on, I'll show you the dining room."

Chapter Fifty Three

"Right lads, it's time to say 'au revoir' to your floozies, those of you not too ugly to have one, so that won't apply to anyone here. We're on twelve hours' notice to move out." The sergeant ducked and the piece of railway track that three men were lowering into place from enormous hooks clattered to the ground.

"Christ, Hickey," he yelled, "Be careful, you nearly got me killed then."

The men had been working on building a railway siding. The weather for the past fortnight had been hot and the work hard. Stripped to the waist, Maurice and Joe were sunburnt and fit. They'd spent the evenings drinking, playing cards and sometimes going into the village where Maurice had been trying out his French on the barmaid who invariably replied in English. He had been trying to summon up the courage to ask her out, so the news that they were to move on was unwelcome.

"Where are we going?" he asked.

The sergeant simply replied cryptically, "Ours not to reason why, lad. But I'm putting you in charge of loading the officers' deckchairs. Don't touch the instruments. If you can nearly smash up a piece of railway track I shiver to think what you could do to a trombone."

Maurice looked around. They hadn't finished the job. They'd only been here a couple of weeks and already they were being moved.

Joe came over and said, " Reilly says we're going to the front. He heard in the village that the Germans have got into France. They've flattened Rotterdam and the Dutch have surrendered. So..."

"But they said we wouldn't be fighting. We can't be. We haven't got any weapons."

"Listen," said Joe, "I'm only telling you what I heard, all right? Anyway, right now I'd rather be doing anything than hoiking these bleedin' sleepers around."

In the camp the battalion was busily loading up the lorries with tents, provisions, and all the general paraphernalia that had been collected over the past few weeks. The sergeant saw Maurice and yelled, "Get the deckchairs and put them on the second lorry, and for God's sake be careful."

Maurice ran about the camp feeling like a beach attendant at Blackpool. By two o'clock the first lorries were pulling out amidst clouds of dust and diesel fumes. He was one of the last to climb into a cab and asked the driver, "Where are we going?"

"Rennes, mate."

"Where's that?"

"Don't ask me, I've got no idea. I'm just following the geezer in front, and if you ask him he'll give you the same answer and so on to the bloke who's leading and who's probably bloody miles away by now and completely lost. If you haven't noticed, that's what life's like in the British army."

After an hour of bouncing around on rough roads they arrived at Rennes station. A train with wooden cattle trucks was billowing steam out into the summer air while officers shouted orders for them men to climb inside, thirty to a carriage, and French policemen were walking up and down with their sticks directing the soldiers like sheep dogs. Joe and Maurice clambered into a truck. "Bloody hell," said Joe, "stinks of horses. I hope this stuff is clean," and he sat down in the straw with his back pressed to the wall.

Maurice gingerly lowered himself next to him. The carriage was almost full. Small cracks of light appeared on the side walls when the door was slid shut from the outside and the men were left in almost total darkness. The train gave a jolt and a sigh and creaked forward a few yards before stopping again. It waited for what seemed like hours before slowly dragging its way along the track. Nobody seemed much like talking. Maurice put his knapsack under his head, stretched out and stared up at the roof. Joe had already fallen asleep when a voice said, "Give us a tune, Bingle, it's like a bloody mortuary in here."

A harmonica began to play slowly, "Show me the way to go home" and the men joined in so mournfully that after a few bars someone said, "Jesus, I wanted a bit of music to cheer me up because I was feeling depressed and now I just want to shoot meself. Haven't you got something a bit more jolly?"

In the early evening the train stopped and the door to the carriage slid open. The men climbed out stiffly and looked about. They were directed to a pump where they could wash and bully beef, tea and biscuits were handed out. Maurice had aching joints and his eyes had hardly adjusted to the light before they were ordered back into the wagon, the door slid shut and they train moved off again. He felt completely disorientated. He lost all sense of how long the train stopped for, or for how long it clicked over the tracks before stopping. Sometimes the doors slid open and he was surprised to see it was daylight outside. There was no shortage of the endless bully beef, so he rarely felt hungry, but all the men seemed to have fallen into a stupor and the fetid air made each hour more unpleasant than the last. At the last stop it was announced that they had left France and were now in Belgium.

The men stumbled down onto the platform and marched painfully along the road towards a farm.

Suddenly there was a cry from the station. A porter was running towards them shouting, "Cachez-vous, cachez-vous, vite." He gripped the last soldier in the line by the shoulder and pointed towards the east. Maurice heard the planes before he saw them, flying low along the line of the track. He stood watching as if transfixed before the station platform appeared to rise in slow motion and pieces of rubble flew into the air. He felt himself being dragged backwards and hauled down into a ditch by the side of the road.

"For Christ's sake, lad, are you trying to get yourself killed? Stay down." The sergeant was lying across him watching the Stukas as they peeled away and circled above them before returning and opening their guns again.

For a moment Maurice felt as if he had lost the use of his limbs. He lay in the ditch breathing heavily. "What happened?" he asked at length.

"Stukas," said the sergeant matter-of-factly, "they'll be back."

They waited until the drone of the last plane had gone and then scrambled back to the road. "Get back to the train," the sergeant shouted, "We've got to get out of here before they come back."

It was still swelteringly hot. Outside the station two army lorries were parked and soldiers were transferring anti-tank rifles into the front carriages of the train. The older soldier behind Maurice groaned at the sight of the guns being manhandled across the damaged platform.

"Oh, God, look what rubbish they're sending us now," he complained as he climbed into the wagon. "He turned to Maurice and gave him a hand up, "Bloody things weigh a ton, kick like a bleedin' mule, you have to use a bipod with the them and the noise they make is deafening. And when they go wrong, which is often, they're a bloody nightmare to repair. Tell you what, even with the padded buttpad it'll near as dammit break your shoulder. Best thing'll be if they've forgotten to send any ammo with them."

The hubbub of voices died down as the door was shut again, the men straining to hear whether the planes were returning. When the train finally stopped for the last time and the men climbed out of the wagon it was dark. In silence they climbed into the lorries that were waiting outside the station. They left at five minute intervals so as not to form a convoy that might attract enemy aircraft, and headed east . Maurice and Joe sat by the back boards and looked out. Their lorry had to keep stopping. After a particularly long delay a sergeant appeared and said, "Hickey, they say you speak French. Get out and explain to these people that they've got to stick to the side of the road to let us through," and he disappeared before Maurice could reply. He looked helplessly at Joe who laughed.

"Don't look at me, mate, you'd better get on with it."

Maurice climbed out of the back of the vehicle. Ahead of him he could see another lorry which was surrounded by a group of people trying to squeeze past it. They were of all ages; an old man was holding a small girl of five or six by the hand and carrying a leather suitcase. He looked exhausted, his eyes glazed over while the girl looked up at Maurice, and seeing that he didn't react, she pulled the old man with both hands and said quietly, "Viens,Papa." Behind them a shabbily dressed man was pushing a handcart that was piled high with furniture, bedding, boxes and a cot. Clinging to the side and stumbling was a young woman clutching a bundle to her chest. She was crooning gently, apparently unaware of anyone around her.

"Hickey," come a shout from ahead, "Get these people off the bloody road or we'll all be dead meat."

He had never felt so hopeless in his life. There was no room for them to get off the road, and the weakened state of nearly all of them meant that they couldn't even if they wanted to. He went around to the front of the lorry where a woman dressed in a headscarf and a thick overcoat was leaning against the bonnet. She was breathing heavily and shaking her head. Maurice looked up helplessly at the driver who leant out of the window and said, "Get her over to the side. I'll pull over to the left. Just make them come in single file and keep the fucking road clear."

Maurice took the woman gently by the arm and tried to usher her towards the row of trees. She tried to pull her arm away, and said, "Non, je ne peux plus, laissez-moi, je vous en prie."

"Come on," implored Maurice, "You can't stay here." This time he held her more firmly and helped her to the verge where she stumbled down with a moan. He went back to the cab and started waving at the mass of people to move to the verge. The lorry started up and inched forward. The shuffling crowd scarcely seemed to notice the woman who was now lying on the ground. Once the lorry had passed him, Maurice felt in his pocket. He'd got a half eaten piece of bully beef left and his hip flask. Squeezing past an elderly couple who were dragging what looked like a child's cart along, he knelt down by the woman and lifted her head. "Eat this," he said. She took it and bit off a small mouthful. "Good, now drink." He lifted the flask to her lips and she gulped it painfully, looking up at him as she drank.

"Hickey, where the fuck are you?" the sergeant's voice roared above the sound of lorry's engine.

Maurice stood up with a last look at the woman who was mouthing something at him.

"Get up here and keep these people moving." Another lorry crept past him.

"Come and stop these people, we're turning right up this track. Get in the last lorry and for God's sake keep this road clear." Behind him Maurice could see the dimmed headlights of three more trucks. The tail-lights of his own suddenly accelerated away to the right. He jogged up to the junction where the sergeant was waving at the oncoming crowd of people to stop as a second lorry rumbled up the track.

"Bloody Germans," he said, "they've driven these people onto the roads to stop us from getting through. There's a farm up there. We're stopping over till dawn. Stay here and keep these people back and make sure no one follows us."

Then he waved down the next lorry and jumped on to the running board as it slowed. There didn't seem much danger of anyone wanting to follow. In the moonlight Maurice could make out dozens of people coming down the road. They stopped and looked at him wearily while he waved the remaining lorries through, and then he climbed onto the running board of the last truck before it followed the others. There were no visible lights on in the farm. They pulled into a yard and Maurice jumped down. It was a large house with several outbuildings.

Inside the early arrivals had lit a fire and blacked out the windows.

"Make the most of this, gentlemen, it may be the best meal you have ever had. Fresh chicken straight from the hen house, new boiled potatoes done in the French style and the coup de grace and you won't be able to believe your taste buds, I give you," the cook laughed and held up a bottle, "a pint of champagne for every man here." He took a swig. "If you don't believe me, go and have a look in the cellar. Best burgundy, best claret and enough champagne to sink a bleeding battleship."

Two soldiers appeared from the cellar carrying crates of red wine. "No point in leaving it for the boche. We'll take the lot with us in the morning."

The sergeant stood in front of the fire,"Right men, get your clobber and find somewhere to kip down. Don't get pissed, we're leaving before sun up and enjoy the meal."

Maurice thought he had never tasted anything so good as he tore off pieces of chicken with his clasp knife. It was the first time he had drunk champagne- the bubbles went up his nose and made him hiccough. By the time he had finished eating he was feeling light-headed. All the chairs and beds had already been taken and the floor was hard in the kitchen. Eventually he found a space on the landing where he could use his knapsack as a pillow. The last thing he saw as he drifted off to sleep were the eyes of the old woman looking up at him. He turned over and hugged his chest tightly.

Chapter Fifty Four

Esther Hart's Diary

Saturday 18th May 1940

Douglas has just gone off to work having eaten a quick lunch. Charles says he is feeling unwell and so has taken himself off to bed. Went to have my hair done this morning and also made a quick phone call to Barbara. The government's started employing researchers to go round asking people about how they feel the war is going in order to assess morale. They should have had someone in the hairdresser's. While she was perming my hair, Valerie said that she'd been talking to her brother who lives in Abingdon. He told her that a lot of German parachutists dressed as nuns had been seen landing in a field just outside the town. They knew they were Germans and not proper nuns because they had machine guns. I wondered whether anyone had opened fire on them. She put her head close to mine, looked at me in the mirror and whispered, "My brother would never have done anything like that, we're Catholic. That's what's so cunning about that Hitler." I did wonder whether Hitler knew that Valerie's brother was a Catholic but decided not to go any further with that particular conversation. Another woman said she'd heard that the Italians had bombed Paris. Someone else said the whole problem was that you never got the truth from the BBC. Everybody knew things were bad, but they must be a lot worse than is being let on, otherwise there would be good news and there never is any. For all we know the Germans have already landed on the south coast. She laughed and said that that was why she was having her hair done, so that she'll be looking her best for when they arrive.

When I came out I phoned Barbara who said she's had a call from Lotte saying that several men from the Austrian Centre had been arrested and could she try and help find out what has happened to them. One of the men was Herr Niedermayer. The news really shook me and if someone hadn't been waiting to use the phone I think I would have just slumped down and cried my eyes out. As if he hasn't suffered enough, and just when he thinks he's going to be reunited with his wife and daughter, he's taken away to God knows where.

Then Barbara said the best hope we have of helping him is through Douglas who would be able to find out where he's gone. I pointed out that he has a new job, but she said she knew that, but that his contacts would be able to provide information. She said Herbert agrees. I'm trying to pluck up the courage to ask him to help.

Monday 20th May

Thank God it's Monday. Had a dreadful row with Douglas yesterday over breakfast. I thought I'd better talk to him before Charles was up. He went to get the Sunday papers while I cooked breakfast and then sat reading them while he ate. I said I thought Mr Churchill's speech last night on the BBC was honest but also frightening, saying the Germans had broken through the Maginot line. But it was much better to be told the truth than to be kept in the dark as we had been before he became Prime Minister. Douglas just grunted and went on reading. Then I told him about the conversation in the hairdresser's and laughed and he just said people will talk any kind of nonsense. He didn't even bother to look up. Finally I said that I'd heard that a man I'd interviewed at the tribunal back in January, an Austrian Jew, had been interned.

He put the paper down and asked me coldly how I had come by the information. I said that Barbara had told me- I wasn't going to lie. He then accused me of being no better than 'those stupid gossipmongers' that I'd been happy to mock. I was livid and said I would be going to the Austrian Centre to find out whether it was true, in which case it wouldn't be gossip, it would show that we are no better than the Germans, locking people up, not for what they've done but for who they are.

Douglas went white with fury and forbade me to do any such thing. He said in case I hadn't noticed, that we are at war, that if people are being locked up it is to protect them as much as anything else. There was a real danger of 'fifth columnists'. I said it was absurd to think that a Jew who had fled to this country because he was being persecuted in his own could possibly be an agent of the

Reich. He looked at me so scornfully that I wanted to throw something at him and then he asked if 'this man' (he said it with such derision) had a family in Germany. I said his wife was trying to come over from Prague with their daughter.

"Well, then don't you think," he said as if talking to an imbecile, "that as Prague is under Nazi control, that the Germans might make a condition of her leaving, the providing of information from England which would prove useful to them?" "But what possible information could he have?" I shouted, "That's the point. That in this country we drive on the left? That it's lovely weather for an air raid? Don't you think they know that already?"

And then I remembered that she'd left Prague and was writing from Switzerland. At which point he slammed his fists on the table, shouted "Very bloody convenient." and stormed out of the house. I've never heard him swear before, and that was even more of a shock than his treating me like a cretin, which I've become increasingly used to.

When Charles eventually appeared he said he thought he'd heard shouting and asked me if there was anything wrong. He put his arm around me and said all marriages have their ups and downs, and then, "We were married for forty-two years and Olave wasn't the easiest woman either." He didn't appear to have any recognition of what he said, as if I knew that any disagreements were my fault really.

Douglas back at four and not speaking to me.

Tuesday 21st May

The only thing Douglas said before going off to work was that he would very much appreciate it if I stopped visiting the Austrian Centre and found some useful way of supporting the war effort. It could lead to difficulties for him because of the nature of the work he is doing. He left without waiting for an answer, and obviously thought that was the end of the matter. Since he won't tell me what work he is doing, I have no way of knowing what sort of difficulties I might cause him. I thought about phoning Barbara to cancel and have been worrying about it all morning. As I see it, the plight of the refugees hasn't changed at all, except the situation has become worse for them since some of the papers are accusing them of being fifth columnists, of spreading rumours, of receiving secret instructions from Lord Haw-haw etc. Even if Hitler has got spies amongst the refugees, which I think very unlikely, does that justify locking away people who are clearly genuinely fleeing from an oppressive regime? As Barbara says, surely a spy would have a better disguise than posing as a refugee. The only thing I do agree with Douglas about is that there is real danger from ignorant people who are simply anti-German and who might take it on themselves to attack anyone with a foreign accent. There have been horrible reports of Belgian and Dutch refugees being mistreated. I've never directly gone against Douglas's wishes before, but I think on this issue I must. I'm meeting Barbara at two.

Later. There was a terrible air of depression at the Centre. No one could tell us what had happened beyond five of the men being taken away in vans with the assurance that they would be taken for questioning and if found to be completely innocent of all wrong doing, would be released in a few days. But no one had been told what they were accused of or where they had been taken. Lotte did say that all the men who were there regularly were frightened that they were about to be arrested soon.

Barbara promised that we would find out what we could. Once outside she said we should write to all the MP's that were sympathetic to the refugees' cause. I'm to write to Fenner Brockway and Major Cazalet. I can't do this behind Douglas's back and will have to tell him.

Wednesday 22nd May

Heard a broadcast asking women to train in First Aid so that they can take in people who are slightly wounded, and have phoned to find out where I can do this. Told Douglas, when he got home, that he was right, that I could do more for the war effort and that I'd applied for a training course to help people who are wounded once the bombing starts. He said that he was very relieved that at last " I had begun to see sense" which absolutely infuriated me and I said I had also been to the Austrian Centre that day and it was true that five innocent men had been arrested without any explanation of what they were supposed to have done. He reacted in a way that I had never seen before, grabbing me by the arm and manhandling me into the bedroom and slamming the door. He said he had signed the Official Secrets Act and so he couldn't discuss his work with anyone. However there was a lot of evidence from both the army and from the secret services that there was a movement to undermine the government from within the country and that a number of arrests would be made tomorrow. One of these people had been feeding sensitive information to Lord Haw-haw and had access to telegrams sent between the Prime Minister and the President of the United States. He finished by hissing at me, "Do you really think you know better than MI5 and the other secret services? " I said that of course I didn't but he just snapped, "Good, then stay out of what you don't understand." Then he went out, closed the door behind himself to show that I wasn't wanted in the drawing room. I could hear him muttering with his father. I sat on the bed in tears. I know he's not right about this, I ABSOLUTELY KNOW IT.

We're all scared because the German army has so far beaten off every French attack and is now turning north towards the Channel. Reynaud says quite openly that only a miracle can save France. He should know, he is, after all, the Prime Minister. Drafted letters to the MP's.

Friday 24th May

Oswald Mosley and members of some right wing organisation were arrested yesterday as Douglas said was going to happen, so he must have a very good idea about what the Home Office is thinking. I sent off my letters to Fenner Brockway and Major Cazalet. I haven't told Douglas yet; there's time enough for that before I'm likely to get a reply and he's still being very shirty with me so I don't want to anger him again so soon. Feel I'm treading on egg shells. If Charles wasn't here I'd move into the spare room.

The news from France is truly terrible. The German army has moved up to Boulogne. I heard that we've lost 100,000 soldiers but I can't believe that can be true. There's a lot of anger in the papers about the French which is new. They were regarded as our allies who would help us win the war and until recently there was a lot of sympathy for them, but that has certainly changed in the last few days and they are blamed for being weak and ineffectual.

The other really worrying thing is that it'll soon be impossible to cash a cheque because there is a run on the banks. Parliament has passed the Emergency Powers Act, which I understand means that not only spies can be executed but anyone who is accused of helping the enemy or who is found guilty of sabotaging the war effort.

Decided to tell Douglas about the letters on Monday. Daren't leave it much longer in case I get a reply quickly and he intercepts the post.

Monday 27th May

I'm afraid I took the coward's way out and told Douglas over supper I'd written to a couple of MP's who were sympathetic to the refugees. I wanted Charles to be there because I thought Douglas would be less likely to cause a scene in front of his father. When he didn't reply I also said that Barbara had also written to Eleanor Rathbone and to JB Priestley and that Herbert thought that this was a good idea. Douglas replied that the reason that Herbert was no longer his manager was that it was felt that his sympathies were too much with refugees whose loyalty to the country could not be guaranteed and who were therefore a potential threat to national security at a time when there was the greatest danger from the enemy. He delivered the words as if he were giving a speech in Parliament and then finished his meal without further comment. When I had cleared away the dishes and washed up, he said he had something that he wanted me to see, and told me to sit down. He took out of his briefcase a folded piece of paper which he lay on the table. Keeping his hand on it, he said, "This is a report written by Sir Nevile Bland, the British Minister to the Dutch Government who arrived back in the country a couple of weeks ago on a warship. He was asked to write this by Lord Halifax. Everybody agrees it is such an important account that Sir Nevile is going to be broadcasting it on the wireless on Thursday evening so that no one can be in any doubt about the danger we are in." He pushed it towards me. It was quite brief, entitled 'Fifth Column Menace' and recounted how German parachutists, boys of sixteen, dropped on people's houses and caused as much death and destruction as they could before being killed themselves. They had lists of Dutch officials who were to be 'shot on sight.' They had got their information from 'the paltriest kitchen maid, who is a menace to the safety of the country.' He concluded by saying that he had no doubt that Hitler has satellites all over England who will embark on widespread sabotage and attack civilians and the military indiscriminately. He concluded by saying that 'ALL Germans and Austrians ought to be interned at once.'

When I had finished reading Douglas looked at me pityingly. "That's not the only report like that," he said. "That's how the Germans conquered Norway so easily, and what they did in Holland and Norway they're doing in France. And it'll happen here. Now do you understand?"

I didn't think it was the moment to point out that Holland and France share borders with Germany, and I still didn't believe Jewish refugees would be supporters of Hitler- how could they? But Douglas clearly felt that the argument was won and finished by saying, "So if you get replies from the MP's, I want to see them, as I want to see the letter you wrote. You know, what you have done is not only foolish, it could also be very damaging for my career."

I went to bed and pretended to be asleep when he came in an hour later.

Wednesday 29th May

Yesterday the Belgian king surrendered, apparently without telling the allies what he was about to do. There is a real fear that France will sue for peace as well, and we will be alone. The Germans have captured Calais and the only way that our army in France can survive is if the soldiers can be evacuated, and though some have managed to get home, there are thousands who are being backed into the sea.

I'm so relieved that the children are safely out of London. The gloom everywhere is almost tangible and everyone is just waiting for the invasion to begin.

Friday 31st May

Listened to Sir Nevile Bland last night on the Home Service. He said there were lots of obvious Nazi sympathisers interned but enough remained free to carry out the instructions they received from Germany.

There is quite a lot of relief that so many soldiers are being rescued from Dunkirk, but behind that is the fear that Italy is about to join the war and that the army, in particular, has been too weakened to defend the country when the invasion comes. Charles very subdued and clearly not well. My husband indescribably smug as if he's enjoying the whole thing.

Chapter Fifty Five

Busch had put the finishing touches to the model of his ship and was examining it critically. There was something not quite right about it, but he couldn't think what. Perhaps it was the proportions - the hull was too short in relation to its breadth, though it had seemed right before he had begun to mount the cabins and the mast. Weiss came in and stood behind him.

"It looks good," he said, " Are you pleased with it?"

"No, it's not right, but I can't do anything about it without starting again." He shook his head, "But I can't see where I went wrong."

"Come back to it later," suggested Weiss, "You'll see it differently. Come outside, I want to show you something."

Relations between the two men had cooled slightly over the last couple of weeks because of Weiss's friendship with Niedermayer. Busch had refused to speak to the Austrian and for the first few days had also had nothing to do with Weiss. Instead he had thrown himself into getting his model finished. The news that France had been invaded and that Belgium and Holland had surrendered had given the Nazis in the camp renewed confidence that the war would soon be won and that the British would immediately surrender.

He followed Weiss outside into the bright sunshine. "What do you want to show me?" he asked irritably. Weiss nodded towards the perimeter fence where two lorries had pulled up just outside and an elderly man was trying to get a guard to take his suitcase as if he were asking a doorman to take his luggage up to his hotel bedroom. Behind him a taller man with thick pebble glasses was looking on quizzically.

"Do you think he's even German?" asked Weiss laughing.

Busch couldn't prevent himself from smiling. "Perhaps he's in disguise, one of these famous fifth columnists that they're so worried about. I heard Müller talking to one of the guards talking about it this morning. I got him to translate for me and he said that the English think that all German civilians are in secret communication with Berlin. The monocle's a bit over the top though. Whoever wears one of those any more?"

They watched the new internees being lined up and ushered through the gate that two of the guards had opened before it swung back and was locked once more.

The man with the monocle set down his case and looked up at the building. He nodded approvingly and said something to his companion that Weiss couldn't quite catch. Then they were led towards the main house.

"Oh God, here comes trouble," whispered Weiss.

Wirth and a group of fellow Nazis marched up to the small group of men and stood in front of them, blocking their way. "Heil Hitler," he snapped, giving the salute.

The older man took off his monocle, rubbed it with a handkerchief, replaced it, and smiled.

"Delighted, I'm sure, old man. Now, if you'll excuse me..."

There was a silence while everyone waited to see how Wirth would react. Busch whispered to Weiss, "The man who's with him, the tall one, I know him, I've seen him before, at Seaton."

"He was in the camp with you?"

Busch shook his head. "No, he was a doctor. He was very good to me. He..."

Wirth had recognised Dr Dobel at the same moment and he smiled. He turned to his group, "This is the gentleman who was good enough to translate for me when I was at the last camp." He turned back to Dobel. "I think I have to thank you for getting me transferred here. I think you know you know how it was that I lost the election to be the internees' representative. It's something I've often wondered about. Now that you are here to, I think we are all looking forward to your explanation."

Two of his henchmen moved forward threateningly. The older man put down his briefcase and cleared his throat. "If I may.." he began.

"Den Mund halten!" shouted Wirth, "Who are you, anyway?"

"Reinhardt," said Reinhardt. "My name is Links Reinhardt. I'm sure Dr Dobel can offer a rational explanation, but in this country we have elections. I expect you've just forgotten how they work, not having had one since the Weimar Republic, which was an awfully long time ago."

Wirth stepped around him and pressed his face into the doctor's. "Then I'm sure we would all be very interested in his 'rational explanation'."

Before Weiss could stop him, Busch ran forward and stood next to Dr Dobel. "Don't you dare touch him," he hissed.

By now a small crowd had gathered around the group of men and the guards were whispering nervously to each other. Wirth's supporters started jostling Busch who was staring at Wirth, refusing to be intimidated.

At this point there was a shout from the direction of the house and the camp commander, Captain Howarth marched over with five guards following closely behind him.

"Take these men," he nodded towards Reinhardt and Dobel to their quarters, "and Mr Wirth, kindly explain what is happening here."

Two guards stepped forward and beckoned to Reinhardt who picked up his case and stepped aside for Dobel, who was looking terrified. They followed the guard along the path to the Garden House. Busch took a step back and looked at Captain Howarth who addressed himself to Wirth.

"You are the Lagerführer by my agreement, and it is your responsibility to maintain discipline, sir. I know your English is excellent, but I want a translator so that you and your men are absolutely clear about what I am about to say to you."

He looked around at the faces of the men, some of whom were looking confused, others who had expressions of anger. He called after Reinhardt and Dobel. "Just wait a moment, I'd like you to here this as well, and will either of you please translate."

Wirth said caustically, "I am perfectly able to communicate your meaning to my men, Captain."

Captain Howarth ignored him. Reinhardt and Dobel looked at each other and Dobel whispered, I'd rather not do it. I have a history with Herr Wirth. Would you mind?"

Reinhardt nodded and walked back to the group.

Captain Howarth raised a piece of paper above his head and said loudly and slowly, "This is a letter I have received from the Home Office. It states that last month questions were raised in the House of Commons, that is in Parliament, to the effect that complaints from internees in this camp had been received. They claimed that anyone who was not a member of the Nazi party has been beaten up in this camp. While the Home Office denied these allegations, nevertheless the behaviour of your men, Herr Wirth, is being closely scrutinised and that immediate action will be taken if any such incidents are found to have any justification."

He paused and waited for Reinhardt to translate, before continuing. "I should like to point out that as a signatory to the Geneva Convention, our government ensures that you men receive a level of privilege, especially with regard to the food that you get, that British internees in Germany will certainly not receive, as the German Government has seen fit not to sign up to the convention. In fact, you have a far better diet than the majority of British people who are strictly rationed, whereas you have exactly the same food as our British soldiers."

He stopped and looked around. "If I receive any more complaints, or if I witness any threats to other men in this camp, I shall take immediate action. I hope I have made myself clear."

Reinhardt translated. Wirth looked around scornfully and walked away. Captain Howarth nodded towards Reinhardt and said, "Thank you," and returned to the main building.

Reinhardt and Dobel were lodged in the Garden House. Their room overlooked the lawn that over the past few weeks had been covered in tents. They unpacked the few possessions they had managed to bring and then decided to go outside and stretch their legs.

"So, tell me," said Reinhardt in English, "What is this history that you've got with this Wirth. And what's his background, anyway?"

Dobel explained how he had been the doctor at Seaton and how Wirth had challenged Captain Burfeind as camp leader, intimidating the rest of the internees into voting for him by having his henchmen examine the voting slips before they were put into the box.

"I caused a diversion and substituted a lot of other voting slips, in support of Captain Burfeind," he said, smiling at the memory. "And the lad who came up and stuck up for me just now - I can't remember his name - he was put into solitary back in January and I had to make sure he was given enough food and warm clothing or he would have contracted hypothermia. He'd broken the arm of a young Jew that he'd got into a fight with. God knows why they put Nazis and Jews in the same camp, it's asking for trouble, or why they put us in with Nazis, for that matter. They don't seem to be able to distinguish between internees and prisoners of war."

"I suppose that we're all the enemy now," suggested Reinhardt, "but I can't say I mind sitting the war out here. It's a damned sight better than some of the places I got sent to in the last war."

They passed a tent which still had the flaps drawn. Inside Niedermayer was writing yet another draft of a letter to his wife. Sitting uncomfortably on his camp bed, he was trying in vain to find a form of words that would explain to her that he was all right, that he had been taken to somewhere in the country and that he was sure that he would soon be released and able to meet her in London. Except that he wasn't really sure at all, and the singing of the Horst Wessel song by the Nazis who marched around at night terrified him so that he had decided some time ago that Weiss was right and that the only safe place to be was in his tent. Rereading his letters made him feel that the constant panic that he felt just below the surface was communicated in his writing. He tore up another page, sighed and started again. And the situation was only getting worse. Germany was going to win the war. The thought stopped him from being able to sleep, but the constant fear and his tiredness made him long to be unconscious. He stared at the blank page and then threw himself back on his bed.

Chapter Fifty Six

Franco had been right; it had taken a lot more than the 'two days tops' that Mr Harper had suggested it would need to get the rented shop into any kind of condition to open the ice-cream parlour. For one thing, they had had problems getting the necessary materials to do the place up. Mr Harper, surprisingly as far as Franco was concerned, came to the rescue.

He'd been dropping by on most days to see how the renovation was coming along. Franco said he was having problems getting hold of new brackets to support the shelving; for some reason all the ironmongers he visited said they couldn't get hold of nails and screws.

"It's the war effort." said Mr Harper, "Steel and iron and is being used to make planes and weapons and stuff. Let me talk to my contacts I reckon we'll be able to sort it out."

When he came back the next day with everything on the list, Franco was both amazed and grateful, though the price seemed somewhat higher than he'd anticipated. "Don't thank me," said Mr Harper as he slipped the ten pound note into his wallet, "I'm just protecting my investment. The sooner you start selling your ice cream, the sooner we'll see a return on our outlay. It's just good business, that's all."

A fortnight later the place was ready to open. All that was needed now was to persuade Julia and Giovanna to start making the ice cream. Giovanna hadn't seen the place. Franco had told her it was to be a surprise, that she would be delighted.

The night before he was planning to bring her along, he stayed late to make sure everything was perfect. It was almost ten o'clock before he had got it exactly as he wanted it. He and Eugenio stood back in admiration and were congratulating themselves on the job and were about to lock up when Mr Harper appeared, smiling broadly.

"Well, I must say you've done the old place proud," he said, "I never knew it would come up as good as this."

He looked round admiringly and nodded, "Nice touch," he said, pointing at the portrait of the king that was hanging on the wall behind the counter. "Very diplomatic. I'd be worried in your shoes as well, but that should help a bit."

"Why should we be worried?" asked Eugenio.

Mr Harper looked at him in surprise, " Oh, well, I just thought," he paused, "No, no, forget I said it. I'm not one for putting the wind up people. I expect you're right."

"No, please tell me," said Franco, "I don't understand."

Mr Harper took a step towards them, "Well," he whispered, and his breath smelled of drink, "the thing is, you know, what with all the talk of old Mussolini joining the war, I mean, if he did, things might start getting a bit ugly for you lot."

He looked from Franco to Eugenio, "I'm not saying he will, but you know the effect that rumours can have." He tapped the newspaper in his jacket pocket. "They're saying they ought to lock up all the krauts 'cos they're at war with us. And I for one agree with them. We can't be too careful. And it's not like you're in the same boat, but some people might start getting a bit shirty, if you catch my drift."

Franco didn't.

"OK, I'll spell it out. I'd hate to see anything happen to your business if the Italians come in with the Germans. Under those unfortunate circumstances you might feel you could do with a bit of protection. See, I'd hate to see all your hard work go to waste, and like I've said before, I want to protect our investment."

Franco was looking blank.

Mr Harper sighed and shook his head. "Right, then I'll lay my cards on the table. Mr Shaw has authorised me to offer you protection at a very fair price - only £4 a week to ensure that nothing untoward happens to your premises. Of course you can turn it down, but speaking as a friend I'd advise you to take it. Regard it as an insurance policy. Then you can sleep in peace knowing that your business is safe when you're not here to look after it yourself."

Franco looked doubtful. Nothing had happened to the parlour so far and he wasn't sure that they could afford another £4.

"I need to think about it," he said.

"Well of course, it's up to you. Let me know tomorrow. I'll drop by at lunch time. Tomorrow's the big day, isn't it. I might come and try one of your famous ice creams myself." With that he disappeared into the darkness.

Franco and Eugenio discussed the proposition on the bus on the way home.

"He's just trying to get more money out of you," said Eugenio. "I've had my restaurant ten years and nothing's ever happened."

"But you did paint it in the colours of their flag. I know you were worried. Maybe he's right."

"That was just to show everyone that we're on the side of the British. I thought it was important to demonstrate that we're more English than Italian."

When they reached Franco's flat Francesca, Giovanna and Eric were sitting around the kitchen table.

"Don't you think Eric looks smart in his new uniform, Papa," said Francesca. Franco nodded and shook Eric's hand.

Giovanna was obviously in a bad mood. "Where have you been all this time?" she demanded, "I've been worried sick, it's so late."

"We've been finishing off the place" said Eugenio, "It's all ready for you and Julia to come and see it in the morning. It looks great- the kitchen's all been done up, there are new cupboards and shelves and the counter looks just like the one in the piazza in Lucca. You're going to love working in there, Giovanna."

"So why's he looking so miserable?" asked Giovanna looking at her husband.

Franco shrugged, "I'm tired, that's all, it's been a long day, and I suppose there are always new worries when you're trying to start up a new business."

"What kind of worries?" asked Francesca, "We're all looking forward to seeing it and tomorrow the money should start coming in. Mamma and I have been out buying the stuff we need. It's powdered eggs and klim, but we can get all we want. I made some this afternoon. Eric really likes it don't you, Eric?"

Eric nodded, "It's very nice, especially the raspberry flavoured one."

"So what's worrying you Papa?" Francesca put her arm on her father's and kissed him on the cheek.

"We'd have been home earlier, except the man we're renting the shop from came just as we were locking up and said that he'd heard that there was a lot of feeling against the Italians. He said if Italy joins the war, then...." he paused. "He said we would need some protection and that he could provide it, that's all. But it would cost us. £4 a week. I don't think we can afford it."

Giovanna threw her hands up. "I knew it. I've never trusted that man. You never told me how much he charged you for the things he got you and I know why. Because you were frightened to say how much it cost. And now he wants more for what? You are so stupid, Franco." She blurted it all out in such a rapid Italian that Eric clearly had not been able to follow. Francesca whispered a translation. "It's just like Cosa Nostra," screamed Giovanna.

"Don't be silly," remonstrated Eugenio, "this is England, and you don't know the man. Tell her Eric, there's nothing like the Mafia in England. He said it himself. They've got a lot invested in Franco's business."

Eric looked embarrassed while Giovanna glared at the two brothers and then stormed off to her bedroom.

"Anyway," said Francesca, "Eric's here because we've fixed a date for the wedding. It's going to be on the 21st September - it's a Saturday and we want to get married in the register office in Islington. We went and fixed it up this morning."

"Hey, that's great news," said Eugenio, "We must celebrate. "I've got a bottle of Barolo that I've been saving for the baby, but we must have a toast. I'll go and get it. Franco, you and get Giovanna and I'll get Julia and some glasses," and he hurried out.

"Mamma didn't take it too well," said Francesca to her father. "She thinks it's not a proper marriage if it's not in a church with a priest, but it is, isn't it."

Franco nodded and put his arm around her. "It takes her a bit of time to get used to things, and there have been a lot of changes lately. But she'll come round, but I don't think it would be a good idea to disturb her just now."

When Eugenio reappeared with six glasses and a bottle, he was looking sheepish. "I thought it was best not to wake her," he said, "and anyway she says alcohol makes her sick when she's pregnant, but we can celebrate without her."

He placed the glasses on the table and poured the wine. "Where's Giovanna?"

"She'll be asleep as well," said Franco, "and she doesn't really like wine either."

Still standing, Eugenio raised his glass, "To the happy couple, may they be happy and rich and make lots of babies," and he downed his glass and lifted the one meant for Giovanna, "and here's to Franco's new business, and may he make lots of money and," he added as an afterthought, "bugger Mussolini."

The following morning Franco and Eugenio set off early for work. Giovanna said she and Francesca would follow later. The men had kept her awake, or rather Eugenio had with his ridiculous toasting everybody and then starting on how he knew he was going to have a son and how he was going to teach him to play football and how one day he would play for Italy but before that he would get a proper education so he wouldn't have to work hard all his life. "I don't know who is crazier, you or your idiot brother," she'd finally said.

When they got to the shop Franco's heart sank. The door was half off its hinges and in huge letters on the inside wall and opposite the picture of the King were written the words 'FASHIST SCUM GO HOME' in the same gloss paint that Franco had used to paint the outside sills. The remainder of the paint had been smeared over the front counter.

The brothers stood staring and looking dazed. Eventually Eugenio said, "We can clear this up. We've got to get it done before the women arrive. It won't matter if I'm a bit late opening. Get some white spirit and you deal with the counter. I'll try and paint over the wall."

An hour later, as Eugenio was applying the fifth coat, Mr Harper arrived looking grave. "It's a crying shame, lads, it really is, but don't say I didn't warn you. There's a lot of ill feeling. Have you thought any better of my offer?"

Franco continued to scrub and without looking up said, "Can you guarantee this won't happen again?"

"You don't know Mr Shaw. One word from him in the right ears." Harper trod on his cigarette butt. "No one crosses Mr Shaw, they wouldn't dare, after all, who wants to be taught a lesson by him? I'll be by later for one of your ice creams and the first payment."

By the time Giovanna and Francesca arrived they had managed to get the place looking almost as good as new. They'd had to find a locksmith who promised he would be round later in the day.

Much to Franco's surprise Giovanna said very little but moved about in a pall of sullen fury. She examined the kitchen, pulling out all the drawers and inspecting the fridge and the cooker. Franco was unsure whether to follow her about and point out how well everything fitted, or to ignore her and get on with unpacking the ingredients for the ice cream that Francesca was busily finding places for. In the end he did neither, but kept giving Giovanna sidelong glances. A voice from the street said, "So this must be your beautiful daughter and your wife, eh, Mr Baldini. I was just passing and thought I'd drop by to see how everything's going."

"This fridge isn't cold enough," said Giovanna, "and I can't find the settings." She looked up at the man in the black trilby and dirty white shirt with a frayed collar.

"I've been giving your husband a hand with one or two things," said Harper, "Nothing much but you do what you can. Name's Mr Harper. Business acquaintance as you might say. I've promised to keep an eye on the place - he's probably told you."

Giovanna gave him a withering look and started to help Francesca.

"Thing is," said Harper, apparently undeterred by the frosty welcome, "I've been thinking. In addition to the protection I was talking about, of course it's not just the business that needs protection. I've had a word with Mr Shaw and he says that for no extra cost he can arrange for you and your family to be covered as well. I mean, you heard what happened to Sabini. "

Franco said he didn't know who Sabini was.

"No?" Harper showed surprise."He's one of your lot, Italian, I mean. Complete bloody crook of course, but that's not why they banged him up. He was notorious. In fact some geezer even wrote a book about him. Somebody Green. The book was called 'Brighton Dock' or something like that. Anyway he was interned because they said he was an enemy alien. I'm not much of a reader myself, but Mr Shaw says that book didn't tell the half of it, but even so, with the contacts he's got in high places, he could have stopped him getting sent to the jug.

Franco didn't understand, but turned his back on his wife and slid £4 across the counter.

"Sensible," said Harper, "Very sensible."

Chapter Fifty Seven

Maurice was in a daze. The last couple of days, or was it weeks? were a blur. He was so tired that he could scarcely stay awake, but when he closed his eyes images kept coming back that shook him and made him open his eyes in terror. And he was starving. He couldn't remember his last meal, but when he thought about food it only increased the pain in his stomach. His lips were parched and the acidic taste in his mouth burned.

He was lying in a slit trench watching a gentle breeze sway the corn on the other side of a canal. Next to him Joe was lying in a crumpled heap snoring gently. They had been there for hours.

A captain they hadn't recognised had ordered them to hold the position. It was expected that Germans would come out of the wood and through the field to the bridge that had been there some time earlier but that had been blown up a few hours ago. His joints were aching, but every time he moved to try and get more comfortable the pain in his legs only made things worse.

During the previous night, when they had been walking west there had been a sudden downpour which soaked them right through. He didn't know whether his rifle had got too wet to fire, but he hadn't dared try it out to see since the men had only been issued with ten rounds and they had been told not to use it unless they could be sure of success. So far he had never shot a bullet in anger, in fact neither of them had. It had become clear days ago that the officers had no idea what they were supposed to be doing and the men had no idea where they were. The captain had explained that they were using maps from the war over twenty years ago, the last time this area of France had been surveyed.

He and Joe had been separated from the rest of the company when the deserted village they had been in had come under attack from half a dozen Messerschmitts that had flown low over the main street, strafing and sending up clouds of dust. The gutteral juddering sound of their engines had sent the men throwing themselves into alleys and behind buildings. He and Joe noticed the front door of a house that was slightly ajar and dived in before slamming it shut. Joe sat down panting and leaned against it, listening as another aeroplane came in from the east and sent up yet another shower of splinters and stones. The room was dark, the heavy shutters keeping out any light and it took a while for their eyes to adjust. Maurice fumbled for the door handle above Joe's head.

"There's a lock here, they must have left in a hurry," he whispered turning the key, "Can you feel a bolt?"

"Yeah, but hang on, we'd better check there's no Jerries hiding in here before we lock ourselves in." He slid the bolt on his rifle, "And if there is, I'm gonna shoot the fucker."

Maurice heard him curse gently as he crawled away from the door and bang his head on something.

A few moments later a whisper came out of the darkness, "Nothing down here, I'm going upstairs."

The planes appeared to have gone, but then Maurice heard men marching along the street from the west and then a burst of machine gun fire. There was silence for several minutes while he strained his ears and then a pistol shot.

"Christ," he thought, "they're here." He scrambled away from the door, trained his rifle on it and waited. He jumped as he felt a hot breath in his ear. "It's the fucking Germans," whispered Joe, "I saw them from the upstairs window. They've shot one of our blokes. Couldn't see who."

Loud voices were coming up the street and they both jumped when there was the pummeling of a rifle butt on the door. From the other side of the blinds a German voice was loudly shouting orders and a motor bike revved its engine and drove off.

They sat in silence for what seemed like an hour until Maurice finally said, "There's no point in trying to get out of here tonight. I think we should wait till just before dawn and then try and get away. What d'you think? We could even get some sleep."

"Yeah, OK, but which way are we going to go?"

"We'll go west and see if we can get to the coast."

"That's the way the Jerries came from. I vote we go east."

"That's the way the planes came from. Which would you rather, get killed by the Luftwaffe or by their soldiers? I don't think the Luftwaffe take prisoners."

Joe thought about this and then said, "OK, we'll take it in turns to get a lie down and see if there's anything to eat. I don't know about you but I could eat one of their bleedin' horses. Kitchen's back there. I'll take a look."

He shuffled off into the darkness and Maurice saw the reflection of a torchlight flicker on the wall of the kitchen before it was switched off and Joe came back. "Not unless you fancy French bread," he said. "Is it supposed to be green?"

"No. Anything to drink?"

"Water, but I wouldn't trust the Jerries not to poison the wells. There's something called Pistas. You want some of that?" He passed Maurice the bottle.

"Pastis? Nah, the girl in the bar gave me some when I asked her what the froggies drink. You have to put water in it and it changes colour. It gave me the farts something shocking and a bloody awful hangover. Pissed arse is the right name for it if you ask me."

Maurice started to giggle and then Joe joined in. In a moment they were so helpless with laughter that neither of them could speak. Eventually Maurice wiped his eyes on his sleeve and spluttered, "Christ, Joe, what the fuck are we going to do?"

They took comfort from being so close to each other and neither wanted to suggest that they could take it in turns to get some sleep in one of the bedrooms upstairs. They dozed and were woken by the slightest sound- the creaking in the rafters or a dog barking in the distance. Eventually Joe crawled across to the window and pulled aside a shutter.

"It's still dark," he whispered, "I think we should get out of here. I can't hear anybody around."

They were stiff from having crouched for so long, tentatively slid the bolt on the door and crept out, silently pulling the door behind them.

"Go left," said Maurice, "and keep to the wall."

Almost immediately he stumbled on something metallic that clanged against the wall and then rolled away onto the road. They held their breaths and listened, but the only sound was the steady patter of rain on the hard ground. He knelt down and felt along the gutter.

"There's someone here," he whispered, trying to conceal the panic he was feeling. "Here, give me your torch."

Joe hesitated, "Don't be fucking stupid. Let's just get out of here."

Ignoring him, Maurice bent over the figure lying on the ground and opened his jacket. He lit his lighter close to his chest and using his body to screen the flame from the rain, he peered down and then shrank back. The rain was washing blood from the dead soldier's mouth and running down his cheek to his neck. In the half light Maurice could see the man's eyes staring up and the pallor of his skin.

"It's Jimmy Croft," he said, He's been bayonetted in the neck. The bastards."

"Mo, he's dead." Joe was pulling at Maurice's shoulder, "We've got to get the fuck out of here and quick."

Maurice hauled himself to his feet. He wanted to scream and run along the street firing his rifle into every window and alley. He ran his hand over the back of his neck where the rain had started to run down beneath his collar and stepped over the dead soldier. They half ran, half crawled along the length of the house and towards the canal which they had crossed the previous evening.

After half an hour the rain began to ease off and they paused, panting as a weak sun begun to rise. By now they were on an open road. There was a ditch to their left and beyond that a low wall. Jo grabbed Maurice by the arm and indicated to him to lie down. They strained their ears. From on the other side of the wall came the sound of a heavy footfall and then a cough. The two men lay flat on the ground on the edge of the ditch and held their breath. Maurice heard the bolt being pulled back on Joe's rifle as he slithered on his back and looked up. The cough came again, louder this time, and then slowly the head of a horse appeared over the wall, looking down at them and silhouetted against the sky. They let out a sigh of relief and clambered to their feet and ran on. After a mile they came to the canal and crossed the wooden bridge on all fours and finally stumbled into a slit trench when they heard the thick Scottish accent telling them to hold their position.

That had all been several hours earlier. They had taken comfort when the bridge had been blown up, but still didn't dare leave their position and waited for the order to move.

Maurice nudged Joe awake.

"Look," he said, "follow the line of those trees on the horizon and then come this way. Does it look to you like that corn is moving?"

Before Joe could reply there was a shout from a trench fifty yards along the canal and a small group of soldiers broke cover and started to run up the hill towards the road. At the same moment a tank appeared from behind the wood beyond the field and began to rumble towards them.

"Christ," gasped Maurice, "Let's get the fuck out of here." A mortar shell landed behind them, spitting up clods of earth. The last thing Maurice saw before turning and fleeing towards the road was a group of Germans who had suddenly appeared below them and who were pushing dinghies into the canal. Another mortar came whistling through the air to his left and he threw himself onto the ground. He gasped at the searing pain in his thigh that made him feel sick and then he passed out.

He came to at the sound of voices a little way off. "This one's gone, sir, can't do nothing for him."

Maurice opened his eyes and looked up into the face of a soldier who was kneeling over him, staring at him intently.

"You all right, mate. Can you walk?"

Maurice had no idea, but the moment he tried to stand up, his legs gave way beneath him.

"Here, let me give you a hand." A second soldier had come over and taken Maurice under the arm. "Come on, soldier, we've got to get you out of here now." He put Maurice's right arm over his shoulder and between then they lifted him from behind the knees. Maurice yelped. "It's my left leg," he tried to say, but his voice came out as a pained scream.

"OK, I'll take your weight, just led the bad leg go limp."

They ushered him towards the road where a steady stream of trucks and soldiers was moving slowly westwards.

An army lorry loaded with men hanging off the running board and sitting on the roof stopped. "Make room for one more."

The passenger door opened and a young private clambered out. "Here, mate, take my place, I'll get in the back - you're bigger than me and it looks like you need the seat more than I do. Let me give you a hand." The three soldiers managed to haul Maurice up alongside two other men and then closed the door that pressed into Maurice's leg and made him grimace with pain. The convoy moved on slowly, Maurice dimly aware of the driver's voice giving a running commentary on everything that he could see.

"I wish that bugger would stop waving his bleedin' feet around," he was saying, "I know it's raining but they're bloody useless as windscreen wipers. It's the horses I feel sorry for," he muttered as he swerved to avoid a dead horse, "Poor bleedin' dumb beats, they didn't ask to get in this war. How can they understand, but it makes me sick the way they're treated."

The soldier who was crushed up next to Maurice whispered in his ear, "He's been rattling on like this all day. I reckon he thinks if he stops talking he'll buy it. But if he doesn't shut up soon I'll fucking well shoot him myself."

Maurice tried to smile but his head was heavy and he fell asleep, his head lolling on the shoulder of the other passenger.

He was woken sometime later by the pain in his leg. There wasn't room to get it away from the door against which it was pressed. The driver was still talking.

"They've thrown a cordon round Dunkirk. Jesus, look at that smoke. They must've bombed an oil distillery or something, Christ what a mess."

He drew up by the side of a derelict house where a captain leaned into the cab. "Get your men out and then destroy the lorry. Any injured men, take them to the medical centre on the dunes behind those buildings."

Maurice was helped down from the cab and he looked around. "Where's my mate?" he asked. The driver called out, "Anyone seen this lad's mate?" and then he leaned across and said quietly, "I think you got on alone, son."

The soldiers who had found Maurice came from behind the truck. The older of the two put his hand on Maurice's shoulder. "He's dead. I'm sorry."

Maurice blinked at him, unable to take in his words. "No, he can't be. We swore we'd always be there for each other. I saw him running. I've got to go back. I promised."

"I promise you, he is dead. Got the full blast of the mortar that got you in the leg. Come on, you need to get it seen to.'

Maurice was still in a daze when he was placed on a stretcher outside the medical tent. He gazed up at a cloudy sky and for the first time became aware of the chaos around him. Thick, black smoke was drifting cross his line of vision while the roar of artillery pounded from the direction of the sea. Occasionally a low flying Stuka whined above his head dropping its bombs to his left. A man was groaning in pain below his feet. After a while an orderly came to examine him. Maurice indicated the pain in his leg. The orderly cut away Maurice's trousers around his thigh and examined it carefully and then stood up.

"You're OK," he said, "You'll live. It's nasty but it's only a flesh wound. We'll get it cleaned up and bandaged when there's a space on the table. In the meantime I'll get you some water and something to help with the pain. Here, have a fag."

Maurice closed his eyes and drew deeply on the cigarette. He couldn't make out if the pounding was guns or his head throbbing. For a while he drifted in and out of consciousness until he felt himself being lifted and a voice say, "He's lost a lot of blood."

He felt a sharp stab of pain and then he passed out.

When he came to again he was lying on the ground by the wall of a tent. People were hurrying around him, whispering and he couldn't make out what was being said.

"You just lie there for a bit, mate, just till you're feeling better. There's no bones broken. When you think you make it you can get yourself down to the mole."

Maurice turned his head. There was a forest of legs, but as far as he could see, no sign of a mole. He thought he must have misunderstood.

He tried to speak, but his lips and mouth were parched and his voice came out as a gutteral croak. He laughed. An orderly bent down and lifted some water to his lips. Maurice gulped it down and said, "I thought you said get down to the mole. What mole?"

The orderly nodded through the open door of the tent. "There's a jetty called the mole. If you can get down there there'll be a ship to get you home. Mind you, there's a bit of a queue at the moment. I should stay here for a bit till you feel a bit stronger."

At the sound of the word 'home' Maurice felt galvanised. He pushed himself up onto his elbows, but immediately felt faint and collapsed back again.

"When you're ready, mate, don't rush it." Maurice slept.

It was dawn when he woke up. Throughout the night he had been dimly aware of people working behind him, of men groaning in pain and orders being shouted.

He climbed painfully to his feet and felt down his left leg. There was a thick bandage around his thigh and his trouser leg had been cut away. His shin and calf was blue with bruising, but at least he felt he could walk. He made his way past three operating tables and stepped outside. The noise from the guns and the smoke drifting across the dunes that filled his nostrils immediately made him feel disorientated. He staggered on for a few steps and then sat down. A soldier was lying on his back clutching a bren gun which he was pointing into the air.

"The thing is," he said, without looking at Maurice," If I'm going to die here, I'm going to take one of those fuckers with me."

The sky was a dirty grey, and every few minutes a plane came roaring out of the clouds and dropped its load onto the beach. "Stukas," said the soldier. "They're not a problem, not unless you get one of their bombs right on the bonce. Sand absorbs the impact, see. Messerschmidts, they're the real bastards. There's one," and he let off a volley of fire.

"Have you got any yet?" asked Maurice.

The man shook his head. "Nope, but it doesn't half make me feel better." There was a pause, and then he asked, "You been injured?"

Maurice pointed to his leg. "Can you walk?"

"Dunno, I think so."

The soldier fired at a Messerschmidt that had strafed the beach and was now circling before starting another run along the dunes."

"Thing is, I've been down on the beach waiting for a ship for two days. And yesterday I was about to get on a destroyer when this fucking captain asked where my regiment was and when I told him he said they're not taking odds and sods. I had to find my regiment. Like I'm going to hitch a lift back to Armentières to drag a frigging corpse back here." He spat into the sand.

"Tell you what," he went on, "you stay here and keep taking pot shots. Geyser told me where I can get some buckshee fags. I'll get us both some and then I'll help you down to the beach. You might change my luck."

He put the gun down beside Maurice, clambered to his feet and headed off in the direction of the town.

Half an hour later he returned with a woman's pink hat on his head and swinging a handbag. "Method in my madness," he said. "I've got eight hundred fags in this bag. If they think I've gone bonkers and you're badly injured, then they might take pity on us. If not, you can give this hat to your best girl."

He helped Maurice to his feet. "We'll leave the bren. Run out of ammo. Come on."

The scene on the beach was one of complete devastation. A thick pall of smoke hung over the sea which was black with oil. A long line of soldiers snaked around the far end of the beach leading to a destroyer that was being bombed as it embarked men from a jetty. There were abandoned vehicles, some of which were still burning to their left, and beneath his feet an assortment of empty tins, broken bottles and empty cigarette packets.

"There," said the soldier, pointing to a line of lorries that had been driven as far as possible into the sea to form a makeshift jetty, "We'll try and get one of those little boats. Do you think you can climb along those trucks?"

Maurice nodded, spurred on by the thought of getting away and home. "If we don't get away today we're fucked," said his companion. "There's some of our blokes and the Frogs holding the line around the town, but they reckon the Jerries'll break through by tomorrow at the latest. I'm Phil, by the way. What's your name?"

Maurice told him.

"Well, Maurice, me old son, I hope you can swim. See that little motor boat trying to get round the wreck over there? That's our man. But we'll have to wade out."

They had reached the sea edge. The waves lapping the shoreline left a black tide mark as they retreated. The two men removed their boots and socks and paddled out into the greasy water. Thirty yards out a motor boat was being moored to a trawler that was partially submerged. In front of them a dozen men were already up to their waists in the water. Two men were hanging over the side of the boat helping the soldiers up.

"Get over here quick," one of them called. A Messerschmidt swept along the coastline and everybody ducked. Maurice slipped as he did so, and spat out a mouthful of salty oil. He shoved his way through the shallows and by the time he reached the boat the water was up to his neck.

He was thrown a rope and grabbed hold of it.

"I can't get up," he said hopelessly, "My leg's too sore."

"Oh, for fuck's sake." Phil lifted him as high as he could and then bent so that he could get his shoulder underneath Maurice's buttocks and then he stood up. The seamen manhandled him over the side and he collapsed onto the deck which was already black and wet with oil. A moment later Phil was sitting next to him.

"Sorry," said Maurice, "I just couldn't do it by myself. Thanks."

"That's all right, Mary. Here you'd better wear the hat. It suits you better than me," and he gave it a brush before placing it on Maurice's head.

The dozen men sat in silence as the motor boat chugged its way towards a second destroyer that was lying half a mile out to sea. German planes were circling when he climbed the ladder onto a ship that was crammed with soldiers. He found a corner and lay down and fell asleep.

Chapter Fifty Eight

Esther Hart's Diary

Saturday 1st June 1940

Charles not at all well, though I don't know what is wrong with him. Took him a cup of tea this morning at nine and had a job waking him. When he eventually came to he said that he was too unwell to get up. I offered to bring him up the paper but he wasn't interested, which is so unlike him. Mercifully Douglas went off to the office very early saying he'd get breakfast there. He can still hardly bring himself to speak to me. There was a time when I would have found that absolutely mortifying, but I'm ashamed to say that now it comes as something of a relief.

The papers are full of the BEF being rescued from the beaches of Dunkirk. It is wonderful that so many have been saved, though apparently there has also been an enormous loss of life as well as equipment and ships. But people are talking as if it's some kind of victory. A piece in yesterday's "Daily Express" describes how, in 'one of the most magnificent operations in history' ships of all sizes and shapes brought back thousands of men. Three destroyers have been lost, but according to the article the Germans' advanced forces have been shattered by naval guns. Then, on an inside page, another piece describes how Amiens has been almost wiped out by German bombers, and yet another that the French army on the Somme is 'progressing favourably.'

We used to complain that there wasn't enough news, and now there is so much that is just plainly contradictory. But then for a long time were were being informed that the Norwegian campaign was going well until it suddenly turned out that the whole thing was a disaster. I want to believe the best, but find it very difficult when so much of it is probably just propaganda. It is also reported that when King Leopold of Belgium surrendered, he intended that all the Belgian's army's equipment would be made over to the Germans. That explains why there is so much hostility to Belgian refugees from some people here.

Monday 3rd June

Not sure if I should continue with this diary, though I sometimes think that it and Barbara are the only things that keep me sane. Having spent all of Saturday in bed, Charles made a miraculous recovery yesterday, I suspect because Douglas was home all day. While I gardened all morning, they sat on the bench in the sunshine watching me and chatting, and then at one o'clock Douglas had the temerity to say that they were peckish and wasn't it time I fixed a spot of lunch. I know he works hard all week at whatever he does now. Civil servants have been asked to extend their hours from 48 to 54 per week, but still, I felt the way he said it was a bit thick.

And I was still furious from what happened on Saturday afternoon. Barbara phoned, and when I said that Douglas was at work she said she'd pop round, she had a letter she thought I ought to see. She sounded unusually serious, and I naturally assumed it was from one of the the MP's that she's agreed to write to. When she arrived she said that the letter had arrived at Herbert's office and that she was so sorry. She took it out of her handbag and looked at me pityingly before handing it over. At first I didn't understand and just stared at it and then she asked if I'd ever suspected that he had another woman. It was true that the handwriting on the envelope was clearly a women's - large, mean and self-satisfied, just like its author's. I recognised it at once. I laughed and said that this wasn't from a mistress, it was from his sister. Barbara looked relieved and asked why ever she would be writing to him at his office. I could only guess that it was because she, or they, didn't want me to know that they were corresponding. I held it, staring at the writing until Barbara said, "Aren't you going to open it?" I was shocked, but also intrigued, because I couldn't imagine why they were having to write so secretly unless it was about the children and I said so. Supposing one of them was very ill and she didn't want me to know, but on the other hand, how could I open it without Douglas finding out? Barbara said that was very simple, she knew how to steam it open and reseal it so Douglas would never know. She was very good at it, having had lots of experience when she was a teenager.

We stood over the steaming kettle, giggling like a couple of schoolgirls but the letter was simply horrible and it was clear that they had been writing to each other like this for some time and that he had told her to write to him at the office. She said that she had asked him 'several times' to visit, that the children were completely out of hand, that Lydia was still wetting the bed and that Gordon had started stealing money. It was my fault of course. I had always been far too lenient with them and that she was reaping what I had sowed. She also needed more money. She ended by saying that she had always known that I was quite unsuitable for him as a wife and the mother of his children, who I had turned into 'perfect little brats.'

The letter was far worse than if Douglas did have a mistress. Barbara was absolutely furious and said I should confront him, but I said I needed to think and changed the conversation to what was happening in the war, trying to work out if there was a way that I could get them home. And I still don't know what to do about the letter.

Tuesday 4th June.

I've burnt the letter.

Thursday 6th June

Mr Churchill made a stirring speech over the radio a couple of night ago saying we'd fight everywhere and will never surrender. Listened to it alone as Charles has resumed his lethargy and had gone to bed early and Douglas was not back. Decided I'm not going to be bullied by him and his awful sister any more, so I wrote a long letter to Gordon and Lydia saying how much I miss them and that I knew it must be very hard for them to be away from home for so long and enclosed a five shilling postal order for each of them.

Then I went and cried on Barbara's shoulder. I told her that Douglas had wanted me to take Charles and go and stay with Ada and how Charles had flatly refused, and at the time I'd thought it was a terrible idea. Now I was having second thoughts, for the sake of the children. She said she thought that was a very bad idea, three adults all living in the same house who hated each other. It sounded like the plot of an Agatha Christie novel. If it didn't work out, and she didn't see how it could, what would happen to me and the children then? We couldn't come back to London, since so many children were being evacuated and everybody knew that London could be bombed at any time. At least the children were safe where they were, and was I sure that in going I wasn't wanting to leave Douglas as much as protect the children? I don't know the answer to that, and that shocks me.

We then talked about Mr Churchill's speech and she really surprised me with her views. She said he was undoubtedly the right man for the job at the moment but she mistrusts all politicians. She laughed when she quoted Voltaire, "If God didn't exist, it would be necessary to invent him". She wasn't sure that was true-there was still a lingering agreement with Marx that religion is the opium of the people. But what is true is that if enemies didn't exist, it would be necessary for governments to create them. All governments rule by fear. During the thirties it was fear of communism. Then it was fear of Nazi Germany. When I pointed out that that was entirely justified she agreed, but said Hitler was the best example. He created a fear in Germany of an international Jewish conspiracy, which was obviously utter rubbish, but which is costing thousands of people their lives. She said I knew she was right really. All those refugees who are coming over here are now demonised as fifth columnists with no more justification than Jews are accused of being in some kind of grand plot. She said in her view any man who wanted to become a politician should be disqualified from becoming one on the grounds that the desire proves he is completely unsuited to the role. "Twas ever thus," she smiled, "and ever shalt be." Then she said that in her experience the vast majority of men (she excluded Herbert from this, which is one of the reasons she married him) are driven by fear. This makes them aggressive and politicians especially create a nightmare world in which everyone is out to get them. So they need more power to overcome these bogeymen they've dreamt up, with the result that they create even bigger bogeymen. Unfortunately they surround themselves with like minded people, including newspaper editors who spend their time writing up stories to reinforce the picture of a nightmare world. She pointed to an article which said how Belgian refugee children were being refused admittance to a play centre because of their nationality, and shook her head. Madness.

I walk home very confused. I like Barbara very much and admire her, although I didn't think she was capable of such cynicism. But I can't argue against her. What I got from what she said was that I need to distance myself emotionally from both Douglas and from Charles.

Friday 7th June

The Germans have broken through the Somme with their tanks and are heading towards Paris. Meanwhile there has been a lot of bitterness from the army saying that the RAF did nothing to protect them at Dunkirk. And yet people seem to be remarkably sanguine about all the bad news as if resigned to the worst.

It's been the most glorious day. I worked in the garden again all morning which I do find takes my mind off things. Still no replies to the letters I sent, and I wonder how they could help anyway. Decided it would do Charles good to get out and so took him for a short walk. He commented on how many people in the neighbourhood had dug up their gardens and were growing vegetables. There was an air raid warning in the late evening and so sat in the Anderson shelter for half an hour wondering whether this was really any protection from a bomb. People who haven't put up their Anderson shelters by the 11th are going to be liable for 'penalties'. If they can't manage to do it, they can apply to the local council for help with it as long as they can give good reason why they need it. Anyone failing to put up their shelter who hasn't applied for assistance will have their shelter confiscated and be punished, presumably by having a fine and a bomb dropped on them. I wonder what the authorities are going to do about all those people who are using their shelters to grow vegetables in. Too much going on in my head to write it down. Keeping a secret diary feels like an act of disloyalty but is it as bad as Douglas's secret correspondence with Ada when it concerns my children? I don't know.

Monday 10th June

Slept very badly because of the heat and this gnawing anxiety about the children, about how things are with Douglas and the constantly worsening news about the war. Was worried that he might pop into his old office to see if there was any post for him there and that he would be told that it had been sent here. Decided the only thing I could do anything about was to try and make things better with Douglas so got up and cooked him breakfast. Had a pleasant enough conversation about the heat and what it must be like for the soldiers having to fight in this weather, but we were like a couple of strangers sitting across the breakfast table, chatting inconsequentially in order to be polite and pass the time. He did kiss me on the cheek before he left which he hasn't done for a long time. Then I realised that I could be nice to him because I was so relieved that he was going to work and would be out of the house for the best part of a week. Compared with what other people are going through, this all makes me feel incredibly selfish.

Douglas phoned just before six to say that I shouldn't wait up, that there was a new crisis but that I should listen to the news. Then came the announcement that Italy had declared war on us and on France. The news from Norway over the weekend was terrible and there now seems no possibility of preventing the Germans from establishing bases along the coast from where they can attack Scotland and the eastern counties. In France the German tanks have almost reached Paris and the fear of invasion is now so great that there has been mass evacuations from the seaside towns.

During the day heavy thunder clouds rolled in and in the afternoon it poured, which the garden certainly needs. At the greengrocer's I'd seen a rather sad looking lettuce selling for one and six so felt very virtuous that I'm growing my own. Charles was scandalized, saying he buys three packets of his 'Black Cat' cigarettes for the same price.

Tuesday 11th June

Slept fitfully again and then woke up to find that Douglas hadn't come home. Went into the living room at midnight and listened to President Roosevelt's speech. It's clear where his sympathies lie and he criticised what he called the 'isolationist' views of many Americans, saying that a small number of dictators had in their hands deadly machines that threaten democracy around the world. Didn't get the idea that America is keen to come to our aid, though. He talked about 'the gods of war and hate' - a clear reference to Hitler and Mussolini.

The lunchtime news reported that there were riots in Glasgow. Groups of hooligans smashing the windows of Italian restaurants and ice cream sellers and then looting them. Police baton charged the youths. Charles came back from the shop with a copy of 'The Times' that showed that Italian restaurants in Soho had also been attacked. When I expressed disgust he said it served the blighters right. They should all be locked up as fifth columnists, I should know that. When I asked him how he knew he was astonished and said Douglas told him and that it was Douglas's job to know. Then he looked embarrassed and asked whether Douglas hadn't told me - it was what his new job was all about. Then he added as an afterthought that if I hadn't got all sentimental about these damned refugees no doubt Douglas would have confided in me too. He finished by saying that I mustn't breath a word of this conversation to Douglas.

Barbara rang to say she's got two tickets for tomorrow evening for 'The Light of Heart' at 'The Apollo'. Herbert couldn't go as he had an evening meeting and did I want to go? Of course I jumped at the idea and then told her about my conversation with Charles. She said Herbert might know something about it, that there'd been talk of some new committee being set up under Lord Swinton that was terribly hush-hush.

Wednesday 12th June

Announcement from Mr Churchill that all Italian males between the ages of 16 and 70 who have been in the country for less than twenty years were to be interned.

Met Barbara in Shaftesbury Avenue for a drink before going to the theatre. She said Herbert told her that the responsibility for internees had suddenly been taken away from the Home Office and it was generally assumed that it had been given to this new committee. Anderson had lost the fight within the government to retain control of the internees which was a tragedy for them. There was a rumour that Sir

Joseph Ball was also on the committee. He had been heavily involved with the magazine 'Truth' that had been vehemently anti-semitic and it was suspected had tried to get Churchill de-selected from his Epping constituency before the war. We both wondered why Churchill would ever have agreed to have this man sit on a committee that he had set up, but apparently he would be Chamberlain's choice and presumably Churchill doesn't know the history.

We sat talking in a smoke-filled pub feeling increasingly depressed until a couple of young soldiers came over and offered to buy us a drink. Barbara did her best Hedy Lamarr impersonation and said, "Darlings, we'd love to if you weren't too young to buy a drink and we weren't too wise to have to disappoint you." They went off muttering about 'stuck up bitches.'

She said there was a real feeling of depression in the Home Office because almost nobody believed all the propaganda about fifth columnists which is being put about by the government and the press and which has led to the imprisonment of thousands of innocent men and now women and to the mindless destruction of so many Italian businesses. She said in Herbert's view there had been a turf war between the Home Office on the one hand and the secret services, the army and the War Office on the other. In the end we talked until so late that we missed the play, but neither of us were feeling much like 'Light of Heart' by then anyway.

Friday 14th June

One of the things that Barbara said last night was that when she was in Germany, Hitler was famous for keeping the crowds waiting for hours at the Nazi rallies so that by the time he arrived they had worked themselves up into a hysteria of expectation. I read somewhere that he predicted that Paris would fall on the 15th June. Today the German troops marched into the city. He also predicted that London would be taken on 15th August and I find there's a part of me that can't wait for it to happen, just so this unbearable tension is finally over. Barbara showed me a poem that she had copied out and kept in her handbag. It was by a Greek poet called Cavafy, I think, called "Expecting the Barbarians."

It started,

"What are we waiting for, gathered in the public square?

The Barbarians are to arrive today."

It tells how nothing happens except that the people grow more and more restless and finishes with everyone going to their homes lost in thought because night has come and the Barbarians haven't arrived. It has been reported that there are no longer any Barbarians. The last lines

"And now what shall become of us without any Barbarians?

Those people were a kind of solution."

People seem to be going about their ordinary everyday lives as if they haven't a care in the world. This afternoon I was washing and ironing and listening to the music on the wireless, planning meals for the weekend, wondering how I was going to endure another weekend with Douglas and his father. Then I thought, suppose when the Germans come they billet a soldier in our house. Where would we put him and what would he want to eat? Do the Germans eat the same food as us? Then Charles came and read me bits out of the paper and was outraged that the Germans had had to have their dogs put down because of food shortages. I didn't like to point out that lots of people here had their dogs put down when war broke out, but I found myself thinking that if we do have to billet a German soldier Charles would have to have Alexander put to sleep, in which case he would undoubtedly try to shoot the German and be bumped off himself. In that case the soldier would be able to have Charles's room. I felt relieved at having discovered the solution while Charles carried on reading out loud, the Incontinent Cat on his lap. I snapped out of my murderous thoughts when Charles asked me for the hundredth time if I knew how Alexander got his name. I said he had, but that I'd forgotten and he said, for the thousandth time it wasn't after Alexander Haig, oh no, but after Major General Alexander who had fought against overwhelming odds and saved his battery which he then had removed out of harm's way by hand. That was in Belgium, he couldn't remember where exactly but it was definitely in 1914, of that he was quite sure.

I said I thought we both needed a cup of tea. I'm desperate to see the children, and feel it may be for the last time. But I'm stuck in this house by an old man who has lost his mind, the Incontinent Cat and at the behest of a husband that I can barely bring myself to look at any more.

Reading back over this I really do wonder who is going mad.

Chapter Fifty Nine

Maurice sat at the kitchen table with a blank piece of paper and a full ash tray in front of him. He lit another cigarette. All evening he hadn't been able to concentrate on the conversation around the table. He'd been trying to think how he could tell Joe's parents what a great mate he'd been, how they'd been together until the very last minute. But he had decided that he wouldn't try and write to them until he had a bit of time to himself, so now he had come downstairs, got some paper from the shop, made himself a mug of tea and tried to find the words. Although he'd never met them, and Joe had rarely spoken about them, he kept on imagining them asking, "What happened? What was it like?"

His father had endlessly asked, "What was it like, son?" while his mother kept crying, a handkerchief clutched to her mouth and shaking her head. Occasionally she'd say, "And both my boys are safe, thank God. Thank God."

He couldn't describe what it had been like and he didn't want to try. How could they possibly understand? His father had saved cuttings from the papers that he had stuck in a scrap book and had shown Maurice with pride. Maurice nodded when he saw the photographs of the devastated ships and the black smoke rising from the beaches, of troops wading in line towards the small boats.

"We hoped there'd be a picture of you," said his father. "Of course we couldn't be sure that you were there. That was the worst thing for your mother. Not knowing."

Maurice stared vacantly at the pictures. He felt there was a ravine between him and his parents, that even if he could explain what it had been like, they would never be able to understand, and with everything that his father said he felt more and more alienated from them.

During supper he had kept glancing across the table at Don. His brother had been on leave for a week and was due to rejoin his ship in a few days. Maurice having arrived back yesterday, the brothers had had little chance to speak beyond saying, "Yeah, it was pretty bad," at which point their father had started a tirade about how the RAF "had let the Navy down in Norway and then, bugger me, made a complete balls up in Dunkirk."

"Language, Stanley," said Mrs Hickey sharply, "there's no need for language."

Don had pushed his chair back violently from the table and stood up. "Right, I'm off to the pub. You want to come, Mo?"

"Maurice is going to dry up while I wash," said Mrs Hickey, "I've hardly seen him. Stanley, you still haven't cashed up last week's takings. Go and do it now please."

She stood at the sink with her hand in the bowl and didn't move while Maurice watched her back. In the few weeks he'd been away she appeared to have grown older, her hair greyer and she stooped as she walked. He didn't know what to say.

Eventually she broke the silence and whispered, "I couldn't bear it if they made you go back. Don't go, son. I'd rather you were in prison than this. They can't send for you again, can they? Not with your wounds."

"Don't worry, Ma," Maurice could never cope with his mother's emotions, "No one's going back to Dunkirk."

"But they might want you to go somewhere else just as dangerous, like Norway. Don won't talk about it, but if they send for you I don't want you to go. Don's going again soon and I've asked him not to but you know how stubborn he is. He says it's his duty and your father agrees. But isn't a boy's life more important than any stupid ideas of duty?"

Maurice wanted to comfort her but he felt repelled by the shaking shoulders and the loud sniffing as she sobbed. He put down the tea towel and said, "I'm on leave for two weeks. I wasn't badly wounded. Let's enjoy the next few days while Don's here and we'll talk about it later. But I doubt that we'll get sent to fight. It's down to the French now."

She nodded and started wiping the dishes furiously. Nothing more was said until Mr Hickey came back from the shop. "I've got bits from the papers about what happened in Norway if you want to see them. Now that was a victory. And your brother played his part, I'm proud to say. I'll fetch them."

Maurice held up his hand, "Dad, show me in the morning. I want to write this letter to Joe's folks. D'you mind?"

Mr Hickey stroked the cover of the scrapbook and laid it on the table. "No, of course not son. I'll leave it there. You write your letter. Come on, Mother, we'll go up."

He ushered his wife through the door and then turned and said, "He won't talk about it either. I expect he thinks it'd be boasting, but I'm proud of him. I'm proud of you both," and he quietly shut the door.

Maurice still hadn't written a word when Don came back from the pub and sat down heavily. He helped himself to one of Maurice's cigarettes and they sat in silence until Don reached across for the scrapbook and opened it. He gazed at the first page and then shook his head.

"He collected all this stuff and wanted to show it to me. I didn't want to know. I mean, how could I tell him it wasn't like that at all. He was so proud and just like he did with you, he wanted to know what it was like. I couldn't explain. You can't, can you?" He drew deeply on his cigarette. "In May in Norway it's like a sunny day, even at midnight. There were Norwegians and French all running round the ship. No one could understand what they were on about. We were told we were going to attack this little village, We went in with 'Vindictive' and five destroyers. We got close to the port. There was snow on the hills and a gang of us had to lower the tanks on landing craft with cranes while the troops got ready to row across to the beach. Our gunners had to cover them. When the first dinghies were in the water they looked like ants crawling across the sea. We didn't hear the order to fire but the whole ship rocked and the noise was deafening." He sucked hard on his cigarette and stubbed it out. Then he gave a dry laugh."I had this fag on and it burnt straight up to my fingers. I thought I'd gone blind until I saw a whole lot of houses go up in flames like they were kindling covered in petrol. The whole sea was suddenly lit up and then there was another blast and the church that had been there a moment before just sort of, well, it exploded. The Germans had been using it as an ammunition dump. The mountains looked like they were on fire. We shelled the beach till the first troops landed but even from the ship you could hear the crackling machine guns. By the time we'd got the tanks onto the landing craft it was dawn and we were nearly dead with tiredness. Anyway, a couple of days later we picked up some blokes from the twenty-fourth brigade. They'd been on a Polish ship that had been sunk by German bombers. And this geezer, Billy Flynn, nice guy from Birmingham, he told me," Don took another cigarette and lit it and inhaled deeply before continuing, "The Norwegians said the town had been evacuated and it hadn't."

He paused. "There were babies and little kids and women. It was a massacre. They made out it was our first great victory in the war, that's what they said. Anyway, five days later we were taking troops and supplies down to Bodo from Harstad and hit this rock. We lost steering and were drifting till we were grounded. The thing was that a couple of German planes flew over so it was decided to get us all off as quickly as possible and then torpedo her so that the Jerries couldn't get her. That was another load of equipment lost, it was only a miracle no one died. So the troops lost one load of equipment on the Polish ship and another on ours. And you know what the Admiralty said? That we'd hit an uncharted rock. That's what they put out. Some of the lads said the navigator was a Norwegian German sympathiser. They said Captain Howson had him arrested, taken up to the bridge and he shot the bloke himself. Bollocks. He was as English as you and me.. What I do know is that those waters have been completely charted and the navigator made a balls up, and if he didn't someone who ordered us through that passage did and he deserves to lose his job. We were sitting ducks and if we hadn't been picked up by the Echo and transferred to the Coventry, well, I wouldn't be here now. But that was a bloody big rock we hit. One of the lads said that when the navigator was plotting our passage he put down his pencil on the map and obscured the rock. That's more like it. They took us back to Harstad to twiddle our thumbs, over a thousand of us. But I'll never forget the way we hit that rock. Jesus. The smoke, the din, blokes running around like crazy bastards...."

He looked at Maurice expectantly. Maurice nodded. "Yeah, the smoke, the noise. Fucking chaos. My mate was killed."

Don nodded, "Yeah, I heard. I'm sorry."

He lit another cigarette. "See, I knew you'd understand because you've seen what it's like. But you can't tell someone who's never been there. For Dad it's all bloody heroic stuff, just like they say in the paper. It's not the RAF's fault like he says. It's the bloody commanders. We were alongside Poles, Frenchies, Spaniards and Christ knows who else and no one talks anyone else's language. The way they packed our cargo - you should have seen it. There was all sorts of rubbish thrown in any old how. We even had fucking bicycles in the hold. What use are they going to be to anyone? There was six inches of snow."

Maurice smiled. "I know. We had the officers' deck-chairs and a whole load of musical instruments, but no weapons and no ammo, not to begin with anyhow. They said we didn't need them because we weren't there to fight. They were right about that anyhow. And the maps were crap. No one knew where we were half the time or where we were supposed to be going."

Don laughed scornfully. "Don't talk to me about fucking maps. You know what we found in the hold? There wasn't a map of Norway or anything like that. No, a map of frigging Belgium. But what I still don't get is this. We obey our captain, right? He gets orders from the Vice Admiral. He gets his orders from who? The war planners in London. They get their orders from the War Cabinet, so by the time all of that lot's come down the line the whole situation has changed. We bombed the shit out of that little village to prepare the attack on Narvik, and then once we have captured it things are so bad in France that we have to evacuate Norway altogether. What a mess." He stared thoughtfully at his brother. "But I've got some great mates and to be honest with you, I can't wait to get back to a ship. It's doing my head in being here, you'll see what I mean when you've been home a few days, with Ma crying and Dad telling me what the Navy and the RAF should be doing and them arguing all the time. The best bit of the day is doing the deliveries for them. Get a bit of peace and quiet. By the way, old Mrs Bawden was asking after you yesterday. I think she's got a bit of a soft spot for you."

Maurice thought back to the conversation he'd had with her what seemed a hundred years ago and how, because of her, he had finally decided to enlist. He nodded. "I'll do her next delivery." He pushed the writing paper across the table and thought, she'll know what to say to Joe's parents. She lost her husband after the last war. She'll know what they'd want to hear.

The following morning he knocked on Cassie Bawden's door. When there was no reply, he walked round to the back garden and found her working on her vegetable plot.

"Maurice," she said when she saw him, "I'm pleased to see you but I've had my delivery. Didn't they tell you? Your brother brought it round a couple of days ago."

Maurice nodded, "Actually, I've come to ask you a favour, Mrs Bawden."

She laughed. "My word, the army has made you formal. You've never called me 'Mrs Bawden' before. It must be a big favour."

Maurice blushed. "I know and I should have done. We all called you Cassie and we shouldn't have. Sorry."

She shrugged. "You can get used to everything. I know what the kids in the village said about me. You thought I was a witch. Who calls a witch 'Mrs'? So what's this favour. I can't think of anything I could do for you." She stopped and looked at him out of the corner of her eye and smiled, baring her four blackened teeth. "But if I'm going to do you a favour, you can do one for me. There's a load of bamboo canes over there. I want to make a frame for my beans. You can tie them up for me. I just can't reach. And while you're doing that you can tell me what you want."

While she passed him the pieces of string and supervised the tying of the knots in the way that she wanted, Maurice explained how he wanted to write to his mate's parents and how he just didn't know what to say to them.

"No, the sticks have got to be in a straight line and they're too close together," said Cassie, "What was his name?"

"Joe," said Maurice.

"That's better, now make sure they're really firm." She passed him a piece of string. "Same as my husband. So you want to know what I'd like to have heard from his best mate."

Maurice nodded and began to tie a knot while she watched intently. "Good. They'll get a letter from the army, very formal, maybe one from the captain saying what a grand chap he was, how he'll be sorely missed. I wanted to know two things. That he didn't suffer when he died. I told you, my Jo suffered terribly. Did yours?"

"No," said Maurice, "He was there beside me one minute and gone the next. I think the mortar that killed him knocked me out, I don't really know, but they told me it was quick."

"They're too close together," said Cassie, nudging a cane with her foot, "twelve inches, do it properly. The other thing I wanted to know is about the good times they had together, you know, what's going to make them remember him enjoying life. There must have been lots."

Maurice stopped and thought. There was the laughing about the pastis. But they probably wouldn't understand that. There were the jokes about French beer. Before that there was the collecting of the baths and putting them round on the golf course to the anger of the golfers. And there was his terror at Joe's driving. He wiped his sleeve across his face.

"Thanks, Cassie," he said. "I know what to say."

"Go and do it while you remember, but come and help me finish this off as soon as you can."

At home he found his mother in tears and clutching a letter. It was marked 'Official' and addressed to him.

"It can't be important, Ma, I've only been home a couple of days. I've still got twelve days of my leave left."

He ripped it open. "See', he said, reading it aloud, "On completion of your period of leave on 19th June 1940, you are to report to Internment Camp 58, The Hayes, Swanwick, Derby at 1200 hours where you will be assigned guard duties."

He looked at the letter. "I don't get it," he said, "I don't even know what an internment camp is."

"You jammy bugger," was his brother's reaction when he heard.

"But won't it be dangerous?" asked their mother, "Guarding Germans and people we're at war with?"

Don scoffed. "Honestly, Ma, what's dangerous about opening gates and closing them again? Most of the people in those camps aren't even soldiers.

They're people who've come over to get away from Hitler. The worst thing about it'll be that it's dead boring."

Their father agreed. "Fifth columnists who are too stupid to avoid getting caught. Don't you read the paper, Mother? Even the Prime Minister says most of those men support us. They're locked up just in case."

Mrs Hickey wasn't to be convinced. "People aren't locked up for no reason. Not unless they've done something wrong. These must be bad people. Maurice, I don't want you to go."

Mr Hickey clicked his tongue in irritation. "There's a bloody war on woman. Just be glad he's not being sent to the front again. He'll be in no more danger than you or me - less in fact. At least he'll have bloody gun when the Germans arrive."

Chapter Sixty

By the middle of June, Swanwick internment camp was full. Rows of tents covered what had been lawns. Extra guards were drafted in, though if anything the atmosphere had become more relaxed as the daily routines had become more familiar. The committed Nazis were by now completely outnumbered by men who had been interned simply by virtue of their being German or Austrian. Although there was a ban on radios and newspapers, it was common knowledge that Paris had fallen and it was only a matter of time before France surrendered. Wirth and his supporters waited eagerly for the attack on Britain that would bring about their freedom. They strolled around the camp with the assurance of those who know that it is only a matter of time before Hitler would be marching through London.

Dr Dobel had offered his services to the medical team and had been gratefully accepted. As the Nazis had grown in confidence, the Jews in the camp had become more and more despondent. He had been the first on the scene when an elderly man had locked himself in the lavatory and tried to hang himself with his belt. The cistern pipe hadn't been able to take his weight and broken, flooding the place.

When he told Reinhardt about the incident, and how the only damage he'd done was to sprain his ankle as he tumbled off the lavatory seat, Reinhardt shrugged and said, "You can't blame him for trying. A lot worse'll happen when the Germans do arrive. To you and me too probably. There's another bloke who goes around by himself who looks as if he could cheerfully end it all. Funny thing is, I know him from somewhere but damned if I can think where. I'll point him out to you next time I see him."

Weiss and Busch had got over their earlier arguments, but now Busch was again becoming increasingly withdrawn. Like everyone he believed that Germany would begin an attack on England and like nearly all the internees in the camp, he also believed that Germany was invincible. The exception was Dr Dobel. They met one evening in the dining room.

"What are you going to do when we win the war, Herr Doktor?" he asked.

Dobel put down his knife and fork and peered short-sightedly at Busch to try and gauge the meaning of the question.

"I mean, will you stay here or will you go home to Germany?"

Dobel shook his head. "Well, assuming that there is an invasion, I rather think I'll be needed here, don't you think? Wars create casualties and it's my job to help casualties."

Busch frowned. "But you're German. Why would you help enemy casualties? That's the British doctors' job."

Dobel was wondering how he could explain when Reinhardt sat down next to him. "This is the chap I was telling you about, he said. "Name's Niedermayer. He remembers that we met at the panel when they were interviewing what they called 'aliens'. I'd forgotten. In fact all I remember was the rather attractive lady who never said a word."

Busch glared at him and leant forward. "You haven't answered my question, Herr Doktor."

Dobel sighed. "Germany hasn't won the war yet. But to answer you, first I'm a doctor, then I'm a German. My family are here, my children practically English. In fact my wife is English. My home is here."

Busch was incredulous. "You weren't born a doctor. You were born German. Your first duty is to your country and we are at war. You really mean that you are willing to treat English soldiers so they can go and massacre your fellow countrymen?"

The men along the table had stopped talking and were listening as Busch shoved his chair back and stood up. "And Jews?" he shouted, pointing at Niedermayer.

Dobel also stood up and was about to remonstrate but Busch was pushing his way through the line of men queuing for their food. Reinhardt turned to Niedermayer and held out his hand. "Sorry about that," he said, "Please come and join us."

Niedermayer moved round to the chair vacated by Busch and stared at the table. Reinhardt wondered what to say to the gaunt figure sitting opposite him who was looking round with a haunted expression as if expecting to be attacked at any moment. He was wearing a dirty jacket that was at least two sizes too large for him and that had a tear in the seam of the shoulder. His collarless shirt had a grey stain down the front and the round glasses that he wore with their heavy metal frames and his sharply pointed nose gave him the appearance of a befuddled owl. He picked at his food with a look of disdain before putting down his knife and fork.

"You're not hungry?" asked Reinhardt.

"Niedermayer opened his palms in a gesture of hopelessness. "It's pork," he said.

He pushed the plate away and looked from Dobel to Reinhardt. "Can I ask you, have you sent out any letters?"

Dobel nodded, "I write to my wife twice a week to tell her I'm all right. Why do you ask?"

"And does she write to you? I mean, do you get a reply?" Niedermayer was leaning forward eagerly. "Do you write in English or German?"

Dobel smiled, "She doesn't really speak German so there wouldn't be much point. No, I always write in English."

"I don't speak English," Niedermayer said, "and nor does my wife. I told someone who said I probably haven't had an answer to my letters because I've been writing in German. So I tried to write in English to let her know where I am, but I've never had a reply."

Dobel nodded sympathetically. "I've never had a reply either. I don't know anyone who has received a letter from home. Do you?" he asked, turning to Reinhardt.

Reinhardt shook his head. "But that's not to say there haven't been letters arriving. During the last war we often got them but they always took ages to arrive. I remember my wife at the time sent me some oil paints and a few canvasses. I think it made her feel better about divorcing me, which I only discovered when I got out. I got quite good actually and used one of the canvasses to paint a portrait of my new lady friend." He smiled at the memory. "And that made me feel better." He turned to Niedermayer, "Where is your wife?"

Niedermayer looked as if he was close to tears. "I don't know. She was coming to England from Switzerland. She should be there by now. I've been writing to her at the Austrian Centre in London where I was working. I've also written to Lotte Staengl who worked there as well asking her to look after my wife when she arrives, but I haven't heard from her either. She's German so I suppose she might have been interned as well. So I wrote again saying the letter should be opened by anyone at the Centre. I don't know what else I can do. I mean, my wife and my daughter will know to go to the Centre but they won't have anywhere to live unless someone helps them."

Dobel said, "Look, we haven't been here very long and I'm sure Reinhardt is right. These things do take time. I'll help you to write a letter in English, if you like and one of the guards will know if anyone is receiving letters. And I'll write to my wife and ask her to find out what she can. She has a sister in London who will be pleased to help."

Niedermayer thanked him profusely, but after a second he looked panic stricken. "But suppose they are interning German women. What would happen to my daughter? She's only eight."

Reinhardt shook his head. "I understand your fear, but the truth is we just don't know and I think we've got enough to worry about with what we do know. Otherwise we'll go mad.

If I were you I'd go and get your letter written with Dobel. Doing things takes the mind off problems. At the moment my problem is that I've eaten my bread so I can't offer to exchange it for your pork and potatoes."

Niedermayer smiled thinly and pushed his plate across the table.

"If we can eat together tonight I'll have your milk.

Reinhardt, his mouth full, nodded his agreement.

Chapter Sixty One

Franco was collecting an order from the kitchen in Eugenio's restaurant when they heard the crash. Amid the shards of glass lay a large stone. The only two customers, a young woman and her mother were sitting by the wall and were visibly shaken. While Franco went to make sure they hadn't been hurt, Eugenio rushed out into the street where a bystander pointed up the road. "They went that way, mate, three of them. Sorry, it happened so fast I couldn't stop them. But it's a shame, it really is."

Eugenio looked up the empty street. "They could have gone anywhere," he said. "Did you see what they looked like?"

The man shrugged. "Young. Two were wearing caps so I couldn't see their faces. It happened so quick," he repeated. "You all right?"

"Si, grazie." He went back inside to find the two women putting on their coats while Franco was apologising profusely. They said nothing and left, picking their way gingerly over the glass.

Eugenio locked the door and started to help his brother move the tables and shake out the tablecloths. He fetched a broom and dustpan and brush while Franco tried to find something with which to cover the broken pane. They worked in silence until there was a loud knocking on the door.

"We're shut," shouted Eugenio loudly. "Come back tomorrow."

"Police," shouted a voice through the letter box, "Open up now, sir."

Franco hurried to unlock the door. "We didn't see them," he said, "It was so quick. Look at the mess." He waved towards his brother. "I haven't been to see if there was any damage to my place. Can you catch them?"

The two detectives looked at him in bewilderment. The older one asked, "Are you Mr Baldini?"

"Yes, I'm Franco and this is my brother Eugenio. This is his place."

The detective took out a piece of paper from his breast pocket and then turned it over.

He shook his head, "You're not on my list, sir. But you may as well come

374

along as well. It'll save us a trip."

Eugenio put down his broom and said, "I don't understand. Come along where? Didn't someone tell you that they threw a stone through my window."

It was the detective's turn to look confused. "We haven't received any reports like that. No, sir, I'm afraid you are under arrest. You have to come with us. Both of you."

"But why? What have we done?" Eugenio was panic-stricken. "We haven't done anything. They are the criminals, the people who did that." He waved his hand towards the broken window. "Aren't you going to try and catch them?"

The detective glanced at the window. "Don't worry, we'll make sure that it gets boarded up." Then he added as an afterthought, "You were lucky not to have been hurt. If whoever did this comes back, the next time you may not be so lucky. It'll be best if you come with us for you own protection. We'll take you home so that you can pack a few things. I'm sure you won't be away for more than a few days."

While Franco was in the bedroom deciding what to take with him, Giovanna was tearfully remonstrating with the policeman. He paused at the open suitcase on the bed as he listened to her struggling to explain in English that her husband was a good man, that he do nothing wrong, but the effort was too great and she burst into a volley of rapid Italian, yelling that she couldn't manage without him and that she and her daughter would surely starve without the money that he brought home from the ice cream business.

When he had packed he went back into the kitchen and put his arm around her. "Non ti preoccupare," he whispered, "They say it'll only be a few days." He was about to tell her about the attack on the restaurant, but thought better of it.

Eugenio, however had told Julia. They were standing on the landing outside the two flats with the older of the two detectives who was struggling to understand Julia's English. He was making placatory gestures and saying, "We'll see to everything. We'll let you know where he is. Please don't worry, it won't be for long." Then they hustled the two brothers down the stairs to the police car."

They drove in silence through the blacked out streets, Eugenio trying to work out where they might be taking them. Franco was gazing down at his lap, wondering why he was clutching the book, and how it had got into his hands.

"What is it?" asked Eugenio.

Franco passed it to him. "It's that book that Francesca was reading, isn't it?" He shrugged and handed it back to Franco who carefully placed it in his suitcase.

They eventually parked outside a police station and were ushered into a room where they joined a queue of Italian men who were lining up in front of an army sergeant seated at a desk. Two guards stood at the door, with their rifles and with bayonets fitted. When Franco reached the desk, the sergeant looked up at him and asked to see his passport, identity papers and asked him to open the suitcase. He took out the book and flicked through the pages.

"Is this yours?" he asked.

Franco shook his head. "It's my daughter's."

The sergeant examined the first page. "So why have you got it? What language is it anyway, Italian?"

Franco was at a loss for words. "I must have picked it up by mistake. My daughter was studying it. Her boyfriend is in the Home guard and he was teaching her about it."

The sergeant looked up at him incredulously. "So he's Italian. What's his name?"

"No, no," Franco found himself reddening. "He's English. They're getting married in September. It's an English book."

The sergeant read a couple of lines aloud and then closed it. "You must think I'm stupid," he said, "We'll be keeping this. Go through there," he waved at a door behind him. "Next."

They were given a cup of tea and taken down to the cells where mattresses filled with straw were laid out on the floor.

A policeman told them to make themselves as comfortable as they could- they would be moving on in the morning, this was only for one night.

"Where will we be going?" Eugenio asked.

The policeman ignored the question and locked the door and turned out the lights from outside. Fully dressed, the men fumbled for a place to sleep. Lying in the darkness, Franco sensed that everyone was awake, but no one felt like talking. Using his suitcase as a pillow he closed his eyes and lay worrying about Giovanna and Francesca. The noises of the night kept him awake until dawn when guards appeared and led the men in groups of four to the lavatory. When they returned to the cell they were brought sweet tea in tin mugs and a piece of bread and margarine.

"Don't get too comfortable," said a guard cheerfully, "You'll not be staying here for long."

"Where are we going?" asked the old man sitting against the wall next to Franco."

"Don't ask me mate, we don't get told anything, but there's another lot outside waiting for this cell. You'll find out soon enough."

An hour later a coach carrying forty Italian internees was travelling south. Although they hadn't been told not to talk aloud, there was an unspoken understanding that it would be wiser to remain as quiet as possible. Franco kept glancing at the guard who was standing next to the driver; the sight of his rifle and bayonet was enough to keep everyone on edge.

Eugenio was staring out of the window and kept shaking his head. "We're leaving London," he whispered, "where can we be going?"

The man across from the aisle leant across. "We're going south," he said. "They couldn't be sending us back to Italy, could they?"

He was overheard by the man in front who started to become very agitated. He leaped to his feet and shouted, "You can't send us to Italy. Don't you understand, most of us hate Mussolini."

Another man at the back shouted, "My son is in the English army. He was at Dunkirk. Why are you sending us back to Italy?"

The guard at the front, who appeared at least twenty years younger than anyone else on the coach, looked terrified. "Sit down," he shouted. He leaned towards the driver and had a hurriedly whispered conversation, his rifle pointing straight down the aisle of the coach.

The driver pulled over to the side of the road and stood up and faced the passengers.

He shouted very slowly, as if addressing a group that he wasn't sure would understand.

"We have orders not to tell you where our destination is, but I can tell you that we are not on our way to Southampton which would be the obvious place to be going if you were being sent to Italy. Now sit down."

The hubbub of voices and questions increased and the driver looked despairingly at the guard who raised his rifle menacingly. The old man in the front seat that Franco had earlier noticed had had a problem hauling himself up the steps into the coach stood up painfully and turned to the passengers. He raised his hand and said quietly, "Silenzio, per favore. We have no choice but to accept what this man says. Those of you who know me will know that I have more to lose than most by being sent back to Italy. I would certainly be imprisoned or shot. The authorities here understand that, so why would they want to send us back? Let these men get on with their jobs- we'll find out soon enough where we're being taken."

He was right. An hour later the coach pulled into a car park. All around barbed wire had been laid out, though there had clearly been no time to construct fences. Franco and Eugenio climbed down and looked around in bewilderment. Towering over them was an enormous grandstand. To their right, beyond the first row of barbed wire, white wooden railings, twenty yards apart curved away into the distance. In front of the grandstand Franco caught a glimpse of a neat line of horse boxes.

The guards told them to form an orderly queue and then walked the men around to a large tent where they lined up waiting to be examined.

It was years since either of the brothers had been out of London. Franco looked around him and whispered, "It's all so green. And the sky is so big, but where are we going to sleep?"

The whole area was teeming with men, some queuing at an outdoor canteen, some sitting up in the stands, while others were lying asleep in the open horse boxes, stretched out on sacks of straw. Eugenio stopped a couple of men who were walking purposefully towards the grandstand. "What is this place?" he asked.

"This is Lingfield race course," they replied. "You've just arrived?"

Eugenio nodded. "Well, then," the shorter of the two men pointed to the grandstand, "If I were you I'd try and make your bed under there. There's plenty of room. But they say we're not staying here for long. This is just a 'clearing station'" He used the English words. "But no one will tell us where we're going next." He turned away and said, laughing over his shoulder, "The place isn't as bad as the food, but you'll find that out for yourselves."

Two days later a train was taking them north.

Chapter Sixty Two

Esther Hart's Diary

Monday 17th June 1940

Terrible row with Douglas last night. Listening to the radio and we heard JB Priestly suggest that as many children as possible should be evacuated to the colonies until the war is over. Said I thought this was a wonderful idea. It would mean the children would be safe in Canada or South Africa and I could go with them. For a moment it seemed the answer to my prayers. We could start a new life far away from the war. Douglas said scornfully that the children are perfectly safe where they are, that it was 'my duty' to be there for him and his father. When I didn't reply he got quite angry and said he really didn't know how I could be so selfish. There were still 130,000 young men still in France who were desperately trying to get back to England and all I could think about was how to save my own skin. I replied that the children might be physically safe at the moment, but that his sister obviously didn't have the faintest idea about how to look after children properly and that they needed their mother, that if Gordon was stealing money it was because he was deeply unhappy and the same with Lydia wetting the bed. I realised too late that I had said too much. He demanded to know how I knew these things and I had to confess that I had seen the letter that his sister had sent to him at the office. He went purple with rage, talked about 'betrayal' and that I had no right to read his private correspondence. He was far more angry about that than he was about the children being miserable, which, in turn, infuriated me. He finished up by yelling that they needed 'a firm hand', that I had always been much too soft with them, that their being away was no different from his having been at boarding school, and a lot less strict and then the old saw that I had heard so many times about it never having done him any harm. I said as calmly as I could that that was a matter of opinion and went to bed. When he came to bed some time later he tried to be affectionate and said he was sorry to have lost his temper, but I couldn't bear his touching me and replied coldly that he had better give his sister his new office address so that I wouldn't be able to find out what they were saying about me and the children. He snorted and turned away, which was what I wanted.

Tuesday 18th June

Resolved to get in touch with the Home Office and see whether I can't act as a children's escort to go to Canada. Went through the papers for the last couple of days to see if I could find any details of how to apply. There have been more evacuations from France as the Germans now occupy the northern coast and the French government has fallen. Marshal Pétain is the new president and he has immediately asked Germany for armistice terms. Everybody is very worried about what will happen to the French fleet. If it falls into the hands of the Germans we are in even greater trouble. And that useless old codger, Chamberlain, says that the safety of children cannot be guaranteed.

Mr Churchill announced that the Battle of France is over and that the Battle of Britain is about to begin. He says that if Hitler wins the war we will sink into a new dark age. We must 'brace ourselves to our duties' so that in a thousand years men will say "'This was their finest hour." He sounded tired and not at all as optimistic as the last time he was on the wireless.

In the queue at the grocer's I talked to a Belgian woman who was there with her two children who were about the same age as Gordon and Lydia. She asked if I knew how they could get out of London and where they could go to, at which point the woman in front of us said she didn't need to worry, Hitler wouldn't want to destroy London as he would want to preserve it at least until he could march his troops in and have his photograph taken outside Parliament. In her view he was going to invade along the south coast and now he had Norway, probably along the east coast as well. She sounded remarkably sanguine about the whole situation and then said finally, "Well, when he comes he'll get rid of the useless old men we've got now and we can start living again instead of spending our lives queuing for a lot over over-priced muck they try to pass off as food."

I asked her if she'd listened to Mr Churchill's speech and she said she hasn't got a wireless and wouldn't listen to it if she had. "When they locked up Mosley they locked up the wrong man." When we got to the counter I used my ration book to buy some chocolate which I gave to the two children and then was accosted outside the shop by the woman without a wireless who said that I was one of the bloody do-gooders who were responsible for the country being in the state it is. I can't begin to understand her reasoning.

Got home feeling upset and decided to do some work in the garden. Couldn't find the spade, and asked Charles if he's seen it. It was under his bed where he's hidden it so that he could 'bash a Jerry'.

Wednesday 19th June

Went to the Education Office to find out about being evacuated with the children. Canada seems the most likely destination; we have to apply in writing, but the government seems very reluctant to move on this, and is urging parents to stay put in London. As if reading my thoughts, Douglas brought up the topic over supper. Said I had to make sure I had my gas mask with me whenever I went out and then that parents who sent their children abroad were being hysterical. There was far more danger of ships being sunk by U-boats on their way to America or Canada than there was from any German attack on this country.

I protested that surely the Germans wouldn't attack a ship that was clearly unarmed and that was flying the Red Cross flag and he replied that that just proved that I didn't know the first thing about German brutality. In any case, yesterday's announcement in Parliament of the evacuation scheme only applied to families who had relatives abroad who would accept them. And parents would have to make a contribution to the cost, and he for one would not pay a single penny towards seeing his children shipped abroad and to be exposed to the dangers of a U-boat attack. He ended by saying that if the Queen of England said she wasn't going anywhere without her children and was refusing to countenance the idea of leaving the country without the King, and the King would certainly never leave, perhaps I could learn from them. It was one of his best Parliamentary Speeches, to which Charles said 'Hear, hear!"

I replied that if that were the case, I really failed to understand why our children had to be evacuated at all and why they couldn't have come back at least for Christmas. He said angrily that I wanted it all ways - that they should be either here in London or four thousand miles away in Canada and that there was no point in arguing with someone so irrational. The best and safest place for them was with his sister. He also thought that my real motive for wanting to get the children to Canada was to get away from him. It was more by way of a plaintive question and I didn't bother to deny it, though some part of me suddenly had a little flash of remembrance at what our marriage had once been like and I recognised his vulnerability that had once attracted me. I apologised to Charles for having had to witness such a scene and went and got on with the washing up.

Thursday 20th June

Met Barbara for an ersatz coffee at Lyons and told her that I really felt it was best for the children and for me if we could find a way to get to Canada but that Douglas was absolutely refusing to countenance it and as he won't pay towards our passage and I don't have any money, I didn't see how it could be possible. She thought for a long while and then said that she had got money and would gladly lend it to me, because she would hate to think that the only reason I couldn't go was financial. On the other hand, did I really think it was the best thing? Even if I was accepted as one of the mothers to accompany evacuees, would it really be the right thing to do? I said I really thought it would. I imagined sailing off with the children and waving good-bye to the war, to the terrible emptiness I've felt ever since they went to Rutland and waving good-bye to the ghastly tension that has surrounded my relationship with Douglas for ages and which is getting worse. We would be able to start a new life.

Barbara said those were all the positive things, but what were the negatives? I haven't really got a skill beyond being a housewife and mother, so although I would have to go out to work I'm not sure what I could offer to a potential employer. We'd have to find somewhere to live and for the children to go to school which might not be easy, though presumably there is help if lots of children are being evacuated. Douglas says it would be a very dangerous trip across the

Atlantic because of U-boats and he may be right, and that's the worst thing. Supposing I was responsible for their deaths when all I was trying to do was get them to safety? Hearing it coming from me, rather than Douglas made the prospect too awful to contemplate. I said that I realised it wasn't a risk I felt I could take.

Walking home I felt strangely relieved and happy although nothing outwardly has changed at all.

Friday 21st June

Something that Barbara said yesterday struck a chord. If we felt we were really able to contribute to the war effort, we would feel very differently. I applied for First Aid training weeks ago and haven't heard a thing and she said that a lot of her friends are saying that they wish that they could do something constructive to help but the government just doesn't seem interested in involving women. I'm sure that we could do a lot of the jobs that young men are doing which would enable them to join up. A large part of the problem is feeling so useless. I'm writing this having just come back from the vet. Charles was worried that the Incontinent Cat has lost a lot of weight recently so I suggested we go and have him looked at together. We're going back at five once they've had a chance to examine him. Charles gone for a nap. It's ridiculous I know but I feel buoyed by having done something for somebody which is not expected of me. Charles was pathetically grateful and told me I'm not such a bad stick, before tottering off to bed.

Later. The cat had to be put down as it had cancer. Now I feel terrible about having been so mean about it. Charles very stoical and just nodded curtly when I said I was sorry and that he must be very upset. He didn't say anything for a long time and then suddenly burst out with, "It was just a bloody cat, Esther. There are young men dying not a hundred miles away. No point in being sentimental." Then he went to his room.

Monday 24th June

Douglas brought back five rolls of tape that he told me to put up on the windows. It's to prevent flying glass in the event of a bomb blast. I quite enjoyed doing it actually - it's made the windows look quite mock Tudor. Charles said he didn't want his bedroom windows done, it made his room look gloomy and he'd rather take the risk. Did it anyway, saying that I would rather he complained than I had to pick shards of glass out of his face.

The French have surrendered to Germany and were forced to sign the armistice in the same carriage that was used when the Germans surrendered in 1918. Apparently it was got out of the museum expressly for the purpose. Hitler doesn't simply mean to win the war. He obviously needs to humiliate his enemies completely. I suppose it's excellent propaganda at home and now everyone here feels that the invasion will happen at any moment.

Reread the leaflet that arrived last week 'If the Invader comes' with the exhortation to STAY PUT because in Belgium and Holland people fled their homes, clogged up the roads and made it too difficult for the army to get at the enemy. But from what we hear and read about German atrocities it is asking a bit much to wait and find out how they are going to behave towards us. And I'm not sure the ARP's are going to be a lot of help. Contrary to what it says in the leaflet, I absolutely do not like ours - no one does. He's an officious little know-all. Mrs Roberts says she knows his wife who hen-pecks him terribly which is why he's the way he is. Mercifully he hasn't been issued with a gun. Apparently a policeman was shot yesterday by an ARP when he didn't hear the command to stop.

Over 150,000 children have been evacuated from London to the country and up to Scotland. Somehow that makes me feel better about Lydia and Gordon.

Tuesday 25th June

We were woken up by an air raid warning in the early hours. Douglas got Charles up who refused to come out into the garden without putting on his tie, which did look a little strange over his pyjamas. It was almost dawn when the all clear sounded, by which time we were cold and thirsty. I had offered to go and make a thermos of tea after an hour of sitting in the cold, but Douglas said not to be such a damned fool woman, as if my stepping one foot out into the garden would trigger the destruction of the whole of London.

Then at about five people were cheerily calling to each other from their gardens saying that it wasn't too bad, to remember to take a decent book and playing cards next time, and then back to bed only to be kept awake by the dawn chorus.

France has signed an armistice with Italy which has led to more mumblings about the Italians over here and sympathy for the French people, though not for their politicians who everyone agrees have let their people down shockingly. I don't get the feeling that ours are much cared for either and people are angrier with the government than they are with Hitler. As the man in the newsagent said, whatever was the point of guaranteeing support for Poland without support from Russia?

Anyway, everyone is very tired from having such a broken night, is very tetchy and fears that this is only the beginning.

Thursday 27th June

Another air raid warning last night. Charles slept in very late and when he got up complained of having a head ache. We were out of Dispirin so I went to Boots to get some. Met Mrs Hughes who said her son is an ARP working in St John's Wood. According to him the internment of so many Italians as well as Germans is proof of the 'fifth column menace.' I was quite surprised to hear her say that she was sure that he was absolutely right. If you know how to look, there are hidden signs everywhere of 'fifth column activity'.

When I asked her if she could give me an example she led me outside and pointed to a painter who was working on a first floor window frame, painting it green. She said that was exactly the same green as on the Italian flag, and three doors down there was another with the same colour front door. She said she'd said hello to the painter, just so she could hear his accent. He didn't reply and that, to her mind, proved that he was Italian and showing the invader where the enemy supporters live. The moment she got home she would tell her son about it, but she doubted he would be able to do anything. To change the subject, I asked after Mr Hughes and rather wish I hadn't. She was in Boots because his piles had flared up again. She put it down to not being able to get a proper diet. But it was he who first noticed the suspicious signs everywhere, and now spends his days decoding German messages in the daily papers in the light of Lord Haw Haw's broadcasts. The invasion from Germany is coming at 4am on July 2nd. She said if I didn't believe it I should get yesterday's 'Times' and then she gave me a list of columns and numbers to follow that were far too complicated for me to remember. The old man in front of her said he was going to the racing on Saturday and wondered if her husband could find out whether Lord Haw Haw had left a tip as to who the winner of the 3.30 would be. That led to quite an argument that most of the people in the shop got involved in, but I was surprised at the anger against Italian and Germans. There was lot of agreement that the government isn't doing enough to mobilise the general population to help with the war effort, especially women, and there are far too many young men who are wandering the streets who could be employed doing useful work. Also heard that a lot of refugees are to be sent abroad, but that may just be a rumour. All the government propaganda about keeping mum and not gossiping seems to have set off a positive storm of speculation. As I was leaving a woman was saying how this she was sure that this new government survey that interviews people to try and gauge morale in the country is really just spying and she wouldn't be a bit surprised to find out that it was a plot by Nazi supporters to snoop on unsuspecting people.

Another beautiful day. Finished reading 'Cold Comfort Farm' in the garden.

Friday 28th June

Received a very polite letter from Major Cazalet which both made me feel very supported but also filled me with some dread. He says that he is sorry not to have replied earlier - there has been a great deal of concern over the internees amongst the general public. As Chairman of the Parliamentary Committee on Refugees he has been trying to discover the whereabouts of a number of men who, in his view, have been quite wrongfully interned and who have clearly demonstrated themselves to be loyal to the United Kingdom. Unfortunately it is clear with the huge numbers arrested in a very short space of time that the authorities have lost track of a large number of individuals. He would seek to find out the whereabouts of Herr Niedermayer. Underneath his signature there was a hand-written sentence "It may well be that your husband can be of more help to you in this instance than I" and signed VC.

I phoned Barbara who came round. Having read the letter she said that Herbert believed that Douglas was working for the Swinton Committee in some capacity. This committee had been given responsibility for all refugees, POW's and aliens. It was terribly secret but it was believed in the Home Office that it wasn't answerable even to the Cabinet. Lord Swinton was known to be in favour of sending as many as possible abroad so as not to risk harbouring enemies in the camps here. In her view, so many had been wrongfully interned that the important thing now was to try and ensure that the conditions in the camps were as comfortable as possible. Then she asked me if I was going to show Douglas the letter.

I was so nervous. I knew he would be absolutely furious with me and would probably accuse me of telling Major Cazalet that he was somehow involved in this committee. Barbara said she'd come back later if I wanted to show it to him and she really felt I should. Felt sick with worry most of the afternoon, dreading the moment when he walked through the front door.

Barbara came round at six with a bottle of wine and we shared a glass with Charles. In fact we'd finished it and the butterflies in my tummy were just beginning to settle when Douglas phoned to say that he was delayed and not to wait up for him.

Came to bed to write this, feeling immensely relieved, but knowing that it's only putting off the evil hour, and there's the whole weekend to get through yet.

Chapter Sixty Three

Walking to Swanwick Camp from the station on a warm June morning, Maurice felt the gnawing trepidation that he'd been feeling for the last few days grow into a sickening sensation in the base of his stomach. He'd been sleeping badly, having flashbacks of the Germans pushing their dinghies across the canal before he and Joe had turned to run up the hill and Joe had been killed by the mortar. The thing was, he had never seen a German face - the soldiers wore their steel helmets and the last he had seen of them was their lying flat on their stomachs as they pushed away from the bank. But in his recurring dream they looked up and their faces were a mixture of blood and skull and eyes staring at him that froze him to the spot as they clambered out of their dinghies and up the bank towards him. He screamed and turned towards Joe who had suddenly vanished.

The nightmare woke him up in a hot sweat . He invariably put on the bedside light and fought against falling back to sleep. Sometimes he succeeded and dozed until dawn, when he got up feeling exhausted. At other times he drifted back to sleep and heard the drone of a Stuka as it swept along the beach at Dunkirk. He knew that the pilot was looking for him and no one else. He couldn't run in the soft sand and finally tripped and looked up as the pilot, a grinning skull swept over him and circled over the sea before returning in a blaze of machine gun fire.

He slowed down and looked around. There were men working in the fields nearby and a pair of buzzards hunting above a copse in he distance, their mewing cries carrying across a landscape that shimmered in the heat. He knew it was ridiculous but he couldn't help feeling that the camp would be full of Germans just like those in his dreams. And they had powers. How else to explain the way they had suddenly appeared with absolutely no warning and would have completely destroyed the British army had it not been for the fog that had kept their planes grounded for three days? Even if he hadn't seen a German face, he had heard the voices when he and Joe were hiding in the house in the village. The rasping tone followed by the sound of machine gun fire fitted completely with the picture he had in his mind's eye.

Trying to reassure himself with Don's words, "They can't be that bloody clever or they'd have never got themselves captured, Ma."

He quickened his step. He reported for duty to a young private who was smoking in the guards' hut at the gates. On either side of the gates were watch towers and a long drive led up to a large house. The private took his name and picked up a phone. "Private Hickey's here reporting, sir."

He nodded and put it back in its cradle. "I'll show you up mate, Larry can man the gate." Maurice saw a young soldier who looked about fifteen sitting on the grass verge. He waved to another guard who opened a second set of gates and then closed them behind Maurice and the private. Maurice looked round apprehensively. There were small groups of men talking as they walked along the path to the rows of tents on the lawns. Beyond that there was a rather disconsolate game of football going on.

"Where are the German prisoners?" asked Maurice.

The private waved his arm in the direction of the house. "Most are inside cos of the heat. Those silly buggers playing soccer are practising for the match against our lads next Saturday. There's a lot out working with the local farmer planting veg. I'm surprised you didn't see them on your way up the road. There's four in clink at the moment and there's probably about thirty in the sick bay. We're here. I'll show you the quarters and then you've got a briefing at two with the other new lads."

As far as Maurice was concerned this wasn't so much an internment camp as a country mansion. True, the place was surrounded with barbed wire but nobody seemed to notice it. And there were blokes working on the farm outside. He'd had a good look at several men and they hadn't looked like Germans at all. They just looked like regular blokes and when they spoke their language it just sounded somehow like English but without any meaning.

Things became a little clearer at the briefing. He was one of eight guards who were new to the camp. Captain Bryant, a short, smiling man of about forty, welcomed them. He explained that the majority of internees were men who had received 'C's' at their tribunals, in other words, they had been deemed as being 'generally supportive' of Britain's war aims, but it was now thought that there might be some 'bad apples' amongst them and so it would be 'better safe than sorry.' There were a fair number of refugees who had left Germany and Austria either because they were Jewish or for political reasons - 'opposed to Nazism, or Communists, that kind of thing.' Of course, there were out and out Nazis in the camp, 'thoroughly unsavoury characters' who needed watching , but as long as they didn't cause any trouble it was always best to 'let sleeping dogs lie.'

The new guards were given their instructions and timetables. Maurice would be doing his first shift at five. Looking out of the dormitory window after unpacking his kit, he laughed at the memory of his fears. It was all right here.

Reinhardt was preparing a lecture he had been cajoled into giving by the education committee. He had made some remark about British racing cars being superior to German ones at a talk given by Doktor Schneider who had been extolling the virtues of the new German Autobahns in a talk that he had given last week. Reinhardt had been interested, but said he didn't really see the point of having very fast motorways if the cars weren't as quick as the English ones. It was meant light-heartedly, but it caused offence and he agreed to speak about the development of British racing cars, but insisted that his lecture would have to be in English since he didn't know the technical German word for some of the vital engine parts that demonstrated British superiority. As he confided to Dr Dobel, this wasn't altogether true, but he was hoping that the Nazis would boycott his lecture once they found out it was to be in English.

Dobel had just laughed and said he didn't think it in the makeup of Nazis to boycott anything. If they disapproved of something they just smashed it up. "I'll come and bring some bandages,' he smiled. "Anyway, aren't they more likely to give you a hard time if you're speaking in English?"

Reinhardt had to agree that this was probably true. "The thing is, I don't actually know much about how German cars are made beyond the fact that they've got some of the fastest in the world. Mercedes and Auto Union. And that Hans

Stuck agreed a a bet with some Austrian Count about the relative speed of their cars as long as the prize was the Count's wife. Needless to say Stuck won, but I've never been able to work out whether this was a useful way of getting rid of a wife that one has no more use for or a way of getting revenge on an opponent who has just defeated you. I mean, a chap would certainly need a certain amount of audacity to arrive home and say, 'Darling, I'm back. And look who I've won.' Wasn't she a famous tennis player?"

Dobel picked up his book. "I think I should leave you to it. I'll have a look in the library to see if they've got anything, and I want to look in on Weiss."

In the main house Weiss and Niedermayer had been given permission to play a rather out of tune grand piano. There was a rota for the internees of an hour per day, but they had got round this by trying to remember Schubert's Fantasy for four hands. Niedermayer was all for trying to write it out, at least as much of it as they could remember. Weiss was more interested in improvising and didn't have the patience. But the joint project had completely changed Niedermayer's attitude. He still wrote to his wife every two days and would suddenly become withdrawn, but he also became completely absorbed in the music, though it hadn't started well.

The first time they had walked into the music room, Weiss had sat down to play and almost immediately Niedermayer had shouted, "Nein, entschuldigung, not that." Weiss had turned in alarm to find Niedermayer racked with sobs. "I'm sorry," he said, "My wife used to play it. Haydn was her favourite composer. She used to say that he wrote this in memory of his lover. The last time I heard it was just before I left and she said she wouldn't play it until we met again."

Weiss had apologised and Niedermeyer had sat down and played a Bach fugue. They had quickly formed the idea of playing duets and eventually of giving a concert.

Even Busch had got involved in the project. They had found a violin with the bridge missing, and a cello with a broken neck. Busch, having finished his ship, was looking for another project and was delighted to try and mend the instruments.

Although he was wary of being seen with Niedermayer, he did enjoy his playing and sat at the table in the music room while Weiss and Niedermayer played. Mending the bridge didn't pose too much of a problem.The the cello was more of a challenge. Dobel came and sat next to him.

"I heard that they might be moving us soon," he said.

Busch shrugged, "I'd like to hear this being played before they do. But I don't know anyone who plays, do you?"

"No, but there must be a cellist in this place. I'll ask around."

"Here," said Busch, "See if you can find a violinist as well. I think I've fixed it, but someone needs to tune it."

Dobel watched him working. "That's amazing," he said, "you could have been a surgeon."

Busch laughed and looked up. "No, it's just that I have to use these or I'd go mad." He looked at his hands and then turned them over. "If I can't fix or make things with them I want to hit somebody with them. Do you understand that?"

Dobel shook his head, "Not really."

"So," said Busch, "I don't care where they send us as long as I can find things to do with these."

Chapter Sixty Four

Franco and Eugenio had been relieved to be leaving the race course. Coaches full of Italians had kept arriving. Some men were immediately summoned to the office where they were interviewed at length. When they reappeared they were invariably surrounded by groups of men desperate to find out what they had been asked and, more importantly, what they had found out. The only topic of conversation was what was going to happen next. Some conjectured that the older men would be sent back to Italy in exchange for any Britons who were there when Mussolini had declared war. They wouldn't risk sending younger men who would be forced to join up. Franco listened sympathetically to Pietro Mancini who was sitting on his suitcase in the shade of the grandstand. Every morning he put on his three piece suit, cleaned his shoes as best he could, carefully adjusted his tie and took up his place leaning against a stanchion out of the sun, his suitcase beside him as if he were waiting for a train.

With an arthritic forefinger he jabbed towards his son who was talking to a group of young Italians a few yards away.

"Look at him," said Pietro in a whisper, as if worried his son could overhear him, "He would make a fine soldier just like his brother. He wanted to join the army as well but we persuaded him to stay because who was going to help me with the shop?" He shook his head. "Antonio was at Dunkirk. Did I tell you that? We had him home for just three days before we were arrested. If we get sent back to Italy and he has to join up he'll be fighting against his very own brother."

Franco tried to persuade him that that couldn't happen, but the old man was adamant. "We have to guard against the worst," he said.

Later that day they were marched to the station by guards who had their bayonets fixed. Franco saw him again falling against a carriage door, clutching his case to his chest with a panicked expression as he was manhandled by a Scots Guard who jabbed him in the back with a rifle butt.

"We're going north," said Eugenio and there was a palpable ripple of relief throughout the carriage. The Scots Guards had been relieved by a group of soldiers who were a lot more sympathetic to the internees. Still, when they were asked where they were being taken the answer was invariably the same. "Couldn't tell you mate, we know as much as you do."

As it grew darker the men in the carriage gradually began to fall into a fitful sleep. Eugenio whispered to Franco, "No matter what happens, we have to stay together. Agreed?"

Franco nodded. "Perhaps it will only be a couple more days, like the policeman said."

He was exhausted from having slept so badly at the camp, and his mind kept returning to Giovanna. Francesca was a sensible girl and would support her mother, and maybe Eric would go to the police and point out the whole thing had been a terrible mistake as they had at first believed. But seeing so many of his fellow countrymen made him think that, after all, every Italian in the country was suspected of supporting Mussolini.

Eventually the rocking rhythm of the train lulled him to a shallow sleep. He was woken a couple of times by the cold and then found it difficult to doze off again. His last picture of Giovanna kept haunting him, standing at the top of the stairs, she was clutching the bottom of her apron to her mouth, her eyes wide with fear and shock.

It was just growing light when the train eventually slowed to a halt with a grinding screech and a cloud of steam drifted past the carriage window. Voices telling them to get out quickly and form a line along the platform sounded along the corridor. The carriage door slid open and a soldier that Franco thought looked quite friendly said, "Out you get lads and jump to it. We've got a bit of a march."

Outside it was cold, though it was also a relief to be out of the fetid air of the carriage. The men were marched briskly away from the station and out of the town.

Pietro Mancini was a few yards ahead of Franco and was limping badly. His son had his arm around him and was encouraging him on. "He'll have to have a rest," he said to the guard who was accompanying them. "How much further is it?"

"Not far." The guard wasn't unsympathetic, "Sit down here and join the ones at the back."

After a couple of miles they arrived at what Franco took to be a factory surrounded by barbed wire. It had obviously been laid out in haste as it wasn't attached to any posts but lay curled along the ground.

The men were marched through two guarded gates and told to halt in a space between the two factory buildings. A group of men came over smiling and offered coffee in metal mugs. Behind them a young priest joined them.

He followed the gaze of the newcomers who were looking up at the derelict buildings with looks of astonishment and horror, nodded and smiled. "Welcome to Warth Mills," he said in Italian. "As you can see, it needs some improvements making, but we are working on that. We don't know how long we will be there, but please come and see me if you think I can be of any help to you. We have mass on Saturday, that's tomorrow morning here, in this area." He waved his arms as if indicating a place of special importance and then went back to the table where more coffee was being poured.

Franco and Eugenio drank the coffee gratefully. It was far better than either had expected. Franco's spirits began to lift. The day was getting warmer and the atmosphere in the place was much more welcoming than it had been at the race course. But the mills were derelict, with broken windows and bits of rusty machinery abandoned against a broken wall.

The line of men shuffled towards an entrance. A guard came out an called, "Baldini F. and Baldini E."

They entered an office where four soldiers were sitting behind a long desk.

"Confirm your names," said an officer, holding out his hand, "and give me your papers. Hand your belongings here," he signalled to his left, "and strip."

Franco took his identity papers out of his jacket pocket and passed over his suitcase. The soldier on the left undid the clasps and lay it open on the table. "Two shirts, wash bag, two pairs underpants, pair trousers," he held them up and shook them. Then he felt in the pocket. "Is this yours?" he asked, holding up Franco's watch.

Franco nodded. "It's very unusual. Where did you get it?"

"My wife gave it to me for my birthday. It was in her family for a long time. She had it repaired."

The soldier passed it to the captain who examined it carefully and then looked up. "We'll keep it safe for you," he said, "There are some pretty unsavoury characters in here," and he slipped it into his desk drawer. Then his tone of voice changed, "And I told you to get undressed. Eugenio was about to protest when Franco took him by the arm. "Best do as they ask," he whispered. Still, he felt acutely embarrassed as he took off his underpants and waited for the doctor to come round the desk and start examining his teeth, his eyes, his chest and his groin. The doctor nodded, made a mark on his clipboard and told him to get dressed again and then went to examine Eugenio, who, Franco, could sense, was on the point of exploding. But the four soldiers were apparently bored with the routine of having to explain the same thing to so many men. As Eugenio was dressing the officer intoned, "Your quarters are in the building opposite. The guards will issue you with sacking and straw with which to make your palliasse. Your bed. You are not permitted to use it during the day. If you have paper and pen you may write home in English a letter of no more than twelve lines. You may attend mass, but all other large congregations of internees are forbidden. Roll call is twice a day at six and again at nine in the evening. You may go."

Outside they joined a group of six other men and a guard who led them to a small room where they were issued with sacking and armfuls of straw. "Make it nice and tight lads," said the guard cheerfully, "the tighter the better. Then follow me."

He led them into the mill which smelt of oil and where the machinery occupied most of the space. The guard pointed to a line of mattresses against the wall. "Anywhere there, choose your spot."

Under the machinery there were balls of cotton waste and grease. It was clear that the men sleeping here had done their best to create a clean place for their palliasses. Further along the wall were several camp beds.

The guard caught Franco looking at them. "First come, first served, old son," he said. "They've been there for days and we didn't know we was going to get so many of you lot in here."

Franco looked around. Rusty pulleys hung from the ceiling. What light there was came through the broken windows high above them. The floor was caked in grease that made the whole of the vast room smell strongly and along the walls there were holes that looked suspiciously as if they were used by rats.

"You're one of the last lot," explained the guard, "so this wall's the one closest to the river, see? There's no space left on the other side. I'm not keen on a rat myself but they don't do no harm."

Eugenio and Franco looked at each other helplessly. "It's not as bad as it was last week," said the young guard defensively. " Father Rossi's organised quite a clean up. I mean, if you think this is bad you should have seen it back then. We've got lime for the lav's now," he said proudly. " They really was bad. They're round the back when you need them."

Franco did. Beneath a wooden board that was precariously attached to the wall of the mill there was a line of metal buckets. Franco joined a queue of four men who were trying to avoid looking at an elderly man who was squatting in front of them, his hat pulled over his head and his jacket held tightly across his waist to try and cover himself.

"Merdaio", whispered Franco, appalled. The man in front of him turned and looked at him.

"You just arrived?" he asked. Franco nodded.

"You're lucky, then. They were all cleaned out earlier. Where are you from?"

"London, Clerkenwell. I worked at the Savoy."

"I'm from Glasgow. But you'll meet a lot of people you probably know here. The food was so bad that in the end they agreed that the chefs who worked in the big restaurants could take over. At least it's edible now. You could probably get work in the kitchen if you wanted it."

"Not unless there's a job for a waiter. How many men are here, do you know?"

"Difficult to say. They keep coming and going. You arrived this morning, what, about a hundred of you? A couple of hundred left yesterday. I heard there's getting on for two thousand. Scusi."

He turned around to use the vacated bucket. Franco turned away and in the distance thought he saw Federico, his colleague from the Savoy. After he had relieved himself he walked over and called. Federico ran to greet him. "Eh, Franco, how long have you been in this dump?" he asked delightedly. He led Franco back to the area between the two buildings. "Listen, we'll catch up in a bit. But it's my turn on the box. Stay and listen." Along the wall a number of wooden boxes had been placed at intervals of about twenty yards. On each box a speaker was exhorting his listeners to pay attention to what he was saying about, in one instance, the betrayal of socialism by Mussolini, in another why Britain should make peace with Germany, in a third, why Italy had to declare war on France and England. Some men were laughing and jeering, some were listening intently and some were heckling, but it seemed to Franco that it was all very good-natured. Federico was shouting that the reason for the war was capitalism and corruption, which, he said, was the same thing, the exploitation of the poor by the rich, of poor countries by rich countries. Italy was a poor country. Her best workers had to go abroad to survive. The reason that they were now here, in this camp was that whenever times are hard, the rich have to punish the poor, as if it's poor people's fault that the country is in a bad way.

When he had finished he jumped off the box and grinned at Franco. "You should try it," he said, "it makes you feel good being able to let off steam."

Franco and Eugenio soon discovered that the worst times were the nights. They had no pillows for their palliasses. They had to keep their clothes on because of the cold and they were aware of feeling increasingly dirty as there was nowhere to wash. It was also almost impossible to sleep for any length of time as several men suffered from nightmares and would wake up screaming. And the rats were fearless, scurrying around the mattresses and amongst the machinery. On the first night Franco had had his arm stretched out on the floor in front of him and was suddenly shaken by feeling his hand being nibbled. He gave a shriek which woke Eugenio.

"Shsh," he'd whispered, "Keep your hands inside your pullover, then they can't get you.

The roll call was taken each morning in the larger of the two mills. A week after they arrived del Giudice, who had been elected the camp leader, read out a list of names in alphabetical order. Franco was on the list, but not Eugenio.

"We've got to stay together," he protested.

"You heard the list," said the guard, "I can't change it." But Federico took the brothers on one side after the men had been dismissed. "My name was called out," he said, "but this place is so chaotic they'll never know if we change places. They're not interested in people, only numbers. Say that you are me. They won't know."

That evening, when Franco's name was called out, Federico answered. "You're doing me a big favour," he whispered. I can't wait to get out of this stinking hole." Once the last name had been called, an officer stepped forward.

"Those of you who have heard your name read out, you may return to your quarters. The rest of you, who have not been called, have yourselves ready to leave the camp at dawn. Dismissed."

"We won't hold you to that," Franco said to Federico as they walked towards their building, but Federico shook his head. "It'll probably all turn out the same in the end. You and Eugenio should stick together, I'll be all right."

At the roll call next morning, even those who were to stay behind had come out to see their friends off. There was a strange mood of foreboding.

"I know it's a fucking pig-sty but I wish we were the ones staying," said Eugenio as he tightened his jacket round himself, and shivered.

Once the head count had taken place of those leaving for a third time, the officer signalled to two of the guards. " It's going to be a cold walk to the station for these men," he said, "Go and get them blankets. They can return them when they get to the station."

As Franco was wrapping the blanket round himself he said to the officer, "Thank you. May I ask you something? We've all written letters to our families to let them know we're safe and where we are. But as far as I know, no one has yet received a reply. What will happen when letters from home come here?"

The officer said, "They'll be forwarded to you. You needn't worry about that."

Eugenio asked, "But where will that be?"

And for perhaps the thirtieth time they heard the reply, "I can't tell you that."

Before they left, Franco embraced Federico and looked over his friend's shoulder and was surprised at the emotion being shown by he men who were being left behind.

At the head of the line Father Rossi was giving a blessing to a group of men who had come to see them off.

"I don't understand it," said Eugenio, "Wherever we're going can't be as bad as this place, so why are we all so sad about leaving?"

Franco shrugged as they passed through the gates. "Don't know. We just are."

Chapter Sixty Five

Esther Hart's Diary

Monday 1st July 1940

Spent the most dreadful weekend feeling guilty, remorseful, furious and quite unable to sleep and all because of Major Cazalet's PS. That sentence kept going through my head like a broken record -"It may be that your husband can be of more help to you in this instance than I." If only he hadn't written it, then I could have shown Douglas his letter and would have been prepared for his reaction - anger. I'm used to that. As it is, Douglas will think that I somehow found out that he's on this wretched committee and told Major Cazalet. Since the Swinton Committee is apparently answerable only to the Prime Minister and not even to Parliament or the Cabinet, then Douglas could be in the most awful trouble for breaching the Official Secrets Act and he wouldn't have done. I would be responsible. On the other hand, if Barbara is right, and I can't help thinking she is, this committee is responsible for the imprisonment of thousands of entirely innocent men who haven't had the semblance of a trial. The right time to show him just didn't arise over the weekend. He went to the office for most of Saturday and said he had several urgent calls to make on Sunday and asked me to take Charles for a walk in Green Park. While we were out we heard that the Germans have occupied the Channel Islands. Charles's reaction was unusually pessimistic. He said, "There we are then. The Channel Islands today, the rest of England tomorrow, just like Hitler predicted." He has suddenly aged and lost his vim.

I shall have to show Douglas the letter tonight.

Tuesday 2nd July

He wasn't even angry but he did make me promise not to tell anyone at all, not even his father that he is working for the Swinton Committee. If I promised, he would tell me what he could, which isn't much because he is absolutely bound by the Official Secrets Act and he would certainly be imprisoned at the least if it was discovered that he had talked about his work to anyone. Also I wasn't to write any more letters about internees. I had to agree. He said that the Swinton Committee has been given responsibility for the internment camps and for giving instructions to the police on who should be interned. Obviously the police know their local populations best, but they have been given permission to intern any men or women in category 'C' where there are doubts about the reliability of the individual. I said that meant locking up innocent people without any trial. He said that was true, but the experiences of Holland, Belgium, Norway and France and now Italy, meant that that the government couldn't afford to take any risks. Besides, there was so much public feeling against the aliens that they were a lot safer behind barbed wire. It was true that there had been a desire on the part of the Home Office to avoid mass internment, but the time was past for that. The Secret Services had a great deal of evidence of fifth column activities and was represented on the Committee. Given the gravity of the international situation it was essential that it could get on with its work without being hide bound by Parliament. He said he couldn't say any more, but that he was just a civil servant, and had no role in making policy. I asked him if he thought it was right though, and he said that yes, under the circumstances he really did.

I'm grateful that he told me and thanked him. But I couldn't believe that the conditions in the camps could be very nice and he said on the contrary, internees are fed the same as our soldiers and are open to inspection by the International Red Cross. As far as he knew, there hadn't been any complaints for several months. He said he had no idea where Herr Niedermayer might be. There are literally hundreds of camps throughout the country and for obvious security reasons, internees aren't allowed to give their address when they write home.

Wednesday 3rd July

The German invasion that everyone was expecting yesterday didn't happen after all but the night sirens caused more fear than usual, though it might just be that the constant broken nights are shredding everybody's nerves. Mr Chamberlain made a broadcast last night and one really has to wonder why they let him. His thin, reedy voice is just a reminder of all the past failures, whereas Mr Priestley's talks do inspire confidence.

I can't stop thinking about what Douglas told me. Hundreds of internment camps? That means there must be many thousands of men who are locked up who are absolutely innocent of any wrongdoing, many of them refugees who escaped from Germany and Austria and who themselves were in camps in those countries. Part of me thinks it is a hysterical overreaction on the part of the government to lock people up indiscriminately, and then again if it really was the case that Germany defeated Holland and Norway with such ease because of a fifth column, then I suppose it is justified. Barbara says that the French government interned all aliens the day that war was declared and it was defeated in just six weeks, so there has never been any suggestion that their defeat was anything but military incompetence. I've promised Douglas I won't tell Barbara about his work.

Later.

On the six o'clock news it was announced that the Arandora Star had been sunk by a U-boat. The tone of the news reader was disgusting. He was positively gloating in the way that he reported that 'great hulking brutes' of Germans pushed the 'poor Italians' out of the way in the mad scramble for the lifeboats and the high loss of life would have been prevented were it not for the fighting that broke out between the Italians and the Germans and which the British guards had to break up. Then it was announced that the first Nazi prisoners to be deported had arrived on another ship at Montreal. They were described as 'swaggering louts.'

Thursday 4th July

I shouldn't have asked Douglas when he got home last night why he hadn't told me that internees were being deported to Canada because he had obviously had a very bad day at the office and he immediately flew into a temper and said he had told me everything he could. The men on 'The Arandora Star' were all category 'A' POW's - proven Nazis and Fascists. The only people who deserved my sympathy were the guards and seamen who had drowned because of the stupidity and cowardice of the aliens. Then he stormed out again.

Two years ago we sailed to the Mediterranean on 'The Arandora Star." It was so idyllic. She was nicknamed 'The Wedding Cake' and it did feel as if we were having a second honeymoon. I remember how much I missed Douglas when he had to leave the ship for a few days to go to a meeting in Florence and how Captain Moulton was so kind and solicitous. I'm writing this in the book that Douglas gave me last Christmas and that he bought on that trip to Florence. It is nearly finished. Now Captain Moulton is dead and the ship gone down and the whole thing makes Douglas angry. It just makes me terribly sad.

The papers have the same horrible way of reporting as the BBC did last night. The Daily Express says that the Germans punched and kicked their way past the Italians and that the British soldiers had to restrain them forcibly. But then another seaman said that the Italians were 'just as bad. The whole mob of them thought of their own skins first. The scramble for the boats was sickening.'

Friday 5th July

Today it is raining and that is good for the garden. We desperately need it. Couldn't get any eggs when I went shopping this morning. There was a lot of discussion about our sinking the French fleet. Most people agreed that it was a shame it had to be done, especially as so many French soldiers died in the attack and everybody expects that the French government will at least break off relations with us. One man said he thought the French would now declare war on us. Another said he had heard that they tried to torpedo our base in Gibraltar. Anyway, we don't seem to have any allies left but the reaction of those in the shop was simply to shrug and say that the French were never very good allies anyway.

I'm quite concerned about Charles. I think his cat being put down has affected him badly. He's not eating and complains about a pain in his side. He's refusing to go to the doctor, but if he's no better by Monday I shall insist.

Monday 8th July

Writing this in the hospital while Charles is being seen to by a doctor. He went quite white this morning and was in a lot of pain. Douglas scarcely home at all, except yesterday afternoon when he looked after his father and I went for a walk. As I was walking past the park there was an air raid warning. Most of the children ran off home but there were three who were panic stricken and a little girl who just stood in the middle of the park and burst into tears. An older boy was trying to comfort her and find out where she lived, but she was much too upset to be able to respond. I picked her up and the boy, who said his name was Raymond, said he thought that she was living with her aunt and her mother. They had just been evacuated from Guernsey. We were walking towards where Raymond lived when the little girl's mother came running out looking for her. When she took hold of her daughter she, too, burst into tears. She said that the last few days, with the arrival of the Germans on the island and losing their home had been impossible to cope with. She was staying with her sister and her husband who was in the RAF. It struck me that they have come to London to be safe, as have so many families evacuated from along the coasts, and we're sending children out of London for the same reason. It is impossible to know where is really safe and since the government refuses to give details of bomb damage or casualties it is very hard to know what to do.

Later.

Charles has been kept in. They suspect kidney stones.

Tuesday 9th July

Feel like a complete idiot this morning. Government starting campaign to get more aluminium. "Housewives, bring us your pots and pans and we'll turn them into Spitfires and Hurricanes." Feeling very virtuous I took three saucepans and a frying pan to the Council Offices only to notice on my way home that the ironmonger's window had lots of saucepans. Went in and asked him why he was still selling them he winked at me and whispered, "Don't let on, lady, but they can't get what they need out of your old kitchenware. It's all a ruse to boost aircraft production -you know, to get people to work in the factories. And I daresay Lord Beaverbrook's got shares in saucepans." So I replaced the ones I'd given away because it would have been difficult to do without them.

Visited Charles in hospital. he looked terrible, ashen grey and very drowsy. They want to keep him in. It certainly is kidney stones but the matron said there seemed to be other problems.

It struck me that the saga about the saucepans was also to make the tea rationing that was introduced today easier to get the public to accept. Two ounces a week isn't very much and the men do take theirs very strong.

General de Gaulle is understandably very angry about what we have done to the French fleet. Very damning also of the Pétain government.

Wednesday 10th July

Air raid warnings throughout the night. Charles still in hospital. Asked me not to tell Douglas that there were complications to his kidney problems. Douglas can't go to visit him because of the fact that he is working during visiting hours. Came back from work too preoccupied and tired to discuss anything so I just said I'd visited Charles and that he was a little more himself.

Barbara came round and said she'd had a response at last to her letters and asked me if I had. I said I had but that I had promised Douglas that I wouldn't discuss it with anyone or write any more. It could put his job in danger and because of his position he could even go to prison if it came out what his job is. I felt very bad telling her all this but mostly because of the pitying way she looked at me. I said I was sure she was right, that the important thing now was to concentrate on the conditions in the camps and that Douglas had said that there had been no complaints from internees for several months.

She nodded curtly and said, "Well, that's good," and then left. I don't know that I 'll see her again, and that makes me so sad.

Friday 12th July

Felt too miserable to write yesterday. Visited Charles. No change. Wrote long letters to the children.

Monday 15th July

Charles came home on Saturday and spent the day in bed. He got up last night for Mr Churchill's speech on the wireless which we all listened to. It was very stirring and for the first time for a long time I felt quite optimistic. The RAF does seem to be winning the battle in the skies and our navy is stronger than the German one. I thought Douglas would be more buoyed by the news than he was and the talk of the sinking of so much of the French fleet reminded me of the Arandora Star. I said, stupidly, that I had no idea that internees were being transported to Canada and did he remember what a wonderful voyage we had had. He said I may have forgotten that there is a war on and that with food shortages, it was essential to get rid of useless mouths.

Chapter Sixty Six

The train carrying the Italians from Bury halted in a tunnel. In the distance they could hear the sound of an air raid siren that, echoing faintly, sounded more than ever like a wailing banshee in the darkness. Then the train crept forward as if seeing that it was all clear, and accelerated into the sunlight. It had been a long day. The men were mostly elderly and the walk to the station in the early morning cold had tired them. They had been given hot tea and a slice of bread when they had arrived on the train. There had been a lot of speculation about where they were being taken.

"We've been going west so I reckon we're going to Liverpool," said Eugenio. He opened the door slightly and said loudly in English and making sure that the guard outside in the corridor could hear, "So I think we must be going to the Isle of Man." He stared expectantly at the guard who smiled and shook his head, "Nice try, mate," he said, "but honest, I don't know any more than you."

Eugenio had been talking for most of the journey. Those who had felt inclined to answer him had long given up and either drifted off to sleep or avoided his gaze by staring out of the window.

"It's the only thing that makes any sense," he went on to no one in particular, "and there was that thing on the radio, you know, about the German women who are servants spying for Hitler. You remember, Franco."

Franco nodded with a pained expression. "What I'm saying is, if they don't trust German women and need to lock them up, why would they trust Italians? I reckon they could already be there waiting for us. I think that by tonight I could be in bed with my Julia and Franco, you'll be seeing Giovanna and Francesca. It's the only thing that makes any sense."

Franco looked down at his jacket that had been impossible to keep clean in the conditions at the mill. He hadn't been able to wash properly since his internment. He felt that he smelled badly, and he couldn't help noticing how rank the atmosphere in the carriage had become. He didn't think Eugenio could be right, it was just wishful thinking, but if he was, he would be ashamed of seeing his wife in his present condition.

The train slowed to walking pace down a steep incline and through another tunnel before curving sharply to the right and eventually pulled into a massive steel and glass vaulted terminus.

"See, said Eugenio, grinning broadly, "Liverpool Riverside Station, what did I tell you. We're going to the Isle of Man." He nodded at the guard knowingly. "You knew, didn't you," he said, "You can tell us now."

The guard lit a cigarette and shook his head, "I don't know why you don't believe me, mate. Don't think I didn't ask myself, but all I got was 'You're an escort guard.' That's all they said to any of us and that's God's honest truth."

The men filed off the train. The sun shining through the roof threw geometric shadows across the platform and the train. They walked stiffly along the platform and through the covered walkway. Franco suddenly smelt the river and heard a jabber of excited voices ahead of him. As he turned the corner he understood why. Those in front had stopped and were looking up at the enormous hull of a ship that had been painted grey. The portholes had been blocked up .

"We've got a bit of a wait," sang one of the guards. "Line up along the wall so as not to obstruct the traffic, please."

Most of the men slumped down on their cases. "That's not going to the Isle of Man," said the passenger who had been sitting opposite Eugenio. "That'll be going a lot further. Australia or America or Canada. But how can they do that to us, just send us off somewhere?"

Franco felt sick. The prospect of a long sea voyage already made him anticipate spending most of the time hanging over the side, but worst was that he'd never had a chance to let Giovanna know where he was going. "Just a few days," the policeman had said. He had lied. But perhaps he'd believed it. After all the guards obviously hadn't known where they were going. He sat down gingerly and clutched his case to his chest.

"I still think...." started Eugenio.

"Shsh," whispered Franco, "Eugenio. Basta."

Maurice had enjoyed the journey from Swanwick. Sitting in the corridor and listening to the Germans speculate about where they were being taken reminded him of the first few days in France. It all felt very familiar, somehow. Reinhardt and Dobel chatted in English. They, too, were certain that their destination was the Isle of Man and Maurice found Reinhardt, in particular, so convincing that he thought that he must be right.

When the train pulled into the station a young private tapped him on the shoulder.

"I've come to relieve you, mate, while you go and get your briefing. We've had ours."

He peered into the carriage and then turned to Maurice in surprise. "This is the lot that we're escorting, is it?"

Maurice nodded. The private shrugged, "First off they tell us we're taking a couple of hundred kids that are being evacuated, but that didn't make no sense after a while, and then they say it's a load of Nazis. That makes more sense but they don't look much like Nazi soldiers to me. That bloke," he nodded towards Reinhardt, "is old enough to be me granddad. You'd better get going. Briefing's on D deck."

Maurice took his suitcase and joined the group of his fellow soldiers who marched briskly along the platform, through the glass roofed tunnel and onto the quay.

A dispirited and tired line of men were either sitting leaning against the wall or lying down using their cases as pillows. But it was the sight of the massive liner that made him pause. She had been painted grey, but it had obviously been a rushed job because in places the scarlet ribbon around the level of the top deck showed through, as did the blue stars on her funnels.

After they climbed the gangway they were given plimsolls to wear. "This is a luxury cruise ship," said the major "and though she has been pressed into service to escort enemy aliens to the new destination, we will continue to treat her as a luxury cruiser. Your task will be to guard the men who are being transported." He looked around. "As you can see, it has been thought necessary to keep certain elements of the aliens apart for obvious reasons. There will be a full briefing for those of you unfamiliar with the ship at nineteen hundred hours by which time everyone will be on board. In the meantime you will be shown to your quarters and assigned your duty roster."

A corporal stepped forward and called out the lists of names and the room they had been assigned to. Maurice found himself being led along the deck by an older corporal. "We're in here," he said. "My name's Reg Davies. I've bagged this bed already. Stow your stuff and I'll show you around."

Maurice introduced himself and looked about the room. "Are these sheets linen?" he asked aghast. "

"Oh she's the best," said Reg, smiling at Maurice's astonishment. "Swimming pool, ballroom, everything you could wish for. You should have seen the skipper's face when we started painting her. Thought he was going to cry. But they say he really blew his top when they started nailing barbed wire all round the place. Him and Major Bethel - that was him give the briefing, they were locked up for over an hour with some blokes from the War Office. In the end they've taken some of the barbed wire down but it's still lying around on the deck. Must be right vicious buggers we're transporting if they've gone to all that trouble."

"You must be right," agreed Maurice, "but the blokes we brought up from Swanwick were no trouble. Who are that lot along the quay?"

"Italians, poor bastards. Been stuck out there for hours while the arguments went on. Right. We're loading them first. They've got to have a medical as they come on board, then leave any large items they might have brought. Some are going down to A deck and some'll be on D deck. We'll be on from eight till midnight and on A deck making sure they don't wander around too much. So we'll get supper on the first shift. I'll show you around."

He led the way to what had been the ballroom with its wall to wall mirrors that were still in place but which now had palliasses on the floor and bunks lining the walls. The windows had been boarded up, giving the place a surreal feel.

Maurice's mind went back to his grandfather's house that he used to visit as a child. There had been a large living room full of furniture and paintings on the walls. Facing south, the room had always been brightly lit, but when the old man died and Maurice went back for the last time, the shutters were drawn, and the furniture and pictures covered with dust sheets. He shivered at the memory, at the grey, ghostly light. It was the first time that someone he knew had died, and somehow the change in that room became what death meant to him.

Back on deck he noticed the barbed wire that prevented access to the bridge. Reg led the way down three flights of stairs and along a darkened corridor.

"This is where some of the Italians'll be. Four to a twin berth, six to a four berth. We're going to be four times the compliment of what she was built for. War Office tried to spring another five hundred on us at the last minute, cheeky bastards, but the old man put his foot down. Look in here."

The bedroom was larger than the one that Maurice would be sharing with Reg. It had two single beds and the floor was almost completely covered by palliasses. There was an indentation on the corner of the carpet from where the wardrobe had been removed and another at the foot of the bed that had held a dressing table. Maurice turned on the hot tap of the basin. The pipe gurgled and coughed and muddy water dribbled out for a second before he turned off the tap again.

Reg grimaced and shook his head. "This trip's going to be no fucking holiday."

Busch had given up asking why they had been sitting in a carriage for so many hours and what the delay could possibly be. He had even given up being curious about where they were being taken. Eventually, at six o'clock the guards along the corridor began to stir and to shout orders. In the next carriage a rather listless rendition of the Horst Wessel song started up as the carriage doors swung open and the internees stepped out onto the platform.

Reinhardt squinted up at the light and grumbled to Dobel that he was feeling his age today. He climbed down stiffly from the carriage and joined the line that was being ushered along the platform. They turned onto the quay just in time to see the last of the Italians walking up the gangway and onto the ship.

His reaction was one of shock. "Christ," he whispered, "that's never going to the Isle of Man."

Dobel, too, was horrified. "They're expecting trouble as well," he said. "Look, an anti-aircraft gun and cannon. I hope we're going to be well escorted."

Forty yards behind them, Busch had a very different reaction. His eyes lit up as he turned onto the quay. "It's the Arandora Star," he said delightedly. "I saw her in Hamburg years ago, when I was a kid. She had her mast aft then...."

"And wasn't carrying a cannon and anti-aircraft gun," said Müller bitterly.

Once on the ship the guards directed the men to their cabins. Reinhardt and Dobel found theirs on D deck impressively comfortable and were it not for the palliasse on the floor Reinhardt felt that he could imagine himself stowing away his things before going on deck and ordering a gin and tonic. Dobel broke into his day dream.

"Did you notice that the lifeboats are behind the barbed wire?' he said as he pushed his suitcase under his bed. He stood up and looked at Reinhardt. "And how many men do you suppose are on this ship? It must be well over a thousand. I counted ten lifeboats."

Reinhardt lay on his bed and put his hands behind his head. "Do you think we could get a g. and t? I could kill for one."

Franco and Eugenio found themselves dragging their palliasses to a quieter corner of the ballroom. A noisy group of Nazis from Swanwick had hung a swastika on a wall and were complaining bitterly about the accommodation. When Major Bethel entered to inspect the arrangements he was immediately accosted by an angry group of Germans who insisted that they be found proper accommodation. Franco had difficulty following what exactly was being said, but the prospect of a long journey with them horrified him. He lay on his back and stared up at the ceiling. After the strain of being out in a hot sun for so many hours and then queuing to get on board, he was exhausted. He wondered what it must have been like to sail on this ship in peace time. He imagined himself waiting on the gentlemen in their tuxedos and the ladies in their ball gowns, all reflected in the vast wall mirrors. It was, he decided, a floating Ritz with its beautiful corniced ceiling and marble pillars, its huge picture windows and elegant paintings on the walls.

He was enjoying his dream when Eugenio dug him in the ribs. "Franco, listen. Whatever we do we've got to make sure we stay up here."

Franco raised himself onto an elbow and looked into the anxious face of his brother. "What are you on about now?"

Eugenio nodded towards an elderly man who was surrounded by a group of who were listening to him intently. "That man is Dr Zezzi. The captain of the ship knows him, they're friends, I think. I don't really know. Anyway, the captain invited him for supper at his table. He told him to stay up on this deck all the time. We haven't got a navy escort. There's no Red Cross flag. The captain says he thinks we'll be attacked and we haven't got any protection."

Chapter Sixty Seven

At midnight Captain Moulton ordered the anchor to be raised and the gangways to be hoisted and shortly after, the ship, in complete darkness, moved slowly out into the middle of the Mersey, a black sea swirling around her bows. In his cabin that he was sharing with three other Austrians on 'A' deck, the lowest, Niedermayer was already feeling sea sick. He had wanted to go up on deck to get some fresh air but a guard had blocked his path and so he had reluctantly gone back to his cabin and lay down on his palliasse, sweating from the heat that would permeate the lower decks until the ship sailed and the fans would circulate fresh air.

Along the corridor, Maurice was coming to the end of his shift. He was relieved to be guarding mostly Italians. He had heard that there had been some trouble up in the ballroom from an elderly man with a pince-nez who had come down the stairs with difficulty, clutching the rail and muttering to himself. He had stopped when he saw Maurice and said in a strong Italian accent, "Please, sir, where must I go?" Maurice had led him along the corridor, opening bedroom doors to see where there was any room. Eventually a voice had said, "Signor Rivaldi, venga, venga." There had been a shuffling of bodies while the six men in the cabin made room for him and a small balding man in flannelette pyjamas made a show of getting out of bed and offering it to the old man.

The crew of the SS Woermann were in cabins on 'C' deck. Captain Burfeind had insisted on having his men near him. He was sharing the state room suite with Müller and Busch who was wide awake listening to the throb of the engines and trying to identify them. "Four steam turbines," he said at length, "Single reduction geared." Captain Burfeind grumbled. Müller smiled to himself. As long as Busch was so fascinated by the ship and its workings, he wouldn't cause trouble.

Weiss had dragged a palliasse into the cabin being shared by Reinhardt and Dobel. He had managed to explore most of the ship by telling guards that he had got lost and was trying to find his way back to his cabin. Reckoning that if there was an accident, he would be safer on the top deck and seeing that the life boats were mostly behind barbed wire, he had had noted that they were not in a good state of repair. One of them was holed beneath what would be the water line. Most were so securely held in place that he couldn't imagine how they would be released if they were needed. Still, he was a strong swimmer. With a shrug, he took a life jacket to be used as a pillow, and settled down to sleep.

The Germans who had been singing lustily in the ballroom eventually got their way and were moved, under Captain Moulton's orders, to cabins in the stern. Franco had breathed a sigh of relief when they had gone. He was woken at four as the ship lifted anchor and moved slowly moved out into Liverpool Bay.

Maurice had had a bad night. Unable to sleep, he went out on deck and turned away when he saw a figure hanging over the side who was clearly being sick. In the early dawn light he recognised Blackpool Tower. He remembered with a pang that his best friend when he was twelve, Gordon, was going on holiday to Blackpool with his parents. Gordon's mother had invited him as well and the two boys had spent hours discussing what they would do - play cricket on the beach, go for donkey rides, ride on the big dipper that Gordon had described so graphically that Maurice had trembled with excitement at the prospect. But when Gordon's Mum had talked to Maurice's Dad about it, he had just said, "That's very kind. We'll have to see." And then, when Maurice was alone with him, he said, "You're not going and that's flat. If your school report hadn't been such a disgrace I might have thought about it. Anyway, it wouldn't be fair on your brother. He's not getting a holiday and he's worked hard all at school. You've been shirking all year, so why should you get special treatment? You're staying at home and doing an hour of reading and writing every day." When, later, Don had found him crying in their bedroom and asked him what the matter was, and Maurice had explained, Don had said, "It's nothing to do with your report, stupid. He's embarrassed because they can't afford it."

Maurice turned away from the handrail and wiped his eyes. The wind was making him tear.

At seven thirty Franco was nominated by the Italians in the ballroom to be one of the waiters who would go down below to fetch breakfast for those on his table.

He joined the queue where the cooks were handing mugs of tea and plates of bread through the barbed wire. He wasn't hungry and didn't even feel like the tea when the discussion turned to where they were being taken. Eugenio was looking sick. "They say we've just passed the Isle of Man," he said quietly. " I thought that's where were we going. I really did. Now they say we're going to Canada." There was a pall of gloom over the ballroom.

The men in the cabins on the lower decks were allowed up for an hour to exercise before being led back for lunch. Again, men from each cabin were designated to go to the galley to bring back the meal of sausages, egg and beetroot which was served on tin plates.

Maurice ate with the crew and the other guards when he came off duty at twelve. It was the best meal he had had for weeks - meat and two veg with roast potatoes.

Reg was less happy. "There are blokes in here who haven't done guard duty yet, and we've done two. Who the fuck's in charge is what I'd like to know. And when we were sorting things down on 'A' deck last night, there was a whole lot of them getting pissed in the bar. That lad in the next cabin, his mate told me he had such a hangover that he was sick all night and was sleeping it off this morning when he should've been on duty." He thrust a roast potato into his mouth. "Oh well, ours not to reason why and all that crap."

Tell you what, we're not on again till midnight and I'm going to get fucking pickled tonight."

Weiss and Dobel's game of chess was constantly interrupted by Reinhardt reading out passages from 'The Code of the Woosters' which Weiss had lent him in the vain hope of stopping him from talking.

"Oh, this is perfect," he laughed, "Listen. "You agree with me that the situation is a lulu?" "Certainly, a somewhat sharp crisis in your affairs would appear to have been precipitated, Sir." Would you describe our situation as a lulu, Dobel?"

Weiss glanced up at Dobel. "He probably would now. I've pinned his queen."

Dobel lay the king on the board and sighed. "Tell you what Reinhardt, while we're setting up the game again, you read us the best bits and then when we're playing, you save the next best bits until we've finished. How does that suit you?"

Reinhardt nodded and read, "There are moments, Jeeves, when one asks oneself, "Do trousers matter?" "The mood will pass, sir."

He lay back on his bed and put his hands behind his head. "The rumour is that they're taking us to Canada."

Dobel said that the game was starting, but Reinhardt ignored him. "What does anyone know about Canada?" he asked. "I've always imagined it was all red indians and forests and squaws being chased by grizzly bears. We'll probably have to sleep in teepees and be guarded by men in raccoon hats with bows and arrows and moccasins. And learn to whittle. Just as at home it was all, "Dig for Victory", in Canada it'll be "Whittle while you work.""

Weiss picked up a pawn and flung it at him. "I've sacrificed this piece just so I can throw it at you. And before you ask, I don't know what whittling is and furthermore, I don't want to."

Reinhardt hauled himself off the bed and stood in the door of the cabin. "In that case I shall take my umbrage out on deck and leave you in your sink of ignorance."

Dinner was served at seven thirty. Niedermayer ate his in his cabin. He had struck up a conversation with an Austrian socialist, who, like him, had fled to England but who had been living in Manchester. They were discussing whether or not Hitler could be beaten.

"I don't think the British think they can defeat him," said Niedermayer, "at least not without the help of the Americans, and why would they want to get involved?"

"This is a war about markets," said his friend, " America's the most powerful capitalist nation in the world and Europe's its biggest market. They can't afford to allow Germany to win."

The discussion went on well into the evening as 'The Arandora Star' passed Malin Head and set a zig zagging course westward.

Maurice went on duty at midnight feeling ill. He'd had three pints of beer and the rocking of the ship was making him distinctly queazy. The guard that he relieved said that it had been completely quiet on the lower decks. The Italians were all decent blokes as far as he could see; he didn't even know what they were doing there. Maurice bade him goodnight and settled down on a chair. It was all right on the ship, he reflected. The food was the best he'd had for ages. In fact he couldn't remember a meal as good as tonight's. He'd had a good rest in the afternoon on the most comfortable bed he'd ever slept in. The men they were guarding were mostly OK. The only unpleasantness that he's experienced was when an Italian who was old enough to be his father had asked him where they were going. Maurice had answered truthfully that he didn't know and the old man had looked at him disbelievingly and said, "Is it true we're going to Canada?" Maurice had laughed and said, "Like I told you, I don't know," at which the man had said "You're lying. Tell me, please, what difference does it make to you?" Maurice had walked away and heard the old man swear at his back.

He wasn't going to be able to stay awake until four but there hadn't been any trouble. He could close his eyes, just for a few minutes while the feeling of sickness wore off.

Sometime later he stretched out on the ground. His relief shook him awake. "Sorry, mate, I know I'm late, I overslept."

Completely disorientated Maurice struggled to his feet and stared wildly about. The walls of the corridor were spinning. He hauled himself painfully up the three flights of stairs and then groped his way to his cabin. His head was throbbing as he fell onto his bed with a grunt.

He was shaken awake by an explosion that nearly tipped him from his bed. "What the fuck was that?" he gasped and called out, "Reg? You there?"

There was no answer. He reached for the light switch, but nothing happened. He couldn't be sure but the ship seemed to be listing slightly.

In the lowest deck it sounded as if a bomb had exploded deep in the bowels of the vessel. The floor juddered. Niedermayer heard shouting all around him as he groped his way to the door. Behind him a man was pleading, "Bitte, turn on the light, I must find my glasses."

They pushed open the door. A stream of men was groping its way along the corridor in the darkness. Niedermayer hesitated. "There are no lights," he shouted, "Take my arm," and he felt for his friend who was on his hands and knees feeling for his glasses.

"Nein, nein, I can't go anywhere without them."

Niedermayer didn't know what to do. He dropped down and felt between the palliasses that were pushed closely together. There were shoes, socks, trousers shirts and jackets lying around. "Where are you? " he shouted. The man was weeping with frustration, repeatedly sobbing, "I can't see without them." Niedermayer was on the point of giving up when he felt the round metal rims beneath a pillow.

"Here, I've got them. He pushed them into his friend's hand and shoved him towards the door. There were fewer men now. Niedermayer tried to remember how to get up onto the open decks and couldn't . He decided the only thing to do was to follow the voices, some German, but mostly Italian as he pulled his companion behind him.

Busch knew immediately what had happened.

"Torpedo," he said aloud once he had recovered from the initial shock. Captain Burfeind swore. Most of his crew had been relocated to cabins in the decks below from the ballroom the previous evening. He'd kept Busch with him as he didn't trust him not to get into trouble. Now he said, "Go and find as many of the crew as you can and bring them back here."

In the ballroom the explosion was immediately followed by a loud crash as the enormous mirrors were ripped from the walls. In the darkness men yelped with pain as the shards of glass cut into their hands as they tried to crawl towards the doors. Franco was one of those furthest from the exit. Momentarily knocked unconscious, he came to and found himself lying across another body. There were men shouting, but the body beneath him was quite lifeless. "Eugenio?" he whispered, "Is that you?"

He felt the shoulders of the man beneath him and moved his hand up the neck, trying to identify whether or not it was his brother. The face was wet. Franco withdrew his hand hurriedly and tried to stand, but fell back against the wall.

In a daze and with the searing pain in his head, Maurice staggered out onto the open deck. He turned as someone tapped him on the shoulder. "Christ, mate, I've been wondering what happened to you. I've been looking everywhere." Reg stared at him.

"Torpedo's hit the fucking engine room. The bugger's gonna sink and us with it if we don't get those lifeboats down. Use your bayonet. Get rid of the fucking barbed wire."

Maurice stared disbelievingly at the men who were pouring out of the doors to the lower decks. Some were trying to rip at the wire with their bare hands. At his feet an elderly man was sitting on his suitcase, looking around himself with an air of quiet bewilderment.

He looked up at Maurice and smiled. "You agree with me that the situation is a lulu?"

"What?" Maurice was unnerved by the man's calmness. "There are plenty of life jackets over there. I'll get you one."

Reinhardt shook his head. "I've never thought of Canada as a particularly attractive destination. I suppose the squaws might be quite fun, but with my luck I'd probably be scalped in bed by a jealous redskin." He sighed. "There aren't enough lifeboats even if they can get to them." He glanced over at the increasing number of men grappling furiously with the barbed wire. "The sea on that side is black. I've been in oil all my life, but I'm buggered if I want to die in the stuff."

Maurice looked up at the bridge wing. Loudhailer in hand, Captain Moulton was shouting down to the internees who were desperately trying to get to the lifeboats. "Please do not panic. The ship will stay afloat for a long time..." His words went unheeded as guards tore at the barbed wire with their bayonets and tried to smash the posts holding it in place with the butts of their rifles. More internees were groping their way out of the exits to the lower decks. Some were fully dressed, others were in their pyjamas.

Busch had managed to find his crew mates and was leading them to the state room suite. It was slow progress in the dark. The ship was beginning to list to starboard as they groped their way along the corridors and up the stairs. Captain

Burfeind had found his torch and ordered his men to put their hand of the shoulder of the man in front of them as he led them towards the boat deck.

A group of guards and internees had managed to move enough of the barbed wire by a boat station to start trying to release a lifeboat from its davits. Two men wearing life jackets stood by and watched as the group wrestled helplessly with the wires securing the boat. The two men looked at each other and shook their heads, and then climbed over the railing and jumped into the sea forty feet below. A British sailor rushed to the scene and looked over.

"Stupid buggers'll have broken their necks," he said. "Saw the same thing happen on 'The Lancastria." He turned to the crowd of men and shouted, "If you've got a life jacket you must tie it tightly and pull down on it as you jump or it'll ride up and break you neck when you hit the water." He looked at the uncomprehending faces staring at him and then drew his hand across his throat. "Comprendi?"

Eugenio had gone down to fetch the breakfast when the torpedo struck. Abandoning the tea, he rushed back to the ballroom. An elderly priest was blessing the men around him who were kneeling in silent resignation. Desperately searching for his brother, he eventually found him clutching his cheek and lying next to a man who was lying in a pool of blood. He grabbed hold of Franco, "Come on," he shouted, "We've got to get out of here." Franco pulled away and fell back against the wall. "Non è possibile," he whispered. Eugenio bent down, "There are life boats. We can escape." He looked round for support, but in the half light all he could see was men lying or kneeling and all he could hear was the quiet whispering of the priest and the moaning of those who had been hurt by the mirrors breaking. The atmosphere of resignation infuriated him. He pulled at Franco's arm, but Franco again pulled away. "Non posso farlo," he said, "You must go. Think of Julia and the baby. I'll only slow you up."

"Are you hurt?"

Franco nodded, lay back and closed his eyes. "Va'! Va'!" A sudden lurch of the ship decided Eugenio. He ran across the ballroom and out onto the open deck.

In his bright blue pyjamas Captain Burfeind was organising his crew into lowering the remaining boats. They worked quickly, releasing the ropes from the davits and helping men over the railings before lowering the boars. One snagged, the lifeboat lurching precariously down the side of the ship and then tipping the occupants into the sea. All around there were men hurling anything that might float - doors, chairs, the casing around the cannon, onto the waves and then leaping in after it.

Several men in the sea were hit by the falling débris. Maurice ran over to Captain Burfeind who pointed to a space in a lifeboat.

"I don't know if I should," he said. It felt like desertion. Captain Burfeind said slowly, "Das Schiff sinkt," and pointed again at the empty space. Maurice had never disobeyed an order and he climbed in. The boat was full with men squatting in the well. Two internees took the oars and pushed the craft inexpertly away from the ship and began to row. There was a growing swell to the waves as they moved away from the ship. To his horror, Maurice saw an oar hit the head of a man who was floating in the water, his life jacket riding high around his neck and his head at a strange angle.

Below decks the sea had roared in through the gaping hole created by the torpedo. Franz Niedermayer momentarily heard, but never saw, the wave that poured along the narrow corridor and engulfed him and the others who were desperately scrabbling up the staircase.

Within twenty minutes Captain Burfeind had organised his crew into lowering the remaining lifeboats. When the last one was safely in the water he turned and looked up at the bridge from where Captain Moulton was urging those still on the deck to jump. The ship was now listing dangerously, her bows lifting clear of a sea that was coated in black oil and the floating detritus that had been thrown overboard.

Captain Burfeind gave a last look and turned towards the stairs leading up to the bridge. Busch followed him but the older man turned and shook his head. "Go and save yourself," he said. Busch hesitated, confused. He wanted to remonstrate that this wasn't their ship, that they could both be saved and that he wanted to be with his captain no matter what, but Captain Burfeind added, "Das ist ein Befehl."

Busch watched him as he hauled himself up the stairway and turn onto the bridge.

Busch pulled off his shoes and ran to the railings. He climbed over, and grabbing a rope that had been used for lowering a lifeboat, he slid down it and dropped into the sea. He surfaced, spitting oil and swam towards a raft to which were clinging three Italians. The oldest of them flailed in panic as his oily hands desperately tried to cling to the side. Busch put his arm around the man's waist and with the help of the other two internees managed to bundle him onto the deck.

Eugenio had lost consciousness for a moment when the lifeboat he had been in suddenly lurched as it was being lowered into the water and he had been tipped into the sea. He came to with a loud ringing in his ears and found himself lying at the bottom of the boat.

"We've got to get away or we'll be dragged down," he heard someone shout. He hauled himself onto his knees and sat down heavily and looked around. The the men behind him were urging the oarsmen to row as hard as they could. A sailor was standing in the stern shouting orders while their lifeboat slowly slid its way through the oil slick. It gave a slight tilt as a man covered in oil grabbed the side and shouted for help.

The man nearest him asked "What are you? English or German?"

"German," he said.

"No room, we're only saving English," but the sailor protested.

"We're at sea. We save everyone we can. Help him up."

Reluctantly the two men closest to him put their hands under his arms and dragged him on board. His pyjama top was covered in oil but the bottoms had slipped off and he lay shivering at the bottom of the boat, half naked. The sailor took off his jacket and tossed it to him. "Here, cover yourself up, and you men, row as fast as you can."

In his lifeboat that was now full, Maurice watched in horror as the ship's gun broke from its station and rolled down the deck, sweeping everyone before it into the sea. A little further off, Eugenio turned away and cried. The image of scraping vegetables off a chopping board and into the water came to his mind, and a few seconds later, as the Arandora Star's bows rose into the air, there was another explosion. The portholes were blown open and amid the escaping smoke, men were hurled into the air.

The ship's anchor was swinging like a pendulum and then, with what sounded to Maurice like a terrible groan, she sank from sight.

For a moment there was silence as a wave rolled towards the lifeboats and rafts making them bob and the men in them groan. Busch heard a familiar voice call his name. He turned towards the sound. Initially he couldn't see anyone alive and then he caught sight of Weiss waving to him and clinging to a plank.

With his free hand, Weiss paddled towards the boat and was pulled on board. He squeezed in between Busch and a young British soldier who was turning away and retching over the side. Most of the men in the boat were at the point of exhaustion, but charged with adrenalin, Weiss couldn't stop talking. Between breaths he told Busch, "I knew I'd be all right. I can swim well. The old men didn't have a chance. So many old men drowned and Dobel and Reinhardt."

Busch looked up at him, "Doktor Dobel?"

Weiss nodded. "I saw him just before I dived. He'd been helping a bloke who'd got himself entangled in the wire. I told him that he couldn't do anything for him, I mean, even if he could treat his wounds the bloke wouldn't survive in that sea because all the life boats had gone by then. It was as if he couldn't hear me. He was kneeling on the deck bandaging the man's hands completely calmly, as if it was a normal day in his surgery." He paused. "So many dead, and for what?"

A couple of hundred yards away, Maurice covered his ears. The sound of voices carrying across the waves and crying out for help sounded to him like a field full of sheep. Then he fell asleep and when he awoke there was silence except for the chugging sound of the ship's motor launch and a voice calling to keep the lifeboats together - they would be rescued but they must stay together.

A short while later a plane appeared out of a cloudy sky. The men cowered in the boats and on the rafts, unsure of whether it was an enemy or a friendly aircraft. Soon the cry went up, "It's one of ours." Water proof parcels were dropped and as the boats came closer together, cigarettes and food was handed out and a message that was swiftly circulated amongst the survivors. "Keep your chins up. Help arriving."

A few hours later a thin plume of smoke appeared on the horizon. Maurice and Busch had been staring to the east, praying for a ship to pick them up, but when it came, it came from the west. Barely conscious, Maurice found himself being winched up the side of a destroyer and laid carefully by a hatch. Within an hour the deck was full and the St Laurent was steaming as fast as possible towards Greenock.

Chapter Sixty Eight

Esther Hart's Diary

Tuesday 16th July 1940

It's been raining for hours. Charles in bed very lethargic and refusing even the tea I've been taking him. Barbara came round unexpectedly. I was very pleased to see her, though somewhat on my guard after the last time we met. However she acted as if our last conversation had never happened and bought some real coffee which I interpreted as an unspoken peace offering. It was delicious. I'd forgotten what real coffee tastes like.

After some small talk she came out with the real reason for her visit. She said that Herbert had told her that there had been crowds of Italian women outside the Brazilian Embassy trying to find out what had happened to their husbands. Brazil is acting as the intermediary between Britain and Italy. Switzerland is doing the same for Germany and Britain. The trouble is that once men have been sent to internment camps, the authorities have very little idea where they are. And the sinking of the Arandora Star has terrified those poor women who had no idea that anyone was being sent abroad.

This made me feel very uncomfortable and I reminded her that I had promised Douglas that I wouldn't discuss it, so I just said that he had told me that all those on the ship were either known fascists or Nazis. She shook her head and said that she knew that that was the official line, but she knew of at least one Jewish refugee from Austria who had died on the ship. Then she went on to say that Mr Churchill had asked for twenty thousand internees to be shipped to Newfoundland or St Helena and had made that request at the beginning of June. I said that couldn't be right - that was even before Italy joined the war and there couldn't have been anything like that number of Category 'A' Germans.

She looked at me pityingly and said that was just the point. Category 'B' and 'C' refugees were arrested and interned, and the Italians didn't even have the benefit of a tribunal. When Italy joined the war, Mr Churchill had simply said

'Collar the Lot'. The Home Office reckons that there are thirty thousand men in the camps. But apparently neither the Home Office nor the War Office really know how many Italians are in the camps or where they are. That's why their wives are besieging the Brazilian Embassy.

Then she said that there had been questions about the internees in Parliament last week. It may be that our letters have had some effect, because both Major Cazalet and Eleanor Rathbone asked why it was that anti-Nazis were interned and why could the families of internees not find out what had happened to them. And the answer was that it was nothing to do with the War Office. She paused for a long time and looked at me and then added that Mr Peake from the Home Office had explained that the decision to send internees abroad was not taken either by the Secretary of State for War or the Home Secretary. It was taken by a Committee of the Cabinet which is chaired by the Lord President of the Council. In other words, by Mr Chamberlain. But he wasn't in Parliament to answer questions. "Don't you see, Esther, that's the Committee that your husband is working for."

Before she left she said that Herr Niedermayer's wife and daughter should have arrived by now and that she was going to try and find her since she would have absolutely nowhere to go.

Felt completely miserable after she'd gone. Kept remembering Douglas's words about it being important to send the aliens overseas in order to 'get rid of useless mouths.'

Wednesday 17th July

Lovely letter from Gordon that made me laugh and cry and a birthday card from Lydia that she had drawn herself. It showed the three of us standing outside our house, with Lydia holding what I take to be a cat and Gordon with a dog standing next to him. In his letter Gordon said he asked Lydia why she hadn't included Daddy in the picture and she said that he was at work. In response to my saying he really mustn't steal, he said that he'd done it in order to buy a stamp so that he could write to me. Aunt Ada hadn't yet let them cash the postal order I'd sent them.

Douglas wasn't very interested in the letter and simply commented that there was never any excuse for stealing. Charles all day in bed.

Thursday 18th July

Barbara phoned to say that she had heard that some of the survivors from "The Arandora Star", Italians and Germans, had been deported to Australia on a ship called 'The Dunera'. Somehow Herbert had found this out, because responsibility for the management of the camps had been handed back to the Home Office. It had also been decided that people who were known to be ant-Nazi should be released from the camps. Herbert has colleagues who have been charged with conducting an inquiry into how the selection methods for 'The Arandora Star.' Asked if I'd go to the Austrian Centre with her tomorrow.

Said I couldn't because I can't leave Charles.

Friday 19th July

This can't go on. The people I care most about in the world - the children and Barbara I can't even see, and Douglas so aloof and off-hand and brusque that we haven't got any kind of relationship at all left. He came home very late last night and only said he'd had a terrible day. Told him I was really worried about Charles and all he could say was that it was just as well that I was there to look after him then. I said I felt I couldn't even get out to do the shopping and he replied that he would have to work on Saturday morning but he'd be here in the afternoon and that I could 'pop out to the shops' for half an hour. He brought his papers to bed and suddenly said, "That bloody Rathbone woman. Stirring up trouble in the House again." I must have looked surprised because he lay the papers on the eiderdown and asked, in a very accusing manner if I'd been in touch with Barbara. I admitted having spoken to her and he went into such a rage that I thought he would wake Charles. He demanded to know what she had said to me and I answered that she had told me that the responsibilty for the camps had been given back to the Home Office and that survivors from 'The Arandora Star' had been sent on a ship to a camp in Australia. Through gritted teeth he said it was bloody women who can't keep their mouths shut who are going to cost us this war.

Monday 22nd July

I don't know what to do. I'm writing this now to try and help me decide but can scarcely hold the pen I'm shaking so much. I don't know where Douglas is. It's 10 o'clock so probably at work.

On Saturday afternoon I got back from the shops to find him not speaking. Eventually he started shouting see what you've done you stupid stupid woman. I didn't know what he was talking about and then icily calm he said that the Swiss Embassy had been on the telephone asking for me because they'd got an Austrian woman called Frau Niedermayer and a little girl with them. The only contact she'd got in this country was a woman called Mrs Esther Hart. Her husband had written two letters to her that mentioned my name. They'd sent her to the Austrian Centre to see if her husband was there but she had returned two hours later, very upset because she'd been told that her husband had been taken away a few weeks before and nobody knew where he was.

I said that I was going to the Swiss Embassy to find her. Douglas said if I left the house I wasn't to come back. I said in that case he'd better make alternative arrangements for someone to look after his father and then I put on my hat and coat and left. I didn't even pack anything - I just needed to be away from him. I caught a bus into the City and then realised I had no idea where the Swiss Embassy is so I phoned Barbara. I was crying so much that she found it difficult to understand what I was saying. When I finally explained she told me to stay where I was and she'd ring back in a few minutes when she had got the address of the Embassy and that she would meet me there. It seemed like hours, but probably was only five minutes. She gave me the address in Montague Place so I got the tube to Baker Street and walked. When I got there Barbara and Herbert had already arrived and were waiting in a little office with Frau Niedermayer and Clara, her daughter.

There was no news of Herr Niedermayer. The Swiss official was very sympathetic and from what I could understand said they would be receive news from the Home Office as soon as there was any and asked her to leave a contact number and address. Herbert said they would be the contact. I kept looking at Frau Niedermayer and wondered at all they had been through. I wanted to hold Clara. She was so lost and waif like and I couldn't stop thinking how they had stuck together all the time through I couldn't imagine what, and how I had let my own children be taken from me and I hadn't had the courage to defy my own husband. At that moment I hated him.

When the official had gone, Frau Niedermayer came over to me and said thank you, and put her arms around me. I burst into tears again and just couldn't stop. I think Clara must have been frightened by this strange woman convulsed by crying because she came and held on to her mother's coat and said, "Mutti?" I bent down to hold her to reassure her and suddenly the memory of holding Lydia came flooding back and I started off again. Herbert gave an embarrassed cough. I wiped my eyes and apologised.

He drove us to their flat. Squeezed in between her mother and me in the back seat, Clara stared out of the window while her mother held her hand and I stroked her hair feeling such an gnawing emptiness mixed with relief that sometimes I was laughing and sometimes sobbing stupidly.

Barbara made up a bed in their spare room for Ilse and Clara while Herbert and I washed up after supper. He said that Hitler had made one last appeal to our government to 'see reason' and negotiate peace terms, which were going to be refused. We could then expect an all out attack on the country, probably within days. He also said that it really wouldn't be possible for Ilse and Clara to stay with them for more than a couple of nights. I said it would be quite impossible for them to come to us, and explained what had happened with Douglas.

When Barbara had settled Ilse and Clara down, I recounted all that had passed between Douglas and me. Herbert asked if I thought that Douglas had meant it when he said that if I left the house I couldn't go back. I didn't know - I wasn't sure I even wanted to. All I knew was that I wanted my children back - the memory of holding Clara brought home just how much I missed them, and I told them about Gordon's letter and Lydia's birthday card. Douglas hadn't even remembered it was my birthday.

Yesterday I took Ilse and Clara for a walk in the park. When we got back Herbert took me on one side and said he'd been in touch with his brother who lives near Ripon. He and his wife had taken in three evacuees who had since returned to their families. He's a vicar and has a large house. He would be willing to have the three of us until we've sorted ourselves out. But what about my children, I asked. Herbert said they would have them too if I'd be prepared to help with the garden and the Sunday School. Herbert said he would lend me the money for the train fares. I could get the children from Ada's and take them up to Ripon. It seems such an enormous step.

This is the last time I'll sit at the kitchen table writing this diary. I've packed. I half expected Douglas to have had the locks changed, but then realised that yesterday being Sunday, he couldn't have got a locksmith. I've asked Mrs Clark next door to come in and look in on Charles every couple of hours until Douglas gets home.

I've phoned Barbara. She's picking me up in half an hour to take Ilse, Clara and me to Kings Cross. We're going to get the 12.53. I shall tell Ada that she really ought to be looking after their father. it'll be so much easier than having to care for Gordon and Lydia. It'll probably be a relief for her.

Epilogue

The number of men who died on the Arandora Star has never been finally determined, but the latest, and probably most accurate figure is

446 Italians

146 Austrians and Germans

58 British Crew

95 British military guards [1]

On the 10th July the Battle of Britain started, with the Luftwaffe attacking shipping convoys off the south coast of Britain.

On 1st August Winston Churchill announced in Cabinet that, "it should now be possible to take a less rigid attitude in regard to internment of aliens," and later in Parliament, that he had always believed that the "Fifth column danger...somewhat exaggerated in this Island."

On 10th August, after a storm, 'The Western People' the County Mayo newspaper, reported

"100 Dead Bodies Floating In The Sea Off Inniskea." Over the next few weeks bodies were washed ashore on the Western Isles of Scotland as far south as Sligo in Ireland. They were given burials by the local people.

In the House of Commons, on 22nd August, the Home Secretary, Sir John Anderson said, speaking of the internment policy, "most regrettable and deplorable things have happened.....They have been due in some cases to the mistakes of individuals and to stupidity and muddle. These matters all relate to the past."

In the same debate Victor Cazalet MP said, "No ordinary excuse, such as there is a war on and that officials are overworked, is sufficient to explain what has happened...Horrible tragedies, unnecessary and undeserved, lie at the door of somebody....Frankly, I shall not feel happy, either as an Englishman or as a supporter of this Government, until this bespattered page of our history has been cleaned up and rewritten."

On 27th November, the Cabinet convened to discuss the report commissioned from Lord Snell on the 'method of selection' of those on 'The Arandora Star.' He pointed out that 'the need for speedy action, and for sending aliens overseas in large numbers, was repeatedly emphasized in Minutes from the Prime Minister calling for periodic reports on the progress achieved.' He went on to say that 'among those deported, were a number of men whose sympathies were wholly with this country.' However, 'Taking the broad view of the programme for deportation, I do not consider that this number of errors is a cause for serious criticism.'

After a brief discussion, the War Cabinet 'took note of the report and decided that no further action should be taken in regard to it, at any rate for the present.'

48 of the Italians who died were from the small town of Bardi, where a memorial chapel has been built and a street named 'Via Arandora Star'.

There is a memorial plaque in St Peter's Italian Church in Clerkenwell, London.

A number of bodies were washed up on the Scottish island of Colonsay where a memorial was unveiled on the 65th anniversary of the sinking.

On the 69th anniversary, the Mayor of Middlesborough unveiled a plaque in the town hall where 13 Italians were held prior to their deportation and deaths.

On the 70th anniversary, a new memorial in St David' Cathedral, Cardiff was unveiled paid for by the 'Arandora Star' memorial fund.

On 16th May, 2011 at St Andrew's Catholic Cathedral, Glasgow a memorial cloister garden was opened by Archbishop Mario Conti. He was joined by Rando Bertoia, the only living survivor from the Arandora Star

In November 1940 a 'Penguin special' was published - "The Internment of Aliens" by François Lafitte. Written in six weeks while London was being bombed by the Luftwaffe, he dedicated it to Herbert Morrison, the successor to Sir John Anderson as Home Secretary. In his conclusion to the chapter on the reasons for internment, he wrote,

"Internment and deportation of refugees are a sordid and disreputable scandal...." [2]

[1] Arandora Star, from Oblivion to Memory Maria Serena Balestracci MUP 2008

[2] The Internment of Aliens François Lafitte Libris 1988

Printed in Great Britain
by Amazon.co.uk, Ltd.,
Marston Gate.